RED

BARBARIAN

RED BARBARIAN

Margaret Gaan

DODD, MEAD & COMPANY
NEW YORK

Published by Dodd, Mead & Company, Inc.
79 Madison Avenue, New York, N.Y. 10016
Distributed in Canada by
McClelland and Stewart Limited, Toronto
Manufactured in the United States of America

Designed by Claire Counihan

First Edition

Library of Congress Cataloging in Publication Data:

Gann, Margaret.
  Red barbarian.

    1. China—History—War of 1840–1842—Fiction.
I. Title.
PS3557.A2R4   1984   813'.54   83-27493
ISBN 0-396-08296-3

FIC

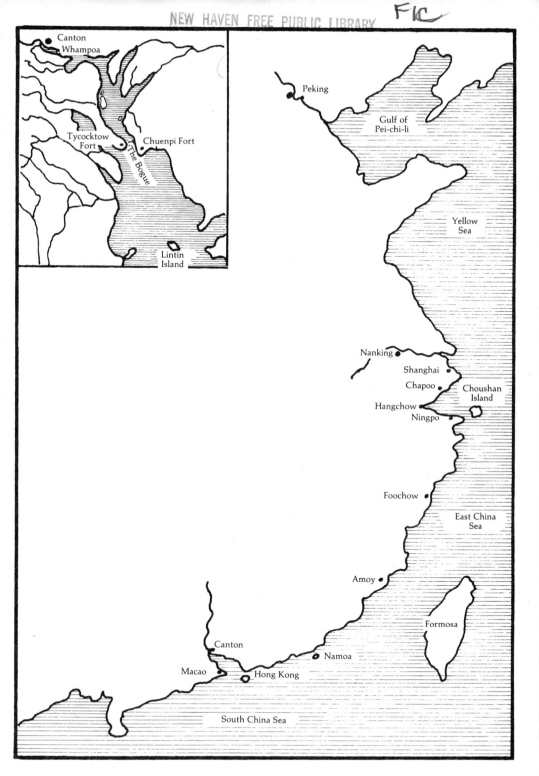

Canton
Whampoa

Tycocktow
Fort

Chuenpi Fort

The Bogue

Lintin
Island

Peking

Gulf of
Pei-chi-li

Yellow
Sea

Nanking

Shanghai

Chapoo

Choushan
Island

Hangchow

Ningpo

Foochow

East China
Sea

Amoy

Formosa

Canton

Namoa

Macao

Hong Kong

South China Sea

THE COAST OF CHINA

Chapter I

1816

ACROSS THE DAMASK-COVERED, CANDLE-LIT table, Sir George Seaton watched his guest apply knife and fork to the thick slice of fresh-killed, perfectly roasted, pinkish-brown beef that the servant had laid before him—watched as he raised a morsel to his mouth, chewed slowly, swallowed, and lifted his small blue eyes to heaven.

"Marvellous! In fact, after four months of ship's biscuits and dried meat, cooped up in that damned H.M.S. *Brunswick*, I would even say divine!"

Smiling dreamily, he lowered his elaborately curled head and feathery sideburns for the next mouthful.

Sir George stifled a sigh. Lord Ambleton, Ambassador of the King of England to the Emperor of China! An exquisite. What the devil could be expected of him in the intricate insubstantialities of negotiating with the Chinese? Sir George, Chairman of the Select Committee at Canton of the Honorable East India Company, the most important foreign trader in China, knew better than most how ungraspable the Chinese could be when they wanted to.

Turning away from the steadily-eating ambassador, George gazed out of the window at *Brunswick,* riding easily at her anchors in the harbor. Of all his memories of China, the most vivid was still of his very first visit, in 1793 when he was only twelve years old, a page in the retinue of Lord Macartney, Britain's first ambassador to the Emperor of China. Now, against the backdrop of *Brunswick's* masts, which seemed to pierce the darkening sky, George saw again the image of the Chien Lung Emperor, tall, stick-thin, eighty-three years old, so frail and ancient among the fat and gaudy mandarins who crowded the gloom of the *yurt.* Lord Macartney had refused to kowtow. He had said he would greet the Emperor on one knee, as he would his own king, and he would bow his head, if necessary nine times, but he would not prostrate himself three times and bang his forehead on the floor three times at each prostration. So the subtle Chien Lung Emperor had received him, not in his Throne Room, but in the *yurt,* a large, black, horse-hair tent, such as used by the wild horsemen who inhabited the edges of China, set up in the gardens of the Summer Palace.

Graciously, the Emperor had accepted from Lord Macartney the letter King George III had sent him, enclosed in a golden box studded with diamonds. Then he had turned to the little page George Seaton. Was it true that George could speak Chinese? George, whose ambitious father had set him to learning Chinese as soon as his appointment to Lord Macartney's embassy had been announced, replied haltingly, but indeed in Chinese. The delighted Emperor had rewarded him with a silk purse in the imperial color, yellow.

After that, the embassy had crumbled. Except for some chiming clocks, the mandarins declared themselves unimpressed by the great display of English-made goods that Lord Macartney had brought as gifts to the Emperor in the hope of generating expanded trade with China. The Emperor had written to King George: "Our ways have no resemblance to yours. As your ambassador can see for himself, we possess all things." And, perhaps in reference to the magical new sulphur matches Lord Macartney had demonstrated: "I set no value on strange and ingenious objects. . . ."

Now, twenty-three years later, another English ambassador to another Chinese Emperor. And this time, George was not the ambassador's page but his chief advisor.

With a satisfied sigh, Lord Ambleton pushed aside his empty plate. A servant hurried forward on silent, cloth-slippered feet to remove it, another to place a platter of fruit on the table, a third to put a finger-bowl of fragrant water at the ambassador's elbow. His lordship observed them, lazily turning his head from one to the other.

"Curious-looking fellows! Those long pig-tails! And those high-domed foreheads, the hair shaved back halfway over the crowns of their heads!"

"Plucked," said George abstractedly. "The hair is plucked out by catching it in twists of thread that the barbers manipulate over the scalp. The scalp stays bare longer that way."

"That must be painful! Why the devil do they do it?"

"Because the first Manchu Emperor thought the Chinese would look more like Manchus with their hair dressed like that."

"Outrageous! And they call *us* barbarians!"

George frowned.

"The expression that has been translated as 'barbarian' is not an epithet. It simply means one who does not speak Chinese. We are the 'red barbarians' because of our ruddy skins and sandy or light brown hair. There are also the 'Black Barbarians'—the lascars and sepoys from India. . . ."

His lordship's eyebrows were rising.

"You know a great deal about the Chinese!"

George shrugged.

"I've studied the language for years and read the writings of the French priests, but there's not much to be known. It's a closed and locked country. . . ."

He paused, regarding the ambassador frowningly.

"My lord, we have not much more time. *Brunswick*'s captain sent an hour ago to say that the ship has been re-supplied to continue the voyage north. You and your party will be sailing in the morning for the Gulf of Pei-chi-li, then by houseboat up the Pei-ho River, about two hundred miles, to Peking. My lord, we have not yet discussed your mission in Peking—had we not better do so now?"

His lordship sighed.

"It is very pleasant here in Macao—how did the Portuguese manage to wrest this nice little town from the Chinese? I had hoped to rest here longer. However . . ." With a grimace, he turned to George. "As you say. Proceed."

George drew a deep breath and settled himself.

"At the risk of repeating what you already know, my lord, I shall begin at the beginning, in order to make sure that the importance of your mission is set forth as clearly as possible."

His lordship closed his eyes and assumed a patient look. George went on doggedly.

"For the last one hundred and thirty-odd years, foreign trade in China has been carried on under the so-called 'Eight Regulations' that were devised by the Emperor who first decided it would be better to allow foreign traders into the port of Canton rather than have them continually raiding the south China coast. . . . Incidentally, that's how the Portuguese got Macao. They were the first, most numerous, and most assiduous of the raiders, and the Chinese thought to soothe them by giving them a place of their own."

His lordship was fumbling for his jewelled snuff box. George waited until the sneezes had subsided.

"As I was saying, the Eight Regulations have governed the activities of foreign traders in China since 1685. Some of the regulations are merely petty. For example, although trade is carried on only at Canton, we can spend only half the year there—September to April, the tea trade season. The rest of the year we spend here in Macao. In Canton, we are confined to our factories—the buildings in which we live and work— which are grouped together in a tiny settlement outside the

4

city walls. Foreign women aren't allowed in the settlement—fortunately it's only about a hundred miles, a three-day sail, from Macao, and the wives are quite comfortable here. We are not allowed to use sedan chairs. We are not allowed to learn the language—any Chinese who teaches it to us is subject to the death penalty. These minor regulations are no hindrance and can be ignored. But there are two regulations which are vitally important."

George cleared his throat as loudly as he could, for his lordship seemed to be falling asleep.

"The first of these vital regulations is that payment for Chinese goods bought by foreigners must be made *in silver.* As you know, my lord, ever since tea became available, the English have bought it—millions of pounds of it every year. As a result, a one-way flood of English silver pours into the Chinese treasury and very little of it trickles back, for the Chinese buy almost nothing from us. Years ago, through your predecessor, Lord Macartney, a great effort was made to entice the Chinese into a trading partnership, but it came to nothing. The Honorable Company, despite all efforts, has not been more successful."

His lordship, eyes still closed, nodded gently. George raised his voice.

"And that is where the second of the two vital regulations comes in. We cannot generate more trade because of the way trade is conducted. A group of ten Cantonese merchants, whom we call the 'Co-hong,' hold the entire responsibility for every aspect of foreign trade, and they are our only contact. We have no access whatever to Chinese officialdom. Any communication we wish to make must be presented in writing at one of the city gates, which has come to be known as the 'Petitions Gate' because our communications must be headed by a Chinese character that means 'petition'—otherwise, the gateman refuses to accept them. If there is a reply to our communication, it comes back to us through the Co-hong, and it is always headed by a character that means 'command.' 'Petition' from us and 'command' from them. You will realize, my lord, that this permits of no negotiation, and makes it impossible for us to develop markets for the goods that we could sell them. Therefore . . ."

His lordship broke in gently.

"And I am charged with explaining all this to the Emperor and persuading him to give us better access to Chinese officials and markets. I understand. Alas, I understand only too well!"

George glanced at him, stifling irritation, and met the twinkle in the little blue eyes. It was amused, quizzical, and very shrewd. George hesitated, irritation shrivelling to surprised respect. His lordship was not as lackadaisical as he seemed! Should George mention the thing he had been about to mention when his lordship interrupted? Better not! The embassy *might* succeed, his lordship *might* be clever enough to pull it off, in which case the thing could be finished with and forgotten.

"Yes, my lord," he murmured. Then, his voice once again strong: "There is one more most important point—the kowtow. You will be asked to kowtow to the Emperor. My advice to you, sir, is not to do it."

The ambassador's blue eyes opened wide and fixed themselves on George's, not at all sleepily. Startled, George went on:

"It's true that if you refuse to kowtow the mandarins may prevent you from seeing the Emperor and you may be obliged to negotiate through an intermediary. But if you do kowtow there will be no negotiations—at least, no sincere ones—for you will have acknowledged that you are inferior to the Emperor and there is no place in Chinese custom for negotiation with inferiors."

A grin spread itself over his lordship's face and his eyes twinkled. Abruptly, he rose to his feet.

"I thank you for your advice. I'll go off to bed now. No doubt my lord captain of *Brunswick* will wish to sail at some unholy early hour."

* * *

The tiny settlement to which the Eight Regulations confined the barbarians at Canton covered an area of about half a mile by two hundred yards. The stone buildings of the factories clung together in a long row between a cobbled courtyard called Jackass Point lying along the bank of the Pearl River, and a narrow, muddy thoroughfare called Hog Lane in which Chinese grog shop owners served First Chop Rum Number One Curio to barbarian seamen.

In early September, three months after *Brunswick* left for the Gulf of Pei-chi-li, the foreign traders began to trickle back from Macao to Jackass Point for the new tea trade season. George, as usual the first to arrive, immediately settled down to the routine he practiced while at Canton. He was inclined to fat, and it was a problem to get enough exercise in the little space available to the traders, so each day he rose at dawn to walk ten laps of the courtyard, about five miles, before the sun rose too high for comfort.

On the morning after his arrival, when he began his pacing, the eastern sky was already reddish and steamy. On his left, the waters of the Pearl River lapped gently. Across the river, the floating village—hundreds of sampans tied hull to hull like an enormous, lumpy, jointed raft—was beginning to stir; the raucous sounds of coughing and hawking up of phlegm from sleep-clogged throats drifted on the breeze. A half-glimpsed sampan slipped by, emitting from its shadows the murmur of voices, a high-pitched laugh. Revellers returning from the Flower Boats anchored further down the river, from whose windows girls twittered and waved all day and half the night. With this new beginning of the tea trade season, the standard warning to the crews of the foreign tea ships would need to be re-posted. They had better control their ardors at least until their ships were in Macao harbor, and even beyond that. Barbarians who visited the Flower Boats were more than likely to be found next morning floating face down in the river, and in Macao they were more than likely to contract the pox. Devil take those pesky seamen! Getting roaring drunk in Hog Lane, breaking up the grog shops for a lark. . . .

George stopped short to peer into the dawn mist. From a narrow lane between two factories, a tall, thin man was emerging, holding by the hand a tiny figure that came no higher than his thighs, its short little legs scissoring sturdily along, trying to keep up. An involuntary smile lightened George's heavy features. Wei and his three-year-old daughter!

Five years ago, How-kwa, chief of the Co-hong merchants, had sent Wei to George to be his valet and majordomo of the factory's staff. It had worked out excellently. Wei was an excellent servant, George liked him personally, and to top it off Wei was from the north and spoke Mandarin. With him, George was able to practice the great, rolling syllables of the northern dialect in which he delighted—the dialects of southern China had always sounded to him like the quacking of ducks.

Last night, on George's arrival from Macao, Wei had come to him, shrugging deprecatingly. It was a great nuisance, but he had a little daughter, a most unworthy and ill-favored child, whom he nevertheless would like to bring to live with him at the factory since, after all, he could hardly leave her in the lanes.

George had considered. It was most irregular, but Wei could easily smuggle the child in, and might do so if George refused permission, in which case George would be in the position of pretending not to know what Wei would know he knew, or of "discovering" the child on the premises and being obliged to discharge Wei for insubordination, which was the last thing he wanted. "Very well," he said to Wei, and only as an afterthought: "Why?"

"My wife has died," Wei said, smiling. George thought with compassion that Wei's heart must be pinching sorely. The careful smile was meant to deny sorrow; it would discomfort George to display it.

"Regret to hear it," George murmured. "What about your sons?"

"I have sent them to my brother in Ningpo. They are older. Ling-ling is only three years old."

And now here she was, clinging to her father's hand, staring solemnly up at George in the dim light, a not at all ill-favored child, round-faced, tilt-eyed, a little beauty.

She tugged at her father's hand and, when he lifted her in his arms, whispered breathily in his ear.

"What does she say?" George asked, amused.

Wei smiled apologetically.

"She says that you are not red."

"Not red?"

"Sir, she's been looking forward to seeing a Red Barbarian."

"Oh, I see!" George laughed, fingering his sandy sideburns. The child hid her face shyly in her father's shoulder. He bowed and walked on, patting her back. George resumed his pacing, glad that he had satisfied Wei by giving permission for the child to stay at the factory, thinking with a sudden thump of his heart that in addition to his personal reasons for keeping Wei satisfied, there was another most important reason. How-kwa had sent Wei. He and Wei no doubt had one of those complicated Chinese affiliations that barbarians could never disentangle. Wei must know about the thing that George had decided not to mention to Lord Ambleton that night in Macao—the thing that always made George squirm to think about.

Opium. Opium produced at Patna in India under the monopoly the Honorable Company had acquired from the Moghul Emperor, sold by the Company at auction in Calcutta, and smuggled into Canton in contravention of two Imperial Edicts under the watchful eyes of old How-kwa and Sir George himself.

If Lord Ambleton's embassy were successful, if the Chinese could be persuaded to buy more English goods and thus send some of England's silver flowing back to its source, the opium smuggling might be stopped. But in the circumstances, the silver earned by the Company at the opium auctions was essential for paying the Co-hong for tea. Opium was keeping the tea trade going—the huge tea trade that was vital both to the

9

Company and the Co-hong. To the Company, because it depended on Parliament for its monopolies on trade in India and China, and Parliament was highly influenced by the extent to which taxes on tea contributed to Crown revenues—in some years as much as ten percent. And to the Co-hong because profits on tea compensated for the high price the merchants had paid the Imperial Treasury for their appointments.

George smiled ruefully, thinking of what old How-kwa had said one day, with his usual chuckle:

"You all same me, Jawgee. How fashion you talkee? Sittee all same boat?"

Yes, you old fox, we're sitting in the same boat. Tea is our fortune, and opium pays for tea, and our boat's been sailing along mighty fine for a long time now. But unless Lord Ambleton is successful with your Emperor, I'm afraid our boat's going to be swamped, and we'll be swimming for it—you all same me! It can't go on much longer!

Sighing, beginning to sweat as the sun rose above the floating village, George turned into his last lap of Jackass Point.

When, three mornings later, *Brunswick*'s gig appeared in the Pearl River, rowed by six sailors of His Majesty's Navy, George, hurrying across Jackass Point to meet it, saw with anxiety that Lord Ambleton appeared to be its only passenger.

As soon as his lordship stepped ashore, he bent to speak in George's ear.

"Came ahead of the rest of my party. Want to talk to you alone. Already been too much confounded confabulation. Can we be private?"

George's heart dipped. "Certainly, my lord."

"The others will follow in the ship's cutter after noon. No doubt you've planned a dinner? Can you hold it tonight? Then tomorrow we can be off again. Four months on that damned vessel before I reach home!"

George's heart sank further.

"Your mission was not successful, sir?"

"There was no damned mission!"

"What?"

"Later—when we're alone."

His lordship started off across the cobbles, then half turned to wave a hand behind him.

"That's my page."

In spite of his perturbation, George, remembering his own paging days, turned to look at the boy who had been hidden behind his lordship. He was stepping out of the gig, eyes cast down to negotiate the slippery steps, the top of his head presented to the viewer. George stared. Great God, what hair! Not carrot-orange. Not just "red." Bright, glowing, startling red, like a sunset, in short-cropped curls like a close-fitting cap. For the rest, he was twelve or thirteen years old, slightly built, and what could be seen of his face was handsome, but it was his hair that snatched the attention. What color would his eyes be, with hair like that?

George laid a kind hand on his shoulder and the boy looked up. His eyes were very dark, almost black, and they stared at George with a fierce, defiant challenge. Startled again, George stared back—what the devil was the matter with him? But his lordship had almost reached the door of the factory and, with a last puzzled look at the boy, George hurried after him.

In the large private office overlooking the bustling river, the ambassador settled gingerly into one of the hot, prickly, wool-upholstered, English-made armchairs in the bay of the window, sipped at the sherry George handed him, and at last looked up with a sardonic smile.

"Well, my boy—you said I'd be damned if I did and in point of fact I was damned because I didn't."

"The kowtow?" George murmured.

"The damned jiggery-pokery of the kowtow! As soon as we got onto the houseboats at Pei-chi-li Point, two mandarins appeared to discuss the matter. Like Lord Macartney, I told the interpreters that I would go down on one knee and bow my head, but I would not kowtow. The mandarins said it would be a gesture of good will. I said my good will need not be proved by any means other than my own word as Ambassador of the English king. There were mutterings and fussings all the way up the Pei-ho river, but I held my ground. When we got to Peking, we were put up in a fine villa outside the Summer Palace and kept waiting for a week. My interpreter said the matter was still being discussed—in fact, he whispered that the mandarins were so perturbed about my refusal that they were even thinking of giving me a push while I was down on one knee before the Emperor, thus causing me to fall forward, which would look like a clumsy kowtow!''

Lord Ambleton made a sound between a snort and a shout of laughter.

''Can you credit it! The Ambassador of the King of England subjected to such tomfoolery! But in the end the mandarins decided to advise the Emperor not to negotiate with me at all, and he's such a stickler for pomp and ritual, it appears, that he was glad to take their advice. So—no audience, no mission, no embassy.''

George looked down at his hands. Fiasco! Well, he'd been a fool to hope for anything! And now he might even be blamed for it! The further the story went toward Parliament, the faster blame would be passed backward. But by God, he'd been right to advise against the kowtow!

His lordship laughed suddenly.

''But you were right, my boy! By God, I was delighted that night in Macao when you warned me so sternly against the kowtow! I was supremely unconvinced of the utility of this mission. As we've just proved in the war against Napoleon, we have the most formidable weapon of war on earth today— our navy. We could blast their defenses into kingdom come before they got those ancient cannon trained. It was fantastical, I thought, to go to a great deal of trouble to attempt negotiations with a ruler who's not even aware of those facts of life! By God, when the world at last breaks into this closed and locked country, it'll be by force of arms, not of negotiation!''

George sighed. His lordship's eyes twinkled.

''Negotiation suits you better? Tell me, my boy—was I right in suspecting that you hoped my negotiations would succeed because you hoped that the opium smuggling might be stopped if reciprocal trading relations could be established?"

George was silent. Put suddenly and baldly like that, it sounded naive. At last he looked up to meet the amused blue eyes.

"Well, there'd be a chance of stopping it. It surely will not stop as long as we have to pay the Chinese millions in silver for tea, with no way of recuperating it but by the sale of opium."

"What troubles you so much about opium? In our own country doctors are recommending it highly. Many regard it as a panacea."

George spoke to his hands folded before him on the table.

"The Chinese believe that opium is deadly harmful, and in allowing opium to be freely imported, I fear, my lord, that the Kings of England are less wise than the Emperors of China. Two Imperial Edicts have been issued against opium. The first was in the mid 1600s, when the Chinese started to smoke opium mixed with tobacco. At that time—I have looked as closely as possible into the matter—it seems that about 200 chests of opium were imported into China each year for the manufacture of medicine. But the habit of smoking opium must have grown very steadily because in 1799, my first year in Canton, four thousand chests were imported. In that year, the Emperor issued a new Edict forbidding not only the smoking of opium but also its importation."

"So now it's smuggled. . . ." His lordship's eyes sparkled with interest. "Belay my curiosity, Sir George. In what form is it smuggled? How much opium is in a chest?"

"The opium arrives from India in raw form—it's a black, pasty substance, rolled into balls about the size of a large apple. The balls are covered with poppy leaves or petals. Forty balls are packed in a wooden chest. The weight of the chest is a Chinese *picul*—about a hundred and thirty-three pounds."

"Ah hah! And how are the chests smuggled in?"

George drew a deep breath.

"The Bay of Canton is a V-shaped estuary, about a hundred

miles long, very wide where it leaves the sea, and narrowing sharply as it nears Canton. The island of Whampoa, about ten miles from Canton, is the closest that ocean-going vessels can approach. Before the 1799 Edict, the ships from India brought the opium right up to Whampoa. That practice continued after the Edict until 1809, when the Viceroy of Kwangtung got around to applying the Edict. He did so by making the Co-hong guarantee that no foreign ship at Whampoa would be carrying opium. The Co-hong merchants are subject to severe punishment if they appear to be unable to control the foreign traders, so they were obliged to give the Viceroy his guarantee. But of course they themselves were powerless to stop the foreign ships from carrying opium to Whampoa. So they came to us—the Honorable Company—for help. We can't afford that any ill should befall the Co-hong, so we saw to it that no more opium was carried as far as Whampoa. Now the opium is transferred from the carrying ships to the buyers' junks in the bays around here."

Rising, George pointed out, on a large map, the area of sea around Macao, on the western tip of the V-shaped estuary, and the uninhabited island of Hong Kong on the eastern tip.

His lordship examined the map.

"Can't be too easy to make the transfers in rough seas. What about payment? Is it also transferred at sea?"

"No—it's made in advance. Silver is too heavy to transfer quickly, and nobody wants to take too long about it, although in fact nobody has troubled the smugglers up to now. They stay too far out for the Chinese navy."

"But here, where the estuary narrows—are not these the Bogue forts?"

"Yes, but they're simply meant to threaten the approaches to Canton. I doubt they could put up a fight. And certainly it's not their concern to enforce Imperial Edicts."

In the little silence that fell, sounds from the courtyard below reached them. George rose to peer from the window. Beneath him, the bright hair of the ambassador's page appeared. The boy was walking toward Wei, who was supervising the factory's servants as they unloaded parcels and packages from the gig that had brought the ambassador. As George watched, a package fell to the cobbles, broke open and spilled its contents. For a moment there was silent dismay as everyone stared at a white lace tablecloth gathering dirt and stain on the ground. Then the boy's tenor voice rose clearly to the occupants of the private office.

"Bad joss! Can do washee-washee?"

"Confound it," his lordship growled. "That's my page talking some infernal gibberish he picked up from one of *Brunswick's* sailors."

George laughed. "That's not gibberish. It's pidgin."

"Pidgin?"

"The language we use to do business with the Chinese. Its made up of corruptions of Portuguese, English, and Chinese words, and there's no grammar to it whatsoever, but it has grown up over the last hundred-odd years and it's remarkably efficient for our purposes. For example, the word 'joss' is a corruption of 'Dios,' the Portuguese word for God, and—logically—'joss' means 'fate' or 'luck.' "

"Enough!" His lordship held up both hands. "I've no wish to learn the language!"

There was silence for a moment. When his lordship spoke again, his tone was conciliatory.

"Well, Sir George, I might as well say it outright . . . I'm leaving my page with you."

George sat up, staring.

"Leaving him with *me?*"

"Yes. You can use him as junior factor, office boy, anything. I trust you can cope with that?"

"I suppose I can. . . ." No wonder the boy had stared at him so defiantly! He knew he was going to be left here, at the mercy of a complete stranger, perhaps a mean and cruel one! Poor lad!

George turned worriedly to his lordship. "But why?"

"Promised his father, my god-son. A country squire. The boy is a fourth son. No expectations. He's an attractive lad.

Likeable. But a rascal, I'm afraid. Drove his father to despair. Refused to study. Persisted in keeping low company—poachers and the like. When my god-son heard I was coming to China, he begged me to bring the boy with me and find him a billet. Only hope of making a man of him."

"But the responsibility! He's still a child!"

"You'll have no more responsibility for him than for any other young employee. I had his father put it in writing, and I'll give you the paper before I leave. You'd be doing me a great service."

"Very well." George sank back. One more worry! "What's his name?"

"Charles Tyson."

Silence fell between them. The cacophony of the river made itself heard—the slap-slap of roiled waters, the shouts of boatmen, the squeak of oars in bamboo rowlocks, the calls of boat-borne vendors, each with his own polysyllabic trill that identified his stock-in-trade.

His lordship broke the silence.

"Now that that's settled—how much bribery goes on to cover the smuggling?"

George had hoped that the subject was closed. . . . He roused himself.

"The standard bribe is about thirty dollars a chest. Bribes go to the Director of Customs and to various mandarins in a position to look the other way—even some of the mandarins of the navy who could create a nuisance for the smugglers."

"Is everybody on Jackass Point engaged in the smuggling?"

"Not the Company, of course." George's lips turned downward. "We only supply the opium. And not the Co-hong itself. How-kwa, chief of the Co-hong merchants, uses an old friend of his, a man named Lee Kwok, to manage the smuggling. Other than that, almost all the traders on Jackass Point are engaged in it to some degree. The biggest of the smugglers is a Scotsman by the name of William Carradine, trading under the Danish flag. He handles more opium than the rest of the smugglers put together."

"Enterprising! How extensive is the smuggling?"

"For the last fifteen years, How-kwa and I have managed to keep it at about five thousand chests a year—it simply wouldn't do to let it get out of hand. But it won't remain at that, I fear."

"Why not?"

George rose again to look from the window. *Brunswick's* cutter was tying up at the dock. The ambassador's party was leaping ashore, followed by the ship's officers, all delighted at the prospect of a meal of fresh meat, laughing, clapping each other's shoulders. Feeling infinitely weary, George spoke out of the window, his voice blowing back unevenly into the room.

"My lord, Patna is not the only place in India where opium is produced. It's produced in several other places, including Rajputana, which is not yet under British control. Opium from Rajputana is being sold at Bombay, at prices well below Patna. Stocks of Patna are piling high in Calcutta."

George turned to face the ambassador.

"In the Company's place, what would you do, sir? The Company must pay for tea in silver, and it gets its silver from the sale of Patna opium. If sales of Patna continue to dwindle, the Company will be obliged to reduce purchases of tea. Revenues from tea in Britain will suffer. Parliament will be displeased. And the Company depends on Parliament for the monopolies that are even now being attacked by those who demand the right of free trade."

He sighed and resumed his seat. His voice became bland and flat.

"If I were to make a prediction, I should say that within the next three or four years, the Company will be forced to cut the price of Patna opium. To make up the difference, it will be forced to increase production. More opium will become available at cheaper prices. More and more, and cheaper and cheaper. Smugglers will cluster like bees around honey. And what will happen then? The Chinese close their eyes to five thousand chests a year, but what when it becomes twenty thousand? Or more?" George quirked an eyebrow at his lordship, whose eyes were no longer twinkling. "The day will come, sir, when we will look back with nostalgia on the present 'enterprising' smuggling!"

Ling-ling crouched in her father's room on the ground floor of the factory. The door was open for coolness, but half covered by a bamboo screen. No one could see in, but Ling-ling on her pallet on the floor could see out, could see and hear everything that happened as far away as the main hallway of the factory. Yesterday, she had seen only Chinese feet, bare or shod in cloth slippers, heard only the slithery sound they made, only Chinese voices speaking words she could understand. But today she was seeing feet in big, hard shoes that clumped across the floor with loud thuds. She was hearing rough, deep voices that made unintelligible sounds. Barbarian feet. Barbarian voices. She was shivering with fright when her father hurried in to say that there would be a dinner for the party of the number-one English master, and he would have to leave her alone till quite late that night.

"You'll be good and quiet? The master has given permission for you to stay here, but if you cry and make a nuisance of yourself, he might send us both away. You'll be good?"

She promised, but when he left she sobbed herself to sleep, missing the mother who had so mysteriously disappeared, the brothers who had waved to her and gone away with strange men, riding horses.

When she woke, it was to a barrage of the barbarian noises— so many barbarian voices that they merged into an echoing rumble, so many barbarian feet clumping so heavily that the floor beneath her shook. She sat up, trembling—but wondering too. The only barbarian she'd seen so far was a strange shade of yellow, not red at all. . . . At last, she crawled to the doorway and cautiously thrust her head out beneath the screen.

Many barbarians were standing about in the main hallway of the factory. They were huge! Any one of them would make two of her father. And they had so much hair! It bunched out on their heads in rolls and waves, grew down the sides of their faces, completely hiding their ears. Some even had great bursts of it growing out of their chins. They all wore thick clothes, like winter, and—strangest of all!—their legs were separated, each leg clothed separately from top to bottom!

But not a single one of them was red. Their skins were light-colored, a little pinkish, perhaps, but not red. Their hair was any color from white to yellow to gray to brown, but not red. . . .

A bell rang, and the barbarians, still talking and hitting each other's backs, though not apparently in anger, began to ascend some steps she had not previously noticed—steps like the ones of mud and stone that went up the little hill behind the house where she used to live, but these were of wood, very sharp and regular, and *inside* the house! In a few moments all the barbarians had disappeared up the steps, and she could hear their feet clumping over her head. There must be another house on top of this one! Not a roof under the sky, but another house, and the steps must lead up to it!

She crawled under the screen and out into the hall. It was empty and half-dark. The outer doors had been closed, but light came from the well of the inside steps, from the unseen house overhead. Slowly, she began to climb the steps. . . .

Indeed, there was another house overhead. At the top of the steps, she found herself at the open door of a huge room in which there was a great table. The barbarians were sitting on chairs around it, eating. From a doorway on the other side of the room, she saw her father come, carrying a tray on which a lump of meat lay steaming. He set it down on the table, and at that moment one of the barbarians looked up and saw her. He laughed and said something and rose from his chair and walked toward her. He meant to touch her! He meant to pick her up! She mustn't cry out! She mustn't run away! If she made a nuisance of herself, her father's master would send them both away!

With desperate courage, she stared up at the barbarian and stood her ground.

* * *

In the main kitchen that flanked the factory's great dining room, Wei had decided that he himself must serve the roast of mutton. To insist that the number-two boy do it would be to invite rebellion. All day the servants had grumbled—the usual grumble, but today emphasized by the size of the meal. How could these Red Barbarians eat so much meat? And not pork from otherwise useless pigs. Beef, from the oxen who helped to till the earth and should be respected, not slaughtered to feed these incredible appetites. No wonder barbarians stank so disgustingly! Not only did they smell of stale sweat and accumulated dirt, for their woolen clothing was never washed and they rarely washed their bodies and the great, untidy growths of hair in which lice nested, but their very pores exuded the revolting odor of the enormous quantities of meat they devoured. And today not only beef but now mutton, that stinkiest of meats!

So Wei himself took up the tray of roast mutton and carried it into the dining room. As he laid it down before his master, the number-one English master looked up and exclaimed, then rose and walked toward the door. Wei turned, his heart sinking. In the doorway stood Ling-ling, the new skirt in which he had dressed her that morning half slipping off her shoulders, bare feet firmly planted, wide eyes fixed on the number-one English master in a mixture of terror and bravery.

"What an adorable child," the barbarian said. He picked her up and went back to his chair, sat her on his lap, chucked her under the chin. Wei watched anxiously from the corner of his eye. She sat rigidly, eyes still fixed on the barbarian's face, leaning back to avoid the whiskers, her nose slightly wrinkled—she was smelling the barbarian stink.

Looking grim, George cut a slice from the roast and laid it on a plate. Wei carried it to the number-one master. He, finding himself overburdened with the child on his lap, passed her to the master of *Brunswick*, who sat beside him. Wei waited for the howl of distress, but there was none. From lap to lap she was passed, holding herself stiffly, avoiding the whiskers, but not crying out. At last she was passed to the boy who sat in the lowliest place at the end of the table. He received her with both arms, pushing his chair back to make room for her. Wei saw her relax—no whiskers to lean away from; the boy had smooth, hairless cheeks. He saw her raise her eyes cautiously to the boy's face, and break suddenly into a brilliant smile. Sagging with relief, Wei smiled too. The boy had hair the color of the red paper in which gifts of silver ingots were wrapped for New Year and weddings. Ling-ling had found a Red Barbarian!

His heart swelling with fellow feeling, Charlie Tyson smiled back at the child. A stray like himself, warily on guard—they had recognized each other! Still smiling, she laid her head confidingly against his chest and, like an exhausted puppy, fell into instant sleep. He shifted to make her more comfortable, feeling her little weight grow heavier. A lovely child, the peach bloom of babyhood still on her cheeks, long black lashes, tiny black pigtails sticking out entrancingly over her ears. Charlie cuddled her close.

The Chinese brought him a plate of mutton, but he shook his head to it. The meal had been big enough for two! The ambassador was passing up his plate for a second slice, at the same time saying tartly:

"I never did see the Emperor. And that, I hope, is the end of that!"

A younger voice laughed.

"Wonder what Carradine will think of that! Heard him say the other day that negotiations with the Chinese are a damnable waste of time! Only way to open up the country is to lay a few of His Majesty's sloops alongside the Bogue forts—"

"Hush!" Sir George was glaring at the speaker.

After the mutton there was a tart, and brandy, and cheroots, and at last they rose from the table. The tall Chinese called Wei came to take the child from Charlie. He handed her to one of the other servants with a whispered word, then beckoned Charlie to follow him. They went up to a small room in the attic of the factory. Wei opened the door.

"Master talkee you stay Canton. This room b'long you."

A narrow bed, a clothespress, a chair, a table, a washstand. All from England—cheap stuff, not like the furniture in the dining room. Charlie went to the window. It looked out over the river, dark now, silent. The little Chinese craft had all homed for the night, but the gig and the cutter were still there, dimly seen, tied up at the dock. Lights appeared—oil lanterns carried by the servants. The ambassador came out with the others, all laughing and talking. Going home. They shook hands with Sir George, the fattish, shortish, chunky man who was to be Charlie's new—employer? master? father? They got into the little boats. The sailors raised their oars, shoved off. Immediately, the boats were lost in darkness, though the voices trailed back on the still, hot air. They hadn't said goodbye to him, not even his lordship. Well, devil take it!

Charlie turned away from the window. The Chinese, Wei, was looking down at him, smiling, a compassionate look in his eyes.

"Maskee!"

The pidgin word for "never mind." . . . Never mind your sorrow, your distress. It'll come out all right. I'm here to help you. . . . All these things were in the Chinese eyes. Charlie grinned.

"Good." The Chinese nodded. "You clever boy. I got two piece boy, go Ningpo now. Far 'way. . . ." For a moment his eyes saddened. Then he smiled again and put out a long-fingered hand to touch Charlie's hair. "Good-joss color!"

When he had left the room, Charlie laid his head against the window frame. What had the Chinese said? He had two sons of his own, far away in Ningpo. He missed them—he hadn't said so, but his eyes had. He loved them. A father who loved his sons. Charlie's father loved his sons too—the three older ones. Well, devil take it, Charlie didn't love his father either! Poppy eyes, like fish eyes, stern and hard. Cold voice.

"Lord Ambleton expects you tomorrow. You will catch the coach from the village." No goodbye from him either. . . .

The green fields of home. The partridge plopping fatly into flight. The stream chuckling over the stones. Crouched on the slippery surface of the big stone, one could see the silver fish flash by, one could dip one's hand into the water and deflect them toward the net. The sudden, great splash as they hit it! And the forest. The deep, cool, dappled woods . . .

Oh, *devil* take it!

It was so black—the Chinese night was blacker than the English night. The forts must lie in that direction. The Bogue forts. Sailed between them yesterday. Thick mud walls, embrasured for cannon, lying close above the water under low, bare hills.

"Them old cannon!" The seaman had spat scornfully to leeward. "Don't know as they'd even fire, let alone hit wot they wuz aimed at. Chinee gunpowder be no good for none but firecrackers!"

The only way to open up this country is to lay a few of His Majesty's sloops alongside the Bogue forts.

Who had said that?

Carradine?

Chapter II

1820

CARRADINE STARED ACROSS THE TABLE, his eyes glinting green in the uneasy light of the oil lamp. Charlie stared back, blood pumping. Let him agree! Let him say yes!

Carradine said, harsh-voiced: "How much? What for? And what makes you think I'll lend it to you?"

Charlie took a deep breath.

"A thousand guineas. To buy *Merope*. And I think you'll lend it to me because I'll pay you good interest—whatever you say."

"*Merope?* Dobell's ship that foundered in the great typhoon? She's nothing but a hulk!" Carradine laughed shortly and rose to his great height, stretching his arms. "How old are you, boy? Seventeen? Does Sir God Almighty George know you're out of your bed? Better run back before he finds you missing!"

He turned away. Charlie spoke quickly.

"Just a moment, sir. May I ask a question? Is it true that when *Betsy* transferred her opium in Lark's Bay last month in heavy seas, twenty chests were lost overboard?"

Carradine sank back into his chair, his eyes hard and green as the great green stone on his table.

"Who the devil told you that?"

Charlie bit his lip.

Wei had told him. Wei came often now to the attic room, at night after everyone was in bed. It had started when he learned that his sons were dead, killed when the caravan with which he had sent them north was waylaid by bandits in the lonely mountains of Kwangsi Province. It had taken a year for the news to reach Canton. Wei had told no one at the factory but Charlie. Standing in the darkness at the foot of the narrow cot, he had said harshly:

"My two piece boy finis'."

"Finish?"

"Finis'. Die."

Appalled, Charlie murmured:

"Bad joss!"

Wei was silent for a long minute. Then he told Charlie about the bandits. And:

"You no talkee Ling-ling. No talkee any man. No talkee more better—bad joss finis' chop-chop."

The less said, the quicker the bad luck would run out. . . .

After that, Wei had started coming almost every night to the attic room, at first to bring some unneeded thing and leave again quickly, later to stay and talk. All the servants of all the factories spied on their masters and passed the information they gathered to the Co-hong. Wei also passed it to Charlie. The "twenny piece ches' bottomside" had cost Carradine two thousand dollars each in Calcutta, and were to have been sold to Lee Kwok in Canton for five thousand. But Charlie had made Wei a promise of secrecy, and now he stared silently at Carradine, gnawing his lip.

"Devil take it!" Carradine growled. "All right, what d'you want with *Merope?*"

Still Charlie was silent, running his tongue over his lips to hide their trembling. Carradine let out a roar.

"By God, d'you take me for a fool? You'll not speak a word,

and you expect me to shell out guineas? Be damned to you! Get back to Georgie, sitting on his fat scut lapping up trade like a cat lapping cream by right of his God-rotted monopolies! You're *his* sucker—why've you come sucking around me? Get out!"

He pushed his chair back violently. For another agonized instant Charlie held his tongue, then blurted:

"What would it have been worth to you if, instead of trying to transfer opium in high seas, *Betsy*'s master could have discharged it into a hulk anchored in the lee of Lintin Island, to be fetched by the buyer at his convenience?"

For a long minute the room was silent. The light flickered on their faces, Charlie's white and strained, Carradine's sharp and craggy. At last Charlie said hoarsely:

"That would have been worth five dollars a chest at least, wouldn't it? That's what I want with *Merope*."

Carradine stared down at his hands, fiddling with the smooth apple-green stone. It was called jade, they said. It was supposed to be valuable. He'd got it off a pirate that he'd scuppered, they said—killed him with his own hands, holding him by the pigtail while he hacked at his head with a short ax. They said all sorts of things about Carradine, talked of him all the time—him and his bloodiness and his wealth.

Carradine put down the green stone.

"I'll think on it."

"But . . ."

"I said I'd think on it. Get out!"

Stumbling back to the Company's factory in the darkness, Charlie cursed himself bitterly. Fool! Fool, to let himself be bullied into saying why he wanted *Merope*! Now Carradine would do it for himself! Four years of *tea!* Four years of Lapsang Souchong, Oolong, Red Congou, Black Congou—God-blasted, muck-raking tea! Four years of filling out papers, running errands, walking Ling-ling around Jackass Point for high jinks in the evenings. And now Carradine would buy *Merope* and leave him out in the cold, working for George forever, or going back home a pauper. For an instant, Charlie saw in his mind's eye the woods, the stream, the dappling sunshine, and his heart yearned for home. But not without money. Not to buckle under to his father—"Yes, Father, as you wish, Father, I'll read for the church, Father." Never! Never until he had silver to throw in his father's face!

Panting, sobbing, he ran into Wei at the door of the factory.

"Wassa matta you, Chahlee?" Wei regarded him with concern. "Maskee—you talkee me after. Just now, chop-chop go Jawgee. He go ship tomorrow."

Tomorrow? George had announced a week ago that he was going home to England for a year, and that was what had decided Charlie to approach Carradine. But no Company ship was due for five weeks.

At George's door, Charlie wiped his face and straightened his clothes before knocking. George was sitting in his shirt-sleeves going over papers at his desk—chubby, kind George, who thought tea was the be-all and end-all.

"Ah, Charlie! Sit down. I've been fortunate to obtain passage on *Hooghley*. Captain Pybus is sailing tomorrow. Charlie, your father put you in my care, and I can't leave you here while I'm away. I propose to take you with me and return you to your father—"

"I won't go!" Charlie startled himself with the loudness of his tone. George looked amazed, and Charlie modified his vehemence.

"I'm sorry, sir, but I don't want to go home. I've learned my job here. I'm useful. Whoever comes to take your place will find me useful."

"Yes, indeed. You've learned your work well. But I cannot leave you here—"

"You can, sir! Lord Ambleton showed me the paper my father wrote. You have no responsibility for me. Sir—you are a good man, but when my father wrote that paper he didn't know that. He didn't even know whom I'd be left with. And I was only thirteen."

George nibbled at the end of his pen, looking troubled.

"I understood from Lord Ambleton that your father had reason. You were—er—rebellious?"

"I suppose I was. I didn't get along with my father, nor he with me. My eldest brother inherits the squiredom. My second and third brothers go to the army and the navy—my father bought their commissions when they were born. I came later, and he didn't expect me. I knew I'd have to make my own livelihood and I was willing, but he wanted to choose it for me. He thought a parsonage."

"I see."

"I had the acquaintance of some poachers who made a better living than our parson!"

George sighed. Charlie's eyes had a bright and reckless look. George remembered the defiant challenge they had held the first time he had seen them.

"Charlie, it's true I've no power to compel you back to England, but—well, I may not return here. I may decide to resign from the Company and stay in England. There are reasons. Parliament has abolished the Company's monopoly on trade in India. We still retain our monopoly on trade with China, but for how long God knows—the 'free traders' are bellowing louder than ever. And . . . the Company has increased subsidies to the opium farmers in Patna and lowered prices in Calcutta. Next season, the price of opium will be half what it is now, and there will be double the quantity for sale. . . ."

George's voice trailed off as he turned to gaze beyond the window at the blackness of the night. Charlie shifted miserably in his chair. More opium! The more opium came to China, the more profitable *Merope* would be, spouting dollars! He'd botched it, botched it all the way to hell! But where by all the devils could he have got money to buy *Merope* if not by loan from Carradine? A thousand guineas was like a thousand pence to Carradine, God rot him!

George straightened.

"I've told you this in confidence, Charlie—though it'll be common knowledge soon enough—because I feel you must know all the facts before you decide to stay on here." He looked hopefully at Charlie.

"I'll not go back, sir."

"Very well." George gave his little cough. "But—stay out of trouble, Charlie. Er . . . you know, I think, the dangers of visiting the Flower Boats here, but in Macao there's danger too. The girls there . . ."

"I know, sir."

One of the older factors had said gruffly: "Give heed, boy. The cheap ones are more than likely poxy. Know what the pox is? Never get rid of it once you've got it. Die young, your body covered with cankers, and your brains scrambled, as like as not. If you must, go to Vargas' place. It's the only one where the girls are safe."

But Senhora Vargas' place was expensive, and Charlie's stipend was tiny. Blasted Carradine had a great villa in Macao where he kept his private mistresses.

George was getting to his feet.

"Good. Well, Charlie, one of the Company's directors will come from India to take my place until I return—if I return. There'll be no difficulty about your staying on. . . . Goodbye, Charlie."

"Goodbye, sir. A safe voyage, and I hope you'll decide to return."

"I like you, Charlie. You're very likeable and very bright. You could make something great of yourself."

"I've every intention of trying, sir."

And he'd well and truly botched the first step—perhaps the only step he'd ever have the chance to take! The thump of his boots climbing the steps to the attic sounded to Charlie like the knell of doom.

Wei was waiting for him.

"You go 'long Jawgee?"

"No. I'm staying. God knows what for!"

Charlie tore off his clothes and flung himself on the bed.

For months, he and Wei had discussed his idea about *Merope*. She had foundered on a rocky spur east of Hong Kong

Island, too late to make the waters between Hong Kong and the mainland where all the Chinese vessels took shelter when the typhoons, the great winds, blew. She had lain abandoned for two years, her masts snapped, her tattered sails dripping over the deck into the surf. Dobell, her owner, would take five hundred guineas to be rid of her. Another five hundred to have her properly stripped and the hull repaired, and have her towed to Lintin Island. A floating warehouse for opium. A floating silver mine! In a year or two, Charlie would have enough capital to start in the opium trade himself!

Wei said, "You talkee Carradine?"

Charlie nodded disconsolately, and Wei frowned.

"Why for? I talkee you, *I* catchee money buy *Merope!*"

Charlie threw him a forlorn glance.

"Where *you* catchee money?"

"I show you!" Wei stood up and beckoned imperiously. "You come 'long me. Maskee clotheses. Come chop-chop."

"Oh, Wei, I'm tired!"

"*Come!*"

Wearily, Charlie rose.

In Wei's room, Ling-ling stirred on her pallet and smiled sleepily at Charlie. She was seven years old now, a pretty little girl. She still adored her Red Barbarian. He took her for a walk every evening around Jackass Point, and when they went to Macao with Sir George in the tea off-season, he took her for walks there too. Not in the flower-bedecked *praças* where the great churches stood, nor along the Praya Grande, nor around the Race Course, but in the narrow, crowded lanes of the Chinese quarter, past the pawnshops and gambling dens and opium divans, to the gate that led into China. All day and night Chinese passed through it, but the few barbarians who came to see it, forbidden to step foot into China, could only stand on the Macao side of it and stare. Once, to tease Charlie, Ling-ling had darted through and danced around in China, just beyond his reach, laughing at him. After that, whenever they went there, he held her hand tightly, talking to her in English—he was teaching her English.

"Ling-ling, d'you realize that barbarians know almost nothing about China? Not even how many Chinese there are—they say hundreds of millions. A barbarian who could get into China and stay long enough to learn the secrets would make his fortune. He'd be richer than Carradine! D'you realize that?"

"Yes, no," she cried, hanging on his hand. "Please, thank you. One two three four five six seven . . ."

"Little monkey!"

"Love you, Chahlee!" Adoring eyes gazing up at him.

Now, Wei spoke to her and she turned over, wiggling her fingers at Charlie. From a cupboard, Wei produced a dark cotton gown that Charlie slipped over his head. It was too long, and Wei hitched it up by tying a cotton sash around the waist. Cotton slippers for his feet. A round black cap topped by a round red button, to the back of which was attached a long queue of black hair. Wei tucked Charlie's own hair under the cap—easy to do, for it was still cropped short, and was tenaciously curly. Then Wei scrutinized him carefully.

"Good. Eyes black, all same Chinee. No can see hair. But you talking all same foreign, so *no talkee*, Chahlee!"

They walked out into pitch darkness, first down Hog Lane and then around several corners. Charlie lost all sense of direction, knew only that they were in narrow lanes crowded on both sides by low houses from which came voices, glimmers of lamplight, the clack of the tiny ivory bricks, like dominoes, with which the Chinese played some kind of gambling game. Dark figures brushed by them, as silent and hurried as they. Then they were in an open space, cobbles underfoot, a shadow blacker than the night looming over them. Wei tapped and a small square of grayness opened. A voice spoke. Wei replied. The square was shut again, and there was the rasp of iron bolts. A gate! A gate into the city forbidden to barbarians! Charlie laughed softly, suddenly tingling with excitement.

They passed through the gate. Dimly seen men rushed up to them, chattering—sedan-chair coolies. Wei bargained, and then they were in chairs, each alone. Rough curtains closed Charlie into odorous stuffiness—uncounted bodies had sat in

31

this tiny place, uncounted breaths had been breathed in it, and all had left their record. But the sensation of being carried was not unpleasant—a slight jolt each time the bearers slapped their feet down in their quick, thudding stride, a slight bounce of the flexible carrying poles between each stride.

At last the chair was set down. Charlie pushed aside the curtains and climbed out into darkness, to be hurried by Wei through another gate, into a fabulous place. A great court-yard, softly lighted by many colored lanterns hanging from the high walls. Creamy marble underfoot. Marble benches. Small, glossy-leaved trees in tubs. In front of them, the low outline of a house with a circular gilded doorway, round and glowing like a huge moon, secret and mysterious.

Charlie looked around, excitement drumming. Wei was speaking to the man who had opened the gate for them, and he bowed and hurried away. Wei turned to Charlie, smiling.

"This How-kwa house."

Charlie goggled. How-kwa! Chief of the Co-hong, multi-millionaire, whose name was spoken a hundred times a day in the factories, with respect, admiration, envy, fear.

"Wei, you savvy How-kwa?"

"He my master."

"But . . . Sir George . . ."

"How-kwa send me Jawgee. How-kwa likee Jawgee. He say more better I work Jawgee, maybe 'nother man no good."

By God, who was Wei? A servant had come from the gilded moon doorway and was bowing to him respectfully. Whoever he was, Wei was no servant, though he called Sir George mas-ter—and How-kwa too! Thoughts whirling, Charlie followed Wei and the servant through the moon doorway into a room that seemed, in the light of a single oil lamp, to be all opulent, polished wood, intricate carvings, and a great golden screen studded with stones like Carradine's. The servant left them, and Wei waved toward chairs of heavy black wood that stood around a marble-topped table.

"This house b'long How-kwa papa, papa-papa, die now."

How-kwa's father and grandfather? Dead? Ancestors? Sir George had spoken once or twice about Chinese ancestors. . . .

"Backside have got more five house. How-kwa four wife, chilluns, four house. How-kwa self, one house." Wei smiled at Charlie's stare. "How-kwa too much plenty money! I talkee you—*I* catchee money for buy *Merope*."

"Wei!" Charlie's whisper was almost a shout. "You're going to ask How-kwa for the money?"

Wei nodded, smiling, and sweat spurted all over Charlie's body. A second chance! By God, a second chance! Reality and unreality began to march together through his head, creating a humming dislocation of his senses. It was hard to draw breath.

The servant returned and beckoned. They passed through another courtyard around which stood four low houses, dark and silent, then through still another courtyard. It was cool and very quiet, the air gently perfumed by the scent of the little tub-grown trees. They came to another house, lighted, with a moon doorway like the first. Inside, the servant slid back a door. The room they entered seemed to contain nothing but a mass of strange, cloth-covered shapes—round, square, tall, short—hanging on hooks from the walls and ceiling. Sleepy twitterings and flutters came from them. Birds, by God! Birds put to bed under covers for the night! Dazed, Charlie followed Wei across an expanse of polished floor to a pair of screens even richer than the one in the first room. Beyond the screens, there was a great, canopied bed, and in it, propped up on pillows, a thin, old man—long, bony face sloping from massive forehead to pointed chin, yellowish skin stretched tightly, black eyes bright in narrow, tilted sockets.

"How-kwa," Wei said.

Charlie collected his senses enough to bow. The old man raised a slender hand, the wide sleeve of his blue gown falling away in silken folds.

"Hah! Chahlee!" His voice was low and chuckling.

33

"Yin-kwa," Wei said.

On the other side of the bed, a young man, about Charlie's own age, rose and bowed.

"I am Yin-kwa, How-kwa's grandson."

Charlie stared. He had spoken in almost unaccented English!

The young man smiled.

"I studied English for many years with the missionary Gutzen, in Macao."

"Chahlee!" How-kwa was waving the slender hand. "Yin-kwa talkee Inglis good?"

Charlie found his voice. "Number-one good! Same like English man!"

Nodding, smiling, How-kwa waved toward the stools that stood around the bed. When they were seated, Wei at once began to talk in a low voice. Yin-kwa turned to listen, flashing a glance at Charlie.

The glance meant something. But Yin-kwa's face, as he listened to Wei, showed nothing beyond interest in what he was hearing. A very Chinese face, flat-eyed, cheekbones high and prominent, cheeks concave. The hairline, newly plucked, cut cleanly across the crown of his head, the hair falling back in a thick, loosely plaited queue. He wore a dark tunic with no ornamentation. What had that glance meant?

But it wasn't the time for speculation. Wei was telling How-kwa about *Merope*. Charlie listened to the staccato Cantonese syllables, feeling as though his ears were growing out on stalks. What a language! Impenetrable! He could not even make out the word *Merope*.

How-kwa was beginning to smile. The smile became a chuckling laugh, and he turned to Charlie.

"You number-one clever boy! Inglis man have got five dollah, use one dollah for makee trade. Chinee man have got one dollah, he can makee *five*-dollah trade. But you—you no got *any* dollah, you all same wanchee makee trade! Very good! Number-one!" His eyes twinkled and beamed at Charlie. "Can do. Me buy *Merope*. You take care trade. Profit—me half, you half."

A great, bright breath of triumph swelled Charlie's chest to bursting. But How-kwa was holding up a finger, shaking it from side to side.

"*But* . . . I no wanchee you buy opium. Storage opium, can do. Buy opium, no can do. You savvy?"

The brightness dimmed abruptly. *Merope* was to be only the first step, to earn the capital for buying opium! Charlie was opening his mouth to protest when his eye was caught by Yin-kwa, leaning across the bed, smiling, flat eyes shining:

"Tell him you agree."

What the devil? Charlie stared into Yin-kwa's bright eyes. Was this something to do with the glance Yin-kwa had flashed him? Yin-kwa said again, gently: "Tell him yes, Charlie." And Charlie turned slowly to How-kwa.

"Savvy."

How-kwa was watching him shrewdly.

"Jawgee number-one good man. Jawgee savvy must have *littee* opium"—he held thumb and forefinger close together to show a small quantity—"for buy tea. But plenty opium very bad. Man smoke one pipe every day, after littee time he finis'. No can think, no can chow, no can do nothing. Only lie bed, smoke, smoke. You savvy?"

Sir George had said something like that. "Opium is heavily addictive. Never try it, Charlie. Never!" Well, he didn't mean to! The sweet, heavy smell that sometimes wafted into the factory, that Wei said was the smell of opium being smoked, sickened him. He meant to get rich on opium, not smoke it!

He nodded at How-kwa. "Savvy."

"Carradine likee plenty opium. Me no wanchee you all same he. Savvy?"

"Savvy."

"Hmmmm." How-kwa's eyes, unamused, remained fixed on Charlie's. "S'pose you forget, I forget half profit b'long you. Savvy?"

"Savvy."

"Smile," Yin-kwa murmured.

Charlie smiled.

How-kwa's eyes were twinkling again. He pushed back the covers and lowered thin feet to the floor. The servant rushed up to place embroidered slippers on them. They all rose.

"Come!"

How-kwa beckoned. They left the room in procession, the old man in the lead on the servant's arm. Yin-kwa murmured in Charlie's ear:

"You did well."

"What did you mean . . . why did you? . . ."

"Shhh! We'll talk later."

He urged Charlie forward. On How-kwa's heels, Wei behind them, they walked back through the courtyards, past the dark houses of How-kwa's wives. Yin-kwa said in a normal tone, pointing:

"That one is my mother's house. I have many aunts and cousins and sisters, but my father was How-kwa's only son, and I am the only grandson. When my grandfather dies, I will be head of the family and of the *hong*—the business."

Charlie mumbled, finding no words. The sense of dislocation had returned, deeper than before. The high walls closed him into isolation in this strange, rich, alien world. The air hummed with languorous quiet, stirred with the faint perfume of the trees. The lanterns hanging from the walls glowed like nearby stars—How-kwa's private stars, Yin-kwa's stars, lighting the kingdom he would inherit. Prince Yin-kwa, heir to this kingdom.

They were back in the first house. The servant pushed aside the screen and slid apart a door that lay behind it. They crossed a high threshold into darkness. There was a heavy, musty smell, and the air was flat and stale. The place was seldom used. Someone made a light, a taper in a saucer of oil, and as the flame sputtered the room wavered into sight. Again, paneled walls and bare, polished floor. At the far end, a long, narrow table against the wall. On the table, some oblong objects that seemed to be made of stone, tall candlesticks, a vase from which protruded thin, dry sticks like the dead stalks of long fallen flowers.

How-kwa spoke to his grandson, and Yin-kwa turned to Charlie.

"This is the house of our family's ancestors. Those stone tablets on the altar are their soul tablets, on which their names are engraved. Twice a year, on the appropriate days, we worship at this altar and send our ancestors what they need to be comfortable in the world to which they have passed. We burn paper effigies of silver ingots, furniture, sedan chairs, servants, so that the spirits of the effigies can join the spirits of our ancestors and serve them in the other world, as they did in this one. That may sound like nonsense to you"—he gave Charlie a quizzical glance—"but we believe it. Now—my grandfather asks, will you honor our ancestors?"

"Why?" asked Charlie cautiously.

"Frankly"—Yin-kwa smiled disarmingly—"because my grandfather wants to put you under a compulsion to obey him. You'd acquire a Chinese kind of moral obligation to our family which in theory would force you to respect your promise not to buy opium. . . . Of course, in return, our family would also acquire a moral obligation to you, which would have its advantages. Take Wei, for example. His father's junk foundered somewhere near here in a typhoon, and he was washed ashore. He was just a boy, the sole survivor, and our family took him in. He honored our ancestors and became my grandfather's bondman, but our family is also bound to him. When his wife died, we'd have cared for his sons if he hadn't chosen to send them north, unfortunately to their deaths. Now that his daughter is getting too big to live with him at the factory, she'll be brought here and raised with our children."

"Mmmm." Charlie still felt dubious. But that glance of Yin-kwa's had certainly meant something. "What must I do?"

"Light a joss stick—a stick of incense—and put it into that vase on the altar. Then make a kowtow."

"You mean, lie down and bang my head on the floor?"

"Yes."

"I can't do that!"

In silence, everyone stared at Charlie. Floundering, he remembered Lord Ambleton.

"But I'll kneel on one knee and bow my head to the altar. That's how we honor our King in our country. And I'll light the joss stick."

Yin-kwa spoke to his grandfather, who smiled and nodded, and turned back to Charlie.

"Good. My grandfather is pleased."

The servant brought an incense stick and a piece of live coal in a brazier. Feeling strange and solemn, Charlie set the tip of the stick to the coal. At once, the heavy, musty smell rose thickly: Many joss sticks had been burned in this room. The stick began to glow. Yin-kwa placed his hand over Charlie's, lifted the stick, and blew on it lightly until the glow reddened and the smoke swirled. Then he released Charlie's hand and pointed to the altar.

Slowly, Charlie went forward and slipped the smoking stick into the vase among the burned-out ones. Then, taking a step backward, he went down on one knee and bowed his head. It seemed, in the silence, in the choking smell of the incense, that something should happen—some ancestor speak, perhaps, or some ancestral hand touch his shoulder like an English king dubbing one of his subjects into knighthood. But nothing happened, and after a long moment, Charlie rose to find the others unchanged, How-kwa nodding with satisfaction, Wei smiling, Yin-kwa looking pleased. It was over, and no one had felt solemn but himself—obviously, ancestors and their descendants were on familiar terms. With no effort at quiet, How-kwa led the way back to the outer room, and the servant unceremoniously blew out the taper and shut the ancestors back into darkness behind their magnificent screen.

In the outer room, a meal had been laid on the marble-topped table—a great number of small, steaming dishes from which rose delectable smells. Charlie was suddenly ravenous. He sat down with the others, who started immediately to eat, chopsticks flashing from dish to mouth, the little dumplings and pastries transported as though by magic between the thin sticks. Charlie watched hungrily until Yin-kwa laughed and handed him a clumsy-looking spoon made of porcelain. He scooped up a dumpling, which melted in his mouth in the most delicious taste he could ever have imagined. Wei smiled.

"More better roas' beef?"

"More better!"

Charlie began to eat as quickly as the others. The dishes were soon emptied. The servant moved them and poured tea into small, translucent, handleless cups. Charlie recognized the fragrance—Lapsang Souchong, the best of teas—but not the appearance. This tea was a light reddish color instead of dark brown, and tiny flowers floated in it. Yin-kwa smiled.

"Chrysanthemums, to enhance the flavor. The English buy tons of tea and drain themselves of silver to pay for it, then ruin it by stewing instead of brewing it, and adding milk and sugar!"

The tea, apparently, was the signal for talk. How-kwa sat back, belched, and turned to Wei. Yin-kwa said softly:

"Now, Charlie. We haven't much time, so listen carefully, keep your voice down, and *don't* use the word that begins with O. They'd recognize that word at once. Understand?"

Charlie nodded.

"Good. . . . My grandfather believes that the barbarians will soon break into our country. The present style of trading has gone on for a hundred and fifty years and he thinks it can't last much longer. That's why he sent me to learn English—so that our *hong* will have the advantage when the English spread all over our country. . . . Don't look so serious. Smile."

Charlie smiled.

"I think my grandfather is right in that, but in another matter I'm sure he's not. He thinks that tea will go on forever as the main article of trade. I think that there will be many other things, both bought and sold, and the big O will be one of them. An important one."

"Me too!" Charlie smiled without prompting. "Sir George

39

told me tonight that the Honorable Company has lowered prices of the big O at Calcutta, and increased production at Patna."

"Ah!" Yin-kwa smiled broadly. "It's a wonderful omen that you came tonight! Wei's been saying that you must have very good joss because of the color of your hair, and it seems to be true. . . . You and I are going into the big O trade together."

Charlie gaped. "How? Your grandfather made me promise never to buy it. He'll withdraw my half of *Merope*'s profits if I forget that promise—"

"*Smile!*" Yin-kwa murmured. "My grandfather is old-fashioned. I, as the future head of the family, have a moral duty to safeguard the *hong*'s fortunes. Without, of course, displeasing my grandfather—that would be unfilial. So you must say nothing about this to anyone, especially not to Wei, who would immediately tell my grandfather. You swear to keep this between us only?"

"I swear. But . . ."

"Chahlee!" How-kwa was leaning across the table. "What you two boy talkee, so serious? About you papa? Wei tell me you papa no likee you, send you come Canton when you littee boy?"

Charlie looked into the kind, twinkling eyes and nodded. Depression clamped down. What were he and Yin-kwa talking about? Two boys playing smuggler, like children playing shop. Babes in the wood.

"Smile," Yin-kwa said again, smiling himself. "He's doing it on purpose to make you feel like a child, to put you in the proper frame of mind to obey him. Actually, he likes you very much. He admired you for trying to get into trade without money, he thinks your idea about turning *Merope* into a floating warehouse is brilliant, and he liked the way you avoided making a kowtow. Don't let him discourage you. We can do it. Listen. My grandfather directs the smuggling of the big O in Canton." He laughed shortly at Charlie's stare. "Surprised? He does it, of course, to keep the smuggling under his control. It would be impossible for us to break into it here without his knowing, but we can do it up the coast."

40

"But we'd need a vessel! We'd have to bribe officials . . . it's impossible!"

"It's entirely possible. In fact, Carradine has already done it on a small scale, with the missionary Gutzen, who taught me English. Gutzen knows many Chinese dialects—he's a wonderful linguist. As a barbarian he's not allowed on Chinese soil, but in fact he's made a number of journeys into China to distribute Bibles that he translated and had printed. Carradine offered to stand the cost of printing more Bibles if Gutzen would sail up the coast on one of his ships carrying the big O and make initial contacts ashore for selling it, and Gutzen did. So it's already been introduced up the coast—and once it's known, it sells itself. . . . I'm doing all the talking. Say something."

"You interest me very much. But I don't want to risk losing my half of the profits from *Merope!*"

"You won't! Here's what I propose. I told my grandfather I should make a journey upcountry to visit the tea growers and see if the middlemen, who buy the tea from them and sell it to us, are making too much profit. He agreed. Along the way I'll meet the mandarins. They make big squeeze out of the tea trade, and they'll not object to making more out of another kind of trade. You said we'd have to bribe officials. I'm in a far better position to arrange that than Carradine or Gutzen."

Charlie sighed, a long exhalation that might have been sorrowful but for the light in his eyes. Yin-kwa grinned.

"Your part will be to find a vessel and an Englishman as captain. We need an Englishman because if a Chinese master should be caught with that kind of cargo he'd be liable to severe punishment and the mandarins could squeeze us dry over that. Then, as soon as *Merope* is at Lintin and has a cargo aboard, you'll buy some of it, load it on our vessel, and send it up the coast. D'you know the name? I'll spell it. Don't say it aloud. L-e-e K-w-o-k. He's the chief of the smugglers under my grandfather's control. I've discussed this with him often. He dares not increase the smuggling in Canton because of my grandfather, but he's eager to help us with the upcoast trade. D'you see how easy it will be?"

41

"Yes," Charlie breathed.

How-kwa was preparing to rise. Yin-kwa said quickly:

"Can you be in Macao on this day, three months?"

"Yes. I'll quit the Company if I have to."

"I'll meet you there for final arrangements. D'you know Vargas' place? Go there. Ask for a girl called Ah Sam."

"I . . ."

"Payment will be made in advance. This day, three months."

Two of How-kwa's private sedan chairs took Charlie and Wei back to the city gate. From there they walked to the factory, Charlie stumbling in a blur of excitement and exhaustion, feet splayed and aching in the unaccustomed looseness of the cloth slippers, thoughts whirling in an incoherent merry-go-round.

The big O! Very bad, according to How-kwa. Addictive, according to George. Poisonous, according to the Chinese. George said the Chinese held opium to be poisonous because it came from India and in India dead bodies were exposed to be eaten by birds of prey, so opium must have bits of human flesh mixed up in it. Everything was mixed up. But whatever it was, whatever whoever said it was, opium was *silver*. Great bricks of bullion. Or lovely, round silver dollars. Or *sycee,* the strange little ingots the Chinese made, walnut-sized balls of silver squashed into shapes like tiny boats. Silver, silver, silver.

Back in Wei's room, Wei said:

"You glad, Chahlee?"

He was too tired to smile, but he said, "I'm glad, Wei," and Wei was satisfied with the tone of his voice. He smiled gently and sadly.

"After my boys finis', you all same my son. . . . Go sleep now."

As Charlie slowly climbed the stairs, the buzz of joy faded a little. He wasn't really cheating Wei, was he? It was just that in the future he wouldn't be telling Wei *everything*, as he had in the past. There was no reason why he must. In any case, Wei wanted him to have what he wanted, and he wanted that money! He wanted it! He couldn't go home without it!

Sleep didn't come at once. He tossed a while, thinking, not of *Merope*, How-kwa, Yin-kwa, the big O, the silver—of Wei.

But when he opened his eyes the next morning, the thought in his mind was: Blogg! Blogg was the man to captain their vessel! Blogg had been master of *Betsy* when she lost the twenty chests overboard. Carradine had beached him for that and had blackballed him with the other owners, though Blogg swore that he'd tried the transfer only at Carradine's insistence. Since then, Blogg had been hanging around, unable to get another berth. Blogg was the man for them!

Chapter III

1821

SENHORA VARGAS WAS oily-skinned, short, stout, rigidly corseted. She flipped over the pages of a ledger, followed a line of writing with her finger, and looked up at Charlie with a ferocious smile.

"Si! Ah Sam. Payment awreddy. You go upstair'. . . ." She beckoned to a little Chinese girl who seemed no more than ten years old. "She tak' you upstair'. She spik Inglis."

The little girl came up and broke into a recitation, looking up at Charlie with unblinking eyes.

"I spik Inglis good. I born here this house. Since I baby alla gen'lman teach me spik Inglis. I tak' you upstair'. You come."

She started up an ornate staircase carpeted thickly in crimson. Gilded mirrors on the inner wall reflected scenes in a parlor previously hidden from Charlie by the half-wall behind the Senhora's desk. As in a series of kaleidoscopes, he saw strutting legs, jaunty buttocks, jutting breasts, counterpointed against the dark clothes and heavy beards of numbers of foreign men. And in the bottom right-hand corner of each mir-

44

ror, he saw the reflection of Senhora's eyes, bright, hard, and watchful.

Head half turned to stare into the mirrors, he stumbled over the child. She had stopped to gaze at the reflection of a man stepping out of the open doorway of a side room, buttoning his trousers, while another man, unbuttoning his, waited to go through. The child shook her head sadly.

"One night, gen'lman pee-pee more dollah than Senhora give me one year! Drink wine, pee-pee. Drink wine, pee-pee . . ."

Sighing, she trudged up the rest of the stairs. Charlie followed dumbly, his bewildered senses momentarily overcome by the child's economic value system. At the top of the steps, the crimson carpet continued down a long corridor, dark as blood except where chandeliers spilled circles of light that showed up scarlet as a bishop's sash. The child stopped again and looked up at him patiently.

"Mister. Ah Sam is number-one girlee. All gen'lman want Ah Sam, but she say only this one, only that one. You good joss, Ah Sam say yes for you. You unnerstan'?"

He nodded humbly. Satisfied, the child led him to a door at the end of the corridor, threw it open with a bang, pushed him in, and slammed it shut behind him.

At first it seemed that there was no one in the blood-red room. Then, from behind the canopied bed, a tiny girl came forward, her tip-tilted face reaching no higher than his shoulder. He stared down into sparkling black eyes, heard a lilting:

"Hah! Good-joss color hair!"

She reached up and ran her fingers lightly through his hair, then down his cheeks.

"*And* no got nit-nit! *And* no got beard! I *like!*"

Laughing, she pulled him to the bed. He sat stiffly beside her, wishing the little girl had not left. In her way, Ah Sam was as frightening as Senhora.

She said cheerfully, "What you name?"

"Charlie."

"Chahlee." Her pronunciation of the name was more accented than Wei's or How-kwa's: a singsong, with the first

45

syllable in a considerably higher tone than the second. Somehow, it made him feel like a different person—not Charlie of the tea, the Lapsang Souchong and the Oolong, but Chahlee of blood-red bedrooms.

"How old you?"

"Seventeen."

"Hah!" She beamed at him. "You boy yet. All gen'lman come here, maybe forty year old, maybe more. Only old man got 'nuff money come here. Fat. Stinky. Nit-nit in hair. Ugh! But you, Chahlee, I like!"

She slipped a hand between his legs and gave him a pat that flashed a sharp, exquisite ache to the pit of his stomach. With the other hand, she pulled a cord at her neck. Her loose pink gown slithered away, leaving her naked, a sudden conjuring of glowing ivory flesh. The ache spread like wildfire through his loins, countered by a wave of panic that snatched his breath, fixed his mouth agape.

She turned his face sharply to hers.

"Wassa matta? You sick?"

For a moment she regarded him warily, then broke into a peal of laughter.

"You first time? No ping-ping before? I teach you, Chahlee! I teach you!"

The crimson silk of the bed's canopy impinged slowly on Charlie's dimmed vision. The ache had gone. The panic had gone. He was bathed in wonderful contentment. Against his side Ah Sam lay, a density, soft and warm, long black hair streaming across his chest. He touched it.

"Ah Sam? Thank you."

She sat up.

"No 'thank you'! Yin-kwa, he pay for all night. S'pose he no pay, I tell Senhora, she make *you* pay *three* time. No 'thank you.' Business."

She grinned at the look on his face.

"You young, Chahlee! I teach you more than ping-ping. I

46

teach you life!" She held up a finger, eyes shining. "I teach you 'nother thing too!"

Jumping out of bed, she draped herself again in the loose pink gown, opened the door, and yelled down the corridor. Then she took from a cupboard a large basin and some cloths.

"Come, Chahlee."

"Why?"

"*Come!*"

He looked around for his clothes.

"No, no—come nekkid."

The door burst open and the little girl entered, struggling with a large jug of water, steaming hot. Ah Sam helped her pour it into the basin. The child hurried away in response to another shriek down the hall, and Ah Sam gestured to Charlie.

"Come quick. Water hot now."

She washed him from head to foot, paying special attention to cracks and crannies, scrubbing hard, rinsing the cloth in the basin and wringing it out many times. It felt wonderful. His very skin seemed to breathe. He glowed all over. At last she sat back on her heels.

"You like?"

"It's marvelous!"

"Mahvalus!" she imitated him, grinning. "Inglis man take bath maybe one time one year. Very stinky! You stinky too, but only little. You make like this every day, never stinky. You come again see me, you bath first. If no stinky, no nit-nit, I make wunnerful ping-ping for you."

"Oh, Ah Sam!"

He dropped to the carpet beside her and put his arms around her. Sir George's anxious face appeared behind his eyelids. His colleague's sardonic "if you must go . . ." echoed in his ears. What was the matter with them? Hadn't they ever *tried* this? There must be something very wrong with any man who denigrated ping-ping! There was the money, of course—"business," she'd said—but she hadn't really meant that.

"Ah Sam, I'm going to take you away from here!"

"Why?" Her voice, muffled in his shoulder, sounded startled.

"Because I love you!"

"Sure. Love. Ping-ping love . . ."

The door clattered open. The busy little girl put her head in, chattered urgently, and withdrew again, all in an instant. Ah Sam struggled free.

"Yin-kwa come. Better you put clotheses."

She dumped the dirty water out of a window hidden behind a blood-red curtain and began to tidy up. Charlie, struggling into his trousers, swiveled to watch her. The tiny little thing couldn't weigh half what any one of those old bearded men downstairs weighed! It was cruel! How much would it take to get her out?

Yin-kwa came in quietly. Charlie, already accustomed to the door being flung open and banged shut, heard only a click and Yin-kwa was in the room. His flat, slitted eyes were unsmiling. The neatly plucked hairline made a high dome of his brow. The queue, as before, was loosely plaited, but this time he wore a dark blue robe of heavy brocaded silk, the neckpiece richly embroidered in many colors. He stood, silent and haughty, in the middle of the room.

"Yin-kwa!"

"Charlie."

His voice was cold and arrogant. He went slowly to the table, seated himself beside it, stretched out his arms, one and then the other, sliding up the long sleeves of his robe to expose his hands. The nails of his little fingers were more than an inch long and beginning to curl inward.

Ah Sam had seated herself on the floor at a little distance. Her eyes were lowered. The child tiptoed in with a teapot and two of the small handleless cups. She poured tea and then backed out of the room, wide eyes fixed anxiously on Yin-kwa.

Charlie moved to the other chair at the table, heart thumping. What had gone wrong?

Yin-kwa burst out laughing.

"How do you like that performance, Charlie? That's how I performed for the mandarins up the coast. They were highly impressed! They all agreed, for a trifling bribe of thirty dollars a chest, that any number of wooden chests—contents unknown to them, of course—may be landed along the coast."

Relief surged through Charlie like a tide. By God, it was true, it was real, it was going to happen! He raised his cup to Yin-kwa and they drank together, emptying the cups at a gulp, grinning at each other.

"And what have you done, Charlie?" Yin-kwa sat back, produced a small pair of scissors from an inside pocket, and began clipping off the long nails of his little fingers.

"I've found a master for our vessel. A man called Blogg. Do you know him?"

"The man who lost twenty chests off *Betsy*?"

"That's him. But Carradine bedeviled him into trying it, and then beached him when the twenty chests slid overboard."

"He's a drunkard."

"He's been drinking a lot, yes, but that's because he's desperate. Carradine blackballed him with the other owners and none of them dares employ him, though they all know he's a fine seaman. He's desperate enough to come to us for nearly nothing."

"Not for nearly nothing. We couldn't trust a ship full of opium to a man working for nearly nothing. If he's as good as you say, we'll put him on a profit-sharing basis. If he's no use, we'll get somebody else."

"Fine! I think you'll agree he's a good man. I liked him."

"And what about a ship?"

"D'you know *San Sebastian*? She's a *lorcha*, western-style hull and Chinese rigging. She doesn't look like much, but Blogg says she's sound, and she's going cheap."

Yin-kwa turned to Ah Sam and began to speak in Chinese. She listened, sparkling. She had shed subservience when Yin-kwa shed haughtiness. Indeed, he was the heir to a kingdom!

They all watched him and followed his signals—Ah Sam, the child, the upcoast mandarins. Ah Sam was nodding. Yin-kwa turned back to Charlie.

"You shouldn't appear in the purchase of the ship. That would be so surprising it couldn't be kept secret. I've told Ah Sam to buy it for us."

"Won't that be surprising too? Someone . . . someone like her . . ."

"They'll know she's buying for somebody, but they won't know who. They won't suspect me because my grandfather can buy as many ships as he likes without secrecy. And"—Yin-kwa grinned—"they won't suspect you. How long have you been here? Since seven? Word's already out that you're the latest bird in Ah Sam's cage. I heard it downstairs from Vargas, then from the child, then from one of the other girls. Nobody will suspect you came here for any kind of business but the business of this house!"

He shouted with laughter as Charlie reddened.

"No need to blush, Charlie! Many men are mad for Ah Sam. My own father—"

"Your *father?*"

"Yes! How old d'you think she is? At least thirty-five! My father would have bought her as his concubine if he hadn't died, so my mother told me. Ever since, she's regarded herself as my stepmother. That's why I sent you to her."

Ah Sam was contriving to look proud, modest, and uninterested at the same time. Charlie stared at her. Thirty-five? That fine ivory skin, smooth and taut, without a wrinkle! The lithe little body under the pink silk! She couldn't be thirty-five! And what if she was? She was marvelous! The delicious, tingling, tightening ache attacked him once again. She knew it—she flicked an amused eye at him.

"Well . . ." Yin-kwa brought Charlie back to the matter at hand. "As soon as Ah Sam lets you know that *San Sebastian* has been bought, Blogg can take charge and recruit a crew. I'll appoint one man—the supercargo who'll deal with the mandarins."

"Good. But we'll need a second ship."

"No second ship. Just the one."

"But a *lorcha* can't go to India!"

"We'll not be going to India. We'll not be involved in bringing opium from India. Just buying it when it's here already, and delivering it up the coast."

"Carradine . . ."

"We'll not be imitating Carradine."

They stared at each other, suddenly hostile.

Charlie said flatly: "He would have stolen my idea about *Merope* and cut me out."

"So?" Yin-kwa's tone was as cold as his eyes. "Listen, Charlie. We can't keep Carradine out of the upcoast smuggling, or anyone else, for that matter—the mandarins will take a bribe from anyone who can bring it to them. We can't prevent Carradine, or anyone else who can afford it, from anchoring hulks at Lintin. We'll be the first, but many more will follow us. You'll have to get along with that as best you can. And we're not going to compete with them to be the best and biggest. We're just going to stick to our own little operation as I described it, until I judge it's time to expand. If you can't agree to that, I'll have to withdraw from our partnership."

Ah Sam shifted uneasily and shot Charlie a warning glance.

"Chahlee, more better you let Yin-kwa fix. He savvy. You no savvy."

Not even ping-ping, her glance said. Charlie glowered. But, by God, she was right! All he knew about trade was what he'd learned from George, and all George knew was the tea trade, which ran like clockwork, all cut and dried, a monopoly in which George had no competitors. He glanced at Yin-kwa and spoke in pidgin, with mock humility.

"All li'. You savvy more better me."

"I do!" Good humor bubbled again in Yin-kwa's eyes. "Now listen. Lee Kwok is going to manage the selling for us, for a one-third share of the profits." When Charlie looked rebellious again, he held up a hand. "Trust me, Charlie. It's well worth it! That way we won't have to handle silver, except for

51

the first lot of bribes for the mandarins. After that first lot, Lee Kwok will manage the bribes too." He glanced slyly at Charlie. "Carradine, of course, must handle all his own silver—sacks and sacks of it, weighing tons, taking up a great deal of space, having to be guarded every instant. Lee Kwok and his buyers upcoast can exchange silver deposits by exchanging bits of paper. Lee Kwok will keep your share of the silver until you want it, and even invest it for you and pay you interest. Otherwise, how would you keep and safeguard your silver?"

Charlie looked sheepish.

"Never thought of that."

"Then it's agreed?"

"Agreed!" Charlie bounded to his feet, swept on a great surge of excitement. "Let's have wine!"

"*Sam shui.* Rice wine. Not Senhora's rotgut." Yin-kwa spoke calmly, eyes glistening.

Ah Sam went to the door. The shriek that Charlie had come to expect followed. The child came running with a clay jug and handleless cups so tiny that Charlie had trouble holding his between thumb and forefinger. The wine was warm and sweetish. One cupful hardly filled his mouth. He tossed it back—why did the Chinese serve wine in thimbles?—and waved at Ah Sam for more.

Yin-kwa went on talking. The shipbuilder had said that *Merope* would be ready in two months' time. The stern bay was being converted into living quarters for Charlie. Belowdecks, *Merope* was being stripped to make two large holds, aft and forward. Between the holds there'd be a space for cooking, and for hammocks for the crew.

"My grandfather thinks you should use lascars—Black Barbarians, we call them. Nobody knows their language, so they can't talk to anyone but themselves."

"Where would I get Black Barbarians?" Charlie roared with laughter.

"From Carradine's ships." Yin-kwa grinned. "They're all manned by lascars. Offer them more wages than they're getting. Blogg will know how to manage it."

Charlie drank to that. And to *Merope, San Sebastian,* Lee Kwok, Blogg, Ah Sam, Wei, How-kwa, Yin-kwa, himself. By the time he could think of nothing else to drink to, the jug was empty.

Toward dawn, Charlie opened bleary eyes to lamplight glowing on blood-red silk above his head. His head ached like the devil. It was the wine—that bland-tasting, sweetish, murderous stuff . . .

The wine!

Slowly, with wonder, remembrance came.

It had come true, the hectic daydreaming, the midnight talks with Wei in the attic. All come true. He'd be going home one day with a mountain of silver, enough to waste handfuls thrown in his father's face. It would take—what? ten years?—to amass the million he'd dreamed of. A *million?* Sometimes he'd thought he was mad—it was mad to dream of a million! But that's what opium generated. Millions in bullion or *sycee.* Millions of bright, shiny, heavy, beautiful silver dollars.

Beside him, Ah Sam sighed and stirred. She was sleeping on her back. So tiny. So smooth and strong and lithe. Yin-kwa had said that the living quarters on the *Merope* were comfortable. The stern bay. The windowed superstructure leading off the main deck. It would be cool there. Open to the breezes, the windows high above the water.

How much would it take to buy Ah Sam out of this place?

He shook her gently. "Ah Sam?"

"Mmmmmm?"

"Yin-kwa said his father would have bought you out of this house."

"Mmmm. But he die. I sorry. If he not die, I get plenty dollah. His wife come see me. She say s'pose I go her husband, he give me dollah, she give me too."

"What?"

"Sure! More husband come Ah Sam bed, less wife have baby, less wife have trouble. Foreign woman crazy, no like husband have other wife. You sleep now, Chahlee."

"Ah Sam?"

"Why no sleep?"

"I'm thinking. I want to buy you out of here. I'll have money soon. How much will Senhora want for you?"

She sat up, cross-legged, and regarded him with serious eyes.

"Senhora and *me*. Yin-kwa can fix with Senhora, but me—how much you pay me, Chahlee?"

He faltered. "I thought . . ."

"You think save me, like joss man Gutzen. I no like save. I like dollah. I work here many year, send dollah my mama-papa. When they die, I send my brother, sister. Now they marry, all proper. So I think I work few more year, when I got 'nuff dollah for me, I stop. So—s'pose I go you on ship, how much you pay me?"

"I . . . don't know! What I can afford. Don't you trust me?"

She sighed.

"Chahlee, if got dollah, no need trust. No got dollah, no use trust. How much?"

"All right!" He sat up too and faced her. "How much d'you want?"

"Hah! Good!" She settled herself, regarding Charlie with bright speculation. "I tell you true, Chahlee. I like go you, live on ship like Yin-kwa say. Every day you bath, shave beard. No nit-nit, no stinky. S'pose we make like this: When your business with Yin-kwa going proper, you pay Senhora, and you pay me ten thousan' dollah. I go you, stay maybe one year, maybe ten year. When I like finis', when you like finis', you pay me more ten thousan', I go 'way. Can do?"

"You mean, when I can pay Senhora, and pay you ten thousand dollars, you'll come and stay with me until we both agree that you're to leave, and then I'll pay you another ten thousand?"

"Yes."

"Can do, Ah Sam."

"Good! I like!" She plonked herself down again. "Now sleep."

"Ah Sam?"

"Wassa matta you, Chahlee!" she cried, exasperated.

"You realize you'll be trusting me for that second ten thousand dollars? What if I haven't got it when you want to leave?" He grinned at her closed eyes. "Like it or not, you'll be trusting me!"

She opened an eye and glared at him.

"Not *you!* Yin-kwa! Yin-kwa business must be good business. You make business with Yin-kwa, you must got ten thousan' dollah!"

San Sebastian lumbered before the wind, her masts creaking under full sail, her scuppers no more than two feet above the water, weighed down by the three hundred chests of opium in her hold. To the east, the empty sea stretched into eternity—the nearest land in that direction was the Spanish islands of the Philippines. To the west, the coast of Kwangtung Province loomed hazily. A gentle sun touched the sea's blue with shimmers of gold. A gentle wind playfully riffled the waters. A perfect day.

The fisher boats past which *San Sebastian* sailed saw an ordinary *lorcha,* one of those bastard half-foreign half-Chinese ships, rather old, rather unkempt, wooden hull scarred, sails dark and stained. But inboard she was spick-and-span, deck scrubbed spotless, ropes coiled, nothing out of place. Her sails were new, purposely dirtied here and there. Her crew, young, lean, bare-chested, their pigtails wound tightly round their heads, went smartly about their duties.

"You've done a fine job, Blogg!" Charlie spoke happily.

"Bain't special, guv'nor. Just proper."

Charlie looked up at the giant beside him, a head taller than he. Blogg had rough, grizzled hair and a full beard. His eyes were deep-set and very blue in a craggy, weather-beaten face. His voice was unexpectedly mild.

"D'you know Namoa Island, Blogg?"

"Know it well. And they know us there. Took the boys up

two weeks ago, cargo of them wee oranges from beyond Canton. Thought it'd be good training for 'em, and good to be seen there with a harmless cargo."

"How long will it take us?"

"Three-four days, weather holding." Blogg scanned the cloudless sky. "Should hold. Beautiful, today. We'll be quicker going back without them fifteen ton of you-know-what. Shouldn't be more than a day at Namoa, s'posing that supercargo knows his job and all be going well there."

"He'll know his job! The owner appointed him."

Blogg glanced sideways at Charlie.

"Be you owner, guv? Or be you shares with some Chinee?"

Charlie hesitated.

"Let's see how this first voyage goes."

"Right. No call to tell me nothing you don't want to. I'm beholden to you. That poxy Carradine would've liked to see me scuppered. I thankee for this chance."

Charlie laughed. "We'll be thanking *you* if all goes well!"

"And so it will!"

"I thought . . . I was afraid the crew might think it bad joss to have a woman aboard. They don't mind?"

Blogg grinned broadly. "That they did, at first. But after she talked to 'em, why, they dassn't be anything but right glad!"

Charlie laughed. Ah Sam had insisted on coming too. She had argued a long time with Yin-kwa, sitting cross-legged on the tousled bed, and at last Yin-kwa had shrugged.

"She says you're too young. You might do something foolish if left to yourself."

Ah Sam climbed off the bed and thumped decisively to the floor.

"No more talk! I go too!"

So now she sat on a coil of rope, her long hair blowing free, looking like a child, enjoying the voyage like a child.

"Chahlee, so many year I in Senhora house, go out only little. I forget now nice the sea. I forget wind. I forget sun."

She slept alone in the one tiny private cabin.

"No, Chahlee. Senhora house, I sleep daytime. Here on ship, I like sleep *night*time."

So Charlie spent the nights in a hammock on deck, staring at the stars, listening to the creak of the masts and the water's whisper, trying to concentrate on why he was here. A million dollars. A dollar for every cold word his father had ever said to him, for every fish in his stream, every bird in his hedgerows, every leaf in his forest. The cool, moist, deep forest . . . But it was hard to hold a thought. He was suspended in time, coming from nowhere, going nowhere, under a spell.

The spell was broken the day they sailed into Namoa harbor, a day as clear and sweet as all the days of the voyage. Blogg ordered the main sails reefed, and they cruised gently around the island to anchor in its lee, at the mouth of a bay crowded with craft, a busy, pretty harbor. Charlie stood in the waist of the ship, stomach fluttering. What now? Would the mandarin come? Would he be complacent, as Yin-kwa said, or would he come breathing fire to enforce his Emperor's edicts? What were Chinese prisons like?

"Well?" Blogg laid a hand on his shoulder.

"I'm nervous!"

"Not you! You're excited, that's what!"

"What are we to do now?"

"That's his job."

Blogg jerked a thumb at the supercargo, who had come on deck dressed formally in a long blue gown, an embroidered band around his neck. He was a fat, jolly man who had kept to his hammock most of the voyage—even the sight of the sea made him ill, he said. But now he was brisk.

"We make ready. Soon mandarin come."

Ah Sam must go to her cabin and stay there—the mandarin must not be distracted from the business at hand. Brandy and cheroots must be set out on the table in the main cabin. The brightly painted wooden tea chest containing the nine thousand silver dollars in bribes must be moved from Blogg's locker to a convenient place beside the ladder leading to the deck.

When the supercargo was satisfied with the arrangements, he handed Blogg a small yellow-and-orange-striped pennant to be run up the mainmast.

As soon as the pennant began to flutter, a large gig, almost as broad as it was long, put out from the side of a gaudily painted junk which was anchored in the middle of the harbor. The supercargo nodded happily.

"Mandarin come."

They watched the gig approach. The mandarin, a fat man in flowing robes, was seated in an armchair in the middle of the clumsy vessel, under a large umbrella. His attendants sat on the boards around him, waving fans to stir the air, flicking at flies with horsehair whisks. Ten oarsmen dipped and lifted the paddles that sent the equipage slowly and majestically toward *San Sebastian,* the little sampans scurrying out of its path. The supercargo sent some of Blogg's crewmen to lower *San Sebastian*'s gangplank, and went himself to bow the mandarin and his retinue aboard.

They all went down to the main cabin. The supercargo poured brandy and selected a cheroot, which he handed to the mandarin, bending respectfully to light it. There was silence for a moment as the mandarin puffed, turning haughtily to survey Charlie and Blogg. Then he lifted the hem of his robe to expose high boots of embroidered satin. From one of them he drew a short stick around which was rolled a piece of silk. This he handed to his chief attendant, who shook it out. Unrolled, the silk became a little banner covered with black Chinese characters. The attendant read it aloud in a sonorous voice. The mandarin turned to the supercargo with a severely questioning look.

The supercargo stepped forward, both humble and eager, bowing from his fat, round waist, and spoke at length to the mandarin, pointing dramatically at the sky, the sea, and the deck below his feet. When he had done, he bowed again, and stepped back. The mandarin nodded and rose to his feet.

Was that all? Was the mandarin leaving? His attendants were already preceding him up the ladder! Charlie glanced anxiously at the supercargo, who gave the slightest shake of his head. All was well. As the last of the attendants vanished onto the deck, the mandarin sat down again. The supercargo waved Charlie and Blogg to seats at the table, and went to sit in the chair nearest the mandarin. They were starting a whole new meeting. The supercargo began whispering confidentially to the mandarin, pointing at the tea chest. The mandarin smiled faintly and nodded. More low-voiced conversation, both men now smiling. Then the mandarin called out, and four of his attendants reappeared. They hefted the tea chest, apparently unsurprised by its weight, and carried it off. The mandarin rose again and this time, after bowing slightly to no one in particular, moved ponderously up the ladder and across the deck to his gig, followed by the supercargo bobbing bows all the way. It had all taken less than ten minutes.

As soon as the gig began moving, two junks from the cluster in the harbor drew swiftly alongside San Sebastian, port and starboard. A horde of coolies, half-naked, pigtails wound around their heads, clambered aboard. Like an army of ants, swarming yet never getting in each other's way, they went to work to empty San Sebastian of her cargo. Some hauled chests out of the holds. Some heaved the chests to the shoulders of others, who trotted off, heads strained forward, arms swinging rhythmically, leg muscles rippling, their burdens perfectly balanced across their upper backs. Reaching the junks, they twisted their shoulders, slipping the chests off sideways into the hands of other coolies who immediately lowered them into the junks' holds. Within an hour, San Sebastian's holds were empty, and the junks, low in the water, were lumbering away.

Charlie stared after them. By God, it was done! By God, it was as simple as loading and unloading tea at Whampoa! By God, the first of the million dollars had just come home to roost! By God! By God! He shouted joyously into the wind.

"Shhh!" Ah Sam came up beside him, smiling. "No awful yelling, please! Chinee man glad, only smile. Look he!"

She was pointing at the supercargo, who was coming quickly

up to the bridge, smiling broadly. Blogg banged him on the back with such enthusiasm that he staggered.

"By God, you know your job, you do! What was all that talk you and the mandarin was exchanging?"

The supercargo regained his balance and began to speak, barely able to suppress his chuckles.

"This silk that mandarin's servant read is Imperial Edict: Foreign ship come to Chinee can go only to Canton. So mandarin ask me: Why this Inglis ship come Namoa? I say"—he began again to shake with laughter, pointing up at the cloudless sky with the same dramatic gesture he had used before the mandarin—"I say very big typhoon, we lost our water, we must come Namoa fetch more water!"

His listeners let out a great shout of laughter, and he laughed with them, hiding his mouth behind his hand, for it wouldn't be modest to delight too much in his own cleverness. At last, when he could be heard again:

"Mandarin say all right, we can fetch water, and he stand up to show meeting finish. All servant go away. Then he sit down again to show *new* meeting starting. I say we very happy he give us water, very kind, so we give him *tea*. I show him tea box. Then he ask me when we come again. He say anytime—typhoon, no typhoon—we can come Namoa for fetching water. . . ."

His voice was lost in a new explosion of laughter, Blogg's belly roar drowning the others. The crew, grinning, gathered below the bridge, well knowing what was going on. Charlie flung an arm around Blogg's shoulder.

"What d'you say, Captain? A tot all round?"

"A double tot! I laid in *sam shui!*"

Charlie gave an exaggerated shudder. "For *them!* Grog'll do me fine!"

No one was entirely sober when they left that night, sailing quietly out of the harbor under a full moon. *San Sebastian*, relieved of her cargo, scudded like a gull on the glass-smooth sea. Blogg stood alone at the helm, his great head a black sculpture in the moonlight. Charlie sprawled against a bulkhead, doing sums in his mind.

Six hundred chests had been discharged into *Merope* the week before—her first storage cargo, the first ever discharged into a securely anchored floating warehouse under the bluffs of Lintin Island. At $5 a chest for storage and handling, that made $3,000, half How-kwa's, half his. Three hundred of those chests had just been delivered at Namoa. They had cost $1,500 a chest—$450,000, advanced by Yin-kwa—and they'd been sold by Lee Kwok at $1,800 a chest, a total of $540,000. Profit: $90,000, of which Lee Kwok would credit one-third to himself, one-third to Yin-kwa, and one-third to Charlie. Of course, the cost of buying and operating *San Sebastian* would have to be amortized, and the bribes to the mandarin deducted, and there'd be other expenses, but all the same his one-third share would amount to a lot of dollars! He smiled up at the stars, and they twinkled back at him—yes, Charlie! A lot of dollars!

Ah Sam settled quietly beside him. He put an arm around her and hugged her to him.

"Ah Sam, I'll soon have the money for Senhora and the ten thousand for you!"

"Mmmm." She put a soft hand in his. "Chahlee, when you first time come Senhora house, I like you because you hair good-joss color and no nit-nit and no beard. But now I like you because you very nice. When I say no come cabin, you not anger. Other man, very anger, maybe break door, maybe beat me."

He laughed and held her gently, and she ruffled his hair and said again:

"Good-joss color. All man crew this ship say you very good joss because color you hair."

He said, "When you come to *Merope*, Ah Sam, *that*'ll be good joss, for me, for *Merope*, for *San Sebastian*, for Blogg, for everybody."

She lifted her face to smile at him sweetly, her eyes lacking their usual tartness.

"I think so. I think you, me, together, very good joss. . . . Chahlee, you like come cabin now?"

"*I like!*"

He helped her up. The moonlight threw their shadows before them, faintly gray against the white shine of the scrubbed deck. The sea murmured in the lovely quiet. Except for Blogg at the helm, the length of the ship away from them, they were alone on the deck, alone on the sea, alone perhaps in all the world.

They had gone three steps toward the cabin when Blogg shouted. In an instant, bare feet were slapping the deck all around them as the crew erupted from their quarters. Blogg was pointing southward. Everyone turned to look.

Clear in the moonlight, dark sails had appeared against the silver sky. The men stared, tensely silent, and then began to mutter. Ah Sam gripped Charlie's hand.

"They say—pirate."

"Pirates!"

He turned again to stare. Already, the sails loomed bigger. The hull of the ship was becoming visible. She was coming fast toward them, rushing to meet them, to engage . . .

Blogg shouted from the bridge:

"Charlie! Send the woman below and come up here!"

Ah Sam slipped away and Charlie ran up to the bridge. Blogg was talking fast to his mate—they communicated in a language that Charlie could not follow, a kind of pidgin of the sea. The mate nodded and rushed away.

"Charlie." Blogg's voice vibrated with excitement. "It's a bloody pirate junk. Bloody great thing, and she's got the wind behind her. She's aiming to cut us off on our next tack. Ram us. I could heave to and run afore her, but she's bigger nor us, carries more sail, she'd overtake us afore we made Namoa again. So by God, I'm going to trick her. . . ."

They were at the end of a long southwesterly beat. Blogg flicked the helm, his huge hands as delicate as a woman's, and altered course to southeasterly. His narrowed eyes never left the pirate sails, but he was smiling.

"Here." With one hand he fumbled off the string around his neck from which hung the key to his locker. "Go break out what you'll find in there. Pikes for the men. Fighting irons for you and me." He flashed a fierce grin, his teeth glinting in the moonlight. "Just in case the trick don't work. But it will!"

Charlie ran for the cabin, pushing through men crowded around the masts, their heads craning upward. He glanced up too and saw men climbing in the rigging, dark bodies against dark sails, hardly visible, moving fast, as surefooted as monkeys. Blogg shouted again, and three of the men on deck sprang to go with Charlie, pressed around him as he turned Blogg's key. Pikes. They clanged against each other as Charlie rolled them out, short-handled, with thick, evil blades. The men snatched them up and ran back on deck. Charlie drew out a fighting iron—a half-glove of heavy leather to which were attached five long, jointed flails. A man wearing a fighting iron had an arm six feet long, with vicious iron fingers to slice strips from his enemy's flesh, slash through to his innocent white bones. Charlie grabbed up two of them. The flails clanged together as he rushed back up the ladder, staggering to keep his balance, clinging to the port rail to keep from sliding across the deck. *San Sebastian* was listing heavily to starboard, moving so fast that her starboard scuppers bounced on the water, slapping up great gobs of hissing, drenching spray. Charlie gasped as cold water smacked his face, stung his eyes.

The pirate junk was very close now, carrying every stitch of canvas. Charlie could see her heavy, iron-clad prow and, protruding before it, the twin prongs of battering rams like the gaping fangs of a furious beast of prey. He could envisage the exact point in the fast-closing gap of sea at which the two rushing ships would collide. There! There! Was Blogg trying to slip before the pirate, show her his stern? He couldn't do it! It was impossible! The pirate was going to ram them! The tendons of Charlie's jaw jumped out, tight as wire, as his mouth yawned in a wild grimace, the rending crash of the ramming already in his ears, the shuddering shock already in his bones.

63

From the bridge, Blogg roared out a command, and the men in the rigging flashed into action. *San Sebastian*'s sails concertinaed. Every sail, an instant earlier bellying at fullest strain, suddenly collapsed into itself. She lost way as though a giant hand had closed upon her. In moments, she was almost stationary, her deck swinging gently level, the roar of her passage subsiding into the whisper of the waves.

The pirate shot past across *San Sebastian*'s bows.

The crew had *sam shui* for breakfast. Charlie and Blogg had grog. Ah Sam had tea. Once again, they were sailing calmly. Immediately after the pirate passed, Blogg had ordered *San Sebastian*'s sails hoisted again, and he had put her back into fast tacking until, at dawn, he was satisfied that the pirate had given them up.

Charlie downed the last of his grog.

"By God, Blogg, that was magnificent!"

Blogg grinned and bent to pat the deck with his huge hand. "The *San Seb* be a good little ship!"

Charlie grinned back at him.

"And you're a partner in her!"

"Partner?" Blogg's eyes flashed, blue darts that matched the color of the sea.

"Yes. A sixtieth share—I think that's what captains get. We'll draw up the papers as soon as we're back at *Merope*."

Blogg murmured quietly, "Thankee, guv'nor."

"What about 'Charlie'?" Charlie said.

"Well—Charlie . . ." Blogg looked up and broke into a wide grin. "Matter of fact, crew's saying 'twas *your* good joss, not my sailing."

"*What?*"

"Aye! Hair that color, heavy good joss!"

They laughed and then sat silent, the tension draining from them. Charlie felt a grateful lassitude. Forty-eight hours and they'd be back on *Merope*. How-kwa's shipbuilder had done a splendid job. Her decks were stripped so clean that the lascars were unimpeded as they hauled the chests and stowed them in the holds—bank upon bank of chests, neat and solid, like tea chests, but richer, much, much richer!

And the wide, windowed stern bay. Hot during the day but cool, as he had reckoned, as soon as the sun had set. When Ah Sam came . . .

Ah Sam jumped up, pointing.

"Look! Look!"

Against the hazy outline of the Kwangtung coast, a derelict floated aimlessly, the wind riffling the tatters of her sails. No one moved on her deck. No hand could be on her helm guiding that erratic drift. The shell of a ship.

"By God!" Blogg spoke in a whisper. "She's *Betsy!*"

He called to his mate at the helm, and *San Seb* altered course to make for the derelict. When they were close enough, Blogg rowed Charlie across in the dinghy. *Betsy* had been ravaged. Her decks were littered with debris, great clots of drying blood, bits of gray, nameless matter, a mound of sprawled bodies carelessly flung on top of each other. In the scuppers a severed English head stared unblinking into the sun.

Blogg picked his way silently belowdecks, Charlie following, his stomach quaking. It was the same everywhere—blood, bodies, litter. Only the hold was unlittered. There was nothing at all in it but the smell of opium.

They didn't speak until they were back in *San Sebastian* and the fresh breeze had swept the cloy of the blood scent from their lungs. Blogg said:

"*Betsy* must have been following us. Carradine must've heard we were sailing with you-know-what aboard, and must've reckoned on getting a share of whatever we was bound for. . . . I thought it was funny, only one pirate coming for us. They usually hunt in pairs or threes. Our pirate must've come after us while his mates cleared out *Betsy*. Then he gave us up, not to be late to their meeting place and maybe lose his share of plunder. . . . Charlie, reckon we need to be armed with more nor pikes and fighting irons. Should have us a little traversing cannon. I can get one from a mate of mine, from Singapore."

Charlie nodded silently. If he spoke, the contents of his stomach might come up with the words. The graying eyeballs of that severed head, staring straight up into the sun, had seemed to be melting.

Blogg said reflectively:

"It's going to grow right quick, this upcoast trade in you-know-what. Our first sail, and *Betsy* following us . . . aye, it's going to grow right quick."

Chapter IV

1830

CURLING BARE TOES against the early dew that slicked *Merope's* timbers, Charlie watched the great ship slide quietly out of the dawn mist. *Red Rover*. The first, and—Charlie thought—still the most beautiful of the clippers. Built by William Clifton on the order of the governor-general of India, who gave him a bonus of ten thousand pounds sterling from Indian revenues when his promise that she would beat the monsoons was fulfilled. In Sir George's day, clumsy galleons like *Merope* had brought opium to China once a year, wallowing from India on the southwest monsoon and back to India on the northeast. Now, the tall, slim, rake-masted ships like *Red Rover* raced over the ocean, clipping the monsoons, bringing opium to China four or five times a year.

We could have one too, Charlie thought wistfully. We could have bought *Eugenia,* the slaver captured by the Royal Navy off the Coast of Africa and auctioned off dirt-cheap. Or *Hellas.* Or *Omega.* Or *Governor Findlay.* Or even *Dhaulle,* built years ago in Boston, old and creaking now, but still the model to which the builders of the fast ships clung.

When Carradine bought *Falcon* and *Sylph,* designed by the Surveyor of the Royal Navy specially for the opium trade, Charlie had pleaded with Yin-kwa.

"Let's buy one too! They're so beautiful! They beat the winds as easily as birds! We'd make a lot more silver. Carradine must have twenty or thirty million dollars!"

Yin-kwa frowned.

"Carradine not only owns *Falcon* and *Sylph*—"

"And *Jamesina*," Charlie broke in, "and—"

"And others—I know," Yin-kwa went on firmly. "He not only owns them, he also owns all the opium in them. If one of his ships should go down—even clippers founder sometimes—or be pirated, or if the mandarins of our great navy should suddenly become smart enough to capture one, he'd lose not only the ship but the opium too. A thousand or more chests on a single ship—more than two million dollars' worth of opium, plus, of course, the cost of the ship. We buy two or three hundred chests at a time and own them for no more than two weeks before *San Seb* delivers them up the coast. Our risk is tiny compared to Carradine's."

"So are our profits!"

"Why compare your profits to Carradine's? Compare them to what you had when we started. When Wei brought you to my grandfather that night nine years ago, you had four pounds a year from Sir George. Now you've half a million dollars in safekeeping with my grandfather and Lee Kwok. Be satisfied, Charlie!" He added, glancing at Charlie's expression: "And don't sulk!"

Charlie couldn't help grinning. Yin-kwa had spoken like a stern but kindly parent. Yin-kwa took very seriously the burdens and dignities that devolved upon him as How-kwa relinquished the leadership of the family. How-kwa was largely retired now. As soon as news was received that Sir George had left the Honorable Company, How-kwa had recalled Wei to the house of many courtyards in what Yin-kwa said was the Street of the Psychics, and, with Wei to keep him company, had begun to devote more and more time to his birds. More than a thousand cages of all shapes and sizes hung in his house and courtyards, Yin-kwa said. Yin-kwa still reported to him every night, but Yin-kwa was now virtually in command of the *hong* and the growing family.

Yin-kwa had married the girl to whom he had been betrothed when they were infants, and there were already three children, all sons. On the day of the birth of the third son, Yin-kwa had said to Charlie, smiling, but very serious too: "Our family was cursed in the last two generations. My grandfather has four wives, but between them they managed only one son, my father. My father had two daughters before me, and he died shortly after I was born. But now there are three sons growing up, and there will be more. Though I'd like a daughter too, eventually."

Yin-kwa would never take concubines, Charlie thought. The siring of sons was his responsibility to his ancestors. That done, he would dedicate himself exclusively to the paramount task of heading the richest merchant family in the south of China. Yin-kwa had inherited his kingdom.

On the day of their argument about clippers, when Charlie grinned, Yin-kwa smiled warmly, pleased by Charlie's yielding.

"The time isn't ripe yet to expand our investment. I'll tell you when it is. And while you're comparing yourself to Carradine, remember all the silver he has to guard! The more he earns, the harder it is!"

That was true, Charlie thought, watching the billow of *Red Rover's* sails, ghostly white in the dawning light. Carradine, they said, paid a fortune to the gang of cutthroats who, fighting irons on their wrists, pistols in their belts, daggers in their boots, stood guard over the hatches that hid his silver from covetous eyes. Blogg said there was always tension on a ship that carried silver—a simmering undercurrent as dangerous as the guns that peered from the decks of the beautiful ships themselves.

The sun's first golden rays, rimming the mist, glinted on *Red Rover*'s broadsides. She carried four twenty-pounders port and starboard, and a traversing forty-eight-pounder amidships. She—like all the clippers—was more than a match for the Chinese navy, the gaudy war junks with bulging eyes carved on their prows to spy out the enemy and fearsome dragons writhing on their pennants to strike terror to his spirit. The mouths of their cannon were painted a hungry red, but the cannon were fixed and the war junks had to be heaved about to aim them. They couldn't catch the clippers and they knew it, though sometimes, when a clipper was sailing away, one of them would venture out, its crew screaming threats and grimacing fiercely, to plop a few cannonballs into the clipper's wake.

"What mandarin can do?" Ah Sam shrugged. "He must tell Emperor what he do, but he no can catch clipper. So he tell Emperor he chase clipper away."

Lee Kwok and the other Chinese smugglers were as contemptuous of the war junks as the clipper captains. Their long, narrow "centipede boats," manned by fifty oarsmen, darted to Lintin with impunity, fetched their opium, and darted back again to lose themselves in the myriad creeks that mazed the delta. Only one had ever been caught, and that by a major maneuver involving four war junks that might have been expected to net a greater catch than fifty coolie oarsmen marched off to punishment tied together by their pigtails.

Red Rover was losing way, shuddering as though she would shake off the seamen who climbed her rigging, reefing her sails and robbing her of power. Charlie picked up a grappling hook and banged it against a bulkhead, the clang reverberating back from Lintin's sullen bluffs. The lascars came pouring out of *Merope*'s insides, their loincloths dirty gray against the dark skin of their wiry bodies. Ah Sam hated them.

"Why no Chinee? Why you pay dollah this black man when plenty Chinee no got work?"

But How-kwa had been right. The lascars were ideal for work on the twenty-one hulks that had joined *Merope* at Lintin.

They never learned a word of Chinese, and the Chinese disdained to learn a word of their guttural language, so there was little chance of news being passed to mandarin or pirate of how many chests lay in the hulks. *Red Rover* would have a thousand chests. That would make fourteen thousand in the hulks, give or take a hundred or so. Fourteen thousand chests, all of which would move into China in the next three or four months, to be replaced by the endless flow brought by the clippers. And Sir George had worried so excruciatingly about the five thousand chests a year that, in his time, had made their way into Canton under the watchful eyes of himself and How-kwa!

Charlie's conscience twinged. How-kwa, and Wei too, were still in ignorance of *San Sebastian's* activities. But How-kwa knew very well that the opium trade was now entirely beyond his control. Yin-kwa said that was one of the main reasons he had turned to his birds. The tea trade still roared along at Canton, but at Lintin and Namoa and even farther north, the opium trade was roaring louder. Nobody could control it now, least of all the Honorable Company. Rajputana too had become part of the British Empire, and the Honorable Company was in the happy position of being the sole supplier of Indian opium, considered better and more sought-after than Turkish and Persian, though among Indian opiums, Patna was still the best and most expensive.

The foreman of the lascars, a light-skinned Anglo-Indian, came up to Charlie. "What ship?"

"*Red Rover*. She'll have a thousand chests. Put them in the aft hold."

"Full."

"I know. Move Lee Kwok's stuff up on deck under canvas. He'll be fetching it this evening."

Red Rover's cutter came skimming across the water, bringing the great ropes that would warp her to *Merope's* side. With the expertness of long practice, the lascars went to work. By early afternoon, the ordered chaos of the unloading was over, *Red Rover* was once more standing in the roads, the lascars belowdecks in *Merope* beginning to open up the chests to repack the balls of opium into straw sacks, for easier handling aboard the centipede boats.

Again, *Red Rover*'s cutter put out from her side, making for *Merope*. Charlie took his fighting iron from its locker and secured it around his wrist, swung it in a vicious, whistling arc. The two lascars who were swabbing the deck scuttled below. The cutter came alongside and *Red Rover*'s supercargo stepped aboard, followed by the bos'n and his mate, also wearing irons and carrying between them a heavy canvas sack. Charlie led the way to his quarters in the stern bay. When the door was closed and barred behind them, they shed their irons and the supercargo cut the heavy cord that bound the neck of the sack. Charlie sat down to count the silver: three thousand dollars, three for each of the chests reposing in *Merope*'s aft hold, now the standard fee for storage and handling of opium in the Lintin hulks. Three thousand bright Mexican dollars, finely milled, embossed on one side with the head of some Mexican patriot and on the other with a sunburst. The preferred currency. High-quality silver, and more easily handled than either bullion or ingots.

Charlie counted ten of the dollars, stacked them on a corner of his table, then swiftly matched the stack in rows of ten until thirty rows were neatly standing as though the worn wood had sprouted a gleaming harvest. When it was done, he rose and poured grog for himself and the men from *Red Rover*. They drank standing, tipping their mugs to each other.

"How fast was your passage this time?" Charlie asked politely.

"Thirty-nine days." The bos'n grinned.

"Blogg will be green with envy!"

"Maister Blogg bain't aboard *Merope*?"

"He's off to Namoa."

"Namoa?" The supercargo gave Charlie a sharp glance. "We heard that Blogg's been delivering as far as Foochow."

Charlie laughed. "Namoa's far enough for us!"

But even now Blogg was beyond Foochow. He'd gone as far as the straits between Ningpo and Choushan Island, to learn the tricky currents of the estuary of the Yangtze River. Yin-kwa might be averse to buying clippers, but he was all in favor of delivering as far north as possible.

The supercargo looked suspicious, but he nodded to his men and they went out on deck, carrying their irons over their shoulders. Charlie followed them. Beyond *Red Rover*, in the gathering dusk, another clipper was sinking her anchors. A white-crossed blue flag flew from her halyards—the Carradine flag. *Red Rover*'s bos'n pointed, grinning.

"There be *Falcon!* We's beat her a good eighteen hours!"

The supercargo laughed.

"You had a wager, bos'n?"

"That we did, sir! Two poun' per man!"

"Well, at least some of us'll be making a profit out of Carradine this voyage!" The supercargo turned to Charlie. "He bought up eighty percent of the opium at the last auction—he must have fifteen thousand chests stored in Calcutta, and God knows how many more on the sea and here at Lintin. King of the opium trade. And spit on you as quick as look at you, God blast him! You know him?"

"Yes," Charlie said slowly.

He watched the men clamber cheerfully back into their cutter. *Falcon* rocked quietly at her anchors—they wouldn't start unloading her till the morning. Below her white-crossed blue flag flew the "owner aboard" pennant. Carradine himself was on her. Carradine . . . Charlie's bitter anger against Carradine had faded; he thought of it now as childish. But still the image of Carradine always loomed over him—taller, bigger, handsomer, richer, more powerful, superhuman almost.

In the living quarters, Ah Sam had come out from behind the curtains that enclosed the bed space and was sitting at the table.

"Chahlee, I tell you before—you must ting dollah!"

She took two of the dollars, balanced them on the tips of her forefingers, and clinked them gently against each other. They sent out a musical tinkle.

"This two piece good. S'pose no ting, no good."

He laughed. "You ting them if you want to! There're three thousand of them!"

She widened her eyes at him.

"You so big man now, Chahlee, you don't care bad dollah?"

She began to ting the dollars so quickly that the sound they made was a continuous silvery ringing. Charlie watched her, contentment a soothing buzz in his breast. She didn't look a day older than the first time he'd seen her. The same Ah Sam, tiny, vital, vibrant, her tongue as sharp as ever. In all these nine years, he'd never sought out another woman. She'd been enough for him—more than enough, for, over the years, love had grown between them. On his side, a deep affection. On hers . . . He stirred uneasily. He was no longer sure. He'd taken it for granted that she felt for him as he did for her, but once or twice lately he'd thought he saw a look in her eyes that astonished him—a brooding kind of look. But it hadn't lasted long, if it had been there at all. When she'd caught his eyes on her, she'd flashed at once to her usual style.

"Chahlee, why you doing nothing? I think you not 'preciate your good joss! Everything I do for you!"

"You think it was good joss for my father to send me away when I was only thirteen years old?"

"Maskee Inglis father. How-kwa your father now. Joss father."

He smiled. It was a good name! Joss father. God father. Indeed, How-kwa had been a godfather to him!

She was wrapping the dollars now, rolling them tightly in thick paper made of pressed straw and rice hulls. She would pack the rolls into opium sacks, padding out the sacks with the paper. When Lee Kwok's boats came this evening to fetch his opium, the sacks of dollars would go back to How-kwa for safekeeping.

The westering sun was pouring through the windows of the stern bay, and Charlie felt sweat gathering on his body. The great, blazing sun! It would glare pitilessly until at last, after an endless time of sweating and itching, the sea swallowed it up. At home the sun was not an enemy. At home, the sun was a grateful warmth dappling through green canopies. At home, one lay on a rustling carpet beneath the trees, smelling the tender fragrances that the gentle sun coaxed from the earth, hearing the murmurous rush of the stream as it laved the rocks in its path, cradled the fish in its depth. Everything soft and muted, warmly cool, coolly warm.

How soon could he go home? Half a million wasn't enough for all that he wanted to do. Once he'd wanted to throw dollars in his father's face—the aching plan of a furious child. Now he had quite other plans. He thought of them often, but spoke of them rarely and then only to Blogg, for their content seemed to go against some Chinese grain. Once, when Ah Sam had detected a hint of what he was thinking, she had said to him angrily: "You crazy, Chalee? Son no can punish father!" But on one of those long days at sea when, the opium delivered, there was nothing to do but sail peacefully back to *Merope*, his thoughts had spilled out to Blogg:

"When I go home, I won't let my father know that I'm back. First, I'll buy an estate somewhere near him. Easterbury, if I can get it. It's bigger and better than his. His is really quite modest—though it was all the world to me at thirteen, when he threw me out. I'll buy good clothes—wool, and the finest cambric. And a carriage. No—a high-wheeled trap, black with red trim. And brown horses, I think—chestnuts. . . ."

Glossy chestnuts, trotting through the woody lanes, clickety-clip, clickety-clip, soft and steady, the glossy sound of the glossy hooves of glossy chestnuts. The sound would change when he turned into his father's driveway. The gravel would sputter. His father would come out to see.

"His eyes are poppy, Blogg, like fish eyes. He'll stare with those fish eyes, and he'll begin to smile because he'll think it's someone grand arriving. He won't recognize me—how could he? The last time he saw me I was thirteen! I'll say, 'Hello, Father!' Casual, you know. I'll say, 'How are you, Father? Thought I'd let you know I'm back. Been back several months. I've bought Easterbury.' By God, Blogg, he'll turn *purple!*"

Now, smiling at the thought, he turned to glance at Ah Sam, and found her watching him. The sacks of dollars, neatly tied, lay on the floor. She sat, for once idle, her hands crossed in her lap, her eyes on his, bright and intent. His heart swelled. By God, she was wonderful! By God, he'd miss her when he went home!

"Chahlee," she said softly. "Soon I go away."

He gaped at her.

She gave a small nod.

"I go away. I leave."

"*You* leave?" He laughed shortly, meaninglessly. "I was just thinking . . . Ah Sam, you can't leave!"

"Sorry!" She turned her face away. "In Senhora house, I tell you I stay maybe one year, maybe ten year. Now nine year. I go."

"But—where would you go?"

"Maskee."

He jumped up and grasped her shoulders.

"You can't leave me! You must stay with me till . . . till . . ."

He floundered. What had he been going to say—'till I leave you'? Her eyes on his were knowing, secretive, prescient. But she only shrugged, jerking her shoulders against his hands.

"No, Chahlee. I go soon."

"*You will not—*"

There was a sharp knock on the door. She wriggled from his grasp.

"Lee Kwok come. More better you go see."

"Not till we've settled this! You're *not* leaving."

The knocking began again, louder than before, and the lascar foreman called out. She darted to the door and was lifting the bar before he could prevent her. The door swung free and the foreman looked in.

"Lee Kwok here."

"I know, damn it! I'll be out in a minute!"

The man withdrew, and he turned furiously to Ah Sam.

"God rot it . . . "

She laid a finger across his lips.

"No talk more, Chahlee."

Then she was gone behind the curtains, and Lee Kwok himself was at the door.

Lee Kwok, the scholar-smuggler, was a tall, thin, hollow-cheeked man with a dignified and courteous manner. Now he was smiling gravely, extending a hand as though to invite Charlie out onto the deck. It was impossible to gainsay him.

The deck was swarming with coolies. The sacks of opium, heaved hand to hand, were disappearing over the side into the centipede boats whose stubby sails were bobbing all around. Lee Kwok led Charlie through the melee to a quiet spot in the bow.

"Chahlee, I want talk about your silver."

"Can't it wait, Lee Kwok?"

"More better talk now."

There was no way to stop him! His slow, deliberate voice rolled inexorably on. He had an opportunity to reinvest Charlie's silver, but he wanted to explain it all to Charlie before making the change. He talked slowly, specifying dates, quantities, amounts, all in meticulous detail. He had it all in his head. That was the way the Chinese did business—no letters, statements, credit and debit notes, just everything in their heads with never a mistake or attempt at fraud, and enormous sums transferred by scribbles on bits of paper. By God, Lee Kwok knew that Charlie knew far less about his own silver than Lee Kwok did, and he knew that Charlie trusted him implicitly! Why all this detail? And why *now*?

Wildly impatient, Charlie half listened. "No talk more," Ah Sam had said. Of course he'd talk more! As soon as Lee Kwok had finished, he'd rush back to the cabin and talk and talk until she gave up this crazy idea! But Lee Kwok went on and on, and the loading of the opium went on and on. It was usually done quickly. The Chinese smugglers didn't take chances, even though they weren't afraid of the war junks. The sacks were usually loaded with expert speed and the centipede boats were off under both oar and sail if the wind was right. Today, by God, they were taking much longer than usual! Almost a hundred sacks still remained on deck, and the coolies were still heaving them around. By God, when would they finish?

It was full dark by the time the last of the centipede boats, Lee Kwok leaping agilely aboard at the last moment, slid away from *Merope*'s side and disappeared. Blowing out a big breath, Charlie strode to the door of the cabin and flung it open.

"Ah Sam!"

Stillness. The eerie stillness that says, clear as words, "There's no one here."

He tore aside the curtains. The bed space was, as always, immaculate—and empty. He tore open the cupboard in which she kept her clothes. Empty—nothing. He rushed out on deck. It was deserted in the blackness of the night—no moon, no single star. His heart pounded. The cool night air burned his lungs. He shouted, but no one came, not the foreman, not one of the lascars who normally jumped to his call.

They must know, the lascars! They must have seen her slip over the side into one of Lee Kwok's boats, while Lee kept him talking interminably! Lee must have known too! And if he knew, then Yin-kwa must have known! But he had seen Yin-kwa a few days ago in Macao, and he'd said nothing! A conspiracy! A plot, God rot it! One of those damned twisty Chinese plots that flummoxed barbarians!

He rushed to *Merope*'s scuppers, peering into the darkness though he knew there'd be nothing to see. If only Blogg would appear in *San Seb* he could set out at once to follow her! Get her back! *Drag* her back! But *San Seb* was slower than the centipede boats, and once they got into the delta, who could find them?

God rot and blast it! He pounded his fists on the rail, tearing the skin of his knuckles till blood flowed, shouting curses that none but the fish were there to hear. At last, sanity began to return. There was nothing he could do tonight. Tomorrow he'd hire a junk and sail to Canton, get a message to Yin-kwa. It would take four or five days, and by then Ah Sam could be anywhere in that vast, village-dotted country, but Yin-kwa must know where she was, and he'd *make* Yin-kwa tell!

He stumbled back into the cabin, fumbled in the lockers under the windows, got hold of a bottle, drank standing, lifting the bottle to his lips. God rot it, it was *sam shui!* The sweetish taste made him gag. But at least it would help him sleep, help him get through the hell of night gaping before him. He drank again, head thrown back, and saw around the bulk of the bottle that light and shadow were weaving crazy patterns on the ceiling. The lamp was lit, the flame dancing and smoking in the draft from the open door. She must have lit it before she left, so he wouldn't be in darkness. Heart wincing, he went to shut the door. The light immediately steadied. The shifting shadows vanished. The corners of the cabin came into sight, softly illuminated. Cursing again, he went to blow out the damned light—the sight of the clean, tidy emptiness was more than he could bear.

But—there in the corner where the bathing tub stood, was the light shimmering? He'd had the tub made years ago, of tightly caulked wood. Ah Sam hadn't liked it at first—she said it looked like a coffin—so he'd had them add a high back at one end, like an armchair, and then she'd mightily approved.

The light above it was shimmering now because it was half full of water, still gently steaming. The water must have been boiling when she put it in. She must have boiled several pots full on the small clay stove on which she cooked, while Lee Kwok talked and his coolies slowed the loading to give her time. It must have been the last thing she did before she slipped away.

"Chahlee, take bath! No stinky! No nit-nit!"

Her voice fluted in the empty silence.

Slowly, he stripped and lowered himself into the water. It was still hot, but it couldn't warm the icy chill that was creeping from his guts up to his heart, freezing the channels of his

79

body. She wasn't coming back. Even if he managed to find her, she wouldn't be persuaded to come back. Her planning had been too careful. Her goodbye was too final.

He snatched up the cloth she had laid on the side of the tub and slapped it into the water with a mighty splash, sloshing waves of water onto the floor. It was unbearable! The silence was unbearable! *Merope* was unbearable! A dirty, old, worn-out, splintering hulk, stinking of opium!

When Blogg returned three days later, Charlie was slumped over the table. Blogg glanced calmly around the mess of the stern bay. Charlie glowered at him from under his brows.

"She's gone, as I s'pose you can see!"

Blogg sat down silently, poured a mug for himself from the bottle on the table, sniffed at it.

"*Sam shui?* Thought it wasn't to your liking."

"Got drunk on it first time I saw her. Got drunk on it when she left. Seems everybody but me knew she was going." He peered at Blogg suspiciously. "You don't seem surprised. Did you know too?"

Blogg said mildly:

"Do no good to get slobbering, Charlie."

"*Did you know?*"

"Nor to try to pick a fight with me. Cain't say as I'm surprised she's gone. That mate of mine let words drop, made me reckon something was afoot. South of Choushan Island, it blowed up mighty hard and he was uncommon anxious. Afeared we'd be delayed because, he said, he got orders from Lee Kwok to bring you to Canton five days hence."

Astonishment jerked Charlie's head up. "Your *mate* got orders from *Lee Kwok?*"

"Aye. Take you in *San Seb* to Whampoa, and from there Lee Kwok'll have one of his boats take you to Jackass Point. Wouldn't do, of course, for you to be seen in *San Seb* at Jackass."

"God rot it! Do they think I'm a puppet that they can pull me about like a Punch and Judy show? I won't go!"

"Reckon you'd do well to find out what's going on."

"Who gave Lee Kwok *his* orders? Couldn't be *his* idea to make me go to Jackass Point! There's nothing he can't tell me when he comes to *Merope!*"

"Reckon it'd be Yin-kwa."

"But I saw Yin-kwa a few days ago in Macao, and he said nothing!"

"He asked you to meet him there?"

"No. I hired a junk to sail over—needed some things. Met him by accident. We didn't talk much—he was in a hurry."

Blogg nodded. "Told you. Something's afoot."

"*What*, God blast it? Did they make Ah Sam leave me?"

"Reckon not. Reckon she don't allow none to make her do what she don't want to do."

"Then, by God, why did she leave?"

Blogg drained his mug and wandered over to the windows. Blearily, Charlie saw the outline of his great head against the dazzling streaks that the setting sun shot over the dark blue water. His voice droned loud and soft, loud and soft, in Charlie's ears.

"Could be 'cause she's older nor you, and childless. Chinee think, being twenty-six year old, you'd ought to've sired three or four kids by now. Could be that's what she wants you to do. . . . Whatever her reason, I lay my oath it's something suited to you. Right fond of you, she is. Right fond."

Of its own weight, Charlie's head sank down on his spread arms. His stomach heaved, rebelling against its load of *sam shui*. His mind heaved, rebelling against the leaping images. Ah Sam, slipping out of the cabin, threading her way among the coolies and the lascars, hiding behind them in case he should look around from Lee Kwok's monologue. Ah Sam going over the side into one of Lee Kwok's boats, no feat at all for her tiny trimness. Ah Sam pouring hot water into the bathing tub, performing a last service, saying a last goodbye.

Outside, the sea swallowed the sun as swiftly as, in the dawn, it would spit it up again. Wind rose and whistled mournfully, *Merope's* ancient timbers groaning in response.

The lascars came out of the hold to breathe the evening air, their bare feet pattering on the deck, their voices humming a dirgelike chant.

When Blogg said softly: "So, Charlie? Sit here and slobber, or sail for Whampoa, see what come?" Charlie nodded wearily, his cheek slithering in spilled *sam shui.*

The wind was right and the sail was fast. So as not to arrive too early in Whampoa, they lay over a morning at the mouth of the Bogue, in view of the first two forts, Chuenpi on the eastern shore, Tycocktow on the west. The crew laughed and strutted, swaggering to the scuppers to stare and point.

Blogg grinned.

"Uncommon for them to have no need to run from mandarins!"

"Order a tot of *sam shui* all around," Charlie murmured.

"No need for them to get too brave neither!"

Charlie squinted against the brilliant dance of sunlight on the choppy waves. It was good to be on the open water, breeze sopping up the sun's heat before it broiled you, free to sail or lie rocking on the sea's bosom, no loom of the sulking cliffs under which *Merope* was tethered—stinking old *Merope,* inhabited only by surly lascars! How could he stand it? He'd spent thirteen years—half his life!—in the few hundred miles between Jackass Point, Lintin, Macao, and Namoa. He could take the half million dollars and go home! But then he'd be no richer than his father. Half a million dollars was a hundred thousand pounds sterling—not enough to buy Easterbury and horses and traps and hire servants and maintain everything in a fashion that would infuriate his father. That callous rejection would remain a stone in his guts—that last ramble in the woods, that last wordless appeal. He'd looked into his father's eyes, trying to force out the plea—"Let me stay, Father! Please let me stay!"—but his father had spoken first in that cold, flat voice: "Lord Ambleton expects you tomorrow. You will catch the coach from the village."

He couldn't go home until he had the whole million! And it

was there to be got. *San Seb* was slow and lumbering compared to the clippers, but she was sound as a rock still, and her little four-pounder traversed as easily as any clipper's cannon. The war junks had let her alone, and so had the pirateers. Blogg's seamanship had become a legend, and anyway pirates were more sophisticated now—they went for ships that were carrying silver, having already sold their opium; it saved the trouble of selling it. It would be easy to carry on with *San Seb* until the full million dollars had been accumulated—if only Ah Sam hadn't left!

Blogg was pointing at the low profile of the Bogue forts, dun-colored like the bare hills behind them, blue water lapping at their thick mud walls.

"Carradine's still talking of British sloops alongside those forts. . . . Ten days past, in Namoa, *Jamesina*'s captain came aboard *San Seb* for grog and talk and boasting about his master, Carradine. Says Carradine's in London, preaching free trade, and all them Manchester millowners are cheering for him, thinking under free trade they'd be selling their cottons and woolens all over China, thinking only the Company's monopoly is keeping them from it."

"But the Chinese don't want their stuff!"

"Carradine's telling them otherwise. He's bought some kind of journal or newspaper to tell them with. Wants them to make a big noise in Parliament for abolishing the Company's monopoly. With free trade, he could do away with his Danish flag and trade under the Union Jack, and there'd be lots more Britons coming here to set up in trade. The more the better, so he thinks, for then the Eight Regulations could be got rid of. If the Chinese ain't willing to cancel them out, the British government'd be willing to lay sloops alongside the forts and force them. He thinks, then, opium would no longer be contraband."

"*Legal* opium?"

"That's Carradine's idea, *Jamesina*'s master says. . . . He's going to bring his son Andrew here. If opium's legal and trade free, and Carradine free to open up a house under the Union

Jack, no telling how rich he could get—him, and Andrew, and Andrew's kids and so on."

Charlie laughed shortly. A Carradine dynasty based on legal opium!

"I laughed too," Blogg said, "Made *Jamesina's* master angry. He said I'd be laughing off t'other side of my face soon enough. 'Pears there's a new Foreign Secretary in London—Lord Palmerston—and Carradine's getting cuddly with him."

"Well . . ." Charlie shrugged and lay back, shading his eyes with his hand. For once, talk of Carradine seemed unimportant, and silly to boot.

Wei came aboard as soon as, in the late evening, Lee Kwok's junk tied up at Jackass Point.

"Chahlee—you fine?" He smiled warmly.

"I'm fine, Wei. But—"

"No talk now, Chahlee. How-kwa wait. Dinner How-kwa house."

"But Wei—"

"Shh! Come quick."

He had brought a bundle of Chinese clothes. Charlie slipped on the long cotton gown, the cloth slippers, the little round black hat with queue attached. While Wei was tucking his red hair under the cap, he tried again.

"Wei, why did—"

"Shh! Talk after. Come quick now."

Wei was jerking him around like a puppet! First Lee Kwok, and now Wei! Anger rising, Charlie followed him through the dark lanes behind Jackass Point, through the gate of the city, and into the sedan chairs—How-kwa's private chairs, this time. Restless and edgy, he risked a small slit in the curtains. The bearers were thud-thudding so fast through streets so dark that he could see almost nothing. But at last they turned into a narrow alley. In the light of smoking oil lamps, people sat on the lintels of doorways, fanning themselves, chatting, relaxing. Overhead a clutter of signboards protruded into the alley, covered with intricate ideograms and pictures—outlines of hands, palms outward, fingers radiating like the tentacles of jellyfish; outlines of bumpy, hairless heads. The chair coolies set the chair down before a high, blank wooden gate and Charlie heard Wei call out. Could this be How-kwa's gate? Was this what Yin-kwa called the Street of the Psychics, this dirty lane of palmists and readers of head bumps? Feeling even angrier because he had imagined a broad avenue paced by dignified scholars, Charlie stepped out of the chair into the fairy-like courtyard—more beautiful, more sumptuous, for the fact of its existence in this commonplace alley. The remembered sense of unreality clamped down tight. Was he real—Charlie of Ah Sam, of *Merope* and *San Seb,* of long, sweaty afternoons under the bluffs of Lintin? Or was this real—this cool and hushed place of ordered splendor where every footfall, every stone and leaf and lantern, bespoke wealth that beggared his half million dollars, elegance that made the proudest English home—Easterbury, even—seem lumpish? Resentment flooded him. Who were they to push and pull him about? To order him brought? Not to say "Come," but to tell Lee Kwok to tell Blogg's mate to fetch him!

They crossed the courtyards and entered How-kwa's anteroom. Dozens of bird cages hung from the ceiling and from brackets on the walls, some no more than a foot square, some six feet tall and half that in diameter. There were no songs now, only sleepy twitterings, for each cage was masked with its fitted cloth cover. It must take some servant an hour or more just to put the covers on!

A dinner table in the midst of the birds was laid for four. How-kwa and Yin-kwa were already seated. They greeted Charlie, Yin-kwa casual and friendly, How-kwa affectionate. For a moment, Charlie's resentment faltered. Nine years ago he had thought How-kwa old. Now he was ancient! The skin of his face was parchment, stretched so tightly that his cheekbones seemed on the point of cracking through. He was stick-thin and hunched at the shoulders so that his head, with its old man's tremor, seemed to have lost its neck.

But his eyes were bright and sharp as ever. Chuckling, he waved Charlie to the seat at his right hand. At once, servants placed on the table the first four dishes—cold dishes, appetizers, it seemed, for they were removed before they were emptied. An endless succession of hot dishes followed, served one by one. The thimble-size winecups were filled and refilled and filled again. There was talk, but it was light and teasing. Charlie sat, eating with his clumsy porcelain spoon, waiting for the last dish to be removed, for the tea to be poured. Then they'd start talking!

But he was wrong. How-kwa picked up his teacup and turned to Wei. Yin-kwa picked up his and turned to Charlie, beginning an account of the season's tea trade. Charlie listened, keeping his face composed, though his blood was boiling. Damn them! By God, he'd be damned before he asked why he'd been sent for! By God, he'd wait them out!

At last, a rustle passed through the room. Someone outside whispered to the servant nearest the door, he whispered to the next, and he to the next. The whisper reached How-kwa, his personal servant bending to his ear.

"Hah!" Eyes twinkling, How-kwa put his palms on the table and slowly pushed himself up. "Chahlee!"

Charlie offered his arm, and How-kwa leaned his feather weight on it. They began to walk, Yin-kwa and Wei following. They passed through rooms that were dimly lit, perfumed with flower scents, murmurous with the sound of sleepy birds. They came to a room which was not lit at all, only faintly illumined by light coming from outside, through a large, unshuttered window, to which How-kwa led Charlie.

The window looked out on still another courtyard, a little different from the others, though no less lovely. The tubbed trees were pushed back against the high walls, leaving a wide space of marbled paving, in the middle an oval pool of still water in which lay reflections of the lanterns—a hundred glowing points of light that doubled the glitter and the sparkle. Around the pool were marble benches, and at its edge a great many silken cushions, startlingly bright against the milky marble.

"The courtyard of the women," Yin-kwa, behind Charlie, murmured.

As Charlie stared, half hypnotized by the serene beauty of the scene, a woman entered the courtyard—a tiny woman in a great black brocade robe, supported on each side by a maid who helped her slow and wavering steps.

"My grandmother," Yin-kwa murmured.

Not necessarily Yin-kwa's real grandmother, Charlie had learned—another of How-kwa's four wives might be that—but How-kwa's number-one wife, and therefore the official grandmother of the family. He watched as the maids led her slowly around the pool and seated her on the far side, on the largest of the benches, with many pattings and smoothings of her robe. Her face was obscured by a veil. She sat there like an image. She might have been made of black marble.

Charlie caught back his slackening anger. This was a seduction, a snare, a twisty Chinese plot. He must not lose himself in this beauty and mystery.

Other women in richly colored robes were now coming into the courtyard, each attended by a maid.

"My younger grandmothers," Yin-kwa murmured. "My aunts. And my mother—the one in green."

The woman who would have welcomed Ah Sam as her husband's concubine! With stately step, she moved to the bench beside the one on which How-kwa's number-one wife was enthroned. As she turned to seat herself, Charlie stared at her face. Not beautiful, not ugly. Masklike. He glanced at the faces of the others. All the same. Actresses on a stage, deliberately portraying nothing.

Now younger women entered—some of them girls. They too moved slowly, trying for dignity and elegance, but their litheness betrayed them. They sank down on the cushions, some seeming to suppress giggles. One dipped her hand in the water, then snatched it back and looked around guiltily—she had forgotten her instructions!

"My sisters," Yin-kwa whispered. "Some young cousins and nieces. And my wife—the one sitting at my grandmother's feet."

The grandmother and the mothers of present and future heirs apparent grouped together, taking precedence. Charlie watched gravely, saying nothing—he'd give them no satisfaction.

Now, another girl entered. Alone, unattended. In a heavy, silvery satin robe that flowed and yet molded her figure, out-lined her as she moved across the marble paving, her back to the watchers in the window. Charlie found himself holding his breath. She seemed to glide, the hem of her robe trailing, one hand fluttering a little painted fan that might be a butterfly hovering in homage before her unseen face. She passed around the pool, the heads of the girls on the cushions turning slowly to follow her passage. Before the grandmother, she sank in a deep kowtow, then rose again to her feet, light and supple as a sapling bowed and released by the wind. She began to turn toward the watchers. Charlie's breath caught in a little sigh, and he cursed himself for betraying excitement, but the moment, contrived as it was, artificial, a cunning pull on the puppet strings, was nevertheless unbearingly tantalizing. At last the girl faced the window, standing perfectly still, looking up, expressionless. Charlie swallowed silently. She was exquisite! Almond eyes, lying in soft shadows. Skin translucent as How-kwa's finest porcelain. Hair a shining black fall. Lips a tender promise. And all her loveliness put together by some sculptor of marvelous genius in a perfection of harmony that invaded the heart. For long moments time was suspended as Charlie gazed, forgetting those around him, forgetting everything but the beauty of the girl in the courtyard.

Then, irrepressibly, the girl smiled—an impish twitch of the mobile lips that, clearly, was not supposed to be, but that she could not help.

Charlie's skin prickled. It was familiar! Who was that girl?

88

He swung toward Yin-kwa, but Yin-kwa was turning away, smiling broadly. Wei was muttering something while he slid a shutter over the window, blotting out the scene. Servants came hurrying in with tapers. Chuckling, How-kwa slid a papery hand through Charlie's arm, urging him toward a group of blackwood chairs that stood around a marble-topped table. Simmering, Charlie guided the old man's wavering steps. They seated themselves. Yin-kwa, still smiling, turned to Charlie.

"I've been elected spokesman. Actually a woman should be saying this, a marriage broker. . . ."

"Marriage?" Charlie gave up all pretense of disinterest. "What the devil is this, Yin-kwa? You knew, didn't you, that Ah Sam was planning to leave me? You helped her leave! You . . ."

His voice was rising furiously, and Yin-kwa put an urgent hand on his arm.

"Wait, Charlie! Listen! Listen! Ah Sam knows all about this! In fact, it was her idea! Did you recognize that girl?"

"What girl?" Charlie shouted.

"Please, Charlie! Did you recognize her?"

"No!"

"It was Ling-ling."

Ling-ling? Wei's little daughter? Ling-ling of the nightly walks around Jackass Point, small sticky hand in his? Ling-ling of the impish smile, adoring eyes raised to his? "Love you, Chah-lee!"

Anger evaporated in a great surge of pleasure. He turned to Wei.

"She's *lovely!* I can hardly believe it!"

Wei's anxious face melted in smiles.

"Chahlee, Ling-ling never forgot you! Alla time talk about you. She no like learn woman thing—sew and cook. Only man thing—read, write, talk Inglis. She say, 'Like Chahlee teach me. By-and-by, I see Chahlee, he be glad.' Everything—Chahlee, Chahlee . . ." His eyes, bubbling with eagerness, grew luminous with love. His voice softened. "Chahlee, you same like my own chillun. When my boys finis', I take you for my son. Chahlee, you marry Ling-ling, you *true* my son."

His eyes filled with tears.

God Almighty! Charlie stared down at the tabletop, his eyes compulsively tracing the veins of the marble, his mind a kaleidoscope of flashing patterns. No wonder all the mystery, the slow escalation of drama! Presented cold, he'd have laughed off such a proposition. Now he'd have to find some polite, unhurtful way of turning it down. . . . Did he have to? Was there any real reason for turning it down? God, she was beautiful!

Yin-kwa murmured, "He's proposed it himself, and better than I could have. Let's go outside, Charlie."

Gratefully, Charlie hurried after him into the courtyard of the women. It was empty now, the marble glowing softly in the lantern light, the pool, still as a mirror, reflecting the lanterns. They sat where the grandmother had sat, Charlie breathing hard, grabbing at the whirl of his thoughts. One thing must first be confirmed:

"Yin-kwa, you said all this was *Ah-Sam's* idea?"

"Yes."

"Where is she?"

"Living in my mother's house."

"I want to see her."

"She won't see you. She wants you to marry Ling-ling. That's why she left you."

Blogg had been right! It must have been in her mind for years—not that she was childless, but that *he* was, that his seed was being wasted in her aging body. He'd basked in her indulgence, enjoyed her ministrations, mindlessly content with the present, while she'd been thinking of the future and the future's future, of the sons and grandsons that, in her scheme of things, he must have. Oh God!

Yin-kwa broke the silence.

"Let's try and sort things out. First of all, Ah Sam will not, under any circumstances, go back to live with you in the old way."

The old way—the old, contented, comfortable way that, of

90

her love, she had created for him. He'd given her lots of silver that he could well afford, and planned to leave her one day, and thought that he would miss her sadly, and seen no other problem. Oh God!

"So," Yin-kwa murmured. "The question is—what are you going to do? You could go home to England, but you'd be leaving a gold mine behind, and I don't think you're ready for that yet. . . ."

No, he was not!

"Of course, you could continue to live alone on *Merope.* . . ."

Alone with the lascars on that stinking old hulk?

"Or get another Chinese girl to live with you, which would be easy if you wanted a servant-cum-bedmate, but you wouldn't easily find another Ah Sam. . . ."

There couldn't be another Ah Sam!

"Or you could marry an English girl—show yourself willing and half the English mothers in Macao would be throwing daughters at your head. . . ."

The English wives in Macao were either battle-axes or cringing mice, and their daughters were coarse or simpering, and grossly oversized!

"Well . . ." Yin-kwa glanced at him. "If you don't like any of those suggestions, marrying Ling-ling would be a fine solution. What Wei said is quite true—she adores you. And of course you know that Wei really loves you like a son. The Chinese don't take readily to their sons and daughters marrying barbarians—the fact that Wei's so eager to have you as a son-in-law proves how much he loves you. My grandfather would be delighted if you'd stay on in China. He wants you to stay—he loves you too, Charlie. And I . . . I'd be very pleased if you stayed. Apart from everything else, you and I are excellent business partners. In fact, when Ah Sam came to my grandfather with the idea that you should marry Ling-ling, we all wondered why we hadn't thought of it ourselves!"

Charlie met Yin-kwa's eyes. They were warmer than any

business partnership called for. He felt his own eyes glow in response. Yin-kwa was as close to him as a brother—closer than his own brothers had ever been! But . . .

He turned away and looked miserably into the pool. Would they expect him to stay in China *forever?* He couldn't do that! He had to go home one day and confront his father. He had to! He had to cancel out that old abandonment!

"You'd have a house in Macao," Yin-kwa murmured. "The business with *San Seb* would go on just as usual. You'd hire someone to live on *Merope,* and go there yourself two or three days a week—it's only half a day's sail from Macao."

God, it would be wonderful to get away from stinking old *Merope!* A house in Macao—a little white house on the Praya, in which his own little wife would live with him. Let Carradine have his great barracks of a place and his dozens of sultry mistresses—he would have a *wife,* a *beautiful* wife, the most beautiful girl in thousands of miles. . . .

"Well?" Yin-kwa's smile was as warm as his eyes.

Heart pounding, Charlie stared into the pool. Surely he needn't stay in China *forever*—he could go home at least for a time. He needn't buy Easterbury and horses and traps in order to humiliate his father. It would be enough—by God, it would be *better!* The thought galvanized him—to display *his own family* before his father. His own beautiful wife, his own son whom *he* would never abandon! To rub his father's nose in it! By God, that would be the best revenge of all! And that would need no more than a short while at home. They needn't be away from China for more than two years altogether. . . .

A breeze stirred the mirrorlike surface of the pool and the reflected lights broke into a thousand twinkles that dazzled his eyes, teased his spirit, sent the blood coursing through his veins, young and red and strong. Charlie! Charlie! She's so lovely! The most beautiful girl you've ever seen!

The breath he was holding came from his lungs in a great burst.

"By God, Yin-kwa, I'll do it!"

* * *

The little house in Macao was at the other end of the Praya from the governor's mansion. It was of brick and stone, painted white, two stories high, with eight rooms. Behind the main house, connected to it by a covered passage, was a smaller house containing the kitchen and servants' quarters and the bathing room. In front was a small garden, a sandy patch reclaimed from the beach, planted with coarse grass and stubby bushes. The Praya, at this point no more than a track, meandered across the end of the garden, a low stone wall between it and the fine sand beach. From the edge of the beach, a pier projected over the shallow waters to a floating jetty.

On the day that the wedding junk was due to arrive in Macao, Charlie walked around the house giving it a last inspection. He was restless, the doubts that had plagued him for the last three months once more seesawing in his mind. Had he in fact allowed himself to be puppeteered? He'd gone that night to How-kwa's house knowing that something was up, had spent the evening growing increasingly resentful and wary, and then in the space of half an hour had agreed to everything they wanted, merely on their say-so that Ling-ling loved him! He'd made a fool of himself! But—the seesaw shifted—by God, she was unbelievably beautiful! And Yin-kwa had assured him that it was Ah Sam's idea, and what Ah Sam wanted for him must be good. And Yin-kwa was like a brother to him. Wei really did love him as a son. How-kwa had approved. Blogg, too, had approved.

"Should have known it! Wei's daughter! You'll be staying in China, then? I'm right glad of that!" Blogg had smiled so widely that Charlie had felt his throat constrict. Did he deserve so well of Blogg? He'd taken him for granted too, as he had Ah Sam—his loyalty, good humor, common sense. "*San Seb*'s sailing fine as ever, and we'll carry right on with you-know-what, clippers or no. You could do a lot worse than marry her, Charlie! Beautiful, you say she is?"

Yes, *beautiful!*

And today she was coming.

That night, after Yin-kwa and he had returned to the sitting room from the courtyard of women, after Wei, beaming, had formally embraced him and How-kwa had chuckled his blessings, Yin-kwa had explained the plan. There could be no real wedding ceremony in Canton, because the presence of a barbarian bridegroom couldn't be hidden from the mandarins. So Charlie would be spared the rigors of a Chinese wedding. He could thank his joss for that—he'd have been making kowtows all day! The marriage rites would be held with a proxy for Charlie—perhaps Yin-kwa's eldest son; the discipline would do him good! Then Ling-ling would be sent to Charlie in Macao in a wedding junk instead of the traditional sedan chair. She would have a full complement of attendants and bridesmaids, but no member of the family could accompany her, for when a girl married she must leave her family and go to her husband.

And today the wedding junk was due.

Completing his inspection of the house, Charlie traversed the covered passageway and went into his favorite room—the bathing room. He had designed it himself. It had a stone floor that dipped in a shallow trench to a hole at the juncture of the outside wall. In the middle of the floor stood the bathing tub, transported from *Merope.* After the bath, the tub could simply be tipped and the dirty water would run through the trench, out of the hole, and into the well that had been dug for it in the back garden. No more bailing, as Ah Sam had bailed on *Merope.* How Ah Sam would love this room!

Ah Sam . . .

The sense of loss swept him again, not stingingly as when she'd first left him, not shamefully as when he'd sat with Yin-kwa in the courtyard of the women, but gently, with a sad inevitability. He stared unseeingly at the bathing tub, thinking how strange it was. She'd accused him of not appreciating his good joss, and as far as she was concerned, she'd been right. He'd taken her lightheartedly for granted. But in a way she'd been pleased by that because it underlined his trust in the enduring nature of her love, and that trust, to her, had been a greater appreciation. In the toss of sleepless nights, that thought had formed itself in his mind, slowly and awkwardly, but bringing with it a kind of peace. He would always treasure her!

He went back into the garden. On the jetty, the servants he had hired were stringing up great hoops of brightly colored paper flowers. He had explained to his number-one boy that the marriage celebrations had already taken place in Canton, but the number-one boy had said firmly that the new Tai-tai would be displeased if her servants did not celebrate her marriage. That meant, Blogg had pointed out, that they would lose a great deal of face if there was no grand display on her arrival in Macao.

In addition to the paper flowers, there were two rows of banners, twenty on each side, marking out a path from the jetty to the steps of the verandah—long pennants of red silk on which were pasted gold-paper ideograms signifying auspicious blessings. And there would be a feast this evening for the neighborhood servants. Three round tables, each seating ten, were already laid in the back garden. The best restaurant in Macao would provide a twenty-course dinner, and wine. When presenting the considerable bills for all these things, the number-one boy had implied proudly that Charlie was fortunate in having servants who knew the right things to do.

Now the number-one boy hailed Charlie from the jetty, pointing out over the water. A crowd had gathered to admire the flapping, snapping pennants, and they all turned eagerly at the call, to stare out over the water too, to point and chatter excitedly.

The sails of the wedding junk were rising over the horizon.

Charlie's heart began to pound. The number-one boy called again, his words indistinguishable over the chatter of the crowd, but his meaning plain. Charlie should go into the house. Yin-kwa had said that he should on no account go down to the jetty or stay outdoors to welcome Ling-ling—he should wait for her in the house, and the women would bring her to him in the correct manner.

Nervously, Charlie hurried upstairs to change into his wedding clothes. Yin-kwa had said nothing about what he should wear to welcome his bride, but he had had a Macao tailor make up for him a dark green frock coat with ample skirts and a high-standing collar. The color made his hair seem redder than ever. He had chosen it a little sheepishly, thinking that he was, after all, Ling-ling's Red Barbarian.

In the bedroom there were more red and pink pennants hung from the walls and ceiling, and a new bright red silk spread on the bed. The number-one boy had not yet presented the bills for those, no doubt because he knew Charlie would have refused to pay them. Grimly, Charlie pulled down the most obtrusive of the pennants and shoved them into a cupboard. Damnation! If only Blogg were here! But Blogg had elected to stay away "till everything settles down again—you'll have no need of me, Charlie!"

Tense and edgy, he changed his clothes from the skin out, putting on fine white linen breeches that were anchored in place by straps passed under his insteps, court shoes of thin black leather—Macao shoemakers were becoming expert at making barbarian shoes—a linen shirt with a flyaway collar the points of which stood out on each side of his chin, and finally the new dark green coat, which fell to his knees in rich folds, buttoned over his chest with gold-colored buttons, and cradled the back of his neck in its three-inch standing collar. He brushed his fiery hair, still short and curly as Ah Sam had liked it, and inspected himself in the mirror. He had shaved that morning. His cheeks and chin were clean and smooth—no sideburns; Ah Sam hadn't liked them. By God, he was presenting to Ling-ling a perfect image of what Ah Sam liked! He grinned ruefully into the mirror. At any rate, he also presented a perfect image of the English gentlemen as seen in various aristocratic and leisurely poses in a glossy-paged copy of the *Illustrated London News* that Blogg had somehow got hold of. No need to worry about the impression he'd make on his father when he went home!

Feeling easier, he went downstairs to stand at the big front window of the parlor. Instantly, tension came flooding back. The wedding junk was in full and fearsome sight. It was monstrous! Every inch of it was adorned in the brightest colors of the spectrum—scarlet, pink, orange, green, purple. Yards and yards of cloth, whole bolts of it, were festooned in drooping arcs, from the tops of the masts to the scuppers, where they were fastened by huge dangling tassels. Great round pom-poms on flexible wire stems jiggled, row upon row, around the deck and the superstructure. Pennants, streamers, flags, banners fluttered from every projection. A nightmare concoction!

But the crowd loved it. The mass of watchers had grown enormously in size and noisiness. A sea of bobbing heads overflowed the Praya and mobbed the beach right to the edge of the water, emitting a great hum of admiration. The number-one boy stood at the edge of the jetty, making huge gestures as though beckoning the junk to its mooring, and this delighted the crowd more than ever. When at last the junk reached the jetty, dozens of eager hands reached out for the ropes to secure it. The number-one boy directed the lowering of the gangplank, waving his arms like a maestro conducting a giant orchestra, and this drove the crowd to ecstasies. Charlie fumed. By God, he'd fire that number-one boy as soon as this was over!

At last the gangplank was secured. Women began appearing on deck, garbed in festive red and pink, flowers pinned behind their ears. Professional bridesmaids, Yin-kwa had said, who commanded handsome fees for their specialized knowledge of the correct rituals and postures. A bride was supposed to be reluctant, Yin-kwa said—and often she really was, because she might never yet have seen her bridegroom. It was the business of the bridesmaids to bring the bride to her husband, whatever it took—persuasion, enticement, coaxing, luring, provoking, decoying, wheedling, and even plain pushing and pulling. That was what these women were preparing to do. . . . Panic struck Charlie's spirit. What if Ling-ling was really reluctant? What if Wei and the rest of them had lied? What if Ling-ling didn't love him? And even if she did, by God, it was monstrous! They called him barbarian, but what could be more barbaric than the spectacle of these strutting, posturing women preparing to deliver a bride to her husband like a lamb to slaughter?

With excited encouragement from the crowd, the women were fussing down the gangplank and, with much pushing and pulling and high-pitched shouting, arranging themselves into a half-circle under the hoops of paper flowers, a kind of reception committee for the bride. It took a long time, but the crowd never tired of gaping, pointing, chattering. At last it seemed that the chief bridesmaid was satisfied, and the bride herself appeared on the deck of the junk—or rather, a brilliant red thing appeared, something like a small tent, under which, Charlie assumed, Ling-ling was hidden. At the apex of the tent was balanced an enormous headdress, a miniature turreted castle hung with dozens of jingling, dangling ornaments, and—completely obscuring the face of the bride—a heavy red veil. Nothing at all could be seen of Ling-ling. Perhaps she herself could glimpse from beneath the veil where she was setting her feet, but to the spectators she was nothing but a splendiferous moving monument.

With tiny, unsteady steps, she came blindly down the gangplank, led and supported by two of the bridesmaids. Everyone watched silently, breaths held, in case she should fall. As she safely reached the jetty, everyone exhaled together in a happy outrush of air and the noisy excitement started again. The bridesmaids crowded around the bride, those in front pulling her forward, those behind pushing.

The procession moved slowly up the beach between the banners, across the garden, up to the front steps. Charlie went to the entrance door and flung it open. The women were swarming up the steps and fanning out before the doorway, leaning forward to beckon the bride with extravagant gestures, twittering encouragement. She came wavering forward, on the arms of the two principal women, blinded by the veil, sagging under the weight of the enormous headdress. At last she stood before him, but he could see no more of her up close than he had at a distance—only the brilliant robe, the veil, the forest of ornaments on her head. Urged by the women, she bowed her head to him. They chorused approval, two of them reaching hastily to hold the turreted castle on her head. He had a wild impulse to shove them aside, to snatch her up and tear off the folderol, expose her face, look into her eyes. Was she glad? Was she afraid? By God, was she a person at all?

But already the women were urging her on, stepping on each other's heels to push her toward the bridal chamber. The three amahs he had hired were standing before its door, grinning, fluttering, waving her forward, claiming their share of importance. Furiously, Charlie turned his back and strode into the parlor. The ghastly farce was reaching its height. They were all crowding into the bedroom to prepare the bride, lay her out on the great bed—the sacrificial altar. What did they care for her herself—for her spirit, her person? Nothing! And for the bridegroom? Even less! Moodily, he stared out of the window. The junk men, their job done, their fee earned, were stripping the vessel of its ornamentation, taking down the tassels and pom-poms, methodically folding the streamers and drapings, leaving an ordinary, shabby, none-too-clean junk which would now go back to fishing or ferrying people up and down the coast. From the hall came the patter of many slippered feet—the women were leaving, their job done too, full value for their fees given by their posturings. He saw them stream out of the front door, going matter-of-factly back to the junk, some chatting, some trudging tiredly, their plumage no longer garish in the gathering darkness. Most of the crowd had dispersed, and the few diehards wandered off when the junk hoisted sail and slid off into the sunset. The peace and quiet of the evening seemed artificial after the hurly-burly of the day. But not for long. From the back garden a hum of voices was rising—the guests invited to the number-one boy's feast were gathering. . . .

Charlie turned away from the window. What now? Would Ling-ling expect him immediately? Or would she prefer to be alone for a while? He hesitated, cursing under his breath. He could almost hear Yin-kwa's teasing tone: The bridegroom should decide what *he* preferred!

99

"Chahlee."

The voice came from the shadowed doorway.

Ah Sam? Impossible!

She stepped out of the shadows, tiny, trim, sparkling.

"More better you wait little time, Chahlee. Ling-ling tired. Too heavy dress, too much people."

He gaped at her, speechless. Smiling, she drew him to the sofa, sat down beside him. Her eyes held the soft and brooding look he hadn't been sure he saw before.

"You think I leave you, Chahlee? Never! You my fambly. Ling-ling too, now. By-and-by, when chilluns, they my fambly too."

He sank back, closing his eyes. Ah Sam, in all her shapes and guises! Lover. Teacher. Taskmaster. And now—matriarch? Had Yin-kwa known? Of course he had! They had all known, the Chinese puppeteers! Over the years they had imperceptibly attached their strings to him, and when it suited them they had twitched those strings, with great delicacy, even with love, but he'd had no chance of doing other than what they wanted. For a moment, fiercely, he saw eye to eye with Carradine: The only way to best the Chinese was by force of fighting ships and men. Otherwise, they ran rings around barbarians.

Ah Sam took his hand.

"Chahlee? You hear me, please? I want tell you something."

He said wearily: "I'm listening."

"Chahlee . . . before, when I work in Senhora house, you know that foreign man like me very much. So I can be cheeky—I can say 'yes' this man, 'no' other man . . . but, same time, I fear. My brothers, sisters—they don't know me, I don't know they. When I old, what happen to me? No fambly, nowhere to go. . . . So when you ask me go to *Merope*, I very glad. . . . Chahlee, everybody say you very good joss because color you hair. But I think *I* very good joss because you so good for me, because I so happy with you, many year, on *Merope*."

From under his lids, he saw that her eyes were luminous.

"But I getting old, Chahlee, and you so young! You must have chilluns. Long time, I think—what to do? Then I have mahvalus idea! Ling-ling love you so much, Wei love you too. S'pose you marry Ling-ling, have chilluns—then I have chilluns too! You have fambly, I have fambly! I can stay with you and Ling-ling till I die! When I go to ask How-kwa, he so happy! Everybody happy—Wei, How-kwa, Yin-kwa, Ling-ling, me. . . ." She paused and raised her eyes to his. Far down in their black depths, he caught the flicker of her anxiety. But her voice was steady. "Chahlee—you happy too?"

He took her face between his hands and looked into her eyes and saw with a pang that she looked old—she had let herself grow old, had slipped by some subtle cunning into the new role in which she had cast herself. Lover no longer. Loving, still and always. He kissed her eyes, whispered against the flutter of her lashes: "I'm happy, Ah Sam."

She sighed deeply, and he felt her body sag as the anxiety drained from it. For a long moment she rested her forehead against his lips.

Then she said, "Good!" and stood up briskly—sharp once again, alert, full of energy. She lit the lamp, placed it on the low table before the couch, drew up a chair facing him across the lamplight.

"Now, Chahlee—before you go to Ling-ling, we must talk something else very important. . . ." She paused impressively, fixing her bright eyes on his. "Chahlee, Ling-ling is Chinee fambly girl. In Chinee fambly, girl live inside house, don't know nothing about outside. In Chinee fambly, father is number one. What father say, all fambly must do. *You must remember this,* Chahlee. Up to today, Wei is number one in Ling-ling life. You must very careful *not* do anything make Ling-ling fight inside her heart—you one side, father one side. You unnerstan'?"

The emotions of the day suddenly erupted in a turmoil of sharp-edged shards that whirlpooled through Charlie's mind and heart. He was in it now—up to the neck in twisty Chinese plotting! Up to now he'd been the object of it. Now he was expected to perpetrate it! He rose abruptly and went to the window to stare out into the night.

Ah Sam followed him, spoke from behind his shoulder, her voice soft and insistent.

"You *not* tell Ling-ling about opium and *San Seb*. If you tell her, she worry because her father don't know, she think she must tell her father. What use she worry? More better you not tell. You unnerstan', Chahlee?"

The sounds of feasting echoed from the servants' party in the back garden, but in the front of the house it was very quiet. Under a half-moon, the sea shifted in restless tossings of light and dark—like the thoughts in his mind, like the feelings in his heart. Secrets. He must keep secrets now, lie and pretend. Pretend that *San Seb* had only lately been bought, just for the weekly sail from Macao to *Merope* and back. Warn Blogg to warn his crew that no mention must ever be made before Ling-ling of the voyages to Namoa and beyond, *San Seb's* hold full of you-know-what.

And the secret about going home to England for a two-year visit—that secret had better be kept not only from Ling-ling but from *everybody*. . . .

Ah Sam had taken his arm and was shaking it lightly.

"You unnerstan', Chahlee?"

"I understand," he said numbly.

"Good. You no fear, Chahlee. You see—everything will be good, everybody happy."

Then, with sudden gaiety:

"Chahlee, I see bath room! Mahvalus! You *clever!*"

It was so blatantly cajoling that he couldn't help grinning at her. She grinned back and gave him a little push:

"Go to Ling-ling now, Chahlee. . . ."

He stepped quietly into the bedroom. The new red silk spread was folded back over the foot of the bed. The few banners he had not pulled down hung motionless in the corners of the room. A lamp, turned low, stood on a table.

She lay in the bed. There was little more to be seen of her

now than there had been in the afternoon—just her hair, black and shining, strewn over the pillows, and a pale sliver of forehead. All the rest of her was hidden by the sheet pulled up over her eyes.

He tiptoed to the foot of the bed and suddenly stopped, clamped tight in a vise of anxiety. He had only their word for it that she loved him—what if she didn't? And what if he should find that he couldn't love her? She had been a lovely child, but he knew absolutely nothing of the girl she had become except that she was beautiful. God, he had been mad to do this! *Mad!* He stood, rooted, heart pounding heavily. The room was utterly still.

Then there was a rustle—the sheet that covered her was being cautiously pulled down. Her eyebrows appeared—perfect black arches against ivory skin. Then her heavy eyelashes, fluttering to free themselves from the sheet. Then her eyes—the beautiful almond-shaped eyes—peeped out from under the sheet, glanced around in a puzzled way, caught sight of him, and at once disappeared again as she snatched the sheet back over them.

But only for an instant. While he held his breath, she peeped out again, and this time her eyes were sparkling.

Chapter V

1837

"HIS NAME IS Ellison," Yin-kwa said.

Charlie yawned. They were sitting in wicker arm-chairs in the garden of the white house on the Praya Grande. Below them, on the beach, a gay and noisy scene was being enacted. Four-year-old Jin-see and his younger sister, screeching with excitement, were struggling to dip themselves in the wavelets while their amahs, shouting cautions, struggled to hold them back. Ling-ling and Ah Sam, sitting on the sand under parasols held by their amahs, were alternately laughing at the children's antics and conducting an animated discussion with the amahs. Ling-ling was pregnant again. Pregnancy made her even more lovely, rounded her cheeks, illuminated her skin, made her eyes more black and brilliant. Watching her, it seemed to Charlie that she glowed with the preciousness of gold. He felt the familiar melting in his breast, the soft, warm swelling that brought constriction to his throat, that made him ache to hold her—simply hold her solemnly against him, marveling that fate or luck or joss or God had given him so wondrous a thing as this marriage, this wife. The traits that had been enchanting in the child had grown and ripened in the woman, but still, in her guilelessness and candor, she remained childlike. To her, no one was king or beggar—everyone was the same, to be treated with the same warmth and consideration. Once he'd asked her why she, the Tai-tai, talked to the amahs as equals, and she'd answered, wide-eyed, "Because they peoples." But somehow, they never took advantage of the equality she accorded them. They treated her like a princess. They adored her, and extravagantly petted and spoiled her, as they did the children. And Ah Sam, whom she called Elder Sister—sometimes he thought Ah Sam loved her more than she did him! He smiled to himself, thinking how magically good was his joss, feeling contentment a luxurious cushion around his heart.

On the chair beside him, Yin-kwa stirred.

"About Ellison—I'd like you to come to Canton and get to know him."

"Why?"

"Because I can't do it myself. I represent my grandfather as head of the Co-hong, and he represents the foreign traders, so we can't have more than a formal relationship, and I have a feeling we should get closer to him than that."

"What did you say is his title?"

"Superintendent of Trade. . . . Charlie, I'm very glad that your marriage has turned out so well and that you're living in such happy domesticity, but it has its disadvantages. You've completely lost track of some of the harsher realities, for example, what's been happening in Canton. Things have changed a very great deal since Parliament abolished the Honorable Company's monopoly on trade with China and allowed free trade. Britishers have come flocking to Canton, many of them opportunists and cheapjacks of the worst kind, and for a time there was nobody to control them, since the Company now has no more power than anybody else. We were glad when the British government sent out Captain George Ellison. I think he's someone to be reckoned with. He knows nothing about trade—"

Charlie burst out laughing. "What's worrying you then? He should be a sitting duck for you! Wasn't very smart of Parliament to send out a Superintendent of Trade who knows nothing about trade."

"On the contrary—it could be very smart. Because he knows so little, he's obliged to depend on the traders for guidance—naturally, on the most influential among them, and I needn't tell you that that's Carradine. And Carradine is said to be very close to the British Foreign Secretary, Lord Palmerston. And Lord Palmerston is the one who selected Ellison as Superintendent of Trade."

For the first time that afternoon, Charlie gave Yin-kwa his full attention.

"You mean, you think Palmerston and Carradine are in collusion?"

Yin-kwa raised his eyes to heaven.

"Ah! You're getting the idea. But Ellison doesn't strike me as a man who can easily be used as a cat's-paw. It's a very interesting position, and you can help us a lot, Charlie, by getting to know Ellison."

Charlie stared out to sea. Hadn't Blogg said once that Carradine was getting "cuddly" with Palmerston? He drew a breath.

"What d'you want me to do, Yin-kwa? I can't guarantee to wean Ellison away from Carradine! I couldn't get to know Ellison any better than whatever face he chooses to show me."

"I'm not asking for guarantees. Just that you get to know him as well as you can and find out what you can about him. . . . I understand that it'll be Jin-see's fifth birthday in a few weeks' time, and Wei wants him to spend it with us in Canton. I suggest you all sail over in *San Seb*. My mother and my wife would love to have a visit from Ling-ling and Ah Sam. They can all spend two or three weeks with us, while you stay on *San Seb* at Jackass Point and cultivate acquaintance with Ellison."

"Well . . ." Charlie frowned. "Last time Wei was here, we did discuss sending Jin-see to Canton for his birthday, but since then Blogg's been to Namoa several times and he says there's some kind of rebellion going on. The coastal towns and villages are in an uproar, he says, and it looks as though it might spread as far as Canton."

Yin-kwa waved a casual hand.

"That's the Triad again!"

"Triad?"

"A rebel secret society, claiming to represent the harmony of heaven, earth, and man against the Manchu. It's been making trouble for years. Normally the viceroy sends out troops who kill a few rebels, and that's that until next time. This time it's more serious, because they've put up a rival to the Emperor, whom they call the Golden Dragon King, and somehow or the other they managed to defeat the viceroy's troops. That's what's causing the uproar in the villages—the peasants are saying heaven must be on the side of the Golden Dragon King because his troops defeated the viceroy's. But it'll all die down soon. Anyway, Canton is absolutely safe."

"You're sure?"

"Of course I'm sure!"

"All right, then. We'll all be at Jackass Point the first Sunday in August." He grinned at Yin-kwa. "I'll enjoy it. Change from happy domesticity."

The sail from Macao to Canton was fine, the weather calm and sunny, *San Seb*'s passengers in a state of happy anticipation. Blogg had torn out the partitions of the little private cabin, thus enlarging the main cabin, had covered the planks with mattresses, and turned it over to the women and children, he and Charlie sleeping on deck in hammocks, laughter and chatter from below coming softly to their ears late into the night. Now, as *San Seb* came in sight of Jackass Point in the afternoon of the first Sunday in August, Ling-ling and Ah Sam were on deck, light veils hiding their faces, each clinging to a child, all of them exclaiming while they looked excitedly around. The amahs were below, packing the innumerable boxes and bundles they had thought essential to bring along for the holiday, hurrying to get out on deck too, for they were all Macao women and just as excited as the children to see the great metropolis of Canton for the first time.

As barbarians, Charlie and Blogg were the only ones obliged to present their credentials at the customs house, and *San Seb* nudged into the customs house jetty to allow them to jump off. The customs house took up the entire width of the jetty, with a door on the river side and another on the shore side which led directly onto Jackass Point. When their papers had been stamped by an incurious customs officer, they walked through onto the cobblestones. *San Seb* was nosing her way through the mass of craft to her mooring. Wei was already on the dockside, waiting. The people on *San Seb* were all waving at him, Jin-see almost falling overboard in his excitement. He hadn't seen his grandfather since the last time Wei visited Macao, almost four months ago.

Wei turned to greet Charlie with a big smile.

"One month, Chahlee? How-kwa very happy to see Jin-see, he want Jin-see stay long time. I bring them back one month?"

A month! Yin-kwa must have suggested that, to give Charlie a good long time in which to make Ellison's acquaintance. Charlie shrugged. "A month's a long time."

But Wei had already turned to Ling-ling, who was coming down the gangplank, her face hidden behind her veil. She bowed to her father and then, standing a yard away from Charlie, bowed to him too—a proper Chinese wife taking leave of her husband in public. Smiling, he took a step toward her, but Ah Sam quickly moved between them. From behind her veil, her eyes flashed a warning. Jackass Point was not the place for foreign-style displays of conjugal affection!

Wei too was anxious to get the women away, and he started the party off immediately toward the sedan chairs in the mouth of Hog Lane. He and his grandson led the way, Jin-see clinging to his hand, looking up at him with shining eyes, chattering volubly. Jin-see's amah followed on their heels. Little Sister's amah came next, carrying her. Then Ling-ling and Ah Sam, side by side, their amahs following. And behind, the coolies Wei had brought, carrying the luggage. As Charlie watched them disappear into Hog Lane, discomfort descended on him with unexpected force. It was always *he* who left *them*, to spend a few days on *Merope*. . . .

Blogg was laughing.

"A captain for each crewman! What costs it to you—all them amahs?"

"Not much." Disconsolately, Charlie followed Blogg up to *San Seb's* narrow bridge. "They just get food and lodging, and a set of new clothes at New Year. The only cash they get is tips from visitors to our house. Ling-ling and Ah Sam tip their friends' servants, when they visit them. Adds up to quite a bit for the servants, and costs the employers no more. Chinese system—you pay your friends' servants, and they pay yours."

Blogg laughed again, and Charlie grunted. The little procession must be in the sedan chairs now, proceeding to the city gate, Jin-see no doubt sitting on his grandfather's lap in his grandfather's chair. By God, he was going to be spoiled rotten in the next few weeks—if he wasn't already! Charlie, who spent two or three days a week on *Merope* and while at home in Macao was preoccupied with Ling-ling, had been shocked during the sail from Macao to discover how spoiled Jin-see was. He'd been fascinated by the hammocks in which Charlie and Blogg had slept and had demanded one for himself, but they flipped over too easily and Charlie had said a firm "no." Jin-see had sulked, but what had really astonished and dismayed Charlie was that his pouts had sent not only the amahs but also Ling-ling and Ah Sam into a fever of appeasement. By God, it was high time to apply discipline! As soon as they got back to Macao, he'd start putting a stop to that kind of extravagant spoiling!

The mate appeared with mugs of grog. Charlie leaned on the rail beside Blogg, sipping, surveying Jackass Point. Yin-kwa had been right. It was a mess. Crowded. Dirty. More traders meant more factors, more factories, more ships, more seamen, more defilement, more pollution. The whole row of factories looked shabby and neglected, new gimcrack buildings tucked in cheek by jowl with the old ones, somehow making their dignified lines look squalid too. Where once the Honorable Company had had a neat green garden before its front steps, there was now a patch of dead earth littered with broken crates.

"Scurvy!" Blogg said, wrinkling his brow.

It was that!

Blogg raised his head to sniff the breeze.

"Curse this August weather! Fair all the way from Macao, and now the air be tainted. Typhoon blowing up, I'll lay my oath! Early for it. Should have towed *Merope* to Si-tao Bay afore we left. If we're here a month, we're like to find her atop Lintin Bluff time we get back."

At Lintin Island, in the middle of the estuary, the tethered hulks were easy prey for the great winds of the typhoon season. In August each year they were all towed to Si-tao Bay for shelter.

"Yin-kwa'll take care of it," Charlie said sourly. "He arranged all this, and if we're to be here a month, he'll have to see that Lee Kwok gets *Merope* towed to Si-tao."

"How you going to meet Ellison?"

Charlie laughed shortly. "Yin-kwa'll see to that too, no doubt!"

A drop of sweat from the end of his chin plopped into his grog. It was growing muggier by the minute—not the slightest stir of air on the land or the river, and great dark clouds creeping ponderously overhead. The world was holding its breath, awaiting the typhoon's onslaught.

"This'll be one of the twisty ones," Blogg said uneasily. "Blowing somewhere about, swirling. No telling which way it go."

Moodily, Charlie sipped at his grog. Blogg's mate slipped up to the bridge and began talking to Blogg in their private pidgin. Charlie heard a word that might have been "Ellison." A message from Yin-kwa?

"Huh!" Blogg turned to Charlie as his mate left the bridge. "Message from Yin-kwa."

Charlie shrugged. "Yin-kwa'd make a fine general. His spy net is marvelous—all the servants on Jackass Point are in it. What's the message?"

"Ellison's aboard that schooner we passed at Whampoa—*Lily*. Appears he's moved to her for his base quarters. Doesn't like Jackass Point—can't say as I blame him! He's living and working on *Lily*, sending messages up and down by cutter. He expects a visit from you tomorrow."

"Tomorrow!" Yin-kwa wasn't wasting any time!

"Aye. If you want to be there tomorrow, Charlie, best we sail now. If we wait, typhoon'll likely hold us up here three-four days."

"It won't catch us on the way to Whampoa?"

"Might, but we'll get through anyway. It's not so far, and in the river still."

"All right." Charlie shrugged. With his family in Canton, he might as well be in Whampoa as here.

The crew asked no questions when Blogg ordered sail to be hoisted, and the customs officer asked none when, two hours after their arrival, they stopped to report to him their departure. The ways of barbarians were not to be fathomed—his job was to stamp papers.

It seemed, at first, that the blow would hold off. The sky lowered and the silty brown waters of the Pearl River stirred sluggishly, thick as oil, but the little Chinese craft, which would be the first to scurry for shelter when the blow was imminent, still darted about, busy as ever.

Charlie went to lie in his hammock. *San Seb* was strangely silent. The sultriness of the air muted her usual creakings, and, of course, there were no twittering female voices, no high-pitched cries of children. The women and the children were by now ensconced in the house of many courtyards in the Street of the Psychics. Ling-ling and Ah Sam were no doubt in Yin-kwa's mother's house, but Jin-see would be in How-kwa's house, in Wei's room. He'd spend the next month constantly in Wei's company, and Wei would do just as he liked with his beloved grandson. He would never dream of consulting so unimportant a person as his grandson's mother, and neither Ling-ling nor Ah Sam would dream of interfering between Wei and his grandson. God Almighty! Charlie wriggled uncomfortably in the narrow confines of the hammock. Why the devil had he agreed to this lunatic idea of Yin-kwa's!

When he woke some hours later, it was to heavy gusts of wind that jerked roughly at the hammock. *San Seb* was groaning, her half-furled sails snapping as though they strained to break free of her masts. He rolled out of the hammock and went to join Blogg on the heaving bridge. *San Seb* was beating erratically, becalmed for moments, then flung forward on great, moaning blasts that tugged at Charlie's limbs and threatened his balance. He clung to the rail, deafened by the roar of the wind and the rolling drumbeat of thunder. There was no rain yet, but dazzling streaks of lightning continually tore jagged rents in the black sky, revealing sudden visions of racing clouds and furious water.

"Not far now," Blogg yelled in Charlie's ear. "West channel."

The western shore of Whampoa Island, the sheltered side. The harbor was on the eastern shore, wide and comfortable in fair weather, bustling with the to-and-fro of barges ferrying tea to the great ships. But in foul weather the harbor became a hell of chopping water, and at the first sign of a blow all the craft on the eastern shore moved to the west channel.

There seemed nothing, now, to guide Blogg through the huge flurry of water and spray and the almost visible swirl of the wind, but he stood solid at the helm, and *San Seb* inched forward against the rising fury. They must almost be at the entrance of the west channel, Charlie judged, when Blogg's bellow suddenly bucketed in his ears.

"By God, *Lily's* still in the east channel! Bain't the sods got sense to move her?"

Charlie lurched to the side, straining his eyes to search the howling void, but could see nothing. Then, all at once, more felt than seen, the pale cliff of a ship's hull loomed so close that he jerked backward. If that was *Lily*, she was adrift. She could smash into *San Seb* and turn both ships into driftwood. Charlie turned to yell a warning at Blogg, but the tumult snatched his voice from his mouth. He started to make his way back to Blogg, clutching at every projection, blinded, deafened—and was suddenly aware that the roaring in his ears was not the wind but Blogg's voice, shouting exultantly, "By God, typhoon's veering! By God, she's veering!" In a flash of lightning, Blogg's raised head looked strangely fragile, the great bush of his hair and beard plastered flat by rain, for rain was falling, in sheets, in waterfalls, and the wind was dropping.

Charlie raised his head and bellowed too, bellowed his relief, the rain flooding his wide-open mouth. The crew echoed him from all over *San Seb*. The lightning showed them clinging to ropes and struts, for the ship was still bucking like a wild horse, laughing like madmen because the wind was going, it was almost gone!

But *Lily* was still there, half hidden by curtains of rain, tossing like a dinghy on the leaping water. By common consent, the crew of *San Seb* rushed to the scuppers to make ready with ropes to fling to *Lily*'s crew when she came within reach, and Blogg, his great, delicate hands playing the helm like a violin, began to maneuver toward *Lily*. It took a long time and *Lily* seemed unable to do more than wallow, but at last a crest brought the two vessels close enough together for ropes to be flung across the gap. They were seized and fastened, and, to the cheers of the crew, three men, one after the other, made their way dangerously, hand over hand across the ropes, from *Lily*'s scuppers to *San Seb*'s deck. Blogg left the helm to his mate and came down with Charlie to wring their hands.

"By God, your joss is good! If not for the wind veering, your schooner'd be broke up, fit only for the devil to sail! What happened? Well, later. . . . Take 'em below, Charlie. I'll see us in west channel first."

In pitch darkness, Charlie led the way to *San Seb*'s cabin, which was chokingly stuffy after the wild wet freshness of the deck. He floundered over the soft mattresses until he found the candle and matches that Blogg kept stowed in a bracket. By the flickering light, he found the rum, also stowed carefully by Blogg in brackets. It was safe—four bottles of it! He lifted one, drew the cork with his teeth, and floundered back to the three refugees who stood, dripping, at the foot of the ladder.

"My dear sir!" The taller of the three lifted his hands protestingly. "You first!"

Charlie gulped and passed the bottle, and the others drank in turn, grinning at each other, breathing hard, filthy, tattered, soaking wet.

"Sir." The tall man bowed. "My name is George Ellison."

"And mine is Charlie Tyson."

"Charlie Tyson? By God, are you the gentleman I expected to visit me tomorrow?"

"I am."

They stared at each other curiously. Charlie couldn't tell what Ellison looked like. His hair dripped in rattails over his forehead and watery blood leaked from a cut on his cheek.

Ellison's teeth, very white, flashed in a grin.

"Mr. Tyson, do I look as awful as you?"

They thought it uproariously funny. When Blogg came down a few minutes later, having left the mooring of *San Seb* to his mate, he found them squatting on the mattresses, laughing riotously and passing the bottle. Ellison jumped up to shake Blogg's hand.

"Sir, I and my secretaries"—he waved at the two young men—"are eternally grateful! You've saved us from a fate worse than death." He threw back his head and laughed like a boy. "I'm not jesting. My rank, sir, is Captain in England's Navy, and I'd never have outlived the shame of foundering in a schooner!"

"What betook you?" Blogg stumbled over the mattresses to

lift the second bottle from its bracket. "How came you caught without sails?"

"Her sails were stowed!" Ellison cried. "She wasn't meant to sail! I took her over as a floating home and office when I got tired of landlubbing it on Jackass Point. I was the only seaman aboard, if you don't count the coolie oarsmen who take the cutter to Canton and back with messages and papers. I'd sent them off yesterday, and today, when it began to blow, I thought to go ashore at Whampoa. Looked for the servants to hail a junk, but by God every last damned one of them was gone! Vanished! Galley was empty! Food in the pots, half cooked, but the stove fires carefully banked and not a blasted one of them about! Before we could hail a craft outselves, the blow started, and *Lily* broke her moorings."

They drank while they discussed the mystery of the vanishing servants. Carradine's number-one boy had recruited them, Ellison said, and they'd been good. The cook had been excellent. . . .

Charlie and Blogg glanced at each other. If Carradine's number-one boy had supplied the servants, they must have come through the Co-hong, like all the servants on Jackass Point, and must have been a part of Yin-kwa's spy net. Yet they had vanished, apparently without Yin-kwa's knowledge. Yin-kwa had made the arrangements for Charlie to meet Ellison, and it seemed unlikely he'd have done that if he'd known the servants were about to disappear. There must be some reason for their disappearance—nothing in Yin-kwa's spy net happened without a reason—yet it seemed that this time Yin-kwa couldn't have known . . .

"Charlie!"

Ellison was holding out the bottle. His hair was drying out, standing up in spikes, a light corn color. His eyes were blue. His nose was long, and so was his clean-shaven jaw. Not handsome, Charlie thought, tipping the bottle, but pleasant. Very pleasant. Nice face. Boyish laugh. About the same age as himself. . . . He passed the bottle back.

By the time the fourth bottle was broached, the two young secretaries were asleep, sprawled on the mattresses. Charlie was dozing, listening inattentively to Blogg and Ellison discussing ships, wishing himself in his bathing room in Macao steeped in a steaming tub. The air in the cabin, tightly closed against the still-pouring rain, stinking of rum and half-dried bodies, was nauseatingly fusty. Ellison was saying slurrily:

"It was noble, Blogg! Protest as you may, it was noble to come to our aid as you did! You could have lost your life, and Charlie's and your crew's!"

"Couldn't have saved you but for you aboard *Lily,* keeping her steady as could be without sails," Blogg answered solemnly. "Ask me, 'twere crazy-mad, take a seaman like you off the ships, make you sup'rintendent of bloody trade!"

"Superintendent of bloody *smuggling,* you mean!"

Ellison's voice was almost a snarl. Startled, Charlie glanced at him. Frowning darkly, he was reaching for the bottle. He tipped it with exaggerated care, swallowed, wiped his mouth on the back of a hand, and blinked owlishly at Charlie.

"My instructions from Palmerston were to see that the tea gets shipped, to keep the traders in order, to protect them if needed. It sounded simple, till I learned that the traders I'm supposed to protect are bloody *smugglers!* I wrote to Palmerston for new instructions—God blast it, does he want me to countenance *smuggling?* But I've had no answer from him, though there's been ample time. No bloody answer. . . ."

His voice trailed off and his head lurched forward, coming to rest against his propped-up knees. Charlie shook his own head, trying to clear it of the fuzzy fumes. By God, Yin-kwa was right as usual! Whatever kind of man Ellison might be, he was not complacent! He glanced at Blogg, but Blogg was leaning back, chin on chest, snoring gently. Ellison's voice began again, sounding disembodied, coming fitfully to Charlie's ears.

"You're in it too, you and Blogg. You own one of those opium hulks at Lintin, and you run some opium up the coast, though nothing to what Carradine himself runs, as he proudly informed me. . . . 'S my business to know everything I can about the British traders here. . . . Asked know-it-all Carradine. . . ." His tone became accusatory. "You've got a Chinese mistress in Macao, and a couple of bastards by her. . . ."

"She's not my mistress!" Charlie's head suddenly cleared. His words came loud and clear. "She's my wife, damn you! The children are my son and my daughter!" He glared at Ellison, fury beginning to rise.

Ellison looked up, his blue gaze wavering until it focused on Charlie's face. He broke into a wide, sweet smile.

"Your *wife?* Why, that's wonderful!"

For a moment longer his smiling eyes looked into Charlie's. Then they closed of their own volition. His body slipped sideways until he was lying curled on the mattress. He began to snore.

Charlie lay back slowly, automatically stretching out his right hand. But of course Ling-ling wasn't there, devil take it! This was *San Seb,* not the bedroom in Macao, and there were only snoring men in this stuffy cabin fuddly with many stenches. . . .

There was much to tell Yin-kwa, clever Yin-kwa who had sensed the rift, honorable Ellison versus cuddly Carradine and palmy Palmerston. Ellison, who sounded as though he'd have the guts to challenge the whole rock-solid opium establishment. . . .

And what about those vanishing servants? The mystery of the vanishing servants, who must have gone without Yin-kwa's knowledge . . .

It took two days to find *Lily,* tow her to a secure mooring in the now calm and sunlit harbor, and set her to rights. Blogg's crew, with the promise of extra pay, worked with a will. Ellison was cheerful as a happy boy.

"By God, she's not much damaged, is she, Blogg? By God, that's good! If she'd been damaged, I'd have had to go back to Jackass Point for a while at least. Nearly a year I spent in that hellhole, in Carradine's factory. He turned over his top

117

floor to me, but I insisted on paying him rent. I didn't want to be beholden to him! By God, it's good to walk a deck and sleep in a cabin, hearing the sea shush-shush against the bulkheads!"

Blogg's mate went ashore to try to find some trace of *Lily*'s servants, and came back empty-handed.

"Says he can't find hide nor hair of 'em," Blogg said. "Don't see why—Whampoa is not so big a place. Something's going on, I lay my oath!"

"Never mind." Ellison was in no mood to care. "Get more in Canton if they don't come back. Let's eat!"

They sat down to dried beef from *Lily*'s stores, a bottle of wine that Ellison carefully opened, and a cabbage brought back by Blogg's mate that Blogg himself had cooked.

"In England they boil cabbage," Blogg said. "Boil it till all the good of it is gone in the water. Then they chuck out the water and put limpy rags of cabbage on the table. Chinee way of cooking cabbage is best."

He chopped the cabbage and put it in a pot sizzling with oil, stirred it quickly for a few moments, then covered the pot and pushed it to the back of the stove.

"Cabbage has its own water. Get that out by hotting it quick, then let it stew a bit. Comes out still crispy, all the taste and good of it still there."

They all agreed that the cabbage was superb. It was almost demolished, and the wine was gone, when a voice said from the doorway:

"Good afternoon, gentlemen."

The speaker stepped over the threshold, and suddenly the gaiety in the cabin died.

Carradine.

As tall as Charlie remembered him. As slim—no trace of a paunch, though he must be in his fifties. Handsomely dressed— fine dark woolen coat, white breeches, a lacy stock at his throat. Clean-shaven and bewigged. But there was something strange about his face. The eyes were still as green and hard and shiny as that lump of jade of his, but the rest of his features might have come loose from their moorings. The jaw protruded a little too far. The brows overhung the eyes a little too deeply. The bridge of the craggy nose seemed to have caved in a little. Everything was a little out of kilter.

Ellison had risen and was standing stiffly.

"It's the custom, sir, for visitors to ask permission to come aboard."

"Beg pardon." The green eyes mocked. "Shall I go back to my cutter and start again?"

"No, of course not." With an effort, Ellison smiled. "You know Charlie Tyson? And Captain Blogg?"

Carradine raised the heavy eyebrows.

"Sir George's sucker, eh? All grown up! And good old Blogg! Lost any more chests overboard lately?"

The attack was so unexpected and uncalled-for that hot anger flashed through Charlie, but Blogg only laughed good-naturedly.

"Not since you gave me crazy-mad orders to transfer cargo in high seas!"

He turned his back on Carradine.

"Goodbye, Cap'n Ellison, and thankee. No doubt we'll be seeing you again. Charlie, I'll see *San Seb* ready for sailing."

He ambled unconcernedly away. Charlie made to follow him, but Ellison placed a hand on his arm.

"Wait a bit, Charlie."

Reluctantly, Charlie turned back to see Carradine bowing ironically.

"*Captain* Ellison, I've come to fetch you back to Canton. In a hurry, I'm afraid. Are your servants here? No? Nor are ours at Jackass Point. Vanished, every man jack of them."

Charlie's stomach suddenly tightened. Carradine went on, green eyes glittering.

"By order, no doubt, of the new viceroy. . . . As Superintendent of Trade, it's your place, Ellison, to deal with viceroys, but since you chose to leave Jackass Point, I took the liberty of having the announcement opened and translated. He arrived on the night of the typhoon. The next day, the old viceroy was marched off in chains. Quite a coincidence, isn't it? New viceroy arrives, old one is disgraced, all our servants vanish—and no food is coming into the market on Jackass Point." He grinned ferociously at Ellison. "Even if it discommodes you, don't you think it expedient to return?"

Ellison, all his boyish glow gone, said: "Yes, of course."

Carradine turned toward the door. "Shall we start, then?"

Ellison glanced at Charlie. "I'll see you there?"

"Yes. *San Seb*'ll be tied up along the dock somewhere."

"Goodbye for now, then."

He hurried after Carradine.

Carradine's cutter was a dot on the horizon by the time *San Seb* was under sail. Charlie stood by Blogg on the bridge, staring after it.

"D'you think this business of the servants vanishing might mean—well, some kind of danger? I'm worried about my family in Canton."

"Nay!" Blogg shook his head decidedly. "Whatever happens, they'll certain-sure be safe in How-kwa's house!"

Charlie was silent for a moment. Then: "Ellison doesn't like Carradine."

Blogg grinned. "That he doesn't! Nor does Carradine like him. Yin-kwa knew what he was doing when he set you onto this. . . . Did you notice Carradine's face, Charlie? I've heard that the pox does that to you. Cankers get into the bones and rot them."

"God Almighty!" Charlie turned to gape at Blogg.

"Aye. My mate says all the Chinee know it. Pox can drive you mad as well—could be Carradine's gone a bit mad too, as unmannerly as he was to all of us, with no reason. Makes you sorry for him, don't it? All that wealth, and can't buy himself cured!"

Sorry for Carradine! God-rotted Carradine, with his wealth, his arrogance, his tons of opium, his beautiful clippers, his great green lump of jade. Rotted by God, for no man could save him. . . .

Charlie stared out over the shining water, a kind of wonder dawning in his heart as the image of Carradine, the superhuman image that for so long had diminished him, itself became diminished, itself shrank away into pitifulness.

So one day would the image of his own father be diminished. So one day would that old abandonment be canceled out. So one day would the shame it had buried like a stone in his entrails be exhumed. . . .

"What are you thinking, Charlie?" Blogg was regarding him quizzically.

"Of my father. . . . One day soon I'm going home to see my father."

"Mmmmm. . . . What about Ling-ling and the children?"

"They'll come with me."

"Wei won't like it."

"It'll only be for a couple of years."

"You think Wei'll let you take Jin-see away, even only a couple of years?"

"How can he prevent me? Jin-see's my son."

"And Wei's grandson. Could be he'll make trouble."

"Oh Blogg, could be you're getting more Chinee than the Chinee!"

"Could be." Blogg looked up, smiling.

Charlie met his glance affectionately. Blogg knew a great deal more about the Chinese than how they cooked cabbage. On those peaceful sails from Namoa back to *Merope*, when he had talked to Blogg about his father, Blogg had talked too, bit by bit told his own story, in words and in silences.

Blogg's earliest memory was of sitting by his father in a noisy place, everyone talking loudly, only his father silent, head sunk on a table. "Thought he was asleep. Tried to wake him. Couldn't. I was frightened. Took me a long time to know it was the drink. But seems I always knew it was on account of my mother."

121

A long silence. Charlie had thought of his own mother, a soft, fragrant presence, then a mystery behind a locked door. "She's deaded," his older brother had whispered, big-eyed.

"The day my mother left," Blogg said, "she set the rozzers on him—said he'd beat her, though it was that other did it. He was in debt too, heavy, on account of her. Press gang came for him in the gin mill, ganged him into the navy. Nobody knew what to do with me, so they took me too. Powder monkey. That's how I started life—age of ten. He died when I was sixteen. We were back in London then. A pauper's grave, but it was June and I found some flowers growing, little yellow ones. Put 'em on his mound. Right pretty, they looked."

He'd gone back to the ships after his father's death.

"Not the navy. Merchantmen. Third mate when I was twenty. Singapore—longest voyage I'd ever been. We all went ashore that night. First time I drank, that night—father's mound seemed awful far away."

First time, too, he'd found himself in a brothel.

"The drink took me hard, and I went with the rest of 'em. Never wanted to before. Girls so pretty and wheedly, but my mother could turn into a harridan, drop of a hat. . . . But in that Singapore place there were Chinee girls. Different. Gentle."

He'd stayed in eastern waters after that, and got his master's papers, and one day gone to work for Carradine. In Macao he'd found a right gentle girl and lived with her for a few years.

"Her parents were fisher folk. They thought it fine for her, and certain-sure it was fine for me!"

When she died, her parents had taken the children. Two of them. Boys.

"I couldn't have cared for them myself, they were too little. They raised them right nice, those old fisher folk, and loved them right well. Made me feel fine. They gave me their daughter, and I gave them back her sons."

He had kept the little wooden house on the island of Kolo-an near Macao where he'd lived with the right gentle girl, but he'd never found himself another. "Don't care to, some-how. She was right nice, that one. Right gentle."

No harridan.

Now, hands light on the spokes of the helm, the mild giant scanned the water, humming a tune.

Blogg's mate set off with a note to Yin-kwa as soon as *San Seb* was moored at Jackass Point. He was back within the hour. He couldn't get into the city.

The gates were closed and patrolled by soldiers—not the usual gatekeeper's ragtag guards, but "Emperor soldiers."

"Must be what they call Tartars," Blogg said.

"What the devil's happening?"

"Mate says it's been like that since day after the typhoon. City is sealed up. None going in, none coming out."

"God rot it! Yin-kwa swore Canton would be safe!"

"Oh, they're safe!" Blogg said consolingly. "None safer than How-kwa's own house. They'll be back soon as the gates are opened, and the gates got to be opened soon, otherwise trade'll stop!"

But the gates remained closed, and trade was indeed sus-pended. Charlie fretted, Ellison worried, Carradine and the other traders scowled and fumed, but the dozens of young men, for the most part the traders' factors, who inhabited Jackass Point saw the cessation of their dull routine as holiday time. They were festive. They played noisy games on the cobble-stones, laughing and joshing. The market remained closed, and they crowded the dockside to bargain for food brought over by the boat people of the floating village—at first, scrawny chickens and grayish lumps of goat meat, but as the market continued empty and the boat people realized their bonanza, fresh fish, sides of pork, even the whole carcass of a calf. The factors bought lavishly, experimented with cooking, feasted at each other's factories on burned-black or half-raw meats. It was all a huge joke. Idle seamen from the tea ships gathering at Whampoa flocked to Hog Lane, drank the grogshops dry, but more grog kept appearing, smuggled from factory or ship stores and sold under the counter to the owners of the grogshops. The seamen drank noisily on, slapping each other's back in enormous drunken fellowship, gouging each other's eyes in sudden flares of fury.

No one had any news beyond speculation, not even Ellison. He came to lean on *San Seb*'s rail with Blogg and Charlie, drinking grog. He was in full dress uniform: white breeches; dark blue swallow-tailed coat, double-breasted, brass-buttoned, epauletted; on his head the great cockaded hat of captain's rank. When he removed the hat, they saw that his long face was gray with trouble.

"Why the devil haven't the Chinese communicated? Not a word since the first announcement of the new viceroy's arrival! His name, by the way, is Teng Ting Chen. I've sent a dozen letters to the Petitions Gate asking what's happening, protesting the withdrawal of our servants and the closure of the market, but the gateman has refused to take them. The traders are clamoring for me to do something, but what the devil can I do? Carradine scowls and sneers—always the same refrain from him! Blast the stupid, obstinate Chinese. Blow them up. And that's the kind of people I'm supposed to protect!"

He came to *San Seb* again a few days later, to say that he was sending to Macao for Gutzen. "You know—the missionary who knows Chinese so well. Might need him. Might be foolish to rely entirely on Carradine's translator."

They leaned on the rail, moodily drinking grog. There was nothing to say that hadn't already been said a dozen times, but Ellison stayed, seeming to take comfort from them, perhaps from the slight heave of *San Seb* as the water shifted her against her moorings.

"Good little ship!" He patted the rail.

"That she is!" Blogg murmured.

"Oh God!" Ellison set down his glass and reached for his cockaded hat. "How long is this damned impasse going to last?"

"No telling." Blogg gave him a friendly pat on the shoulder. "Chinee are patient people. Best you be patient too."

"You too," he added, glancing at Charlie as Ellison marched off. "I know it's hard, but they'll be coming back soon, all safe and sound."

"Should never have agreed to Yin-kwa's idea!" Charlie flung off the bridge, down to the cabin, where he and Blogg were sleeping on the mattresses to escape the hordes of mosquitoes that, in port, pestered them on deck. Why the devil had he agreed? He had his million now, and as long as Yin-kwa continued to refuse to expand their interest in the opium trade because "the time isn't ripe," whatever Ellison did or thought made no difference to himself. As soon as this was over, he'd ask Yin-kwa for some of his silver and start planning the journey home. . . . It was dawn before he fell asleep.

On the fourteenth day, the impasse was broken—in the early afternoon, Jackass Point hot and somnolent under the midday sun, the factors napping in their factories, the seamen sleeping it off in the grogshops.

The quiet was disturbed by the sound of cymbals, distant at first but quickly growing in brassy clangor. Soon the cymbalists appeared on Jackass Point itself—ten men in gaudily embroidered jackets over patched, everyday blue cotton trousers, dirty bare feet slapping the cobbles. They marched raggedly out of Hog Lane, clashing their cymbals with great, dramatic gestures of their arms. At the foot of the flagpole they ranged themselves in two straggly rows, facing each other, still clashing their instruments, but lightly now, with a tinny sound.

Spectators were materializing like magic, traders and factors pouring out of the factories, seamen from the grogshops, boat people from across the river. They clustered in excited groups, pointing, exclaiming, questioning. Charlie and Blogg, on their way back to *San Seb* from a visit to Ellison, found a spot on the steps of a factory from which to watch.

Now, soldiers marched into the courtyard, forty or fifty of them, uniformed in dark blue, queues wound around their heads. Some carried swords, some muskets, some ancient blunderbusses. They marched irregularly, more or less to the beat of the cymbals, until the leaders reached the flagpole. Then they squared themselves off in two rows, facing each other about thirty feet apart, enclosing between them a long rectangle of cobblestones, the flagpole and the rows of cymbalists at the top.

A group of coolies followed the soldiers, carrying a mass of brightly colored burdens. They busied themselves at the bottom of the rectangle, and soon the result of their work became apparent: a large, square tent, open on all four sides—actually, a roof of red silk on poles anchored into great blocks of wood. In the center of the square of shade created by the roof, the coolies carefully set a carved blackwood armchair.

For a while, nothing more happened. The cymbalists ting-tinged their instruments, the soldiers gazed across the rectangle at each other, the silk on the tent roof flapped in the breeze, the armchair stood like a throne in its patch of shade. The spectators began to fidget, the younger men to joke and clown around, their voices rising in crescendo. Then, suddenly, the cymbalists began again to clash their cymbals with such vigor that every other sound was drowned in the hideous blare they produced. On and on it went, people grimacing and covering their ears, until at last, at the height of the cymbalists' frenzy, an ornate sedan chair made its appearance in the mouth of the alley, transported by a crowd of red-and-blue-uniformed men— at least twenty of them—yoked in an intricate harness of short and long poles and tasseled ropes. The harness held them so closely together that it seemed they must trip on each other's heels, but they were expert—their short thudding, rhythmic stride never faltered. On their shoulders, the chair moved majestically forward like a ship sailing on air, and was set down before the tent as though it weighed nothing.

The cymbalists stopped their clanging and there was a moment of exquisite quiet. Somebody beside Charlie began to whisper that only very important persons had so many chair-bearers. His words were drowned in a sudden universal gasp— a great in-drawn "AAAAAH!" of breath—that rose from all over Jackass Point. Four men were coming out of Hog Lane. Charlie, standing on tiptoe to see them better, felt his eyes pop wide open. Were these men or immortals? Tall, erect, swinging splendidly along in a kaleidoscope of color that somehow enhanced their magnificent virility—silvery garments floating loose, bound at waist and ankle with stripings of scarlet, enclosed on the upper body by sleeveless black satin jackets on which great, round medallions of brilliant embroidery were splashed like multicolored breastplates. Their cropped hair, swept back in front, gave a proud lift to their impassive faces. They carried long lances, from which, high above their heads, fluttered pennants in the Emperor's color, yellow.

"Tartars . . . Tartars . . ."

The whisper rustled through the crowd.

Tartars. The legendary "banner men" of the Emperor's handpicked battalions. The bravest, strongest, best. The undefeatable.

In a hush of admiration, the Tartars strode to the tent. Two ranged themselves behind the throne. The other two drew back the curtains that hid the occupant of the sedan chair. He was revealed—a fat, heavy, dough-faced man in a green brocade robe, high boots of padded satin, a round hat with swept-back brim to which was pinned a cockade of brilliant feathers.

"Peacock feathers . . . high-rank mandarin . . ." The whispers fled from mouth to mouth around the crowd.

The mandarin rose, stepped out of the chair, went haughtily to seat himself upon the throne. The bearers took up the chair and carried it off to one side. The Tartars stood, two behind the mandarin, one on each side of him.

The scene was set.

No one moved.

The sun blazed down.

Then Gutzen stepped into the rectangle. He was dressed in the half-Chinese fashion he affected as a gesture to his converts: a knee-length loose blouse, sashed at the waist, over ordinary, foreign-style breeches. Around his head, in no particular fashion, another sash of a sky-blue color. Under it, his dark eyes swiveled—he was cock-eyed.

Charlie almost laughed aloud. A cock-eyed missionary who sold opium with his Bibles; a disdainful mandarin on a throne beneath a flapping tent; four fantastical Tartars; all on the prosaic cobblestones of dirty Jackass Point. It was whimsy! It was freakish fancy!

Gutzen reached the tent and bowed to the mandarin. They exchanged words. The mandarin bent and drew from his boot a roll of yellow silk attached to a rod of ivory. With a large gesture, he shook the rod and the silk unrolled into a little banner. He began reading from it in a low, droning voice, the words incomprehensible even if the crowd could have heard them. Then he rolled up the silk, thrust it back into his boot, and made a brief gesture to Gutzen.

Gutzen produced from under his blouse a bullhorn such as those used by ship's mates to bellow orders to their crews. It was so incongruous that a titter ran through the crowd, soon silenced when Gutzen's voice, high and rather squeaky, resounded over Jackass Point.

"The announcement just read out by his excellency the mandarin is an Edict of the Son of Heaven. It translates as follows. 'The people have grown careless of previous edicts issued by my venerable ancestors. Once again, therefore, I remind the people that my ancestors strictly forbade the smoking and trafficking of opium. Now, to ensure reverence to the wishes of my ancestors, I proclaim that henceforth the penalty of all who violate the edicts will be death by strangulation.' "

The breathy voice stopped. The mandarin beckoned and Gutzen leaned toward him again, listened, nodded, and once more raised the bullhorn to his mouth.

"His excellency the mandarin has a message from his excellency the new viceroy, Teng Ting Chen. The viceroy announces his determination to enforce the wishes of the Son of Heaven by destroying once and for all the traffic in opium. Let those barbarians beware who indulge their greed by trying to continue this traffic."

Again the magnified voice stopped. Gutzen glanced down at the mandarin, but he remained motionless, haughty gaze fixed on the air before him. There was a long pause. The crowd began to shift and murmur. Here and there rose a snigger. Was that all? All this fuss to announce a warning to barbarians? "They can't touch us anyway! We're *Britons!*" "Let them strangle their own if they want to." The sneers grew in audibility and sarcasm. Charlie, dizzy from the heat, let himself down from his toes, bent to massage his aching calves. It was fine for Blogg—tall as he was, he could see over the bobbing heads without straining.

"By God!"

Blogg's hushed exclamation abruptly straightened Charlie's back.

"They're going to do it! Right here on Jackass Point, under our noses!"

"What? What?" Charlie craned his neck.

"Strangle some poor devil!"

The sniggers and sneers had faded into dead silence. The crowd was staring, motionless, spellbound. Charlie stretched himself. In front of the flagpole, coolies were hammering a tall cross into the ground. Across the cobblestones, a half-naked man was being dragged toward the flagpole, bare feet stumbling, tattered trousers flapping about his ankles. The two men who dragged him were coolies too, raggedly dressed, queues wound around their heads in working fashion . . . no panoply, no trappings, for executioners!

When they reached the cross, they went to work at once, fastening their victim to it by threading his queue through a hole at the top of the upright, pulling it tight, and knotting it. The cross was taller than the victim. His toes, hardly reaching the cobbles, scrabbled for purchase, scrabbled to help support the weight of his body, which otherwise hung solely from the roots of his hair. But a moment later his feet were jerked entirely off the ground—the executioners were winding rope around his arms, tying them to the crossbar. His weight now hung from his arms, but the space between the crossbar and the hole in the upright where his queue was fastened was too short to accommodate his head and neck. His head was twisted sideways at a grotesque angle, chin jutting, tendons protruding like rope. Murmurs of horror spattered like hail around the courtyard. Unheeding, as though their victim were inanimate, the executioners dropped a noose round the tortured neck and secured it loosely with a few turns of a tourniquet. Then they stepped back, looking toward the mandarin: They were ready; they would await his signal to finish the job.

The victim hung alone there on the cross, for the first time clearly visible to the spectators. Blogg clutched Charlie's arm in a grip that threatened to break it.

"It's Lee Kwok!"

With a thrill of horror, Charlie stretched himself to the utmost, saw clearly for a moment over the heads in front of him, felt the breath rush from his body. The man on the cross was indeed Lee Kwok!

Utter stillness had descended on Jackass Point. Every eye was fixed on the mandarin. Slowly, he rose from the throne, raised his right hand into the air, held it poised. Charlie's heart pounded frantically against his rib cage. There was nothing he could do, nothing! In an instant the mandarin would bring his hand chopping down and the executioners would lay hold upon their noose to squeeze out Lee Kwok's life. . . .

"Hoy, Jack!"

The drunken shout rang gaily through the courtyard. Out of Hog Lane a huge seaman, as big as Blogg, came staggering, beckoning his comrades with a great rolling gesture of his arm.

"Look what them sodders be doing! Got to stop 'em! Here's a lark!"

The rest was lost in pandemonium. A stream of drunken sailors poured out of Hog Lane and plunged into the crowd, howling joyously. In a moment, Jackass Point was a sea of struggling, tangled bodies. Charlie caught a glimpse of the executioners hacking at Lee Kwok's pigtail and the ropes that bound his arms to free him from the cross. A moment later, the cross was wrenched from the ground by yelling seamen, smashed into pieces, the pieces raised and thwacked down happily on any head within reach. Someone snatched up a pair of cymbals and began to clash them in a gay, ear-cracking din. The tent was felled, the gaudy silk fluttering erratically over heads and shoulders and finally slithering to the ground to disappear in shreds and tatters under a hundred kicking feet. The throne flew into the air, tossed up to the rhythm of a mighty "heave-ho, heave-ho," and crashed down again, cracking heads, evoking screams that were lost in the gleeful racket.

Blogg snatched Charlie bodily into the shelter of a factory doorway, Charlie struggling, crying, "We've got to find Lee Kwok," Blogg hanging on to him, yelling "Look there!" Charlie looked over Blogg's shoulder and stopped struggling. A Chinese rabble were streaming out of the alleys into the courtyard, their faces filled with hate, their eyes shining with malevolence. They carried sticks and stones which they were wielding in earnest, striking viciously at the backs of unsuspecting foreigners still engaged in drunken romping. And, nothing loath, the foreigners were turning on the Chinese, turning from a joyous lark to lethal combat.

In the middle of the courtyard someone had managed to run the Union Jack up the flagpole. The breeze had snatched it— it was snapping free and triumphant. Around the flag, the struggle had stopped. Men were holding hands, jigging in unison, roaring out a patriotic chanty, while from the fringes of the melee the vicious fighting was erupting inward, threatening to engulf the dancers, to engulf everyone in deadly battle.

"Going to be a bloody massacre!" Blogg muttered grimly.

But all at once, it ended. One of the new gimcrack factories burst into flame. In an instant, flames were dancing as high as the roof of Carradine's factory, lunging out fiercely to lick at hair and flesh and clothing. By common impulse, men fled the fire. The Chinese filtered quickly back into the alleys, the boat people scurried off across the river, the inhabitants of Jackass Point edged hastily to its periphery, leaving the deserted courtyard to the flames.

The fire burned on in isolated splendor, crackling and snapping as though to applaud itself, until the flimsy building collapsed in a great shower of sparks. A sobered line of seamen, bawled at by their officers, began passing buckets to each other, dousing the glowing pile with water from the river. The embers sizzled angrily but at last subsided into sulky black smoke. In a glorious sunset, Jackass Point lay quiet, its bloodstained cobbles littered with debris and moaning bodies, a seaman floating peacefully face down in the scummy water of the dockside. Overhead, the Union Jack waved proudly.

Men began to move about among the wounded. Blogg and Charlie joined them, went quickly through the courtyard scanning the prone bodies, but there was no sign of Lee Kwok. There was not a single Chinese among the quick or the wounded. Jackass Point, scathed and torn, had been returned to the barbarians.

Late that night, Yin-kwa came.

Charlie and Blogg had gone down to *San Seb*'s cabin to escape the mosquitoes, and were sprawled on the mattresses, drinking grog, still too stunned to talk much, when Yin-kwa slipped quietly down the ladder.

Charlie jumped to his feet, exclaiming in relief, but Yin-kwa quickly put a finger to his lips.

"Shhh! Nobody must know I'm here. It's dangerous. . . . Are your crewmen asleep?"

Blogg snorted softly. "They're out chattering up and down the dockside. We had a lot of excitement here today!"

"I know," Yin-kwa whispered.

He was dressed in coolie clothes, barefooted, queue wound around his head. Even so, the subtle aura of authority garbed him. When he squatted on the mattresses and gestured them down beside him, they sat eagerly, their attention fixed on him. He turned to Charlie, his flat eyes glinting in the light of the single taper.

"Before anything else, Charlie—your family is safe. Wei will bring them back tomorrow or the next day, as soon as the city gates are opened."

Charlie blew out a big breath. "Thank God!"

"Ling-ling has been told nothing. Ah Sam, of course, guessed that something was happening."

"By God, Yin-kwa, *what's* been happening? First . . . is Lee Kwok all right?"

Yin-kwa shook his head heavily.

"No. When the riot started, they rushed him back into the city and chopped off his head as soon as they were inside the walls—strangulation takes a lot longer, and by then they wanted it over quickly."

Blogg swore quietly, but Charlie said nothing, his mind conjuring up an instant image of Lee Kwok on *Merope's* deck, smiling his pleasant smile, bowing his courteous bow. No head to bow with now! Charlie's throat clogged thickly.

"My grandfather's taking it very hard," Yin-kwa whispered. "Lee Kwok was the oldest friend he had left. Of the three of them who started it all, Sir George is gone, and Lee Kwok's dead. Now there's only my grandfather. An era is ending."

He sighed and leaned forward, beckoning them nearer.

"I must be quick. Listen. You remember, Charlie, I told you that the latest Triad rebellion was unimportant? Well, I was wrong. . . ."

Outside, the river murmured. A sampan slid by, its single oar squeaking in the bamboo rowlock, the boatman crooning to himself. The little wake it raised slapped softly against *San Seb's* hull, rocking her gently. The tiny, familiar noises and movements made a strange background to the eerie sound of Yin-kwa's tense whisper.

He had been quite wrong. Far from being unimportant, the Triad rebellion had touched off an explosion in Peking. The Emperor had panicked when it was reported to him that the rebel troops had defeated the imperial troops of the viceroy. The power of the tiny Manchu minority rested on the army. If the army failed, the Manchu dynasty was lost. And this time the army had not only failed—it had failed because of opium. Half the viceroy's troops were opium smokers. When ordered to attack the rebels, they had wanted first to work up some opium courage, but had had trouble getting their pipes lit because it was raining. While they were still trying, the rebels attacked and routed them.

The terrified Emperor had banished the viceroy and sent a new one to Canton with absolute orders to stop the traffic in opium, and a whole battalion of Tartars to help him. The new viceroy's first move had been to have all the city gates closed, with Tartars to stand guard over them, to see that nobody left the city. Then the arrests had started. Within a day, Lee Kwok and a thousand other opium dealers were in prison. In the next two weeks, the entire city had been searched. All opium found had been confiscated and the places where it was found burned down. All opium pipes and paraphernalia had been burned on a great bonfire in the Temple of the Queen of Heaven.

And, as the centerpiece of the viceroy's opening attack on opium, the biggest opium dealer, Lee Kwok, had been selected for execution on Jackass Point.

"The viceroy chose Jackass Point because he has no way of directly punishing the foreigners, and he wanted somehow to teach them a lesson, to rub their noses in it. Strangulation is reserved for our worst criminals, because it takes so long and the victim suffers so much."

Charlie felt the hair rise on his forearms. Lee Kwok! Leaping from a centipede boat to *Merope*'s deck, long queue flying, he had looked like nothing so much as a scholar in playful mood. Dead, now. An era ending . . .

But Yin-kwa had resumed his whispering.

"The Co-hong didn't escape the viceroy. Even before he arrived, he sent a messenger to order us to withdraw all the foreigners' servants and stop deliveries of food to Jackass Point—he wanted the foreigners isolated. We were caught by surprise—it was too late to stop you from going to Whampoa to meet Ellison. Then, every day, he sent for us to attend meetings. Half the time, we sat around waiting for him. When he did come, he'd do nothing but stamp and rage. Under the Eight Regulations the Co-hong is responsible for the behavior of the barbarians! If we don't force the barbarians to stop bringing opium to China, he'll chop off our heads one by one—"

"What?" Charlie and Blogg exclaimed together. Yin-kwa smiled thinly.

"Don't worry! He can't touch us, because if he did the tea trade would be finished, and if that happened he'd soon find himself exiled too. According to the Eight Regulations, only the Co-hong can conduct trade with the barbarians, and it would take years to appoint new merchants to the Co-hong, or to change the regulations, so we're quite safe. Its a ritual threat, to demonstrate to the Emperor how zealous he's being. All the same, it has become very dangerous. The days of comfortable smuggling are over. It's rumored that this new viceroy is only the first of the Emperor's moves on opium. It's rumored that the Emperor is going to appoint a high commissioner to stop the traffic. That's a very rare thing. I don't think there's been a high commissioner for the last fifty years. So . . ."

Yin-kwa looked at Charlie and Blogg in turn, his eyes black as anthracite in the flickering light.

". . . be very, very careful. Whatever you do, don't involve me. The viceroy is watching me like a hawk. My grandfather is still nominally head of the Co-hong, but everybody knows that I'm running it now. The viceroy can't chop off my head, but he can make things very uncomfortable for me in other ways."

"We'll do nothing," Charlie said at once. "We'll just lie up in Macao and do nothing!"

And Blogg said: "Certain-sure! To hell with opium!"

Yin-kwa said, "Thank you," quietly, and then, "Did you meet Ellison?"

When they had told him of Ellison, he said somberly:

"All these years of complacency on both sides, and now on both sides there are men who want to stop the smuggling. It was foreordained. It's written in the stars."

For a while no one spoke. The taper sputtered. Charlie's spirit stirred uneasily. The well-known outlines of *San Seb*'s cabin seemed to flicker with the dying taper, to recede from reality, to fade into the vagueness of fate, of destiny. As though impelled to break a spell, Charlie sprang to his feet.

The movement seemed to release them all. Blogg and Yin-kwa rose too. Yin-kwa said:

"I must go. The Tartars have been withdrawn from the city gates and the usual gatemen are back—the bribable ones. I bribed one to let me out, but I must get back while he's still on duty."

He smiled at Charlie, his tired eyes warming.

"No need to worry about your silver. I know how Lee Kwok invested it. . . . Goodbye for now. I don't know when I'll see you again, but as soon as possible."

He did something that he had never done before—stretched his hand to Charlie and to Blogg in the foreign gesture of the handshake. Then he went as he had come, slipping quietly away into the night.

The next day, Wei brought the family back to Jackass Point. They came walking out of Hog Lane in the same order in which they had left, Wei and Jin-see in front, hand in hand, Ling-ling and Ah Sam sedately bringing up the rear. But when Ling-ling caught sight of Charlie hurrying down *San Seb*'s gangplank, she broke into a run, the veil flying off her head, and threw herself into his arms. *San Seb*'s crew, standing on deck to watch the little procession, burst into laughter, nudging each other and pointing. Charlie laughed too, laughed from joy at seeing her, from delight in her impetuosity, but before he could grasp her firmly she jerked back, scarlet-faced, rushed up the gangplank, and vanished into the cabin. He took a step after her, but Ah Sam, scowling, stepped forward, blocking him. Still laughing, full of pleasure and relief, Charlie turned to Wei.

"I'm glad to see you, Wei! I'm glad they're back!"

Wei smiled, but severely—he hadn't been pleased by Ling-ling's display. Jin-see was clinging to Wei's hand, looking doubtfully at his father. Charlie swung him up into the air.

"Jin-see! Did you have a fine time? Are you glad to be back?"

The child nodded shyly, blinking down into his father's face. Then he gave a polite little wriggle—he wanted to be put down. Charlie set him down, and at once he clutched his grandfather's gown. His face suffused with love and tenderness, Wei squatted beside the child, put an arm around him, whispered in his ear, tickled his tummy with a finger. Jin-see flung his arms around Wei's neck and hugged him strenuously.

Charlie's smile grew a little stiff. By God, how horrifically must Jin-see have been spoiled in the last two weeks! But Wei glanced up at him, smiling conspiratorially and so affectionately that Charlie had a twinge of guilt. Time to worry about all that later. Now, it was time for reunion. Blogg's mate had bought sweet cakes from the restocked market on Jackass Point, and there was hot jasmine-flavored tea for the adults and pink-colored drinks for the children. Everybody sat on deck and ate and drank and talked and laughed, even Ling-ling, once again demurely veiled, who sat as far as possible from her husband.

When Wei rose to leave, Charlie walked him back to the mouth of Hog Lane. As soon as they were out of hearing, Wei turned to him, the smile gone.

"Chahlee, now bad time."

He raised his eyes anxiously to Charlie's—old man's eyes, filmy-rimmed, sunk in wrinkles. Looking into them, Charlie felt himself swept back to the night before, to the dim cabin, to Yin-kwa's sibilant whisper—"It has become dangerous. . . ." Again the mystic sense of destiny floated down upon his spirit like a cobwebbed pall. He quickly put an arm around Wei's shoulders, feeling the brittle bones under his fingers.

"No fear, Wei! Everything all right!"

"You think?" The old eyes looked away into the distance. "I think never same like before. I think old time finis', new time come—danger time."

Charlie hugged him lightly.

"No, no! Everything all right. Look . . ." The Jackass Point servants were returning, a hundred or more of them flooding out of Hog Lane, chattering, eagerly reentering the factories they served. "See? They all come back now. Everything same like before. Few weeks more, you come see us in Macao. Everything same!"

The anxious old eyes softened.

"Yes, I come. . . . Chahlee, how many year I know you? Twenny-one year! From small boy to big rich man!" Smiling the old smile from the old days in the stuffy little attic room, he reached up and touched Charlie's hair. "But hair all same. Good-joss color!"

Smiling still, he turned and walked away, his stride quick and youthful.

Charlie went back to *San Seb,* his heart bubbling gently with thoughts of Wei. It was Wei's simple, ungrudging kindness that had evoked from his heart the very first little movement toward trust, toward affection, after that cold dismissal by his father. How could he begrudge Wei the patent adoration he and Jin-see held for each other? How could he begrudge Wei anything? When the time came to take Jin-see home for a while, he would explain it to Wei so carefully and clearly that Wei would suffer no apprehension. He'd miss Jin-see, of course, but after all it would only be for two years. . . .

"Chahlee."

Ah Sam was standing at the top of the gangplank.

"Chahlee, today Ling-ling so happy to see you, she run to you like chillun. Crewman laugh because Chinee man think very funny Chinee woman hug husband in front of other peoples. But why *you* laugh?"

He laughed.

"Because I was so glad to see her, because she was such a darling, running to me like that!"

She did not smile.

"Chahlee, when you laugh, Ling-ling, she cry, because she think you not serious love her. You unnerstan', Chahlee? You *not* laugh Ling-ling?"

"I'll try," he said, but he was laughing even as he said it, and Ah Sam went away, frowning.

*   *   *

But everybody was happy on the sail back to Macao. The sun was hot, the breezes cool, the sea calm. Jin-see cried a little when his grandfather left, but he soon forgot his tears and followed his father about, shading his eyes and squinting as he did when he looked out over the shining waters. Blogg held Jin-see up and let him spin the helm for a while—and he glowed with pride and excitement. Ling-ling forgot her embarrassment and came on deck to play with Jin-see and Little Sister, to sit close by Charlie when none of the crew was around. The pregnancy was beginning to show in soft little roundings of her body. Charlie tingled, wishing old *San Seb* faster on her way toward Macao and the big bed in the cool bedroom.

One moonlit night they stood together by *San Seb*'s bow rail and she consented, after looking carefully about, to come into his arms.

"I love you *serious*," he whispered, and she flung her head back and kissed him deeply, eyes open, the love and joy in them as glowing and mysterious as the dance of the silver moonbeams on the fathomless sea.

Another day, Ah Sam came to sit by Charlie and said quietly:

"What you do, Chahlee, now that Lee Kwok die?"

"Nothing." He glanced around to be sure that Ling-ling was occupied with the children. "Yin-kwa said that the viceroy is watching him like a hawk. So Blogg and I will take a little holiday. It'll be nice"—he grinned at her—"to take life easy in Macao. And watch how much you and Ling-ling and all those servants spoil Jin-see. Time I took a hand. . . ."

She frowned.

"Nothing wrong with Jin-see. . . . But what about *Merope?*"

"I'll just keep on paying the lascars. As long as they're paid they'll stay on. The opium's not ours, you know. Some of it was Lee Kwok's, but I think he'd already sold it, I don't know to whom. And the rest of it belongs to Robert Innes and another Jackass Point trader. It's up to them what they want to do with it. . . ." He glanced at her sideways. "Yin-kwa was right, once again. The time wasn't ripe for expanding our interests in the opium trade. By God, I'm glad now that he refused to buy a clipper and great big stocks of opium from India, as I wanted!"

Her lips quirked in a ghost of her old flashing smile.

"Long time ago I tell you, more better let Yin-kwa fix. He savvy. You no savvy."

They laughed together, remembering. Then he grew serious.

"Ah Sam, d'you know what happened to Lee Kwok's family?"

She sighed.

"Wife die too. She take her hair, tie around neck, hang from bar outside her house front door."

"What?"

She nodded somberly.

"How she can live, after viceroy say Lee Kwok very bad man, Lee Kwok smuggle opium?"

"But he did! Everybody knew it!"

"Maskee, everybody know it. If she live, same like she say 'yes' to viceroy. Same like she say, 'You right, Mr. Viceroy, my husband very bad man.' So she must die."

He stared at her in horror.

"That—that's the most preposterous extravagance I've ever heard of!"

" 'Posterous?" She didn't know the word, but she knew its meaning. "Maybe you think 'posterous, Chahlee, but Chinee wife know what she must do."

Charlie looked back over *San Seb*'s wake, a pretty little trail of turbulent froth on the sea's blue calm. More than twenty years now he'd lived among the Chinese, and still they could flabbergast him!

"Devil take it!"

Blogg was staring through his spyglass at Lintin Island, looming to starboard. All the way from Jackass Point, Blogg had rejoiced in the fine weather. The Lintin hulks would long since have been towed to Si-tao Bay for shelter in the typhoon season, all except *Merope*. Yin-kwa had had no chance to arrange for her transfer. But it didn't matter, because apart from that one abortive typhoon, the weather had been so fine. But now, staring through the spyglass, Blogg was swearing.

"By God, they're *all* still there!"

Charlie took the glass, made out Lintin's bluffs glaring yellow in the sunlight, and below them the whole long line of tethered hulks, all of them, still there, at the mercy of the wind if it should choose to dash them against the bluffs. Charlie turned to stare at Blogg.

"We'd best sail by and find out what's wrong."

"Aye!"

Blogg spun the helm and called to the mate for more sail.

By the time they were within hailing distance, men were crowding the scuppers of the hulks, waving and shouting. As soon as *San Seb* was close enough, they came jumping aboard in an uproar of excitement, all shouting at once.

As usual, junks had been hired to tow the hulks to Si-tao. As usual, they had set out all more or less together, in a long line—and the first hulk in line, *Samarang*, had been shot at by cannon mounted on the heights commanding the entrance to Si-tao Bay!

"Fired on me, by God!" *Samarang's* one-legged captain was hoarse with fury. "Good joss they be old cannon, and gunpowder mucking rotten. Else, by God, I'd not be here talking to you now!"

At the first sound of cannon fire, the junks had tried to throw the tow ropes and flee. Many had succeeded, but *Samarang's* captain and a few others had managed to hold pistols on the masters of the junks towing them. They hadn't been able to force them into the bay, but had at least made them tow the hulks back to Lintin. It had been a terrible mess, abandoned hulks tossing about in the open sea while the captains who were holding junk masters captive went without food or sleep for days, compelling them to sail back and forth until all the hulks were back at Lintin.

And since then, no junk had been persuaded to approach the hulks.

"Won't come anywhere near us! Don't hear no shouts, no hootings, no tootings. As much noise and blather as we can make, they don't hear us!"

And no centipede boats had come.

"Not a one in fifteen days, by God! They don't see us at Si-tao, they knows we be here! But not a one come!"

Food and water and—by God!—rum were running short. The regular supply boat from Jackass Point hadn't come either.

"What be *happening* in Canton, by God?"

The men crowded around Blogg and Charlie to hear what was happening, and burst into a new fever of excitement almost before they had finished speaking. Some were jubilant. This would stir things up, by God! Mucking dull, life on the hulks! Some shook their heads and fearfully forecast doom.

The lascars sat indolently on the bowsprits. They were getting their pay and no work to do. Charlie's lascar foreman shrugged carelessly when Charlie told him that Lee Kwok was dead, but agreed that as long as Charlie kept the pay coming, he and his men would stay on *Merope*.

They set sail again, having handed over all the rum left on *San Seb*. The supply boat from Jackass Point would be following shortly, now that the market was restocked.

Soberly, Charlie and Blogg discussed the possibilities. Lintin had always been beyond Chinese control, too far for the war junks to venture, and the hulks themselves, to say nothing of the clippers, too well armed. But a determined viceroy could easily isolate Lintin by forcing the hulks to stay there at the mercy of the typhoons and systematically destroying the centipede boats at their home villages instead of trying to catch them at sea. He could drastically curtail the upcoast trade by replacing venal mandarins or scaring them into virtue by chopping off heads; by strengthening the patrols of war junks and stiffening the spines of their commanders by chopping off still more heads. The Emperor's new edict allowed any amount of that. Yes, a determined viceroy could make a very great deal of trouble for the opium traders—more trouble than they, complacent for so long, had ever dreamed would be made.

"Yin-kwa was right. The time wasn't ripe for expanding."

"Aye, it certain-sure weren't!"

Charlie looked out over the water. But for that visit to England? Was the time ripe for that?

Chapter VI

1838

RHUBARB.
Blogg thought of it, and Wei confirmed it was a fine idea. Wei was in Macao for a visit, glad that there was no activity on *Merope*, that Charlie and Blogg were keeping quiet and low. The viceroy was still assiduously watching Yin-kwa.

"Alla time! Three-four man. Today one, tomorrow 'nother, next day 'nother. Yin-kwa make one step, watchman make one step."

"Well," Blogg said, "I was thinking that the viceroy might have more to suspicion Yin-kwa about if he found out that *San Seb*'s at anchor doing bloody-all. I thought we should do something. You know rhubarb, Wei? That vegetable with threads coming out of it, like spittle? Seems the English're buying a lot of it now."

"Yes, I know! Very good for making stomach move. Yin-kwa say English buy plenty, send to England like medicine.

Englishman crazy! Eat beef, eat beef, so much eat beef stomach cannot move. Then eat rhubarb!"

"I thought I might take *San Seb* north, pick up a cargo of rhubarb, take it to Jackass Point and sell it there, share the profit with the crew. They're getting restless with nothing doing. What d'you think, Wei?"

"Fine! Make money, and show viceroy good face!"

"I'll go with you," Charlie cried.

Ling-ling glanced at him reproachfully. He pretended not to notice. When Wei was present, it was better to ignore Ling-ling. Wei was all too quick, if he thought Ling-ling less humble than she should be, to frown at her darkly and take a commiserating attitude toward Charlie, as though apologizing for his wayward daughter.

But later, in the big bedroom, Ling-ling said sadly:

"Why you want go with Blogg, Chahlee? You tired see me?"

He tried to explain to her that now that he was spending twenty-four hours a day, seven days a week, in the white house in Macao, he was beginning to feel a little stifled in the almost exclusive company of women and children. Blogg had spent much of his time on Kolo-an Island, repairing the little wooden house in which he'd lived with the right-gentle girl. Then he'd had *San Seb* careened. And now that there was nothing else for him to do, he wasn't proposing to keep Charlie company in the white house, but to go off again in *San Seb*.

"But, Chahlee, you say you love me serious!"

"I *do* love you serious, sweetheart. I love you up and down, round and about, long and short, in the sky and on the earth and in the sea. I love you every way there is, my darling. But I just want to go off with Blogg on *San Seb* for a little while. All right?"

"But my father here now, keep you company."

He laughed ruefully.

"In a way, that's the trouble, sweetheart. I'm always glad to see your father, but when he's here something strange happens with Jin-see."

145

"What?" she asked, anxious, wide-eyed.

"Well, Jin-see and I get along fine, don't we? You must admit he's behaving much better than when I was spending so much time on *Merope*. He hardly sulks at all, and he's given up that awful habit of throwing himself on the floor, kicking his heels and screaming at the top of his lungs. You and Ah Sam and the servants thought the way to stop that was to rush and give him whatever he was yelling for, but one hard spanking from me stopped it for good, didn't it? Jin-see's not stupid! We get along fine—until your father comes. Then, I don't know what it is—it's as though he and Jin-see have a secret that nobody else knows."

"Oh!" She nodded understandingly. "Is because Jin-see is the one who will make kowtow for my father when my father die. You cannot because"—she sparkled at him for a moment—"you are Red Barbarian. So Jin-see must do. Jin-see know, and my father know. This is not secret—this is . . . *knot* between my father and Jin-see. You don't angry, Chahlee!"

"I know Jin-see's your father's—well, *heir*—and I'm not angry about that, darling. But—"

She interrupted, "Chahlee, true, you make Jin-see very good boy now, and my father still little-bit spoil Jin-see. But please, Chahlee, you *not* spank Jin-see when my father here. My father *no like!* And I don' know this Inglis fashion spanking chillun. Your father spank you when you chillun? I know your father send you come to Chinee when you only little bigger than Jin-see!"

"Good God, that's not English fashion! My father is *not* typical of the English fashion of bringing up children!"

Suddenly she abandoned her doubts and gave him a brilliant smile. "All right, Chahlee. But you don' go with Blogg till after baby born?"

"Of course not, sweetheart!"

It was almost time for the new baby to be born. The midwife had already moved into the house. It was the custom, Charlie had learned, for the midwife to move in a few days before the birth and stay a few days after, for it was part of her duties to help the mother with her chores and with the other children. In the white house they didn't need her for such duties, but she had moved in anyway because, she said, otherwise she might not get there in time. Chinese women were much quicker than foreign women to bring their babies into the world—the midwife had been flabbergasted to find out how long it took foreign women, and what a horrible fuss they made about it—but even among Chinese women, Ling-ling was a champion. She'd got Jin-see out in two hours, and Little Sister in one.

The new baby came in fifteen minutes. The midwife laughed so much that she almost dropped the baby.

"A cough!" Ah Sam translated her as saying. "Just a cough, and out popped Little Sister!"

Ling-ling lay in the bed, beautiful as ever, hardly a hair of her thick black mane out of place, looking worried.

"Chahlee, my father want boy."

"By God!" For a moment he felt like shaking her. "You're having babies for *us*, my darling, for you and me, not for your father!"

Though in his heart of hearts he had vaguely wished for a boy who might share the attention that Wei now concentrated on Jin-see alone, he was just as happy with another daughter as he would have been with another son. He looked at the tiny little thing lying on Ling-ling's breast and felt love dawn in his heart in exactly the same way it had dawned for Little Sister. For Jin-see it had been different—for a reason that was, perhaps, not unlike Wei's. In that first moment of looking at his son, Charlie had thought, not of the child or of its mother, but of his own father. He had thought how his father would look when he took the child home and said to his father: "Here's *my* son, whom *I* will never abandon."

But with Little Sister there'd been no such moment of solemn import. There'd just been delighted love, which had grown with her growing. She was an adorable child, so sweet and gentle that in any confrontation with Jin-see she always gave in rather than quarrel—though, recently, he'd begun to wonder whether, when he'd been spending so much time on *Merope,* Ling-ling and Ah Sam and the servants hadn't been *training* Little Sister to give in to Jin-see.

He shook off the thought and put his arms around the mother and the new little baby.

"What shall we call her?"

Ling-ling nuzzled her head against him. "Little Sister."

"But we already have a Little Sister!"

"She is *big* Little Sister. This one *little* Little Sister."

"Ling-ling!" He drew back and gazed at her in smiling astonishment. He had given Jin-see an English name, David, but nobody ever used it. The boy was Jin-see, the name Wei had given him, his "home" name, Ling-ling said—later, he'd be given other official names. Little Sister had an English name too, Emily, which also had never been used. But unlike Jin-see, she had not been given a Chinese name. She'd just been Little Sister, and Charlie himself had always called her that, using it as a pet name. But now . . .

"Our daughters must have names, Ling-ling!"

"After," she said comfortably. "Girl names, maskee. My name is Little Bell—my mother called me that because she say when I cry my voice just like a bell. Elder Sister's name, Ah Sam, means Third Daughter. If you like, we can call new baby Second Daughter. But I like little Little Sister more better. After, if you like, Chahlee, we can go see fortune-teller man, ask him what names for Little Sisters."

She smiled up at Charlie, and then looked down at the baby. After the baby had yelled lustily a few times, the midwife had placed her on Ling-ling's breast, and she had fallen instantly asleep.

"She can feel my heart beat," Ling-ling said tenderly. "Just like when she inside me, she can feel my heart now, so she happy."

"We'll call her Heart's Ease," said Charlie. "It's the name of an English flower."

His own heart suddenly overflowed. He knelt and kissed

the baby's tiny foot, and when Ling-ling held out her hand to him, he kissed it too and laid it, palm up, against his cheek.

"I love you very, very serious," he said, looking into her eyes over the baby's black-haired head.

It was the right season for rhubarb, Wei said. Some of the farmers were working with middlemen, who sold their crops to the British traders before they had been harvested, sometimes even before they were planted. But that was the new-fashion way, Wei said, and most farmers still preferred to wait until they were sure their crops were of good quality before they sold. Namoa would be the best place to go. *San Seb* could stay at anchor in the harbor while Blogg's mate went ashore to buy a crop.

They stopped first at Lintin to inspect *Merope*. It was more than six months since they'd been there, and the changes were astonishing. A small cannon had somehow been hauled up to the bluff and it squatted there, menacing all comers within three or four hundred yards at a sweep of 180 degrees. An armed cutter patrolled the sea up and down the line of hulks. On each hulk at least one of the crewmen was armed with pistol and saber. On *Merope*, the lascar foreman had been armed, he said, by Robert Innes, who owned most of the opium stored in her holds.

Samarang's one-legged captain, sitting in a wicker chair on his deck, a musket across his knees, insisted that they come aboard. When they did, he happily plied them with grog, talking without pause.

Very different it was now from the old days when the crews of the hulks had been a kind of brotherhood, like a village at home in England, everybody knowing everybody. 'Cept for the lascars, of course, but nobody paid them no mind, 'cept for cursing their monkey language and their foul-smelling, rancid-oil, curdled-milk food! But the rest—a real brotherhood, all Britons 'cept for a couple of Spaniards and Americans, and they almost as good as Britons, and English-speaking, even the

149

Spaniards. Remember when *Curlew's* captain—Perkins, wasn't he?—remember when he came back from a voyage home and brought a new wife? Remember how she'd made a right nice little parlor-like, on *Curlew's* deck, under a striped awning, with wicker chairs and a little table? Served tea, every day at four o'clock, to all who came. Right nice, hadn't that been? Right homey-like. And after dark, when she'd gone below, Perkins would put out the rum bottle there on the same table! The old days! The hulks all a-hustle and a-bustle with clippers and centipedes and junks and *lorchas,* all kinds of craft, back-and-forthing, the opium flowing in, flowing out—by God, them were the days!

But now—by God, *nothing!* Dull as ditchwater, sitting around guarding the opium. Not a centipede in months. Destroyed 'em all, he had, that God-rotted viceroy. And not a war junk neither, too far for 'em, always had been. But still the opium had to be guarded account of the pirateers. They'd come more'n a few times and had had to be fought off. Carradine and Dent had clippers not too far off, roving about trying to catch the pirates afore they got to Lintin, 'cause then they could blow 'em right out of the water without worrying about damaging the hulks. By God, there'd been a couple of sea battles around Lintin, clippers against them Chinee pirateers, that would've done the British navy itself proud!

On and on he went. When Charlie glanced at Blogg and made a move to rise, he compelled them down again, filled their glasses to the brim.

"Stay a mite longer! God knows, you be doing an old man a favor! Wish I could go with you! Go in a minute, I would, if anybody'd have me with this cursed wooden leg! You taking opium from *Merope?*"

After a moment Blogg said slowly, "Nay, we be going for rhubarb."

"Rhubarb! I ain't hearing right, am I, Blogg?"

"You said yourself not ten minutes ago—there's no opium trade left to speak of."

"Aye, but by God, we cain't just give up and go for *rhubarb!*

There be millions of silver sunk in them chests of opium! *Millions!* We've bloody well got to force the trade!"

"Pirating, you mean?"

"Well, not wot you'd call *pirating!* Not stealing anybody else's property! Some fights with war junks along the coast, when the cutters goes in to beach the chests."

"Beach them?"

"Aye! Where you been, the two of you? Don't you know nothing of wot's going on? That God-rotted viceroy's got the harbors at Namoa and Amoy blocked up with war junks, and he's chopped off enough heads so them mandarins dassn't look cross-eyed at our ships no more, even for a bribe of a hundred dollars a chest—not a year ago it used to be thirty! But there be places along the coast, coves and inlets and beaches and the like, where the cutters can deliver, and where the mandarins—them that needs the silver bad enough to risk their necks—turn their heads so the buyers can make a dash for it down to the beach to fetch the chests. Been a good few fights, o' course, but the cutters got cannon now, small 'uns wot Carradine brought in from Singapore, and they're faster nor them war junks, so many's the time the cutters come off better."

"You don't call that pirating?" Charlie asked.

"Protecting our investment, that's what Carradine calls it, and he be right, I reckon! All very fine for you two—you don't own the stuff on *Merope*. And Carradine and Dent and some of them others, they got the tea trade and the silk trade and wot-all to fall back on. But me and Innes and the rest of us, we stands to lose everything we got! The bribe's up to a hundred dollars a chest and bloody hard to get any takers, and the price of the opium's down to two hundred and fifty dollars a chest, from six-fifty when that God-rotted viceroy arrived!"

He gulped the rest of his grog, and leaned forward to whisper hoarsely, though there were only the seagulls to hear.

"Carradine's got *Jamesina* anchored off Amoy as a receiving ship, and six fast cutters running inshore with opium wot he moved, real careful, from here to *Jamesina*. And Dent and Innes're doing the same more northerly, near Foochow. They be partners now, hate each other as they do, but needs must, I reckon. . . ."

It took a long time to convince him that they were really not going to try and run some opium from *Merope,* and when he finally believed them, he got furious.

"Traitors, that's wot you be!" he screamed after them as Blogg rowed the dinghy back to *San Seb.* "Sucking up to that God-rotted viceroy! Rhubarb, by God! *Rhubarb!"*

The sail to Namoa was rough, the sea choppy, mist and low clouds obscuring visibility. Only a few fisher boats were about. Once Blogg saw the outline of a bigger ship that he thought might be *Jamesina,* but he couldn't be sure, and they didn't alter their course to investigate.

At Namoa, they had to sink anchor in the roads, in order to keep out of range of the red-mouthed cannon mounted on the row of war junks that blocked the entrance to the harbor. But when a contingent of mandarins had come aboard to search *San Seb* and found her holds empty, they were allowed to sail into the harbor. The mate went ashore and within half a day was back: there were all sorts of cargoes to be picked up cheap. With all the fighting, coastal sea traffic had become so hazardous that many merchant junk owners had moved farther north, or had put their vessels up to wait for safer times. Times were hard, and getting harder.

In the end they bought both rhubarb and a cargo of small, very sweet oranges that the mate insisted were excellent value.

The sail back to Canton was made in the same kind of gray, gloomy weather, the rain clouds so dark and heavy that Blogg said pirating would be suspended. With visibility so low, the danger was too great of the cutters running aground in the uncharted coves and inlets. Once aground, they lost their greatest asset, their speed.

In the Bay of Canton, approaching the Bogue, *San Seb* was hailed by three war junks, and boarded by mandarins in magnificent uniforms who peered haughtily into the holds and seemed relieved when they found nothing but rhubarb and oranges.

"Wonder what they'd have did had they found opium?" Blogg murmured sardonically. "Sunk us?"

They sailed between the forts. The battlements were patrolled by squads of guards. Red-mouthed cannon protruded from each embrasure. By God, the viceroy was indefatigable! What effort he must be expending to keep the mandarins of the war junks so alert, and the unwarlike Bogue forts looking so fighting fit!

At Jackass Point they sold the rhubarb and oranges quickly and profitably. Ships were hungry for cargoes, traders hungry for any kind of trade that put a few dollars in their pockets. *San Seb*'s crew, delighted with their share of the profits, went off to spend their money in Canton. Charlie and Blogg decided not to try to get in touch with Yin-kwa; there was nothing particular to discuss with him, and it was not the time, under the viceroy's voracious eye, for social contacts.

But Ellison was on Jackass Point, and one evening they found themselves sitting with him in his rooms atop Carradine's factory, feeling both disconcerted and compassionate. It seemed that Ellison had the same need as *Samarang*'s captain to talk and be listened to. Elegant, honorable Ellison, and that dirty, crooked old codger on *Samarang*! A sign of the times? Charlie glanced at Blogg and found his eyes fixed on Ellison with gentleness.

Ellison was pointing down into the courtyard.

"You noticed that the Union Jack is flying? It's been up every day since the attempted execution of that Chinese smuggler. I called for volunteers and trained them myself to hoist and haul down the flag with full ceremony, bugles, everything—to rub it into the viceroy's nose that he'd better not try tricks on the British. As long as I'm responsible for the safety of British lives on Jackass Point . . ."

He let the sentence trail and took a gulp of rum, went on talking almost before he had swallowed it.

"D'you know what Carradine and Dent are doing? Running

opium from receiving ships anchored off the coast. Open piracy! D'you know what that blackguard Innes tried to do? Tried to bring opium to Whampoa in a cutter run by armed lascars and flying the Union Jack! Here I'm flying the Union Jack to remind the viceroy that he can't play fast and loose with British lives, and that damned Innes flies the same flag as protection for his bloody piracy! If the viceroy's war junks had fired on Innes' cutter, they'd have been firing on the Union Jack! D'you realize what that would have meant?"

He jumped up and began to pace the room.

"I'm going to ask Palmerston for a warship. How can I protect the traders with nothing at my command? How could I have defended the flag, if the viceroy's war junks had fired on Innes' pirate cutter, with the Union Jack waving over it like a charm? I've got to have a ship! Palmerston can't ignore danger to British lives—even if he does ignore my pleas for instructions about opium!"

He flung himself back into his chair and buried his face in his hands. His voice, coming through his clenched fingers, sounded ghostly.

"*Three times* I've written to Palmerston for instructions about opium. The last time I wrote the strongest words I could think of: 'No man entertains a deeper detestation than I of the disgrace and evil of this contraband traffic. Our government cannot with honor countenance it.' And I got no answer! What can that mean but that he *does* countenance it? That he does condone the smuggling, the piracy, the opium?"

His head swung up suddenly, his eyes glaring.

"And the two of you? Are you pirating too? If you are, there's the door!" He pointed dramatically. "Much as I feel—more than ever now—that you're my only friends around here, there's the door!"

Blogg said compassionately:

"You can keep us your friends much as ever, Ellison. We came here with a cargo of rhubarb and oranges, and with the word 'traitor' flung after us from the Lintin hulks. Of course"— he hesitated—"our reasons for being out of opium may be different from what you think, but you may be certain-sure we ain't pirating."

For the first time that night, Ellison smiled.

"You're out of opium for good, I hope. By God, I'm *never* going to be reconciled to opium, no matter what Palmerston sees fit to do or not do! I'll protect the traders, and I'll see that the tea gets shipped, but by God I swear it—I will do *nothing* to further the spread of opium!"

They left him soon after, his eyes tired and strained, his uniform sagging where flesh had fallen from his frame, but perhaps—Charlie thought—looking a little relieved of the spate of words that had been bottled up in him and had poured out on them.

"Strange, isn't it?" he said to Blogg when, once more, they were sailing between the forts. "Ellison sending for a British warship makes it seem that Ellison is setting the scene for making Carradine's wish come true—to lay some of His Majesty's sloops alongside the Bogue forts."

. . . *Her* Majesty's now. Since Carradine had expressed that thought, the sloops had passed from George III to George IV to William IV, and now they were Victoria's. Charlie's own life had passed through the same successions. George III had been on the throne of England when his father said: "Lord Ambleton expects you tomorrow. You'll take the coach from the village." Twenty-two years ago.

It was time, now. Time to go home.

"Blogg, this orange and rhubarb business'll keep *San Seb* busy enough until we know what's going to happen?"

"Aye."

"You won't miss me then if I go away for a while."

"Nay . . . but . . ."

"It's time for me to go home, to see my father. In a few months, when the baby's old enough to travel and I can take them all with me, Ling-ling and all three of the children."

"Charlie . . ."

"Oh, Blogg, I know I've told you a lot of stuff over the years—throwing silver in my father's face, buying Easterbury, all that. That's all forgotten now. Childish nonsense. But all the same, I have to see him, Blogg. He *threw me out.*"

"The shame of that's on him, Charlie, not on you. Man does a bad thing to you, makes *him* bad, not you."

"Maybe. But all the same, I have to see him. I have to show him Jin-see, *my* son, whom I'll never throw out. Until I do that, Blogg, it'll sit in my guts like a stone."

Blogg said slowly, "I know. But Wei won't like it."

"I'll explain it to him. It'll only be for two years."

After a while, Blogg said again: "Wei won't like it."

Chapter VII

January - August

1839

THE STREAM OF BLACK HAIR hid Ling-ling's averted face, and the piled-up pillows muffled her voice, hoarse with sobbing.

"Wait little time, Chahlee?"

He sighed, sitting on the edge of the bed, gently stroking her back.

"I *have* waited, Ling-ling! I waited for the baby to be born and for her to be old enough to travel—I've waited a long time."

She gave another little hiccuping sob, and he sighed again. Why couldn't she accept it? Ah Sam had, however reluctantly. He'd persuaded Ah Sam first, to ensure her help in persuading Ling-ling, or at least to avert her opposition.

"I'll bring them back in two years, Ah Sam. Don't you see, *now's* the time for us to go, while there's nothing doing here."

"Why you care nothing doing? You got plenty dollah!"

"Ah Sam, I'm thirty-six years old. I've been here twenty-three years. I want to see my father—"

"Why? Father no like you, why you like he?"

"I don't, but I want to see him. I—I can't explain." How explain to her the need of canceling out that old rejection? "I'll bring them back in two years, and meantime you'll stay right here in this house and keep it for us."

"Baby too small, so long voyage."

"She's not. She's nearly a year old."

"No amah look-see chilluns. How Ling-ling look-see three chilluns by self?"

"There're servants in England! Nursemaids. English amahs."

She was silent for a moment, then she came back stubbornly to the main point.

"Wei no like."

"I know he won't, but I'll talk to him. I'll have to go to Canton to ask Yin-kwa for some of my silver. I'll see Wei then, if he doesn't come here before, and I'll explain everything to him."

The argument had gone on for days in the intervals when Ling-ling was occupied elsewhere. At last Ah Sam had said icily:

"You like go, Chahlee, how I stop you?"

"Will you tell Ling-ling there's nothing to be afraid of?"

"*You* tell. I tell only I wait Macao."

And now, two weeks of coaxing Ling-ling and she was still weeping and shaking her head, refusing to admit the possibility that any place in the world other than Canton and Macao might be habitable and safe, not peopled by ogres and fire-breathing dragons waiting to devour.

And, of course, "My father no like!"

Resignedly, he rose from the bedside and went to the window, the sound of her sobs following him. Well, if she absolutely wouldn't go, there was nothing for it but to go alone. If he couldn't show his family to his father, at least he could tell him about them, tell him about Jin-see. . . .

"All right, Ling-ling. I'll go alone."

A long moment of silence. Then a whisper, full of anguish:

"Chahlee, you leave me?"

He almost exclaimed aloud. Had he at last found the right approach?

"I must, if you won't come."

She broke into a storm of weeping, swept off the bed, rushed to him, clung to him. He held her off:

"Will you come with me?"

"I come . . . I come . . ."

He swept her into his arms.

"Oh, sweetheart, thank you! You'll love it once you're there! England is beautiful! There's nothing to be afraid of! Don't cry anymore!"

She raised her blotched face to his, tears still welling from under the swollen lids.

"I don't care beautiful, Chahlee. I care you, and my father. He no like!"

"I know, but I'll tell him myself. I'll explain everything to him. We'll only be away two years. When we get back, Jin-see won't be nine years old yet. And maybe I'll build a factory at Jackass Point, so you can go very often to see your father in Canton with the children."

She sighed—a deep, sad, doomful sound. He laughed and picked her up.

"It's not the day of judgment, sweetheart! It's just a voyage we're going to take, to *my* home, and you'll love it when we get there!"

The next day—a heavy, gray day—they all crossed the garden to the beach, to see Charlie off to Canton in *San Seb*. They gathered in a little group on the jetty, Ling-ling and Ah Sam side by side, the little sisters in their amahs' arms, Jin-see, overexcited, jumping about and shouting.

But when *San Seb* moved away from the jetty and the strip of water between the ship and shore widened, something seemed suddenly to awe him. He stopped clowning and stood still, staring wide-eyed after the ship—a small boy, not yet seven years old, in a miniature of his grandfather's long silk gown, split to the waist over little satin trousers, buttoned up the side with knotted frog-buttons. His hair was as black as his mother's and cropped short—Charlie wouldn't hear of his wearing a queue. His skin was fair—barbarian skin, Ah Sam said. His eyes were shiny jet black, but wide and round and deep-set, like Charlie's—barbarian eyes, except for their color.

As the ship distanced, Jin-see stepped forward and raised a hand toward the diminishing figure of his father. A moment later, Ling-ling left Ah Sam and came to stand beside her son, raising her hand toward Charlie in the same way. A streak of sunlight, escaping its cloud prison, danced a moment on the waves, then, as though it had been seeking them, picked out the mother and son and bathed them in a shining golden aura.

"Beautiful, ain't that?" Blogg said, glancing over his shoulder.

"Yes," said Charlie, smiling. "Beautiful!"

San Seb touched the customs jetty, and Charlie and Blogg jumped off, as usual, to show their papers. The customs house was half-empty. There was an atmosphere of gaiety. Counter clerks called out to each other, joking, paying scant attention to their work. The officer who stamped their papers did so with hardly a glance. As they walked out onto Jackass Point, Blogg laughed suddenly.

"It's twelfth February! No wonder! Chinee New Year tomorrow. They're all readying for the feast—our crew too. They'll be hurrying off soon as we get back to *San Seb.*"

"Blast!" Charlie swore. "I wanted to send your mate into Canton immediately with a note for Yin-kwa!"

"You'll be waiting three-four day, at least. You know what Chinee New Year celebrating's like!"

Indeed! It was frenetic. The humblest coolie, putting on some tiny piece of finery, went off on holiday, refusing to do the smallest stroke of work. Charlie frowned moodily, cursing the delay, but Blogg exclaimed in a pleased way, pointing at the Union Jack fluttering from the flagpole outside Carradine's factory.

"Ellison must be here. At least we'll be able to keep some company with him. He cain't be having too good a time of it,

160

cooped up with Carradine. Carradine must be in a foul mood, with half them twenty thousand chests at Lintin belonging to him and no way of getting rid of them but murderous pirating!"

They walked in silence for a moment, then Blogg again exclaimed and pointed. "Look—there's Andrew."

Andrew Carradine, striding across Jackass Point toward his father's factory. He looked much like his father, but his eyes were blue instead of green, and in him his father's craggy features were less pronounced. A very handsome man—and an arrogant one. He was not exactly elbowing people out of his way, but he didn't care either if they got pushed aside. They watched him enter his father's factory. At the last moment, he shot them a glance over his shoulder.

"Wonder if Ellison ever did ask for that warship."

Blogg spoke slowly, and Charlie gave a short laugh. It was strange. The sight of Andrew had brought the same thought to his mind.

"If he did, it hasn't come yet."

Jackass Point was dirtier, more crowded, more cluttered than ever. By the time they had walked its length, dodging people and obstacles, and come to *San Seb*, the crew were ready to go ashore, scrubbed clean, queues unwound from around their heads and hanging down their backs, newly plaited. They grinned as they departed, putting their fists together, knuckles to knuckles, and shaking them at Charlie and Blogg to wish them good joss for the New Year.

Blogg's mate waited until the others had gone before he stepped forward. He had been with *San Seb* from the beginning, a lean-faced, sure-stepping young man on that first trip to Namoa, now thinner, more wiry, weather-beaten, a little wrinkled. He alone of all the crew knew of Yin-kwa's connection with *San Seb*, but Blogg had sworn him to secrecy and there was no fear that he would tell, for he loved Blogg with a pure and touching trust, and he held Charlie in awe.

Blogg laughed now and said to Charlie:

"He'll like it if you chin-chin too—do as he does, shake your fists at him. He reckons nobody—but *nobody*—can have such good joss as you, seeing the color of your hair!"

So Charlie touched his own closed fists to the mate's, and the mate, grinning happily, went off down the gangplank.

As he disappeared into the crowd on Jackass Point, the first of the firecrackers went off, somewhere behind Hog Lane. Blogg sighed.

"There we go!"

For the entire night, and for most of the next day, the firecrackers went off, banging, roaring, racketing, thundering, trumpeting. Right on Jackass Point the servants, decked out in their best, set up great rockets and pinwheels, some two feet tall and almost as wide across, and shot them up into the air with earsplitting booms. It began to be unbearable.

At last, when night fell again, the noise abated. Blogg got out the rum and some dried beef and hard ship's biscuits, and they sat down to the unappetizing meal. It was as chilly as it ever got in Canton, and they sat in the cabin, Charlie's ears still ringing from the bombardment, the increasing quiet seeming unnatural, the chill seeming unnatural, everything seeming unnatural—except home. He was going home!

"When's your mate coming back, Blogg?"

"Dunno. Could be tomorrow, if he ain't drunk too much."

Charlie fidgeted. Yin-kwa no more than a few miles away and entirely out of reach until the mate was finished with his celebrating!

"Ahoy!"

Footsteps sounded, bouncing on the gangplank, solid when they hit the deck, and Ellison came down the ladder—first his highly polished black boots, then his spotless white breeches, the flapping tails of his navy-blue coat, his brass buttons and golden epaulettes, and at last his long, fair-haired head. He'd already taken off the cockaded hat.

"Why didn't you let me know you were here? I heard it from Andrew!"

"Would have looked you up tomorrow. Too much noise to-day!"

They shook hands, grinning at each other. Charlie felt he'd like to put his arms around Ellison and hug him—he was so proper, so behooving, so redolent of England.

"I'm going home, George! Just for a visit—year or two."

"By God, wish I were going with you!"

The tone of his voice made Charlie glance sharply at him. It was no casual, conventional phrase! He had meant it with all his heart! His smile had faded and deep lines had appeared between his brows.

"What's happened, George?"

"A high commissioner, that's what happened!"

They stared at him. For an instant, Yin-kwa's whisper rustled again through the cabin—"a high commissioner—a very rare thing . . ." Charlie shivered. It seemed that the chill of the air was deepening.

Ellison produced from under his coattails a roll of yellow silk furled around a short ivory rod. Shaken out, it became a small yellow banner covered with black ideograms. Ellison laid it on the table.

"This arrived early this morning. It's dated today"—he consulted a piece of paper—"the first day of the first moon of the eighteenth year of the Tao Kuang Emperor. Chinese New Year day—very auspicious, Carradine's translator says. It announces the arrival in Canton of High Commissioner Lin Tse-hsu with a new edict from the Son of Heaven authorizing him to apply *to barbarians* the same penalties that are applicable to Chinese for violation of the edicts against opium."

"Great God!" Charlie stared at Ellison. "You mean that *foreigners too* can now be executed for opium violations?"

"Exactly!" Ellison drained the mug Blogg had handed him and slapped it down on the table with a crack that threatened to break it. "All this piracy that's been going on—Carradine and the rest of them felt safe because the viceroy could confiscate Chinese-owned opium and chop off Chinese heads, but he couldn't touch foreigners. Now the Emperor has removed that obstacle with a stroke of his brush. High Commissioner Lin Tse-hsu can do what he likes to foreigners—confiscate their opium *and* chop off their heads, if he sees fit. . . ."

They sat in silence, staring at each other. It was a stunning development! The ineffectual Chinese, whose laws the foreigners had flouted so long with impunity, suddenly putting long, sharp teeth into the mouth of the Emperor's new watchdog.

"And, of course," Ellison went on, "these are the same foreigners whom I am commanded by Her Majesty to protect, be they opium smugglers or not!" He shrugged elaborately. "What can I do? I'm having a letter prepared saluting the high commissioner in the most florid phrases that Carradine's translator knows, and stating flatly that Britons are subject only to Her Majesty Queen Victoria. I've simply ignored the rest of his announcement. But it's only a matter of time before I get another little yellow banner from him demanding the surrender of all the opium owned by the British. By God, I *agree* with that! I firmly believe that every ounce of opium should be confiscated and destroyed. But I've no instructions about opium from Palmerston, and there isn't a chance in hell that Carradine and the other owners will surrender their opium on my say-so alone!"

"George . . ." Charlie spoke slowly. "The last time we saw you, you said that you were going to ask Palmerston for a warship. Did you?"

"Yes, I did, thank God! But it hasn't come yet. Palmerston wrote that he can't act on his own in such a matter, he must consult the Cabinet . . . although . . ."

Ellison hesitated, his frown deepening. Blogg had lit a taper, and the flickering light showed Ellison's cheeks to be concave, the cheekbones fine-honed, the eyes heavily circled.

"Although what?" Charlie said softly.

"God blast it!" Ellison slammed a fist down on the little yellow banner. "I confess to you that I don't really know what's happening! Palmerston writes to me that he's consulting the Cabinet, but from things that Carradine's let drop I suspect that Palmerston's writing to him too, and more fully than he is to me! Carradine has bought a London journal—a weekly. I've seen copies of it. It hammers away at the 'sad plight' of British traders in China. Calls them 'pioneers of British commerce' and claims that they're being 'mistreated and abused' by the 'stupid, obstinate' Chinese. It not only misrepresents the situation here, but it does so in a most inflammatory manner. I don't think that Palmerston's directly involved in it, but he must know what Carradine's doing, in which case he's condoning it. . . . Now, with the arrival of this banner"—he flicked the silk on the table—"Carradine's behaving like the cat who swallowed the cream. He's glad that there must soon be a forced confrontation. . . ."

Ellison jumped up and began pacing the cabin.

"Charlie, how long are you going to be in Jackass Point?"

Charlie considered. Time to get in touch with Yin-kwa, for Yin-kwa to call in some of the silver Lee Kwok had invested. Time for himself to exchange the silver with some of the traders for letters of credit on their London banks. . . .

"About three weeks, I suppose."

"Good! Charlie, will you come and spend that time with me, in my rooms? I've plenty of space, and since I pay Carradine rent you needn't feel beholden to him in any way. I'd be very grateful for the company and the . . . support. I must be the most unpopular person in South China today. I've made no secret of the fact that I despise the opium smuggling and if I had my way, all of the opium would be turned over to the high commissioner as soon as possible. But they know I'm powerless because I've had no instructions from Palmerston. And I suspect they know that Carradine has better connections with Palmerston than I have. D'you see my position?"

Charlie was already on his feet, collecting some of his belongings into a bag.

"I'll go with you now, George. Eh, Blogg?"

"Certain-sure! I'll stay on *San Seb* and see that all messages"—he glanced at Charlie—"are passed back and forth as need be."

"Thanks." Ellison grinned with some of his old boyish humor. "At least I've got two on my side now!"

They laughed as they marched off together, Blogg watching them from *San Seb*'s bridge, smiling genially. The firecrackers had stopped, Charlie noticed—the clump of their boots on the cobbles was loud. The Chinese New Year holidays would soon be over. Blogg's mate would be returning in a day or two, and he'd take the note to Yin-kwa, and Yin-kwa would come and get the silver, and—by God, in three weeks at most he and Blogg would be sailing back to Macao, and then on the very next ship, home, to England!

Marching along Jackass Point shoulder to shoulder with Ellison, Charlie began to whistle happily.

Charlie stood at the back window of Ellison's sitting room, looking out over rooftops. A week since he'd moved in with Ellison. A week since Ellison's letter to the high commissioner had been delivered at the Petitions Gate, and four days since Blogg's mate had taken his letter to Yin-kwa to the Street of the Psychics. No answer to either letter had yet been received.

Ellison's rooms on the fourth floor of Carradine's factory overlooked the river on one side, and on the other the myriad low little houses that stretched from Hog Lane to the distant Petitions Gate. In the gathering darkness, the angled mass of charcoal-black rooftops formed a somber landscape, overlaid by a thin network of the narrow lanes that threaded through it, and dotted here and there with the small pale spots of rooftop sculptures ornamenting the ridgepoles. Wei had once told Charlie that they represented the Dragon of the East and the Tiger of the West.

Charlie strained his eyes over the roofs as though he might catch sight of Yin-kwa coming through the Petitions Gate. Why the devil had he not come? The nerve-racking waiting was beginning to take on familiar overtones, like the last time he'd been on Jackass Point when the viceroy had had all the city gates closed and patrolled by Tartars. But this time the gates were open. A constant stream of people passed through them. Why had Yin-kwa not come yet?

Behind Charlie, Ellison was working at his desk, keeping calm, waiting for further word from the high commissioner. He kept his door closed and had ordered his and Charlie's meals served upstairs. For the whole week, Charlie had spoken to no one but Ellison and Blogg on his daily walks to *San Seb* to see if there was news of Yin-kwa. But at all hours the traders could be heard tramping in and out of the factory to consult Carradine. Their voices, loud, angry, jolly, boastful, anxious, floated up the stairs. News of the high commissioner's arrival and of his new edict—the "murder edict," the traders called it—had spread all over Jackass Point within an hour after the little yellow banner was delivered to Ellison, and everybody was agog over it.

Charlie was turning away from the rooftops, opening his mouth to speak to Ellison, when the door crashed open. A man lurched into the room, one of the new traders Yin-kwa had called "cheapjacks." An unkempt man with snarled hair and beard, soiled shirt, filthy scarf around his neck.

Ellison looked up coldly.

"Don't you knock at doors?"

But the trader was already at the desk, leaning down over Ellison, shouting hoarsely.

"You've got to do something, man!"

"About what?"

"We can't leave! They're preventing us from leaving!"

"What the devil d'you mean?"

"What I say, man! I wanted to sail to Whampoa—I've bought space on a merchanter for my tea, wanted to make sure the ship was in. But the customs house is locked!"

"It's their New Year. It might be locked for another day or two."

"But there's a notice on the door. In them damned characters, but in English too, a kind of English. Way I read it, customs house be shut indefinitely. No exit papers will be stamped. We can't leave!"

"What?" Ellison jumped to his feet, forcing the man to fall back.

"I'm telling you, man!" he shouted.

Ellison's temper snapped. "My name's Ellison, sir! *Captain* Ellison."

"Captain be damned," the trader snarled. "You're supposed to protect us, ain't you? You cain't let 'em do this!"

Ellison strode to the window and peered out, but it was dark now, and anyway too far from the customs house to see anything. He turned back to the trader, biting his lip, forcing his voice to calm.

"I'll go down first thing in the morning. Too late to do anything tonight."

"By God, you *better* do something! I'm going to tell Carradine. *He'll* do something if you won't, rot you, *Captain* Do-naught!"

Pale with anger, Ellison closed the door as the trader clattered furiously down the stairs.

"Those scum!" He took a deep breath. "What's the high commissioner up to?"

Charlie shrugged silently. His blood was playing ticktacktoe in his veins. By God, was something going to go wrong *now? Now*—when he'd thought to be in England by May? Thought to see the first tender leafing of the trees, hear the first calls of the nesting birds? *Devil take it!* Was the high commissioner planning some coup along the lines of Lee Kwok's execution? Was that why Yin-kwa hadn't come—because he couldn't, because something was preventing him?

Ellison had taken the rum out of the cupboard, but now he replaced it and slammed the cupboard door.

"No, better keep a clear head for tomorrow. God knows what might come! We'd better go to bed, Charlie. Carradine might come up, and I couldn't stand a long commotion with him now. By God, Charlie, it's really bad luck for you. The second time you've arrived on Jackass Point just in time to be caught in some folderol!"

In his room, Charlie stood at the window looking out. It was very like that first night on Jackass Point. A small room, a narrow cot, a minimum of furniture, and beyond the window the thick, black darkness. To the right, far out there, the Bogue forts. . . . He turned from the window and filled the basin from the jug of water. It was cold, of course, but he stripped and began to wash himself with a cloth, the shock of the water making his skin shiver. But it also cooled his blood a little, slowed the thumping of his heart. Perhaps nothing special was imminent. Perhaps Yin-kwa hadn't come because he was busy or away from the city. Perhaps he'd come in a day or two. Perhaps they'd be home by June. The trees would be in full leaf, the woods deep and dappled.

But when he had dried himself, Charlie lay down on the cot very carefully, trying to prevent it from creaking. There was something in him, some fabric, that was growing thin and should not be subjected to shocks. He felt both solemn and silly; he almost jumped out of bed to lie down again, noisily. But he didn't. Ah Sam would understand, and so would Ling-ling, and so—he smiled to himself wryly—would Blogg's mate. All the Chinese would understand. There was need now to hold himself in stillness, to be very quiet and calm, to guard his spirit.

By noon the next day, Jackass Point was in an uproar.

The customs house remained locked. A crowd of traders milled around in a buzz of question and obscenity, peering at the notice written on yellow paper pinned on the door.

"What's Ellison going to do?"

"What's Carradine say?"

"Where's Ellison?"

"God rot it, what's Ellison going to *do* about this?"

"Where the bloody hell is he?"

"What's to stop us, damn it? We don't *have* to go through that mucking customs house! We can just get in the cutters and *go!*"

169

But already, cutters were returning.

"Got no farther than halfway to Whampoa!"

"River's blocked by war junks!"

"More'n a dozen of them, cannon trained on us, by God!"

Ellison had been down at first light to look at the notice. There was nothing he could do, he and Charlie agreed. Now Ellison stood at the window glumly looking down at the scene on Jackass Point, while Charlie paced the room restlessly, the thump of his boots a counterpoint to the furious clamor of his mind. Two precious weeks wasted persuading Ling-ling! He could have been in and out of Canton, back in Macao by now, packing up, getting ready to sail for home, out of this mucking mess! Devil take it! Devil take it!

"Devil take it!" Ellison echoed Charlie's thoughts. "Never before been in such a situation, where the best I can do is mucking *nothing!*"

Again, as on the previous night, the door was flung open, but this time it was Andrew Carradine who burst in, followed by the translator. Andrew was waving another little yellow banner.

"This just came for you, Ellison!"

He spread it on the table. By common consent, they gathered, quickly and silently, to watch the translator scrutinize the black characters, his long finger running down the lines from top to bottom, from right to left. At last he looked up.

"Well?" Andrew growled. "What's it say?"

The man cleared his throat.

"From High Commissioner Lin Tse-hsu."

"We bloody well know that!" Andrew snapped.

The man pointed to the large character written at the top of the banner that even Charlie recognized—the character for "command." His voice squeaked timidly.

"High commissioner command all opium."

"You mean he wants to buy it?" Andrew said sharply.

The man tittered nervously.

"Not buy. *Give. Give* him all opium."

In the moment of silence that followed this announcement, an indolent voice spoke from the doorway,

"He's mucking crazy!"

Carradine!

They all swung around. Almost reluctantly, Charlie glanced at Carradine's face. But it was no different from the last time he had seen it—in fact, it seemed less askew, for Carradine was holding himself tightly in check, lips folded, green eyes wide and cold.

After a moment, Ellison said:

"He's within his rights. Point of fact, he's doing his duty. He's been commanded by the Emperor to do just that—confiscate and destroy your opium."

Carradine's lip lifted in a sneer.

"Whose rights are you protecting, Ellison? His, or ours?"

Ellison flushed.

"I'll protect the rights of the British traders to the limit of my ability. But as to opium, you have no 'rights,' Carradine. Opium is clearly contraband in China and in Chinese waters."

"And what about our right to protect our investment? Do you know how much that stuff *cost?* Do you know how much silver is represented at Lintin?"

Ellison shrugged.

"It was your choice as to how you invested your silver. If you chose to do so illegally, that's your responsibility."

"We bought what is legally sold by Her Majesty's Government in India!"

"And you brought it to where it is *not* legal."

Carradine smiled grimly.

"We all know your tender views, Ellison. There's no point in arguing them. The point now is: How will you answer the high commissioner?"

"I hope to tell him that the opium will be surrendered at a place and time convenient to him."

Andrew snorted, but Carradine remained impassive.

"Your hope, I believe, is vain. But I'm not the only one involved. There are other owners. I suggest you call a meeting."

"Very well."

They stared at each other. As the silence grew, the translator interposed timidly.

"Sir—there is more. High commissioner say foreigners cannot leave Canton until they give up all opium—"

"We bloody know that already!" Andrew muttered.

"—and tea trade suspended."

"*What?*"

They all exclaimed together, swinging around to stare at the translator, who began to tremble.

Carradine turned back to Ellison, his eyes gleaming.

"Better call that meeting soon, Ellison. Isn't it a part of your duties to see that the tea gets shipped?"

"I'll call it for this afternoon. But I'll remind you, Carradine, that I also have other instructions—to protect the British traders, which means not only their rights, but their safety—if it comes to that, their *lives*. You'll remember that the high commissioner holds a new edict from the Emperor that makes foreign as well as Chinese opium violators subject to execution."

"By God—" Andrew flared, but his father interrupted, his voice dripping sarcasm.

"And you're going to let Lin chop our necks to salve your delicate conscience?"

Ellison turned white.

"That is an insult, sir!"

"Then what the devil did you mean?"

"I meant to call it to your attention that if the high commissioner decides to enforce the edict he holds, I have not the physical means of protecting your lives."

Carradine smiled—a secret, inward movement of his lips.

"Isn't it fortunate, then, that you asked Lord Palmerston for a warship."

"He has not yet said that he'd send one."

"Not to you, perhaps."

Charlie caught a flash of anguish in Ellison's eyes, but his voice remained calm and stony.

"You mean—*you*'ve heard?"

Carradine had turned away. Now he spoke carelessly over his shoulder: "Not one but *two* ships are on the way." He paused in the doorway and bowed ironically to Ellison. "For no other purpose, of course, than to help you protect our lives. . . . Call that meeting, Ellison."

Charlie, leaning on the wall by the window in Carradine's dining room, watched the traders disperse themselves around the table. More than a score of them, all grim and angry, except Lancelot Dent, Carradine's greatest rival, who deliberately made himself Carradine's antithesis, his manner bluff and hearty, his bulky body dressed in workingman's clothes. Now he was smiling and murmuring to his partner, a Scotsman named Innes. Across the table, Robert Innes was glowering at him. A "turbulent man," Sir George had called Innes a long time ago—a jealous, angry, vengeful man. Once, in a fury because he said a servant of the director of customs had insulted him, he had tried to burn down the director's house by firing Congreve rockets at it from a small cannon he set up on Jackass Point. Even Carradine had called that action stupid.

Now, Innes leaned across the table to snarl at Dent.

"What've you got to smirk about, God rot it!"

Ignoring him, Dent turned genially to Ellison.

"I see you've not invited the Americans."

"Bloody well *not!*" Innes roared, and there was a chorus of agreement. The Americans had held small stocks of Turkish and Persian opium at Lintin, and to get rid of them they'd shipped them to Singapore for sale. Word had recently arrived that when the Singaporeans learned that the shipment had been returned from China—from what had been the greatest market on earth for opium—prices had once again tumbled, plummeted to an all-time low. Loud criticism of the Americans began to burgeon around the table.

Ellison said firmly, "This will get us nowhere," and rose to begin the meeting, but before he could say a word, Innes turned fiercely on him:

173

"By God and the devil, Ellison, I'm telling you! You're mucking wrong if you think I'll give that high commissioner a single ball of my opium!"

A hubbub of agreement arose.

"Thievery, that's what it be!"

"Thieving our opium!"

"Paid for it, we did, in good, heavy silver!"

"Let 'em *try* to chop off our heads!"

"Bloody murderer, with his murder edict!"

"Warships coming, by God, *English* ships, blow those bloody junks out of the water!"

On and on. Charlie sighed, a small core of comfort settling in the turbulence of his thoughts. If not for Yin-kwa's refusal to buy clippers and opium, he himself would be sitting here now, swearing and protesting, his silver sunk in chest on chest of unsalable opium in the lonely deserted hulks at Lintin.

Ellison rose and pounded on the table.

"Gentlemen! This is getting us nowhere. May we please consider our situation quietly and logically?"

Slowly, the shouting tapered off. The men glowered, but fell into silence. Ellison cleared his throat.

"First of all, gentlemen, it is useless to protest the fact that opium is contraband in China. *It is.* The Chinese have given us full notice to abandon the trade, and they are fully within their rights to try to enforce their interdiction."

A few mutters rose, but no one spoke out. Carradine kept silent, the green eyes below the heavy brows fixed on Ellison.

"Secondly," Ellison went on quietly, "the two British warships that are on their way here will accomplish no miracles. I grant you that they could destroy quite a few Chinese war junks, but you've overlooked the fact that the high commissioner has announced that until the opium is surrendered, not only will we all be kept here on Jackass Point, but the *tea trade will be stopped.* Could our warships force the Chinese to start the tea trade up again? To bring the tea out of Canton?"

The words thudded into dead silence.

"And if the high commissioner should decide to use what

you call his 'murder edict'—if, for instance, he had some of you kidnapped and carried into Canton—could those two British warships, which can get no nearer Canton than Whampoa, prevent him from executing you inside the city?"

Ellison looked around the ring of glum, silent faces.

"Of course not! I tell you, gentlemen, that the real use of those warships—the use I had in mind when I asked for them—will be to evacuate you in case of need, to take you out of the reach of the high commissioner."

In silence as loud as a shriek, Carradine tapped his hands together.

"Congratulations, Ellison. I didn't think you had it in you."

All heads turned in unison to Carradine. He looked around, smiling.

"Gentlemen, I submit that our superintendent of trade is right. In the circumstances, two British ships of war can be no more than a token of British might. I submit that it would be judicious for us to play for time. We don't want to lose our investment in opium, but we also don't want to lose our profits from tea. I suggest, therefore, that we break the impasse by making the high commissioner an offer. He has demanded all our opium, but he has little means of knowing just how much opium there is at Lintin. Shall we offer him, say, a thousand chests?"

An astonished hum arose. Carradine called to Ellison:

"Do you agree with that proposal, sir?"

Ellison hesitated. "What did you mean—'play for time'?"

"Surely it's obvious! The twenty thousand chests at Lintin isn't all the opium in the world. There are another thirty thousand chests in Bombay and Calcutta awaiting auction, and the new season's crop to be added to that. Lin's demand for the Lintin opium is by no means the end of the story. Who can know what will happen later?"

When Ellison still hesitated, Carradine said, smiling:

"Come, sir! Compromise! You'll not get a better proposal. We all know you'd like to see an end to the opium trade, but that's beyond our decision here. The immediate problem is Lin's demand for the opium at Lintin, and I'm proposing that we take steps to solve that problem. If Lin accepts a thousand chests, that'll solve it, won't it?"

Ellison drew a deep breath.

"Very well. We can try."

Carradine grunted with satisfaction and turned to the other traders.

"Well, gentlemen? I am prepared to contribute four hundred chests. You, Dent—three hundred? Innes—a hundred? And the rest of you, share the remaining two hundred among you?"

After a pause, Innes said, "All right. A hundred."

Suddenly they were all agreed, anxious to contribute, perking up cheerfully. Perhaps Lin would accept a thousand chests! He couldn't know, after all, how much there was in the Lintin hulks, and it would take him a long time to find out! And perhaps all he wanted was to demonstrate zeal. Perhaps he'd accept the thousand chests and destroy them with great fanfare, and after that, why, maybe some new system of bribery could be worked out and . . .

Ellison rose abruptly, stiff-faced, and marched out of the room, signaling to Charlie. When they were alone, climbing the stairs, he said bitterly:

"Pirates and lawbreakers and greedy fools, too! Snatching at delusions! Well—let's find that translator and get him to write out the offer of a thousand chests. I want him to take it to the Petitions Gate today. I want to get all this over as quick as possible."

But it wasn't going to be quick. Charlie, trudging up the stairs behind Ellison, knew suddenly and surely, in the pit of his stomach, that it was going to take a long time. They were no longer dealing with petty mandarins tempted by thirty-dollar bribes, nor with a careless old viceroy who let his troops become opium smokers, nor even with a new and honest viceroy who, indefatigable as he was, nevertheless had no authorization to punish foreigners. They were dealing now with a formidable high commissioner who had the authority to do anything he saw fit, and would undoubtedly dare to do it.

While Ellison talked to the translator, Charlie went back down the stairs and out onto Jackass Point. He wanted to be with Blogg tonight, on *San Seb*, away from the turgid tensions of Carradine's factory. Plodding over the cobbles, he laughed at himself for fancying that the peace of *San Seb* was real, but all the same he quickened his step, longing for the taper-lit familiarity of *San Seb*'s cabin, for Blogg's deep-voiced common sense.

Blogg was glad to see him, and they sprawled on their bunks, talking for a long time about the latest developments. When Charlie told Blogg about the offer of a thousand chests, Blogg guffawed.

"If Lin's honest, what's the use? And if he's dishonest, it's too mingy! Yin-kwa would offer him *five* thousand chests to destroy for the Emperor, and another five thousand to keep for himself!"

Charlie laughed. That was Yin-kwa's way. If you're trusting a man, make it worth his while to be honest, but if you're tempting him, make it *very* worth his while to be *dis*honest. . . .

At some point, the conversation flagged and they fell asleep. Later Charlie half woke, distressed by the fullness of his bladder, and stumbled on deck to relieve himself over the side. Turning to go back into the cabin, he faced upriver and was startled into momentary wakefulness by the weird and beautiful appearance of the river. At this hour, before dawn on a moonless night, the river should be pitch-dark without any reflection of light on its surface. But now it was full of light, a ghostly luminescence coming from dozens and dozens of lanterns, the cylindrical oilpaper-shaded lanterns of small Chinese craft. There must be forty or fifty of the craft clustered a mile or more away, moving jerkily about. What the devil were they doing? A few lanterns would move forward for twenty yards or so, then stop and spin around for a minute, then move forward again. What the hell was going on? For a few moments longer Charlie stared sleepily, but the mystery was too much to solve now. He stumbled down the ladder and fell back onto his bunk.

In the morning, the sun was already high when he awoke. Overhead, on deck, he could hear Blogg and the mate talking, the mate agitated and even Blogg not as calm as usual. He lay awhile longer, eyes closed, reluctant to learn what new thing was causing their excitement. It must have something to do with the lights of last night. If only he could wish it all away, wish Yin-kwa into appearing this moment in the *San Seb*'s cabin, wish those two precious weeks of Ling-ling's dilly-dallying back into viability!

When at last he rose and went up on deck, Blogg and the mate were standing on the bridge, staring silently over the river at an entirely new landscape.

The river had grown a forest of bamboo poles, sticking six or seven feet out of the water, so close together that they barred the passage of any craft larger than a sampan. The forest lay in a wide band on each side of the river just beyond Jackass Point. Between the bands, there was a narrow clear passage through which a craft as large as a cutter might pass. In the foreground, where there were no stakes, three concentric arcs of small junks faced Jackass Point. In each junk, two soldiers stood, fore and aft, muskets on their shoulders.

"Great God!" It came from Charlie's lips, a whisper.

"Aye!" Blogg's voice was sardonic. "That's what the high commissioner thinks of Carradine's offer of a thousand chests. . . . We're going to be sitting here, Charlie, till he's found out just how much opium's in the Lintin hulks. . . ."

The mate brought them tea and they sipped at their steaming mugs, staring silently at the new landscape. The tea was too hot and Charlie felt it burn in a long trail as it descended into the rumbling sickness in the pit of his stomach. They were stuck. God alone knew when—if—he'd ever get back home to England, but it certainly wouldn't be June! Stuck here on dirty, filthy, crowded Jackass Point! Stuck. The ripples slapping against *San Seb*'s hull chuckled the word, and seemed to giggle as they withdrew to slap again.

After a time, they left *San Seb* and pushed their way to Carradine's factory through the crowd that had assembled to gape and point and chatter at the three rows of junks and the mass of gently bending flexible stakes that backed them up. Ellison was standing at his window looking out at the river. He moved to give them room, but no one spoke. From this height, they could see, some hundreds of yards beyond the forest of stakes, two big junks being rowed away from the middle of the river, one toward the west bank, one toward the east. The craft moved slowly, as though held back by some heavy burden, and on each bank groups of men helped pull the craft forward by hauling strenuously on ropes attached to their bows. The sound of the men's rhythmic chanting came faintly on the breeze—"*Heh*-ho, *hahng*-ho . . ." The water between the junks began to riffle in a long, thin line as something rose out of the river—a chain. As the junks reached the banks, the chain came to rest, stretching from bank to bank a foot or so above the water.

And beyond the chain, beyond the waving forest of stakes, beyond the three arcs of guardian soldiers, in the gray haze behind which lay Whampoa, they saw faintly the pennants of war junks.

Ellison turned grimly from the window.

"Well, clearly Lin isn't going to settle for a thousand chests. He's making sure none of us gets out before he finds out just how much opium there is at Lintin. . . . I'm sorry, Charlie. This is the damnedest bad luck for you."

The door opened quietly. Andrew came in.

"See that?"

Ellison nodded.

"And the servants are gone again, all of them. And there's nothing in the market."

Without a word, Ellison took the rum from the cupboard, poured four tots, and set the glasses down carefully, one on

179

each side of the table. They sat and sipped. Not even Andrew said a word.

Every day now there was a great crowd at the dockside, not to stare at the three arcs of junks with their guardian soldiers—that sight had become commonplace—but to bargain with the boat people for food. Once again, the boat people were bringing food from the other side of the river, though this time the prices they demanded were much higher, because they had to pay bribes to the soldiers to be allowed to cross their lines. But there was plenty of silver in the factories on Jackass Point, and the food the boat people brought was good. With practice, some of the factors had learned to cook well, except for rice—no foreigner could ever learn to cook rice properly, they laughed. The traders might steam and stew and stamp about, cursing Lin and Ellison and even, sometimes, Carradine, but their factors were once again on holiday, enjoying themselves hugely.

Charlie trudged from Ellison's rooms to *San Seb*, as he did daily, and Blogg met him, shaking his head. No news. Blogg's mate had been sent into Canton a second time with a letter for Yin-kwa, but this time it had not even been received in the Street of the Psychics. The tall gate of the house of many courtyards had remained closed, though the mate had banged on it until a curious crowd gathered.

Blogg had then suggested that they send the mate to Macao, to tell Ling-ling and Ah Sam not to worry, that they'd be back as soon as possible. The mate could go around the creeks of the delta in a sampan, get out into the river beyond Whampoa, and hire a junk. It might take him a month to get to Macao and back, but it was worth trying. He'd been gone two weeks now.

They leaned silently on *San Seb*'s rail. It was warm and muggy, the sky overcast and sulfurous. Too early in the day for grog, and too hot anyway, and nothing else to drink but tea made from river water. Of all the dozens of laden carts that normally came every day to the market in Hog's Lane, only one came now, with two large wooden buckets of spring water. A committee of factors zealously rationed out the water—about a cupful daily for each denizen of Jackass Point.

"Lin's not going to have it said we died of thirst!"

"Starve us, yes, but . . ."

"He knows bloody well we're getting food from the boat people!"

"Maybe he's getting a cut of the bribes they pay the soldiers!"

"Not Lin! He's a mucking *honest* fellow!"

Lin was honest, the word had got around. An honest man, a fierce man, an adamant man. A great, big, fat man, weighing twenty stone or more. A man who had once put down a rebellion single-handed by talking the rebels out of it. A man who had once ordered a thousand heads chopped off and watched them drop one by one into a growing lake of blood without turning a hair. A poet too, some said. Wrote poetry, by God! How d'you write poetry in Chinee? Make it *rhyme?*

So the factors laughed and joshed and played games on Jackass Point. Blogg suddenly pointed over the heads of a group of leapfrog players.

"Mate's back!"

The mate was scurrying along the cobblestones, keeping to one side, avoiding the players. He came aboard panting, his face working with agitation. For a long time he spoke to Blogg in their seaman's pidgin. At last Blogg turned to Charlie, eyes bright with excitement.

"By God, them warships Ellison asked for must have arrived! Mate ain't seen 'em, but he says he couldn't get a junk to take him to Macao because the estuary's full of fire rafts!"

"Fire rafts?"

"Aye—Chinee weapon of war. Big rafts, piled up high with firewood and straw and sulfur, that the Chinee set ablaze and turn loose to float about every which way. Damned hard for a ship to get around all of 'em without catching fire. Ellison's warships must have sailed right up to the blockage at Whampoa, then the Chinee floated the fire rafts behind 'em, ready to be fired if they should try to run back. They're bottled up 'tween Whampoa and the Bogue.''

"By God, we'd better tell Ellison!"

But Ellison had already heard. Carradine and Andrew were with him in his rooms.

"Well," Ellison was saying grimly. "Is this why you wanted to 'play for time'? For two of our ships to get bottled up in the estuary?"

"D'you take me for a fool?" Carradine was barely under control. "I told you, those two ships are a token! There's not enough time—"

He stopped short, scowling, a concavity suddenly appearing between his eyes, deep and dark, as though the bone had cracked.

"What d'you mean?" said Ellison sharply.

"Never mind! We must deal with this present situation—"

"*I* will deal with it!" Ellison snapped. "I want to know what you meant by that ambiguous statement!"

Suddenly Carradine was roaring, leaning over the table, thrusting his face into Ellison's.

"You're a mucking ninny, Ellison! Opium is 'evil'! Opium is 'evil'! That's all you think about! Opium is *silver*, man! It's produced on British earth in India, and it's got to be sold, and China's the greatest market on earth for it. China's got to be forced to admit it as *lawful import*! But right now we must play for time, because only two of our warships aren't enough to force that! Can't you see that, you ninny?"

He stood over Ellison, panting, his face seeming to jiggle as though its bony parts were separating and were held together only by flesh and skin. His jaw was working to break away from his cheekbones, his eyes to jump out of their sockets. Ellison stared at him, ashen-faced.

"I see that you're plotting to force the Chinese to legalize opium—which can only mean that you're plotting war."

"War!" Carradine spat the word out. "Against these nincompoops with their fire-eating dragons? We warred against

182

Napoleon! It'll need no more than a spat against the Chinese!"

Ellison stared directly into Carradine's eyes.

"Is Lord Palmerston privy to your plans?"

Carradine suddenly took command of himself. His features smoothed out. The hot glaring of his eyes sank to a cool green glow. He ignored the question.

"Well, as you said, Ellison—*you* will deal with this present situation. What d'you propose to do?"

Still gray-faced, Ellison spoke quietly.

"As I see it, the danger does not lie in our ships' trying to make a run for it back through the Bogue. Our captains didn't reach their rank by being foolish. As I see it, the danger lies in their overestimating *our* danger, and breaking through to us, as they could, in their cutters and with the modern weapons our men carry. But that would be an act of war. I propose, therefore, to ask the high commissioner for a safe-conduct to go to Whampoa and meet the captains of our ships. I propose to ask them to do nothing until, one way or the other, we have reached a resolution here. If we cannot settle our present dispute with Lin, if the lives of Britons on Jackass Point are actually endangered, then I propose to signal our captains to break through by firing those Congreve rockets Robert Innes brought here. I believe you still have them in your storehouse, Carradine? And *San Sebastian* has a small cannon."

For a moment there was complete silence. Then Carradine turned abruptly toward the door.

"If you stand by your word, Ellison, I'll apologize for calling you a ninny."

The safe-conduct—another small yellow banner—came within three hours of the delivery of Ellison's request at the Petitions Gate. Ellison set off at once, in a cutter rowed between the stakes in the river. At the chain, he was to transfer to one of the war junks, as instructed in the banner. The war junk would transport him to Whampoa, where he would be allowed to go aboard the British warships.

On the third day, he was back.

183

There was no need to call a meeting. As soon as the cutter was sighted, men began hurrying to Carradine's dining room to hear what Ellison would have to say. But Ellison, looking exhausted, hardly paused. From the doorway he spoke briefly, the traders craning at him over their shoulders.

"The ships are frigates. *Volage,* twenty-eight guns, and *Hyacinth,* eighteen guns. Captain of *Volage,* Harry Smith, is the senior in command. He didn't like the idea of lying up at Whampoa doing nothing, but he saw my point. He's agreed to what I suggested."

The traders broke into loud discussion as Ellison turned abruptly and began to climb the stairs. Charlie went with him. In his rooms, Ellison stripped off his coat, tore open his shirt, and flung himself into a chair, his face gray. When he spoke his voice was hollow with fatigue—and something else, a kind of despairing sorrow.

"It won't work, Charlie! I'd forgotten. . . . Three years I've been here, mixed up with merchants and traders, buying, selling, dealing, tea, silk, rhubarb, opium . . . I'd forgotten that our navy is a *fighting machine.* Captain Harry Smith thought I'd taken leave of my senses when I talked about dealing with Lin! I was shamed, Charlie. By God, I was *shamed!"*

He jumped up and began to pace the room, for once not caring that he was dirty and disheveled.

"I'm not even Smith's equal! He was sent here at my request, but not to do my bidding. *He's* in command of what that two-ship flotilla does or does not do. I had to *plead* with him, *beg* him to listen to me, to shroud his guns and restrain his men!"

He stopped in the middle of the room, eyes squeezed shut, teeth gritted in an agony of bitterness. Shocked, Charlie jumped up, but Ellison shook his head. Slowly, he forced his features back to calm and came to sit again at the table.

"Never mind. I hold Her Majesty's Commission too, such as it is, and I cannot lose my honor by honoring it. Smith agreed, at last. . . . But it won't work, Charlie. When I spoke to Carradine about firing off those Congreve rockets, I thought of rescue—of getting the traders off Jackass Point and into our ships, out of Lin's reach. But there are more than a hundred merchant ships out there, strung out from Whampoa almost to the Bogue, waiting for their cargoes. Two thousand seamen, in addition to our sailors, all nervy and jerky with idleness, and their food and grog running out. They couldn't be held back, Charlie. There'd be no way of controlling them. If I were to order those rockets fired, the whole lot of them would come breaking through. It would be a bath of blood, to God knows what useless end!"

"Then what . . . ?"

"I'll have to do something else. I've thought about it backward and forward and sideways, and there's nothing for it but to give Lin the Lintin opium."

"But you know you'll never get them to hand it over!"

"I know. So I'll buy it."

"You'll buy it?"

"Not I myself. I'll undertake that the British government will pay the traders three hundred dollars a chest if they'll turn them over to Lin. That's fifty dollars a chest more than they could get now *if* they were able to sell to anybody but me."

Charlie gaped at him.

"You've no authority for that!"

"No, nor time to get it."

"George! There're twenty thousand chests at Lintin! That's *six million dollars.* You'll undertake on behalf of Lord Palmerston, without the slightest authority to do so, that the British Treasury will pay *six million dollars* to buy opium that's already British-owned, in order to have it all destroyed?"

"Its better than spilling the blood of God knows how many Britons, and Chinese too. Carradine—all the traders—will jump at it."

"You'll be putting your head into a noose!"

"It's in one now—I put it in when I accepted this bloody commission."

They sat in silence, Ellison leaning back, eyes closed, Charlie staring at him. By God, he was a courageous man!

After a while, Ellison sat up and began to button his shirt, then tore it open again.

"I'll call a meeting for tomorrow. For now, the devil with it. Let's go to *San Seb*, and drink some grog and have a talk with Blogg about the *sea!*"

But as they left the room, they met Carradine coming up the stairs, followed by his translator. In his hand was another yellow banner. They stood on the landing, the four of them, staring at it, the clamor of the traders' voices rising from three floors below. Then Ellison backed into his room and the others followed. In silence, they watched the translator spread the banner on the table and bend over it, following the lines of characters with a trembling finger.

"Very hard, sir . . ." The man's voice shook.

"Get on with it!" Carradine growled impatiently.

"High commissioner say . . ." The man stammered, cleared his throat. "He say maybe Sir Ellison think high commissioner stupid. Lintin have got twenny thousand chest, not one thousand. He want all. All twenny thousand."

The words fell on blank silence. After a moment, seeming to take heart that he hadn't been attacked, the translator went on.

"He say ten thousand chest belong you, Sir Carradine. He want you go to him, go inside Canton."

"Why?" Carradine snapped.

"He don't say."

Carradine threw back his head and let out a harsh bellow of laughter.

"By God, does he think *I'm* stupid? Go into Canton and let him chop my head under his bloody murder edict?"

"Why should you think that?" Ellison was frowning. "I'm sure he simply wants to discuss the matter with you, since you're the biggest owner. We could ask for a safe-conduct."

"What good would that do?" Carradine roared. "D'you think

186

a piece of yellow silk'd protect my neck from his ax? You're mad, Ellison!"

Andrew burst into the room, drawn by his father's roar, and Carradine went on roaring at his son.

"This ninny wants me to go into Canton, to have my head chopped off!"

"I want nothing of the kind!" Ellison shouted, his face contorted with anger. "I simply think we must find out why Lin wants to see you!"

"Let him come *here*, then! To Jackass Point! I'll meet him under the flagpole, under the Union Jack!"

They glared at each other. The silence grew and swelled. At last the translator, glancing timidly from one to the other, broke it.

"There is more, sir. High commissioner writes that Co-hong is responsible for foreign traders. If you don't go in Canton, high commissioner make Co-hong responsible."

"Let him, by God!" Carradine's bellow was raw with rage, his face almost unrecognizable. "That damned Co-hong's made enough money out of us, hiding behind their God-rotted Eight Regulations that should have been blasted a century ago! Let 'em be hoist on their own damned petard now!" He swung on the translator. "Write him that! Write that damned high commissioner that he'll never get our opium—"

"No!" Ellison cut in, shouting Carradine down. "You've no right to speak for the others!"

"But I've a right to say what'll happen to my own head! Write him"—Carradine stabbed a finger at the shaking translator— "write him that I'll never go into Canton, he can hold the whole God-rotted Co-hong responsible, he can chop off all their heads, but he'll never chop off mine!"

"Very well." Ellison turned to the translator, forcing his voice to normalcy. "Write the high commissioner that Mr. Carradine does not feel able to go into Canton. But"—he swung to Carradine—"about the opium, about giving it up to Lin, I'll call a meeting for tomorrow."

187

"Another damned meeting!" Carradine sneered. "What about those Congreve rockets you were going to fire off? You're supposed to protect *my* head too, you ninny!"

"Before any rockets are fired, I've a proposal to make to all of you that I think you'll like."

"I don't like *anything* you do or say, Ellison!"

"Nevertheless, we'll have a meeting tomorrow and you'll hear me out!"

They glared at each other again, Ellison haggard, great black shadows smudging his eyes, Carradine's face like a crumbling monument. After a moment, Carradine, lip lifted in a heavy sneer, turned to Andrew, and the two left the room. The translator timidly sat at Ellison's table and opened his box of writing brushes and ink blocks. Ellison sat down heavily on the other side of the table and put his head in his hands.

Charlie stared from the window, the thumping of his heart seeming to echo in the sudden quiet of the room. The high commissioner was threatening the Co-hong, but it was ritual, Yin-kwa had said. Tomorrow Ellison would hold his meeting and offer Carradine and the others three hundred dollars a chest for their opium, and they'd jump at the offer, and it would all be over! Perhaps, after all, he could be in England by August! He sighed and glanced at Ellison, who was watching the translator write, his long fingers delicately flicking the brush. Charlie went to the cupboard and poured three small tots of rum. At first the translator shook his head, but then he smiled and took his glass and raised it and the three of them swallowed together.

It was almost noon the next day, the sun blazing down on Jackass Point, the traders hurrying to get into Carradine's cool dining room for the meeting Ellison had called, when they heard the cymbals.

Everyone on Jackass Point instantly remembered. At once, people began hurrying to vantage points from where the patchwork of light and shadow that lay across the mouth of

Hog Lane was visible. This time, the sound was not the fast, brassy clang-clang-clang that had heralded Lee Kwok's death, but a heavy, slow-paced bong-bong-bong, each bong dying away before the next echoed. In the vast silence that had descended on Jackass Point, the sound approached, becoming louder, more threatening, until at last the cymbalists appeared—four coolies, pacing slowly, letting their cymbals fall to their sides before raising them again for the next dirgelike clash. Directly behind the cymbalists, borne by four more shabby coolies, came an unadorned sedan chair, its dirty curtains closely drawn. Beside the chair walked a tall thin man in a plain cotton gown. Behind it marched four soldiers, barefooted, queues wound around their heads, blunderbusses on their shoulders.

A very small and plain procession, yet there was something ominous in its very unpretentiousness. The crowd of spectators grew larger by the minute, everyone maneuvering to keep it in sight. On the steps of Carradine's factory, the traders jostled each other for a better view. Charlie, craning to see, found his view abruptly cut off by Robert Innes' tangled, ill-smelling hair pressed against his eyes and nose. Angrily, he shoved Innes, who stumbled heavily against the man in front of him, causing him in turn to fall against others. A scuffle developed, everyone pushing and shoving, and Charlie suddenly found himself hurtling through a crack in the wall of bodies. All at once he was in the front row, his view unobstructed.

Clear before his eyes, Jackass Point lay in blazing sunlight. At the mouth of Hog Lane the soldiers, cymbalists, and chairbearers crowded in a tight little group around the sedan chair, which stood empty, its curtains open. Across the cobbles, the tall, thin man who had walked beside the sedan chair was moving slowly, supporting on his arm a tiny, tottering figure, bent almost double under the weight of a great chain draped from neck to ankles.

Wei and How-kwa.

Charlie's blood spurted through his body in a great, hot surge that forced beads of sweat from every pore. How-kwa, still nominally head of the Co-hong, the only member of the Co-hong whose head the high commissioner could chop off without upsetting the tea trade, without displacing a single leaf of tea!

Mutters and murmurs were swelling all around. People were turning to each other in horror. Charlie neither saw nor heard them. Every sight and sound had vanished from his ken, except Wei and How-kwa. He stepped forward. Hands clutched at him, but he shook them off. Hurried across the cobbles. Put an arm around How-kwa and with the other hand lifted the slack of the chain to take the weight of it from his neck.

"Wei," he said quietly. "Those soldiers don't know Carradine. Tell them I'm Carradine. Say I'll go with them into Canton *now*, to the high commissioner."

Wei's eyes, pinpoints of anguish, flashed at him. Then Wei was calling over his shoulder to the soldiers. They came running—they didn't like what they'd been ordered to do—and knelt to unlock the chain from How-kwa's ankles and remove it. Feebly, How-kwa turned his head sideways—he couldn't lift it—to glance at Charlie, but the wavering eyes under the heavy lids were glassy and unseeing. The bearers had rushed up with the sedan chair. One of the soldiers gently lifted How-kwa into it, and they went off, almost running, Wei keeping pace with them.

The soldiers, businesslike now, formed a square around Charlie. The cymbalists ranged themselves in front, began again to clash their instruments, fast now, brassy, triumphant. One of the soldiers gave Charlie a push between the shoulder blades, and they marched off, to the beat of the cymbals.

"You are not a prisoner," someone said.

Charlie wiped the back of a hand across his forehead. It came away drenched, and immediately more sweat dripped from his hairline. Two hours of marching between the soldiers, in the full onslaught of the sun, through narrow streets between baleful crowds of spectators, to get to this place, whatever it was. A tall, blank gate in a twenty-foot-high mud-brick wall, behind which square green roofs reached up into the sky, one upon the other, each smaller than the one below it.

"You are not a prisoner," the speaker said again.

Charlie peered at him, eyes stinging from the sweat that kept trickling into their corners. A very thin man who looked something like Lee Kwok. He was smiling. His grammar might be correct, but his accent was atrocious.

"Then why these soldiers?" Charlie muttered thickly.

"To protect you," the man said. He turned and pointed up at the green roofs. "This is the Temple of the Queen of Heaven."

"Where's Lin?" Charlie growled. "The high commissioner? He wants to see me. Or Carradine."

"He awaits you in the Great Hall."

Silently, on oiled hinges, the tall gate opened. They entered a huge courtyard, flagstoned, bare and severe, the only ornaments three gaudily painted statues, life-size but dwarfed by the height of the wall against which they stood. The man pointed to them.

"The Queen of Heaven. The Goddess of Mercy, in three of her apparitions."

Charlie nodded vaguely, his attention riveted on the delicious black band of shade under the eave of the temple's lowest roof. The temple was a tall pagoda and its lowest roof was enormous, sheltering a space, enclosed behind carved wooden shutters, that must be large enough to hold a thousand people. They crossed the courtyard and stepped into the band of shade, Charlie sighing with relief, closing his eyes. But at once, against his eyelids, leaped the wispy image of chained Howkwa, twinkling eyes glazed over, that effortful sidewise twist of his head all that remained of his quick, birdlike movements. Rage clotted Charlie's throat. What kind of *animal* was Lin? The proximity of Lin suffused him, and he swung toward the open door of the Great Hall.

Yin-kwa stepped into the doorway, cool and elegant in a satin robe, hairline newly plucked, hair disappearing in a loose plait behind his back.

191

"Charlie." The black eyes gleamed. "Wei told me. Thank you."

Charlie shook his head impatiently.

"How is he?"

"Bad, but alive."

"God Almighty! How could Lin *do* a thing like that?"

Yin-kwa smiled, a soft, bland, meaningless movement of his lips that betrayed to Charlie the strain on his spirit. His voice was as soft and bland as the smile.

"Lin is an adamant man."

"Did he really intend to chop off your grandfather's head if Carradine didn't do what he wanted?"

"Who knows? He doesn't tell what he intends. What we must do now is make sure that he doesn't chop off *your* head for Carradine's. The whole Co-hong is here. We've all told him that you're not Carradine, but he's a hard man to convince. Come in now, but say nothing. Above all, show no anger. Just be quiet. Your head may depend on it. Do you understand?"

"Yes."

Quietly, they walked into the hall. In comparison to the glaring courtyard, it was dim and shadowy, so big and empty that Charlie's leather-soled footsteps echoed on the polished wooden floor like miniature thunderclaps. In one corner, twenty or thirty people sat in a silent circle. In the clear space between them was an empty chair to which Yin-kwa pointed. Charlie went forward alone and seated himself.

Opposite him was a table behind which sat a hugely fat man. His body, clothed in stiff satin, looked like a small mountain and his head like a giant mushroom growing from the mountain's crest. Blinking to clear his vision, Charlie saw that the curious impression was created by the man's thick neck, which joined his head in a single column—the stem of the mushroom—and the wide, round-brimmed hat on his head, which was the mushroom cap. The huge moon face was decorated by a thin, angular mustache, the ends of which drooped wispily on each side of the chin. The narrow black eyes stared icily.

Charlie wrenched his gaze away, his heart pounding. Say nothing. Be quiet. Your head may depend on it.

For a long moment there was silence. Then, with a rustle of silk, someone rose and began to speak, slowly and quietly. When he had done, another rose. They spoke in turn, the merchants of the Co-hong, all but Yin-kwa. It took a long time. From the calmness of their voices, they might be discussing some esoteric point of scholarship. Were they truly trying to save his neck? But show no anger, Yin-kwa had said. Lin was a secret man, and unpredictable, so they were wooing him with courtesy and dignity, making it hard for him to be less than they, to descend to such vulgarity as the chopping off of heads. That was Yin-kwa's kind of tactic. . . . Charlie listened to the singsong of the staccato syllables going on and on, a strange, atonal music.

At last there was a pause. Charlie's heart quickened. Then Yin-kwa's voice. A brief statement. A question, perhaps—his tone rose on the last words. A murmur of assent from the others, and again a long silence. The stillness grew so tense that the air of the vast room seemed to vibrate. Charlie's mouth dried. When he tried to swallow, his throat convulsed. At last he risked a glance from under his brows. Lin's massive face was stony. The narrow eyes, almost hidden in the heavy folds of flesh, stared at a point above Charlie's head. Then, slowly, he raised a pudgy finger. One of the mandarins behind him leaned forward, and Lin whispered in his ear. The mandarin rose. Though no one else moved, it seemed to Charlie that the Co-hong merchants sagged in relief, that a soft sigh crept through the room as they released their pent-up breaths. Had Lin conceded something? The mandarin beckoned. Charlie glanced at Yin-kwa, but his face was impassive. Feeling the blood rush and gush through his body, feeling every precious crimson drop, Charlie rose on spongy knees and followed the mandarin.

They left the hall by a door at the back. The westering sun, straight ahead, struck Charlie's eyes like a blow. Eagerly, he raised his face to it. Had he ever hated the sun? Could he ever have hated that blazing, burning, glorious symbol of *life?* They crossed another courtyard. Charlie glanced around it cautiously, but it was as bare as the first—no sign of scaffold or strangling cross. They passed through a gate and entered still another courtyard, this one dotted from wall to wall with tiny buildings, each one no more than two yards square. Suddenly, the interpreter was beside him, saying pleasantly:

"These are the cells for the monks in contemplation. They are locked in. Once a day the doors are opened and they are given rice and water. The rest of the time they spend alone, in darkness and silence, to help them meditate worthily."

Charlie grinned at the man. Would he be talking of monks and meditation if they were going to a head-chopping? Talk on, man, talk on! The man talked on, and Charlie clung to the hope of his gentle tone, hearing none of his words. They came to a square stone building. The mandarin knocked and the door was opened. They entered and immediately it was cool and dim again. And moist. The stone floor was wet. Drops of water clung to the walls. Charlie looked around, hope burgeoning. This was no execution chamber. It was almost like his own bathing room in Macao! Bigger, of course, and no bathing tub. Instead, a high square stone basin built into the wall, brimming full of water, fed by a pipe of split bamboo that trickled water from some outside source. What a fine idea! When he got back to Macao, he'd have to try and fix up something like that. . . .

"Take your clothes off," the interpreter said. He and the mandarin had stepped up onto a wooden platform.

Charlie grinned. It was as though Ah Sam had said, "Clotheses off, Chahlee!" in those long-ago days on *Merope.* He stripped quickly, dropping his filthy clothes on the wet floor. By the time he stood upright, naked, another man had come into the room, silently, on bare feet. A very calm man, dressed in a yellow cotton robe—but not really a robe, just a long, wide strip of yellow cloth wrapped around the man's body, one end of it draped over a shoulder, leaving the other shoulder bare. What kind of garment was that? And the man was shaven absolutely clean, even his head—his bare scalp gave off highlights where sunbeams through a high window touched it.

The man went to another little wooden platform beside the container of water, picked up a wooden bowl that rested on its rim, filled it with water, and stood waiting.

"He will bathe you," the interpreter said.

Charlie laughed aloud. Not a head-chopping, but a bath! A wonderful bath with floods of water, such as he hadn't had since the last night at home in Macao!

He slid his bare feet across the floor, delighting in the wetness of it, and stood before the man. The first bowlful of icy water made him gasp, but the second was pure sensuality. He stood, head raised, eyes closed, and luxuriated as the man poured bowl after bowl of water over his head. He began to rub his body with his hands, and the man seemed to time the showers to coincide. By the time the showers stopped, Charlie felt marvelous—clean, tingling, refreshed, renewed. He opened his eyes. The man was making signs to him—he should spread wide his arms and legs. It seemed strange, but obligingly he did so. Lifting the hem of his garment, the man stepped down onto the sloshing floor and slowly walked around him, bending, straightening, peering closely at his body from every angle. It took a long time. At last, the man turned and bowed to the mandarin, said a single word, and walked from the room.

"He says you are clean," the interpreter announced.

Obviously! Charlie looked around happily. Now there should be the great bed, sheets that were always sparkling white . . . but there were only the two men on the platform and his dirty clothes scattered soggily on the floor. Slowly he began to put them on, euphoria fading. Why the bath? Why the inspection of his body? Why the pronouncement that he was clean? Perhaps Chinese heads could be chopped dirty, but barbarian heads had to be clean. There were stranger things than that in Chinese culture. . . .

The mandarin was beckoning again. The interpreter had

disappeared, and Charlie followed the mandarin, heart thudding, still pumping his blood, his precious red blood. The thought of Lee Kwok's blood jumped into his mind. It must have poured out of the severed neck like the water from the abbot's bowl. But blood was warm, not icy like the water. Warm and sticky, exuding its sweetish smell. His breath caught, as though the smell of his own blood already cloyed the air.

At the door of the Great Hall the mandarin stepped aside, bowed, turned, and left. Alone, Charlie stood before the door, afraid to touch it. But the hall was not silent now. There were voices, even laughter. Hesitantly, he pushed the door open.

"Charlie!"

Yin-kwa came swiftly. For the second time in all the years they'd known each other, he shook Charlie's hand, shook it many times. The Co-hong merchants crowded around, smiling, nodding. The world spun. The hall spun. The faces blurred. The voices hummed. Charlie smiled and smiled, not hearing, not seeing, just sensing the drops of blood still safe in his veins, pumping, coursing, living. After a time, he and Yin-kwa were alone, walking across the entrance courtyard, Yin-kwa talking. Charlie stopped, conscious suddenly that it was dark, that the three statues of the Queen of Heaven glimmered raffishly, that a star could be seen, that a cool breeze was blowing.

"What did you say, Yin-kwa?"

Yin-kwa put an arm around his shoulders, smiling.

"I was telling you what happened. All of us, one by one, told Lin again that you were not Carradine. But still he wouldn't give in. At last I had the idea of asking him to have your body examined. Everybody in Canton knows that Carradine is poxed. He killed a pirate once, long ago. The pirate's relatives arranged for him to meet a beautiful Macao prostitute who had the pox. He took her as his mistress until he found out, but by then he was well and truly poxed himself. The story is so well known that even Lin had to believe it. He agreed to accept the word of the abbot of this temple, if the abbot examined your body and confirmed that it was clean—no lesions or chancres. But you were so dirty that you had to be bathed first."

Yin-kwa laughed. "In fact, when the abbot came to report to Lin that you were clean, he even said that you're remarkable for a barbarian—you enjoyed your bath!"

Charlie drew a great breath. Air had never smelled so sweet!

"By God, Yin-kwa, I won't forget that experience soon! I was thinking of Lee Kwok, how his blood must have . . ."

Yin-kwa grasped his arm, urged him toward the gate.

"Enough! It's over!"

Charlie stopped dead, dragging Yin-kwa to a stop too. "By God, it really *is* over, Yin-kwa! Ellison's going to give Lin the opium! All twenty thousand chests of it! He's offering the traders three hundred dollars a chest for it, and then he'll turn it all over to Lin."

"*He's* going to pay?" Yin-kwa stared.

"Oh, not he! He's undertaking that the British government will pay."

Yin-kwa started walking again, slowly.

"A very brave thing to do! The traders will accept, of course."

"Yes—and then Lin'll let us go. I understand why you couldn't come to *San Seb*, Yin-kwa—Lin must've been watching you every minute—and it really didn't matter, since we couldn't get off Jackass Point, but now he'll be letting us go soon. Yin-kwa, could you quickly get me some of my silver? I'm going home to England for a visit, taking Ling-ling and the children with me."

"*What?*" Yin-kwa stopped again and stared at Charlie. "You think you're going to take Jin-see away from China?"

"Just for a year or two."

"Wei will never permit it, Charlie."

"By God, Yin-kwa! Doesn't anybody remember that Jin-see is *my* son? Everybody, even Ling-ling sometimes, behaves as though Wei has more rights over him than I have!"

"In a way, he does. Jin-see is Wei's spiritual heir. It's Jin-see who'll perform the rituals for Wei when he becomes an ancestor."

"I've no objection whatever to that! All I want to do is take him home for a year or two to show him to my father!"

"Well . . ." Yin-kwa began to walk again. "I can call in your silver in a week or two, of course, but Lin's not going to take Ellison's word for it that those twenty thousand chests will be delivered to him. He'll want to see all the opium first—see it and destroy it. Have you ever thought how to destroy a ball of opium without smoking it up? Let alone twenty thousand chests of it—two and a half million pounds?"

"By God!" Charlie's eyes widened.

Yin-kwa smiled. "Moreover, the destruction of those twenty thousand chests isn't going to end the problem. What about all the thousands of chests awaiting auction in Calcutta and Bombay? And d'you think the opium farmers in Patna and Rajputana are going to stop growing poppies? If Lin is to finish off the opium trade, as the Emperor has ordered, there's plenty more he's going to have to do besides merely destroying the twenty thousand Lintin chests. . . . I'm afraid, Charlie, it may be a long time before you make a voyage to England, with or without Jin-see."

They had reached the gate. Outside, two of Yin-kwa's sedan chairs were waiting. Silently, Charlie stepped into one of them. The remnants of his euphoria were fast disappearing, like the prospects of that journey home.

In the Street of the Psychics, the tall blank gate was thrown open as the sedan chairs approached. The gateman ran out and spoke urgently to Yin-kwa. Yin-kwa turned to Charlie.

"Quick. He's dying."

They walked swiftly, side by side, through the lantern-lit courtyards, Yin-kwa speaking softly, almost inaudibly.

"Lovely, aren't they? They were lovely when my grandfather was born, and they'll be as lovely after he dies, and he'll live among them still in the house of the ancestors where the progenitors live on with their descendants forever—where I myself will one day live. . . . He's ninety-four years old. For a long time he's wished to go to the other world and be with our ancestors. Now, he's going in peace and dignity. But for you, Charlie, he might have gone this morning, in chains, on

Jackass Point. I thank you, Charlie. My ancestors thank you. . . ."

Charlie heard him wonderingly. He looked as always, elegant and imperturbable. The strange words were the measure of his spirit's sorrow. . . .

In the antechamber, among the sleepily protesting birds, the household was assembled, the women with white veils covering their faces, the men with sashes of coarse white cloth around their waists. As Yin-kwa entered, a little sigh rustled round the room—he had arrived, the Grandson, in time to see the Old One off on his journey to the other world.

They passed quickly into the bedroom. Wei was there, and Yin-kwa's sons, squatting on their heels, their young faces awed and solemn. At a sign from their father, they prostrated themselves, bowing their foreheads to the floor, then filed silently from the room.

Now there were only the three of them with the Old One, Wei hovering by the foot of the bed, Yin-kwa and Charlie kneeling on either side of it.

The Old One might already be dead, his body made such a tiny mound under the silken quilts, but he breathed still, lips quivering lightly, eyes deeply sunken in the ivory face. His hand, fragile as a bird's claw, inched toward Yin-kwa. Yin-kwa held it gently in his own and laid his forehead on it.

For long moments there was no sound but the Old One's shallow panting. Then the heavy eyes opened and looked directly at Wei, a look that had nothing of the present in it—of the darkened room, the approach of death. The eyes looked at Wei with the memory of youth, of the long years together, of the bond between bondman and bondmaster, who loved each other. With a harsh sob, Wei fell to his knees and stretched his gnarled hands over the little protuberances that were the dying man's feet.

Then the head turned toward Charlie, turned with infinite slowness as though it were almost too heavy to move, and the slitted eyes held on Charlie's face.

199

"Chahlee . . ." It was the merest breath of sound. "You . . . cheat . . . me . . . you . . . buy . . . opium. . . ."

Aghast, Charlie stared into the slits of eyes. Oh God! Were they twinkling? Surely they were! Surely from under those drooping lids, the old, amused, little twinkle flickered faintly! How-kwa was teasing . . . *teasing* . . .

But he was gone. The slits of the eyes remained open, but the life in them was gone. If they had twinkled, the twinkle was gone. . . . Charlie let his head sink down on the silken quilt, his pulses slamming.

A hand grabbed his shoulder, jerked him backward, sent him sprawling.

"You buy opium? You cheat How-kwa?"

Wei's voice, rasping like a file on the teeth of a saw. Wei's eyes, glaring like the hot embers of charcoal. Appalled, Charlie stared up into the furious eyes. Oh God! If How-kwa had guessed about the opium, Wei had not! If How-kwa had forgiven, Wei had not!

Yin-kwa spoke sharply from the other side of the bed. Wei swung toward him, snarling. Yin-kwa spoke again, softly, his voice almost pleading, but Wei had already swung back to Charlie.

"I *finis'* you, Chahlee!"

Charlie scrambled to his feet, arms outstretched in a gesture of helpless supplication, but Wei stepped away from him, hand slashing out as though, if it held a knife, he would slit Charlie's throat. They stood for a moment, frozen, then Wei turned and went to the bedside, stood looking down on the dead face, his eyes filling with tears that flooded down his cheeks, rolling a zigzag course among the wrinkles. Murmuring broken words, he leaned forward and delicately closed the lids over the dead eyes. Then, with difficulty, with an old man's stiff movements, he prostrated himself, arms fully extended, fists clasped above his head, and struck his forehead to the floor three times, the three raps cracking loud in the silence. Then he rose and strode from the room without a backward glance.

Shaking with shock and dismay, Charlie turned to Yin-kwa.

"He's repudiated you," Yin-kwa said tightly. They stared at each other, Charlie's eyes as black as Yin-kwa's, sharing the guilt that had taken so many years to come home so disastrously to roost.

Then Yin-kwa closed his eyes and deliberately relaxed the taut lines of his face, muscle by muscle, until he seemed once again calm and impassive. He knelt beside the bed and gently touched his grandfather's forehead, his lips moving in a little smile.

"I think he guessed about the opium—he was a hard man to hoodwink. But he said nothing, so I said nothing—it was a kind of game we played between us. I thought, though, that he must have told Wei. He always told Wei everything. But this time, it seems, he didn't, perhaps because he thought Wei might not forgive you as easily as he had."

Charlie knelt slowly on the other side of the bed.

"Then he had forgiven me? I thought, when he said that to me just before he . . . died—I thought that he was teasing."

"I thought so too." Yin-kwa's voice was no more than a murmur. "But we can't ask him anymore, can we?"

Now, from the antechamber, came the sound of women wailing, soft at first, then louder, more mournful, more terrible. Yin-kwa inclined his head toward the sound.

"The dirge of death. You gave him that, Charlie. You made it possible for him to die here, among those who love him. One day, Wei will remember that, and when he does, he will forgive you."

The small smile was still on his lips, but tears were shining in his eyes.

Charlie stared down at the peaceful old face. It was hard to believe that he was dead. The eyelids seemed on the verge of lifting to reveal the bright little twinkle, the lips on the verge of twitching into the chuckling laugh.

Behind his own lips, inside his tight, aching throat, Charlie said silently:

You'd forgiven me, hadn't you? *Hadn't you?*

But there was no answer.

Chapter VIII

September - December

1839

THE STENCH WAS impossible to escape. It pervaded Jackass Point, ballooning in the relentless July heat, swirling with every puff of breeze. It came from the coastal village of Chen-kou, where the high commissioner had set up a carpeted pavilion, hung with scrolls and paintings, from which he could watch every step of his plan to destroy two and a half million pounds of opium.

The first phase of the plan had been the digging of three trenches, each a hundred and fifty feet long, half as wide, and seven feet deep, lined with stones and timber. The second had been to break up the balls of opium and throw them into the trenches. The third had been to flood the trenches with two feet of water. The fourth and last phase, the one that was producing the awesome stench, was to pour lime and salt into the sludge of waterlogged opium, stir it all up, and run it off into the sea. Five hundred coolies and sixty supervising officers had been busy for two months executing the plan under the ever-watching eyes of the high commissioner and of the American,

Caleb King, one of the oldest traders on Jackass Point, a Quaker who had never touched opium, who had been invited by Lin to witness the destruction.

On the day that the stench first began to swirl on Jackass Point, Caleb King reported to a meeting in Carradine's dining room that Lin had composed a poem to the god of the sea, asking him to hide all the sea creatures safely while the poison was being run off into their watery domain.

"He's an admirable man!" enthused Mr. King.

Charlie and Blogg glanced at each other. An admirable man! Worried about the creatures of the sea, but willing to drape How-kwa in chains and perhaps to chop off Charlie's head, too!

Only Blogg, of all those on Jackass Point, knew exactly what had happened that day in Canton. After Charlie left Yin-kwa beside How-kwa's deathbed—an unfamiliar Yin-kwa, squatting on his heels, head bowed, wrapped in stillness and solitude—he had been carried back to *San Seb* by the waiting chair-bearers. Blogg had embraced him in a hug that lifted him off his feet and thanked God for his safety in a voice that quavered with such fervor that Charlie's eyes had watered. In spite of his exhaustion, he had there and then told Blogg everything, wavering back and forth in his narrative while emotions popped in his mind like bubbles on the surface of boiling water.

When Ellison came at dawn the next morning to see if there was news of Charlie, he had been almost as glad as Blogg to find him safe. They had told Ellison only that the high commissioner had believed the Co-hong's assurances that Charlie was not Carradine, and had released him. He had wrung Charlie's hand.

"By God, that was brave, Charlie! To go marching off into Canton like that, no safe-conduct or anything! I know you did it for the sake of old How-kwa, but all the same you might have had your head chopped off if Lin hadn't believed the Co-hong, and if Lin really had designs on Carradine, you saved Carradine's neck too. He should be damned grateful to you!"

But later that day, at the meeting Ellison called to announce that Lin had accepted the offer of twenty thousand chests of Lintin opium, Carradine had sneered.

"More fool you, rushing off into Canton to save that old fox How-kwa, who's made far more millions out of tea than we've ever made out of opium! If you think I'll thank you for it, you're bloody mistaken! Serve you right if your head had been chopped off, doing a bloody fool thing like that! Only reason Lin didn't chop it off, he must have known you're nothing but a *peddler!*"

The dark spot between his eyes that looked like an excavation of the bone had been deeply in evidence. Now it was again in evidence as Carradine listened to Caleb King extolling the virtues of the high commissioner.

"He's totally honest! I cannot conceive how any business could be more faithfully executed! He has in his hands portable wealth that could be sold for twenty million dollars, and he's destroying every ounce of it!"

Carradine grunted sourly. His share of that twenty million would have been ten million, now reduced to three million under the indemnity Ellison had promised on Lord Palmerston's behalf. Palmerston had been informed of that promise by a letter Ellison wrote him and, with Lin's permission, sent to Macao to be dispatched to England on the next mail packet. But Carradine had not had permission to send a letter, and he was glowering, unsure that Palmerston would pay up on Ellison's word alone. Now he growled at King:

"And you think it's grand to see twenty million dollars run off into the ocean!"

King raised his eyebrows pointedly.

"The government of a *Christian* Queen is growing and selling this poison, and a *pagan* monarch, disdaining to enrich himself by it, has instructed his *pagan* high commissioner to destroy it, which that man is faithfully doing. I do indeed think it noble!" He looked around the ring of frowning faces, his lip lifting.

"I'll make you free of another piece of interesting information. The high commissioner wanted to know what those markings on the balls of opium mean—*VRI*. When I told him they mean *Victoria Regina et Imperatrix* he couldn't believe it! The Queen of England allowing her mark to be put on balls of *opium!* D'you know that he's written a letter to your Queen, which he's trying to get properly translated, informing her of your smuggling activities here? He feels sure that she doesn't know. He cannot believe that a reigning monarch would countenance traffic in *opium.*"

The words fell into crackling silence. Ellison's face was stony, Carradine's lowering. "Bloody Quaker!" he muttered after a moment.

Ellison rose then to break up the meeting.

"That Quaker is a sententious man, and I can't blame them for disliking him," he said late that evening to Charlie and Blogg, drinking rum on *San Seb*'s bridge. The heat had at last dissipated, though the stench still swirled. "But tempers are running high, and this awful smell isn't helping, and I didn't want to risk a row. I can't afford a challenge to my authority, because as soon as the river is cleared, I'm going to order all the British off Jackass Point, out of Lin's reach."

The river was still blockaded, although, on the day the sludge began to be run off into the sea, the factories' servants had reappeared, the market had been reopened, and a number of carts had arrived bearing the carcasses of freshly killed pigs, sheep, and chickens, gifts from a triumphant Lin to the traders whose opium was vanishing into the sea.

Together with the gifts, another little yellow banner had been delivered to Ellison, announcing the next phase in Lin's program of eradicating the opium trade: Any trader who wished to resume trade with China must sign a bond promising under pain of death not to smuggle opium.

"I'm not against the bond itself, by God!" Ellison said, jumping up to pace *San Seb*'s little bridge. "I'd like nothing better than to see that disgraceful business stopped! But I cannot permit any Briton to sign a bond giving a foreign government power of life and death over him. I offered Lin his twenty thousand chests of opium, but I have nothing to offer him now but a straight refusal. Before I make that refusal, I think it safer to have all the Britons off Jackass Point. They can go to their homes in Macao, and I can go aboard *Volage* in Hong Kong harbor. From there I can haggle with Lin."

"Well," said Charlie. "Blogg and I will be in Macao too. I'll welcome you in my home if you can come."

"You've given up the idea of going to England?"

Charlie shrugged. "For the time being."

Yin-kwa had come to *San Seb* late one night to say that some of Charlie's silver was available, but Charlie had asked him to keep it a while longer. He couldn't, of course, transport the silver to England, and now it was too chancy to exchange it with the traders for notes on their banks in London. The big traders like Carradine and Dent already had more silver than they needed locked up in their storerooms waiting to pay for the tea that was still stored in Canton, and the smaller traders were not to be trusted. Their financial condition was poor, no trade having been done for months, and now, with the haggling over Lin's bond, God alone knew how long it would be before trade was resumed.

"Well," Ellison said gloomily. "If you're going to be in Macao, I'll come and visit you if I can, but I doubt it. There's already quarreling about the bond. The traders who've never touched opium or who are prepared to give it up are anxious to sign and get back to trading. But Carradine and Dent and Innes and some of the others are dead against signing, because they intend to start their smuggling again as soon as possible. It's damned ironical, isn't it? I'm squarely on the side of the traders who're giving up opium, and they're furious with me for not letting them sign the bond, while those damned opium pirates whom I hate are full of praise for me for the same reason!"

He left soon after, still marching erectly, still in full regalia in spite of the heat and the stench. But his uniform was very loose on him now, and he looked ten years older than the man who'd drunk and laughed with them in *San Seb*'s cabin on the night of the abortive typhoon, who'd rushed about with boyish enthusiasm putting the schooner *Lily* back to rights.

"By God, he's in a tight spot, poor devil!" Blogg murmured.

"By God, he is!" said Charlie. "I'm glad to be going home to Macao soon, even if not home to England yet."

Four days later, the last of the opium sludge run off into the sea, the stench fading, the river at last cleared of all its blockages, Blogg cheerfully ordered the untying of the ropes that had moored *San Seb* to Jackass Point for six long months.

But Charlie, watching the dirty, cluttered courtyard recede in the distance, was less cheerful. Jackass Point would forever be associated in his mind with Wei, and Wei had disappeared. No one had seen him since the night he walked out of Howkwa's death chamber and out of the house of many courtyards. Yin-kwa thought he must have gone back to Ningpo, his original home.

"Why?" Charlie had cried. "Why did he leave at all? Why was he so angry with me, when your grandfather wasn't?"

"With Wei it's a different kind of thing," Yin-kwa said slowly. "You betrayed his bondmaster. I did too, but it was worse for you because you're Wei's son-in-law and that makes it the same as though he himself had committed the betrayal."

"That's ridiculous! Why should he hold himself responsible for what I do?"

"You may think it's silly, but it's a Chinese kind of thing, and a *Wei* kind of thing. . . ."

Yes. It was the other side of Wei's coin—an anger as implacable as his love was generous. Ranting at Wei for ridiculous behavior wasn't going to do much to exorcise the devil of guilt that was haunting Charlie.

"But he'll come back," Yin-kwa said consolingly. "He'll remember what you did for my grandfather on Jackass Point. But most of all, he'll come back because if he cuts himself off from you, he'll be cutting himself off from Jin-see, and that he'll never do!"

Thank God for that, Charlie thought, watching Jackass Point

fade out of sight. Sooner or later Wei would come to Macao to see Jin-see, and when he came, Charlie would talk to him, get Ling-ling and Ah Sam to talk to him, convince him that Charlie's sin against How-kwa was not his sin, and that anyway, How-kwa had guessed, had known for a long time, and had forgiven.

The river widened, the water became cleaner, took on a greenish tinge. They sailed through the east channel of Whampoa, past the two frigates, which looked quite small—smaller than big war junks—and almost demure, their broadsides hidden behind blank ports. Blogg dipped *San Seb*'s Union Jack in salute, and both *Volage* and *Hyacinth* dipped theirs in return. Blue-jacketed seamen came to the gunwales of the frigates and stared curiously after *San Seb*.

"Reckon they ain't seen nothing like *San Seb* before." Blogg grinned. "Proper bastards, *lorchas* is."

Charlie looked over his shoulder, smiling, and saw the seamen smile back, and wave. He waved too. It was good to be free again, to see ships other than the three arcs of junks around Jackass Point and the war junks patrolling beyond. They looked good, the frigates. Marvelous to think of the power that their innocent appearance concealed.

But when Charlie turned back to Blogg, Blogg's expression was strangely somber.

"British warships in the Bogue. Well—it ain't you or me or Ellison or Carradine makes history. History makes itself."

They were quiet until Blogg cried, "Look!" and Charlie looked and saw the first of the merchant ships Ellison had spoken of, rocking idly at anchor. The first of more than a hundred of them, an endless line stretching almost to the Bogue, some of them trim and shipshape, but most looking as though their condition had deteriorated daily as the boredom and idleness of their crews increased.

The passing of *San Seb* brought excitement to the merchant ships. Seamen came rushing to the gunwales, waving, shouting questions about was the tea coming out and when.

Charlie and Blogg waved back, but Blogg altered *San Seb*'s course so that they were too far away for the men to hear the words they pretended to shout in response. What answer could they give to the men's questions? It all depended on Lin's bond, and who the devil knew what was going to happen about *that?*

On the second day, they entered the Bay of Canton proper, water deep blue and pure, air fresh and clean, nothing but sparkling space between *San Seb* and the bare, unpopulated hills rising distantly on the shoreline. There was none of the usual bustle of all kinds of craft busily plying their trades. The suspension of trade at Canton and the blockage of Whampoa had affected everyone who made his living on the bay. Everyone had suffered. They'd be back soon now, all the craft, big and small, but in the meantime the peaceful emptiness of the bay was beautiful.

"Hoy!"

Charlie looked up to see Blogg's mate pointing excitedly. The great, calm, blue emptiness had been invaded by a large junk sailing toward them.

"From Macao," Blogg said. "Things be getting back to normal!"

Full of excitement, *San Seb*'s crew and the crew of the junk rushed to the scuppers of their craft to shout a conversation, Blogg's mate leaning so far out that he almost fell into the water. Blogg smiled, watching his mate struggle to recover his balance. "Latest news from Macao must be int'resting!"

The words suddenly brought Ling-ling very close to Charlie. Jackass Point had always been a womanless place, a place of men concentrated on the making of money, a place in which sexuality was in suspension. Now, Charlie was suffused with the thought of Ling-ling. He squinted over the water, his eyes turned inward to the image of his lovely wife. His thoughts hummed around her like bees around nectar, his body tingled, his blood sang and leaped and tumbled, his fingers almost feeling the touch of her satin skin, her soft roundnesses, her secret places. . . .

"Charlie?" Blogg spoke hesitantly. The junk had passed out

of sight and *San Seb* had settled down again, the crew back to their duties, the mate having stopped to speak to Blogg on his way to the bridge.

Charlie turned lazily. "Mmmmm?"

"Mate's saying that the crew's saying that Wei was right to turn you off."

"What?" Charlie sat up abruptly. "How the devil do they know anything about that?"

Blogg shrugged. "They hear most things, one way or t'other."

"That they do, by God!" Charlie sat back angrily. "Well, they can say what they bloody well like! It is *ridiculous* for Wei to hold himself responsible for what I do. We'll get that settled as soon as Wei comes to Macao."

"Maybe."

"There's no maybe about it! I'll settle it with him when he comes, and you said yourself he must come!"

"Aye."

Charlie threw Blogg an irritated glance. What the hell was wrong with him? But Blogg was gazing calmly out to sea, eyes squinted.

When at last, on the third day, the white house at the end of the Praya came into sight, Charlie snatched up the spyglass.

"Can't see anyone about! Well, they don't expect us, of course. They couldn't have had any news from Canton yet. We were first off, weren't we?"

"Nay. Carradine was couple hours afore us off to England in *Falcon*."

"To make sure Palmerston pays that indemnity!" Charlie laughed.

"Aye."

"He left Andrew in Canton?"

"Aye."

Why the hell was Blogg so taciturn? But whatever was wrong with Blogg could wait. . . . Charlie turned eagerly to peer again

210

through the spyglass. But it was no use. They didn't expect *San Seb* and they wouldn't be on the jetty, they'd be indoors, sheltering from the sun. It was nap time, and the house would be cool and quiet and dim, blinds drawn, but what a furor there'd be when they realized he'd come home! He'd bang on the door and one of the amahs would come to open it, clattering in those awful noisy wooden clogs that they all, even Lingling, loved to wear—tiny Ah Sam was the only one whose clogs didn't make a racket, just a small, steady clack-clack. And then all the shouting and the welcoming and the embracing and the rejoicing and at last, at last, they'd leave him alone with Lingling in the cool, white bedroom. . . . Charlie drew a deep breath, his heartbeat quickening.

When *San Seb* nudged the jetty, Charlie leaped off, leaving Blogg to see her moored, ran across the beach to the house, and banged loudly on the door. Coming along the corridor inside, he heard, not the clatter of an amah's clogs, but Ah Sam's small, steady clack-clack. She opened the door. He picked her up and swung her around, set her down and bent, laughing, to look into her face.

"Did you think we were never coming back?"

Without a word, she turned and walked away from him into the dark parlor, the clogs clacking. Except for that small noise, the house was silent. There was a musty smell that, more than the silence, more than her withdrawal, triggered alarm in a hot flood through his veins. He followed her quickly.

"Ah Sam, what the hell is wrong?"

She faced him, her eyes glimmering in the dark.

"They gone."

"Who's gone?"

"All. Ling-ling. Jin-see. Little Sisters."

He stared at her as though she spoke some unknown language. "What d'you mean?"

"They go Ningpo with Wei."

The words struck him like a bolt of lightning. His tongue froze and his throat clogged. Stunned into immobility, he stood, staring at the white shimmer of her face. She pushed him back onto the dusty-smelling sofa and stood before him, words tumbling from her lips.

Wei had come two months ago, she said. He had told them of How-kwa's death, and of the circumstances surrounding his own repudiation of Charlie. But Wei had repented of that repudiation, because during the long voyage from Canton to Macao through the creeks of the delta, he had had time to remember that Charlie had saved How-kwa from death on the cobbles of Jackass Point. Because of that, he had concluded, he must forgive Charlie. He would go to Ningpo to rest and calm himself and compose his mind, and in two or three months' time he would come back to Macao and make his peace with Charlie.

Ah Sam's voice faltered, hoarsened.

"Ling-ling very glad when he say he forgive you, but she say more better he wait for you in Macao. If he go Ningpo first, come back two-three month, maybe you and her and chilluns awreddy go Inglan'."

His skin prickled.

"She told him that?"

"You say *you* tell him!"

"But I never got the chance to! Anyway, we're not going now! We can't go!"

There was a despairing note in her whispered answer.

"How she know, Chahlee? She think you awreddy tell him, so she tell him too. He angry like he *die* from angry. He say she go Inglan' he finis' her. No more father. And no more son. He take Jin-see away."

"God rot it!" He leaped, roaring, to his feet, sending a small table crashing. "Are you telling me she went with him because he threatened to take Jin-see? Ah Sam, how could you let her go?"

She yelled back at him, standing her ground.

"How I stop her? She don't want go! She *cry!* But Wei take Jin-see, she must go too, and Little Sisters, and *how I stop?*"

"Charlie!" Blogg stood in the dark doorway, eyes white in the blur of his hair and beard. "They gone with Wei?"

Charlie swung on him. "By God, did you know it? Did that mucking crew of yours know it too?"

"Aye." Blogg squeezed his eyes shut in an agonized grimace. "Crew of that junk we met in the bay shouted it over."

"Why the devil didn't you tell me?"

"Reckoned there'd be no need to tell you if it wasn't true."

"Damn you, Blogg, I'm not a *child!*" He glared furiously for a moment, eyes glittering in the darkness. Then: "Well, to the devil with that. Come on, now!"

He rushed for the door, but Blogg grabbed his arm.

"Where you going?"

"Ningpo, of course! *Come on!*"

"And how do we get into the city? Barbarians ain't allowed in Chinese cities."

"Oh, *come on,* Blogg! We'll get in somehow! I got into Canton, by God!"

Ah Sam said stonily: "*Wei* take you Canton. You think he take you Ningpo?"

Charlie swung on her furiously.

"Whose side are you on?"

"I wait you, Chahlee," she said quietly. "I sit this house two months by self, wait you."

There was a stinging silence. She went to the window, clogs clacking, and flung open the shutters. Light flooded the room, setting a million dust specks dancing, emphasizing that lonely wait.

With a groan, Charlie fell back onto the sofa, buried his face in his hands.

"There must be a way! There's *got to be* a way of getting into that city!"

"You're not thinking straight, Charlie." Blogg's deep voice was gentle. "We hasten off to Ningpo, and what then? Shout for Ling-ling over the city walls? Break through the gates and get thrown in prison, maybe get our heads chopped off? What good would you be to Ling-ling in prison, or without a head? Calm down, Charlie! Only thing's to get Yin-kwa to send a man to Ningpo—"

"*No!*" Charlie wrenched away from Blogg. "That'll take too bloody long! I'm going *now!*"

Blogg got quietly to his feet.

"Then you'll have to get yourself another captain. You know right well, Charlie, I'd do anything that's *good* for you, but I won't help you harm yourself, and that's what you'd be doing rushing off to Ningpo, crazy-mad with anger. Don't you see, that's the best way of *losing* them forever?"

"Damn you, Blogg! Are you telling me to sit here and twid-dle my thumbs while that bloody scoundrel—"

"Chahlee!" Ah Sam cried sharply. "No use you bloody this, bloody that. Blogg *right*. You must wait here, ask Yin-kwa send somebody Ningpo—"

"God rot the two of you!"

He ran headlong from the room and across the garden, leaped the plank onto *San Seb*, shouting for the mate. No one answered. He searched the ship, rushing from deck to deck, above, below, forward, aft, the holds even, shouting at the top of his lungs, but *San Seb* was empty of people.

Lungs bursting, anger burning like fire in his veins, he leaped back onto the jetty. Blogg was standing quietly on the seawall.

"They'll be back sometime," he called. "They went because they was afeared you'd want to do just what you're wanting to do—rush off to Ningpo."

He jumped off the wall and started walking down the Praya toward the town. As an afterthought, he called over his shoul-der.

"I'm going to my house on Kolo-an. You can find me there, if you want."

Charlie watched him go. God, what was happening? Ling-ling gone. The children gone. And now Blogg. It wasn't pos-sible! It wasn't true! The white heat of his fury turned into ice. The blood drained dizzily from his head. Fear twisted in his vitals like a cruel, giant fist. He walked shakily back to the house, into the parlor, came to rest against the windowsill, looking out at empty *San Seb* standing at the empty jetty. He could almost see them there on the jetty—Ling-ling and Jin-see, standing together, hands solemnly raised, in a pool of light from that stray sunbeam. It was incredible that they were hundreds of miles away. It was incredible that for all his fierce longing, he couldn't stride over the water, leap the mountains, fly through the air, to snatch them back from that bloody Wei. . . .

He hardly knew it when Ah Sam took his hand and led him up the stairs to the bedroom. He stared down at the bed, vast and lonely, inimical in its smooth, untouched whiteness. With Ling-ling in it, it was always rumpled, pillows strewn all over as she scrabbled like a small, vibrant animal to make a soft night-nest, black hair streaming, bright eyes peeping. He flung himself down on the bed, his body in uproar. Sweet, fragrant Ling-ling! Satin skin over swelling softness! "Love you, Chah-lee!" Sometimes uttered solemnly, eyes deep and shining. Sometimes whispered between kisses. Sometimes gasped out as she panted under him, arms and legs clutching. God, how could she have left him? That damned, vengeful Wei! That bloody Wei!

Impelled by demons, he leaped up and strode to the window to stare out again at the deserted beach. It was dark now, nothing to be seen but the rippling phosphorescence of the surf, yet it seemed still that the jetty was bright with sunlight, that she stood there, beside her son, hand raised. "I love you," he called to her luminous ghost. "I love you *serious!*" But there was no answer—only silence and stillness, an aching silence, a numbing stillness. He swung away to pace the room and at last to fling himself back upon the bed, devils of fury pounding within him.

When a hand touched his shoulder his heart leaped wildly, but it was only Ah Sam, a candle in her hand, the plume of flickering light making deep shadows of her eyes, limning the wrinkles at the corners of her lips. She laid the candle on the bedside table and held out a steaming cup. When he shook

215

his head, she put it to his lips. Willy-nilly, he sipped and drew back, grimacing at the bitter taste. But in a moment the inside of his mouth turned wonderfully sweet. He took the cup and sipped again. She nodded.

"Good. Drink all. Chinee herb, make your blood cool."

When he had finished, she perched on the bed beside him.

"Now Chahlee, *I* talk, you hear—hear and unnerstan'." Her head was cocked to one side, her eyes wide and stern. "Why you want go Inglan'? For make your father angry?"

He started up to protest, but she pushed him back.

"I tell you before—son no can punish father! But you *want* punish father, you *want* make he angry, so you make everybody here misery!" She stared accusingly into his eyes. "You tell Ling-ling, if she not go with you, you leave her."

"I didn't say that!" he shouted.

"But you make her think that!" she shouted back. "She think if she stay Macao and you go Inglan', same like fish go in sea. You *gone*. You *no more*. She so frightened that she say all right, she go with you, even she know how angry her father will be. *You* don't know, Chahlee. You say, so easy, 'I explain to Wei.' But you no idea how Wei will feel!"

He stared at her, his throat drying. All of them, even Blogg, had tried to tell him how Wei would feel, but he hadn't listened. He'd brushed it off. It was true—he'd had no idea.

Ah Sam nodded with grim satisfaction as she saw that her meaning had penetrated.

"So, you unnerstan', Chahlee? You pull Ling-ling go Inglan', leave Wei behind. Wei pull Ling-ling go Ningpo, leave you behind. You angry Wei. He angry you. He do something you think bad. You do something he think bad. And Ling-ling in middle, pull this way, that way."

"I'd have brought them back," he flared. "Just two years, and then I'd have brought them back!"

"You *say*." She raised her eyebrows. "But how Wei know? How *you* know? Chahlee, you here many year, but you not Chinee. You not like amah talking loud. You not like clack-clack wood shoe. You not like people give Jin-see everything he want. . . . But this is Chinee way of living. . . . In Chinee house, everybody talk, everybody make noise, everybody spoil eldest son. Jin-see is like Yin-kwa—son and grandson. When he big, Jin-see will be number one, take care all fambly, make kowtow for Wei, make sons for fambly go on. When he big, Jin-see life will be very important, very hard. So when he small, everybody spoil him, make his life good. But you not like this Chinee way. Maybe you go Inglan', you remember Inglis way living, maybe you never come back. I know this. Wei know this too."

After a moment, he said grimly: "If you knew all that, why did you arrange for me to marry Ling-ling?"

Great tears started suddenly from her eyes—the first he had ever seen her shed. She said slowly, straining her voice to calm:

"You know why. Because I love you, I want stay with you, I want fambly. Now, this happen. But when I go How-kwa, ask him you marry Ling-ling, I think everything good."

His heart lurched. She had been deprived too. She had watched the family she'd contrived for herself leave her, and then she'd closed the house and sat alone, waiting for him. He reached for her hand, but she withdrew it, impatiently flicked away the tears.

"Maskee . . . I want you unnerstan' why Wei so angry you. Chinee fambly is *everybody*—dead people, people living now, people not born yet. Everybody. If you take away Jin-see, Wei fambly broken. Who make kowtow for Wei when he die? Who make sons for fambly go on?"

He was silent, and again she nodded with satisfaction.

"So Chahlee, you and Wei very angry now, but after, when he forgive you, you must forgive him too."

He snorted. "Forgive that bloody kidnapper?"

"Yes," she said patiently. "When he come back, he forgive you, you forgive him."

"He's not coming back!"

"Yes, he come back. What he can do? He old man now, no money, no work. How he keep them? He must bring them back. Maybe long time, but he come back. Yin-kwa send

217

somebody find him. Ling-ling talk him come back. He love her, he no like she sorrow. He love you too."

"He *hates* me!"

"No. He angry you, but he love you."

Her voice was blurry. Behind her head, the ceiling seemed to ripple. What the devil was in that drink she'd given him?

"Sleep now, Chahlee," she said softly.

The ceiling was no longer white—it was cobbled, like Jack-ass Point. Ling-ling ran across it and threw herself into his arms, but he laughed and she fled and Wei took her place, his arms enveloping Jin-see, his head swelling bigger and bigger, eyes glaring and malevolent. But Ling-ling blocked his eyes out, tiptoeing back across the ceiling, smiling, starry, whispering, "Love you, Chahlee!" He reached for her, heart jumping wildly, but she faded away, and when he leaped to follow her, Ah Sam pushed him back, and sleep felled him like a thunder-bolt.

For a long time he seemed to be floating, half submerged, in a dove-gray place in which time had no meaning, a place so remote that he need not be concerned about anything. Ah Sam came and fed him and he ate and drank. She spoke to him and he listened and forgot what she had said. Once it seemed that *San Seb*'s mate was there, bowing respect-fully, and Ah Sam said that he was apologizing for not having been there the night Charlie wanted to go to Ningpo. He was very sorry. Like hell, thought Charlie, but the thought slipped away before it reached his tongue.

And then one day he woke to the first silver light of dawn, and Ah Sam was shaking his arm and trying to put something in his hand. A thin, white oblong. An envelope.

"Chahlee, I send *San Seb* to Canton, tell Yin-kwa about Wei. Yin-kwa write you letter. Chahlee! Chahlee! You hear me, Chahlee?"

"Yes," he said, and took the letter, and all at once was back in the real world, the world in which Wei had come and taken away his wife and children. The blow that struck his heart was like the hammer of doom.

"Open letter!" Ah Sam urged, and like an automaton he slit it open.

There was a single sheet of paper, covered in Yin-kwa's fine hand.

"I am immediately sending a man to Ningpo, an old servant whom Wei knows well, to find him and persuade him to return to Macao with Ling-ling and the children. I will write as soon as there is news. Stay where you are, Charlie. Be available, so I can reach you quickly. You will do no good by trying to reach them yourself in Ningpo. Keep calm. Wei will eventually bring them back to you. He'll have to. He can do nothing else."

"See?" Ah Sam said briskly—the mate must have told her what was in the letter. "Yin-kwa say too, Wei must come back. S'pose you go Ningpo, Chahlee, and same time Wei come here? You miss he, he miss you! Crazy! You must wait, Chahlee!"

Smiling, she handed him a cup of tea.

"How long have I been asleep?" he muttered.

"Few day."

"How many days?"

"Nine, ten."

Nine or ten days, during which she'd let him sleep, given him more of her devilish brew to *make* him sleep, while *San Seb* sailed to Canton and back.

"Where's Blogg?"

"He say he go Kolo-an."

"He didn't come back?"

"No."

He pushed the teacup aside and rose and went out into what used to be the pretty garden, patchy now, the sand creeping back. He sat on the top step of the verandah and stared across the Praya. *San Seb* was at the jetty, the crew scrambling all over the ship, hanging by ropes from the gunwales, cleaning her, scraping her, oiling her. The mate, in the bow, turned and gave him a hopeful smile. Charlie pretended not to see him. But he'd been right, that night, to absent himself and the crew from *San Seb*. They were all right—Yin-kwa and Ah Sam and

219

Blogg. There was nothing to do but wait and let Yin-kwa's man persuade Wei to return—when and if Wei would.

"Macao like boiling water!" Ah Sam said.

She had just returned from marketing in the town and had come, as usual, bringing the bottle of rum, to sit with Charlie in the shade of a scrubby little tree and give him the news of the day. There was always news. Macao was full to bursting. The British traders, who usually filtered into Macao in the tea off-season, had all come together this year in response to Ellison's order that they must leave Jackass Point without signing Lin's bond.

Everyone knew about the bond, of course. The high commissioner had made his presence felt all around the South China Sea, even in Macao, where the Portuguese governor, Don Adraio Accacio da Silveira Pinto, was reminded by a formal visit from Lin himself that the Portuguese held the city not as a possession but at the grace of China.

And everyone was discussing the bond. Ah Sam said that this year the British presence in Macao was not the usual pleasant holiday, with the British giving parties and dances and Macao merchants reaping a profitable harvest from their activities. This year, Ah Sam said, the British were standing around in the *praças*, arguing and quarreling, drinking heavily in the grogshops, betting more than they could afford at the race course and in the Chinese gambling dens.

Today, when Charlie only grunted at her news, Ah Sam was silent for a while, then:

"Chahlee, you like go Kolo-an, see Blogg?"

"No." Blogg had left him, let Blogg come back. Feeling a little ashamed, he added: "I want to be alone."

She said: "Chahlee, more better you live easy. No use so nervous. . . ." She pointed at the young girl she had hired to help with the cooking and the laundry. "You like she go your bed?"

"*What?*" He turned to glare at her. "Are you crazy, Ah Sam?"

220

"Why crazy? When you in Canton six month, Ling-ling worry 'cause no girl on Jackass Point."

"Oh God!"

He jumped to his feet and walked to the edge of the water. The day had darkened with that ominous darkness that bespoke a typhoon, a darkness that seemed to glow with anger from within itself. A rising wind muttered the first few notes of a typhoon's terrifying howl, then sank down again, to lie in wait.

"August," Ah Sam said. She had come to stand beside him. "Typhoon time soon."

Charlie didn't answer. In his soul a typhoon was already blowing, darkness growing darker, the great wind howling. By God, if Wei didn't come soon . . .

He watched the sea. The days passed and he sat under the scrubby tree, or on the top step of the verandah, or on the Praya wall, and watched for the junk that would bring Wei and Ling-ling and the children. Sometimes he thought of the beach peopled as it had been, children screeching delightedly, amahs chattering, Ah Sam and laughing Ling-ling sitting under umbrellas. Sometimes he whispered to that lovely, laughing image, "I love you *serious*," and stared unbelievingly when it didn't turn and whisper back, "Love you, Chahlee!" Sometimes he thought of Blogg on Kolo-an in the lonely little house, and thought that he should go to Blogg, but some ambiguity kept him where he was, for it was more important than anything else to sit and stare out to sea and wait for the junk that would finally bring them back.

And one morning, toward the end of August, he did see strange sails rising over the horizon. Not dirty, patched junk sails, but very clean white sails that shone in the sun, shaped like no other sails in these waters.

Volage!

Excitedly, he watched as the frigate neared. She was small, clean-lined, very smart, picking her way daintily in the long swells, sails billowing uniformly as though the breeze itself were forbidden to hurry her. Twenty-eight guns, but she looked harmless, her gun ports discreetly blank.

Charlie hurried down to the jetty. *Volage* was sailing past, making for the other end of the Praya, where the official Portuguese government pier was. Charlie followed, keeping abreast of her as her sails were reefed and she slowed.

A crowd stood around the pier, but the pier itself was empty, guarded by Portuguese militia. *Volage* slid in gently and was warped to a berth. Charlie, craning, saw Ellison in full dress uniform appear on deck, followed by his secretaries. *Volage's* ladder was lowered, and he came down. The captain of the militia stepped forward to greet him. They exchanged salutes while the men formed a guard of honor. Then, to a gay blast of trumpets, they all paraded across the Praya to the governor's mansion.

As they disappeared indoors, a hum arose in the watching crowd—mostly men, mostly Britons, milling about, questioning, speculating. The few women present gathered together, whispering to each other, smiling, calling out to admonish children who, quickly bored, were starting to play noisily. They were glad of anything that broke the dreariness, Charlie thought; of anything that might give their husbands something to think about other than that damned bond. By God, things were a mess when the snobbish English wives allowed themselves to look eager and hopeful instead of haughty!

It wasn't long before Ellison reappeared with the Portuguese governor, he too in full uniform. They stood together in the doorway, Ellison stiff and formal, the governor talking, shrugging apologetically. In a moment, Ellison stepped back and saluted, then turned smartly on his heel and marched toward the building a hundred yards away, once shining with importance, now shabby, that housed the much diminished Honorable East India Company and was still the meeting place for Britons in Macao. The crowd followed eagerly. By the time Charlie squeezed in the door of the meeting room, Ellison was already speaking.

". . . bad news. His excellency the governor sent a message asking me to call on him. He wished to inform me that he has heard a rumor that High Commissioner Lin is planning to raid Macao, with the purpose of arresting Britons." Ellison raised a hand to hush the mutters that arose. "Whether or not that rumor is true, I cannot risk having all of you here. If Lin should kidnap even one Briton to hold hostage against the signature of his bond, we would all be in an impossible position. So I'm afraid I must ask you all to move out of Macao."

Cries of dismay rose all over the room. Ellison, face impassive, raised his voice to shout them down.

"I am very sorry, but there is no alternative. Those of you who are not prepared to return to England will have to move aboard the merchant vessels that are now gathered in Hong Kong harbor. . . ."

A roar of protest drowned him out. He waited a moment, almost lost in the turbulence, then climbed up on a table and began to bellow, his voice gradually gaining over the crowd's.

". . . useless to complain! If you don't do as I ask, the governor will find some way of ousting you. He does not want us here, and I can't blame him, with the high commissioner breathing down his neck. Listen! Please *listen!* It will not be too uncomfortable on the ships. I've taken a census. There are fifty-seven British families to be accommodated—assuming that none of you will return to England—and there are thirty-eight ships in Hong Kong harbor. Quarters may be a little cramped, but there'll be enough space for all. I will organize committees to allot quarters, arrange for food and water and so on. I regret this very much, but I've no alternative."

Someone yelled hoarsely: "I'll sign that damned bond, and devil take you, Ellison, *that's* the alternative!"

Yells of "Me too!" rose all round, countered by yells of "Never!" and "For shame!" Men began to shove each other, cursing. A dozen scuffles broke out. In the mounting turmoil, Ellison stamped for quiet, raised his voice to a roar.

"*Think,* you fools! There're thirty thousand chests of opium in Calcutta and Bombay! Anyone might get hold of some and smuggle it in. Who's to guarantee that the high commissioner won't decide that it was *you* who did it? Or *you?* Or *you?"* He stabbed a finger at furious, upturned faces. "Could you prove that it wasn't you? Don't you understand, if you sign that bond, Lin will need nothing else to order your head chopped off. You'll have signed your *life* away!"

Silence fell, sudden and sullen. Men glanced covertly at each other, shuffled their feet. Ellison lowered his voice, which had become raw, and spoke persuasively:

"We'll have to stick together. There's nothing for it but that. We're *British,* after all. I know you'll all rally. . . . Now, I'll leave my secretaries to make the arrangements."

He jumped off the table quickly and pushed through the crowd. His strained eyes brightened when he sighted Charlie, and he caught his arm and drew him outdoors.

From close up, it was clear that Ellison had lost a great deal of weight. His uniform hung from his shoulders. His face was gaunt, the frown between his eyes as though hewn by a knife. His grip on Charlie's arm was convulsive.

"God, I thought they'd tear me apart! That was a rotten thing to have to do to them, but there really is no alternative! I don't believe the governor heard any such rumor about Lin's invading Macao to arrest Britons, but what the devil could I do but agree when he asked me to withdraw all the Britons? It's *his* territory!"

He had been walking fast across the Praya toward *Volage,* drawing Charlie along, but now he suddenly stopped, smiling apologetically, the smile almost more painful to see than the frown.

"I'm sorry, Charlie! Never even asked how you are! Where's Blogg?" But he didn't wait for an answer. "I'm afraid that order applies to you and Blogg too. Lin had hold of you once already, Charlie, and I certainly can't let him get hold of you again! You'll leave?"

"Yes!" Charlie said on a sudden flood of excitement. By God, anything would be better than sitting in his garden watching the sea! But Ellison was regarding him anxiously.

"It'll be worse for you than for the others, because I suppose you'll want to leave your family here in Macao. There'd be no objection, of course, since they're Chinese—"

"Yes, they'll stay here," Charlie said hastily, glad to avoid the necessity of making explanations to Ellison. "And—I don't think Blogg will go to Hong Kong either. He's not in Macao now, he's on Kolo-an Island nearby—he has a little house there. . . ."

He hesitated. *San Seb* would have to be left with Ah Sam, so she could send a message in case Wei should return. . . . Again Ellison bridged the gap.

"If you want to leave *San Seb* with your family, Charlie, you're welcome to come aboard *Volage.*"

Charlie breathed a heartfelt "Thank you!"

"Not at all!" Ellison had brightened. "I'll be damned glad to have you! Harry Smith's company isn't amusing at the best of times, and now he's positively noxious with the prospect of playing guardian to fifty-seven trader families! Can you be ready to sail about midnight, Charlie?"

"I'll be ready!"

Charlie waved and turned to hurry back to the white house. He felt alive again. His blood was flowing again. Anything was preferable to that awful waiting! The sound of his heels on the cobblestones, followed an instant later by the tap of his toes, made a double clop-clip, clop-clip that echoed his excitement at the prospect of action, even such little action as packing some clothes and walking back to board *Volage* with Ellison.

The crowds thinned as he left the town behind. Quickly darkness fell. While he was still a good way off, lamplight appeared in a window of the white house. He thought he saw a shadow crisscrossing it. As he neared, he saw he was right: The lighted window was that of his bedroom, and the shadow was that of Ah Sam, moving about.

He ran up the stairs. She had been packing clothes into his valise; as he entered the room, she snapped it shut and turned to face him.

"You go Hong Kong." A statement, not a question.

"How did you know?" he cried.

"In Macao, everybody know everything. All right, Chahlee. You go. I wait you here."

Again. For the second time in a few months she'd sit in the empty white house and wait. He said:

"I'm sorry, Ah Sam."

She shrugged.

"Don't stay alone, Ah Sam. Keep that girl on—she'll be company. I'll leave you plenty of silver."

She nodded.

"I'll be on *Volage* in Hong Kong harbor." He spoke loudly and quickly to make up for her silence. "I'll leave *San Seb* here. If Wei comes back, or Yin-kwa writes, or anything at all happens, you'll send the mate to Hong Kong with a message."

She nodded.

He said, a little desperately, "I think, in any case, you'd better send *San Seb* to Hong Kong every ten days, so I'll be sure things are all right here, and I can send you a message if I need to. And . . . perhaps you'd better send *San Seb* to Kolo-an, to let Blogg know what's happening. Maybe he'd like to go to Hong Kong too."

She said, "Blogg go if you ask he, not if I send *San Seb.*"

"To hell with it, then!" he cried, anger rankling. Blogg had left him, not he Blogg! Let Blogg sulk on Kolo-an if that's what he wanted! He picked up the valise she had packed.

"I've got to be back to *Volage* by midnight."

Turning to say goodbye to her, he was suddenly struck dumb and motionless. She was so tiny. She looked so lonely and sad, and yet so strong and brave. A jumble of feelings flooded up to his tongue, but no words would come.

She smiled gently. "Maskee, Chahlee . . . you and me, long time good joss. Now, bad-joss time come." She shrugged, raising her shoulders and her hands and her eyebrows and the corners of her lips, in a single all-embracing gesture. "What we can do? Nothing! Only make like in typhoon—shut door, shut window, cover head, wait till finish." She stood on tiptoe and touched her lips to his cheek. "You my fambly, Chahlee. Ling-ling too, and Jin-see, and Little Sisters. But you, I love. Go Hong Kong. No worry. I take care here."

She went to the door and turned back, smiling, her eyes shining with the vital essence of her resilience. A trick of the light made her seem young again, as young as the first time he'd seen her in that blood-red bedroom. He smiled back, and they stood a moment, affection, like a velvet band, holding them close. Then her head jerked around—someone was banging on the front door.

"Who come so late?"

She clattered down the stairs and reappeared moments later, an envelope in her hand.

"From Yin-kwa."

Heart thudding, he tore it open. Yin-kwa's hand covered two pages.

The man he had sent to Ningpo had found Wei at his brother's house, but Wei had denied him entrance, had consented only to talk to him a few minutes on the street outside the house. Wei had repeated his repudiation of Charlie, but would say nothing more. Later, Yin-kwa's man had queried the neighbors, and they had confirmed that Wei had arrived at the house with a young woman and three children, and that they were still there.

"So at least we know where they are," Yin-kwa wrote, "and that they are safe. Unfortunately, Wei hasn't yet recovered his common sense, but he cannot hide Ling-ling and the children forever. Eventually, he'll have to do something, and unless I'm much mistaken, or something unforeseen happens, that something will be to take them back to Macao."

"What Yin-kwa say?" Ah Sam asked.

He told her, folding the letter—and noticed that there was more writing on the back of one of the sheets, a scribble quite unlike Yin-kwa's normal neat hand.

"I don't like to say this, Charlie, but I think I should. I believe the reason Wei is being so cautious, the reason he is hiding your children so carefully, is that the mood of the country is violently anti-foreign, and your children all show clearly that they have foreign blood."

Oh God!

He looked up blindly, a vacuum suddenly mushrooming in his body as the normal courses of life rushed out of it.

"*What?*" Ah Sam whispered.

He had to swallow before he could answer.

"Yin-kwa says Jin-see and Little Sisters look like foreign children, so Wei must hide them in case . . . in case . . ." He could not bring himself to the words, not even to the thought. In case *what*, by God!

She was nodding slowly. All at once she looked old again, not with age, though her wrinkles stood out clearly, but with a kind of age-old awareness, a fatalistic foreknowing. She reached out her tiny hand and laid it against his cheek.

"Not worry, Chahlee. Wei will take care. . . ." Then, very low: "True. Now bad-joss time come. . . ."

She left him then, the clatter of her clogs echoing in the dark house, a small and lonely sound.

It was a beautiful harbor, a stretch of sparkling blue water lying between the barren island of Hong Kong with its crown of mountain and the low coastal plain of the mainland, where the village of Kowloon crowded to the water's edge and spread back into the dimpling hills.

But the harbor's beauty was maimed by the shabby mass of ships of all shapes, sizes, and conditions from trim to filthy that straggled untidily between *Volage* at the northern end of the harbor, where it narrowed into the pass called Lyemoon, and *Hyacinth* at the southern end, where it broke into a dotted mass of islands. A crosshatch of masts and reefed sails obscured the sky, tallest among them the raked masts of *Sylph*, flying the "owner aboard" flag for Andrew—Carradine was still in England with *Falcon*. The blue water was tainted by great brown splotches of effluent washing about just

228

below the surface, and pimpled by the constant oarbeat of cutters, gigs, dinghies, sampans, junks, bumboats. The air hummed and swelled with sounds carried on the water—the creakings and groanings of the ships themselves, and the human noises, shouts and yells and guffaws and voices raised in anger.

In the month that had passed since the fifty-seven families from Macao moved onto the merchant ships, chaos had resolved itself into mere muddle. Ellison's committees worked hard, satisfied no one, resigned, and were reconstituted time after time. But at least they had arranged a constant supply of food and water for the floating colony from the village of Kowloon. The villagers were fiercely anti-foreign, but Ellison's committees managed, by paying without question the fabulous prices demanded, to maintain the daily flow of bumboats full of vegetables and barrels of fresh water. The traders, among whom the exorbitant charges were prorated, complained and protested—the poorer ones cried out in agony—but there was no help for it, the committees insisted. Since the villagers charged even more for water than for food, some of the men from the ships had gone ashore on the island to search for water, but had found none. Then they had tried to help themselves from the wells around Kowloon, and the villagers had promptly threatened to poison the wells. Ellison had had to constitute a force of bluejackets from *Volage* and *Hyacinth* to patrol the harbor and prevent forays ashore by the traders. Captain Smith had been forced to agree to the use of his sailors for such a purpose, but that had increased his bitterness in his new role as guardian of God-rotted merchants and their families.

"If only the *wives* wouldn't insist on coming aboard *Volage* to see me personally!" Ellison lamented. He and Charlie were in canvas chairs on *Volage*'s quarterdeck, sipping rum, undiluted to conserve water. Almost every evening they sat thus in the long dusk after supper, after Captain Smith had grumpily taken himself off to his quarters, Ellison talking nervously of trivia, as though stirring up froth on the surface of his mind would keep more serious worries submerged. Now he went on almost petulantly.

"It's unbelievable, the complaints those women can find to screech about! The cost of food and water, the discomfort of their quarters, even their quarrels! Today one of them wanted me to shift her and her family to another ship because, she raged, she could no longer abide 'that common, coarse woman who's no better than she should be!' Ten minutes later the 'common, coarse woman' presented *herself*—couldn't *she* be shifted to another ship? That hoity-toity madam, cold as a fish, thinking herself so grand, and her poor husband only too glad to get a bit of warmth where he could find it! You wouldn't believe the rubbish they come to me about!"

He took a gulp and wiped his mouth on the back of his hand. His gaunt face was both pale and sunburned, disfigured by bits of reddened skin flaking off to reveal patches of pasty white. Lines of worry furrowed deeply between his eyes and from his nose to the corners of his tight-lipped mouth.

"Don't see the women," Charlie said. "Refer them to your committees."

"I can't!" Ellison groaned. "It's all *my* fault, you see. *I* won't let their husbands sign that damned bond. Bad as the wives are, it's even worse when the men come to urge me to let them sign the bond, some of them with tears in their eyes, on their last legs, facing ruination. By God, its almost more than a man can bear!"

Tears were close to Ellison's eyes, and Charlie looked away compassionately. If only Ellison's feelings weren't quite so delicate! From a nearby ship came a sudden burst of furious shouting, a high-pitched scream. Ellison groaned again.

"Murder'll be done yet, if this goes on!"

"How long can it last, George? You'll have to hear soon, either from Palmerston or Lin!"

"From Lin I've heard nothing at all, and from Palmerston nothing since that dispatch last August. . . . Did I think the time opportune for him to present a bill to Parliament for six million dollars to pay for destroying our own traders' opium? Or did I think Parliament should be asked to vote funds for a British force to patrol Chinese waters to prevent the Chinese from buying what they clearly wish to buy? He has a sarcastic pen, does Palmerston! The only useful thing he said in that dispatch was that Carradine was expected in London shortly, and he would wait to consult him before sending me new orders."

"Lin has let the Americans sign the bond *without* the death clause. Have you written that to Palmerston?"

"Yes, but it doesn't affect the British. The American trade in Persian and Turkish opium was comparatively small, and when Caleb King guaranteed to see that they'd drop it, Lin was safe in accepting. Can I guarantee that the British will drop the opium trade?" He made a bitter sound between a laugh and a snort.

"Sir." One of *Volage*'s officers stood at his elbow. "This just arrived for you, sir."

He held out a little roll of yellow silk furled around an ivory stick.

Ellison sat bolt upright, his eyes almost starting from his head as he stared at it.

"At last!" He looked across at Charlie, his lips twitching with tension, and then up at the officer.

"Will you take that across to *Sylph* immediately, to Carradine's translator? The translation's to be brought back to me as soon as it's done. And will you pass the word to all the ships that there'll be a meeting on *Sylph* at eight bells tomorrow morning? All the traders to be present."

"Yes, sir." The officer saluted and marched away.

Ellison got slowly to his feet and stood looking out over the darkening water. His face was gray, the sunburned patches standing out like sores.

"God!" The word was a prayer, not a blasphemy. "God, let this be the end of it!"

* * *

The crush of small boats around *Sylph*'s ladder was so great that men, too impatient to wait for each boat to discharge its passengers and back away, leaped wildly from boat to boat, and so to *Sylph*'s platform, to push and shove their way up the bouncing ladder. The main cabin was crammed to overflowing, the atmosphere thick with emanations from dozens of overheated, unwashed bodies. The roar of voices was deafening. Charlie tucked himself in beside the door—by the time he had risen that morning, Ellison had long since left *Volage* for *Sylph*, and he had had to hail a sampan to get himself rowed over. Now he stood quietly, knowing no more about what was in Lin's little yellow banner than anybody else. Speculation was flowing like water from an overfull pot. Lin had withdrawn his bond. Lin would let the British sign without the death clause, as he had let the Americans. The Emperor was angry with Lin for having delayed the tea trade and disgraced him. Lin had been led off in chains like the viceroy, and some new official had come. . . . All of it was optimistic. No one voiced fears, but Charlie, looking around, saw many drawn and haggard faces. Except for Carradine and Dent and Innes and two or three others, the traders not already ruined stood on the brink.

When silence fell, it was sudden. It seemed that everyone at once turned toward the back of the cabin, where Ellison's head and shoulders were coming into view as he climbed up onto a table. Charlie's heart pinched—Ellison's prayer had not been answered! His face, if possible, was even gaunter and grayer than it had been last night. But he stood very straight, and his voice, when he began to speak, was strong and steady.

"Gentlemen, I'll not beat about the bush. The news I have for you is bad. As you know, the high commissioner allowed the Americans to sign his bond without the death clause, and I have been hoping that he would extend the same privilege to the British. To put it baldly, the answer is no. We must either sign his bond *with* the death clause, or leave Chinese waters within three days."

It was a shattering shock. For a long moment, there was

humming silence. Then somebody muttered bewilderedly: "An ultimatum?"

"In a way," Ellison said. "The high commissioner has stationed a fleet of twenty-nine war junks in the Bay of Canton between Lintin Island and the Bogue. He has informed me that any British trader wishing to resume trade with China may go aboard the flagship, sign his bond, and proceed to Jackass Point under the protection of the fleet. Any Briton who does not do so within three days must leave China forever."

Still there was silence: The traders were trying to assimilate the proposal. Charlie held his breath. By God, Lin was clever! He had realized how shaky Ellison's authority was, and he was trying to undermine it by offering the traders, not an ultimatum, but an alternative: Defy your Superintendent Ellison, and I, Lin, will give you protection, will bring you back to where you can earn your living, will allow you to trade again, will save you from ruin.

It seemed that understanding of Lin's proposal struck everybody in the cabin at the same moment. A great babble arose, some shouting that they would sign immediately, to hell with the death clause, to the devil with opium, why should they bother about the death clause if they didn't deal in opium, where was the Chinese fleet, where was the flagship, how soon could they get there. . . . And others, a few others, bawling out that they mustn't sign, nobody must sign, it would mean the death of the opium trade or, by God, the death of *them*, the *traders*, for Lin wouldn't hesitate to chop off their heads if he felt like it.

Ellison stood bleakly silent. Charlie watched him with pity. All his years of striving now lay on the block—all his years of balancing on the high wire, torn between his duty to his country and the terrible conviction that, in the matter of opium, moral rectitude lay with the Chinese. Now it was Hobson's choice for Ellison. Whatever happened, the community—Ellison's community, whose charge he took with such seriousness—was divided. Those who signed the bond would do so in defiance of him, although he would sympathize with their motives. And those who didn't sign, who stood shoulder to shoulder with him against signature—they would be the ones whom he despised and hated.

But suddenly, above the jumble of shouting voices, a new voice rang out:

"Gentlemen!"

Andrew Carradine stood on another table, tall, handsome, confident, his eyes traveling slowly around the dozens of up-turned faces. The shouting began to die, slowly trailed off into silence. Andrew smiled.

"We're all getting very excited over nothing very much, gentlemen!" His voice was untroubled, almost amused. "We don't have to accept any ultimatum, you know. We don't have to sign that damned bond. Nor do we have to sail away in three days. Who's going to make us? Those twenty-nine war junks? *Volage* and *Hyacinth* between them could blow that fleet right out of the water!"

For a moment longer there was silence. Then there broke out a tumult of happy shouting. This everybody was agreed on! This everybody liked!

Grinning broadly, Andrew sketched "Hurray!" with his arms. They shouted louder. He reached down and pulled someone onto the table beside him, waving for quiet.

"And here, gentlemen, is Captain Harry Smith, ready to take *Volage* and *Hyacinth* into the Bay of Canton to confront the war junks!"

The screams became hysterical.

"Is that what we're going to do?" Andrew bellowed over the noise, his eyes like beacons of triumph. "Is that our con-sensus?"

"Yes! Yes!" they yelled, jumping up and down, waving their arms, hugging each other. "Blow 'em up!" "Devil with that bond!" "Devil with Ellison!"

In the pandemonium, Andrew looked across at Ellison, grinning, raising his hands palms up, saying as clear as words: "And what are you going to do about *that*?"

234

Ellison, face pale as death, cold and expressionless, began to speak so quietly that at last the most vociferous fell silent to listen.

"I remind you, gentlemen, that in Europe such an act would be an act of war."

Jeers met this statement, more joking than malicious. The traders were too relieved and happy to be nasty, and Europe was very, very far away, and very, very different—civilized, Europe was. This was China!

Ellison went on: "In any case, it is an act of confrontation, and confrontation will solve nothing. Unless the Chinese *want* to sell you tea, you'll not be able to buy tea."

More derisive laughter.

Ellison shrugged. "Very well. So be it."

He turned and looked across at Captain Smith, still standing beside Andrew on the other table. "I will, of course, sail with you aboard *Volage*."

Captain Smith bowed politely.

"You are welcome."

They were an impressive sight, the twenty-nine gaudy war junks strung out in a long line on the deep blue of the bay, under a sky prettily laced with trailing clouds. A multitude of colored flags and pennants fluttered from their masts. Carved eyes, black on white, glared from their prows. The bright red mouths of their cannon made a startling contrast against the blues and greens of the sea and sky, and there was more bright red in the hundreds of tassels strung from the masts of the flagship. But, comic-opera as they seemed, they were huge vessels, heavily armed. In comparison, the two little British frigates were ludicrously insignificant. Pacing the quarterdeck of *Volage*, Charlie wondered for the dozenth time at the gleeful spirit of the British seamen. Partly, of course, it was release from the months of inactivity, but there was more to it than that. A kind of lip-licking anticipation lurked in their laughter, in the stance of the officers walking their watches,

235

in the glittery-eyed coarseness of the men's joking. Was it bravado, or were they really so sure they were a match for those twenty-nine junks?

Charlie looked back at *Hyacinth* bobbing on the choppy waves two hundred yards away and felt his spine tingle. He'd looked over this bay ten thousand times from *Merope's* deck, sailed it over and over in *San Seb.* It was all so familiar, and yet now so alien. So peaceful, and so dangerous. The two little frigates sailed perkily about, as a couple of cocks might strut a barnyard. The huge junks rocked impassively at their anchors, seeming to take no notice. Yet they were all waiting—the ships and the men who worked them—waiting for the fourth day. Today was the third of the three days of the high commissioner's ultimatum. Here on *Volage,* on *Hyacinth,* and across the water there on the war junks, the nerves of the men who commanded, who strode the decks, who manned the guns, must be screwing up tighter and tighter. The air must be silently crackling with hostile emanations. Behind the appearance of peace and calm, everyone's skin must be crawling.

There was a clatter of boots on the deck below Charlie, and he looked down to see Captains Smith and Ellison emerging from the main cabin. Everyone's skin but theirs! They seemed completely unaffected. The antipathy between them had vanished the moment *Volage* sailed out of Hong Kong harbor. They had spent the whole of the past three days in each other's company, standing together on the bridge, pacing the decks together, sitting together at meals gravely talking and listening to each other. Charlie saw in Ellison a somber felicity. For these three days the superintendent of trade had ceased to exist. He was Captain George Ellison, acknowledged and recognized by Captain Harry Smith, and they, the equals, were absorbed in their rightful business, the business of Her Majesty's Navy.

Andrew, excluded like Charlie by the isolation of the captains, sulked angrily. But Charlie, happy for Ellison, was glad of the time and freedom to walk *Volage*'s deck alone. In these long, quiet days, the cobwebs in his head could be brushed aside. He would get his family back! It was only a matter of time and patience. And now there was no need to feel guilt toward Wei, to worry about who would make kowtow for him when he was dead. The scoundrel had himself wiped all that out. Now Charlie could take his family home with a clear conscience and settle them in England. The children would easily become English, forget their Chinese heritage. It would be hard for Ling-ling, but he would lead her, oh so gently, comfort and console her, accustom her, until she too would feel at home. Perhaps he really would buy Easterbury—he smiled to think of those long-ago dreams on *Merope*. Living in England, there'd be no need for a dramatic confrontation with his father, crammed into a brief visit. The balance of power between them would be redressed slowly and steadily, at its own pace, and the scale would at last come down in his favor. He raised his head and looked out over the water, moistening his lips, almost tasting the relief, the satisfaction of it.

The magic in his heart was matched by the magic of the scene. It was dusk. Remnants of the blazing sunset flickered brilliantly on the adornments of the Chinese junks and painted the darkening water with winking streaks of red and orange. The heads and shoulders of the two captains, standing quietly at *Volage*'s scuppers, were black shapes that emphasized the scintillating colors. For a point in time the spectacle was static, reflected on the mirror of Charlie's eye like a troth of peace renewed forever in every sunset.

Then Captain Smith moved, extending an arm toward the Chinese flagship. His voice floated pleasantly to Charlie's ears.

"Reckon we could take her with one broadside."

"Aye." Ellison's voice was as pleasant. "We surely could. But we aren't going to."

There was a moment of silence. Then Smith said gently:

"We are, you know, It's my command."

"And my responsibility."

The two men turned to face each other, nothing written on their faces, their eyes calm and quiet. Smith said without emphasis:

"I'll relieve you of it, then. As of now, Mr. Ellison, you're a passenger."

"Very well."

Ellison bowed and walked away.

Charlie gulped, the breath balking in his throat at the suddenness of it, the frightening implications it had carried. All at once he was conscious that Andrew stood beside him. They had not said a word to each other since Andrew came aboard *Volage*. Now Andrew spoke excitedly, turning toward Charlie, bright blue eyes glittering in a last streak of golden light.

"God, Harry Smith's bloody exactly the kind of man we need! God, that was bloody exactly the right thing to do!"

"*Ellison* did it, you fool!"

Charlie glared angrily at Andrew. Couldn't the damned fool see that Ellison had provoked the incident, to ease the way for Smith and himself to break out of their idyll of the last three days? The fourth day was at hand. Captain Ellison was once again superintendent of trade and as such could have nothing to say about the actions of the British navy. So he'd offered Captain Smith a way out, and Captain Smith had taken it and was grateful for it! By God, Andrew was a fool to think otherwise!

Andrew's handsome face had contorted with anger, and he was leaning forward, furious eyes only inches from Charlie's.

"You bloody dare call *me* a fool, you bloody *peddler!*"

His fist came up from the deck in a roundhouse punch that would have knocked Charlie flying had he not hunched his shoulder and caught it on his upper arm.

"Andrew!" Captain Smith's voice cut sharply between them. "Stop it! There'll be no brawling on my ship!"

For a moment Andrew glared defiantly, then he swung on his heel and strode away. Charlie stared after him, his shoulder aching, his heart suddenly slumping. By God, he'd called Andrew a fool, but he was a fool himself—a big fool! The last three days had been no more an idyll for Ellison than for himself! Those great calm thoughts he'd thought not ten minutes ago about taking his family to England, about redressing the balance of power between himself and his father—all illusion, like the closeness between Ellison and Smith, like the glowing light of peace out there on the bay! Between himself and his family lay not merely a few hundred miles of sea, but an abyss of ifs and buts and maybes. . . .

Icy fingers playing scales up and down his spine, he clattered down the ladders to the tiny cabin that had been assigned to him. It was five months since he'd returned to Macao to hear the clack of Ah Sam's clogs in the empty house. Five long months, and the strain was telling! He tore off his clothes and flung himself onto the narrow bunk, the sour odor of his own body assaulting his nostrils. He could never get into bed with Ling-ling stinking as he did! And the stink was more than that of accumulated grime, it was the stink of deterioration. He was swirling down and down into that abyss, and then he was stumbling over great clods of plowed earth in a dark field, pursuing a luminous vision of a mother and son standing together in a beam of sunlight, their hands solemnly raised, in beckoning or farewell he could not tell, for the stink of his body blurred his sight like a miasmic cloud. And then the dark field disappeared and he was behind a tall, blank gate on the other side of which he could hear Ling-ling laughing, playing with Jin-see and the Little Sisters. He could hear their trilling voices, but though he banged and banged upon the gate, he could make no sound, or if he did make sound they did not hear it, or if they heard it they would not open, and he stood outside alone, alone.

And then dawn was lightening the porthole and he leaped up, aware through a heavy fog that it was the fourth day. He pulled on clothes and stumbled through passages and up ladders, out onto the deck, stood shivering, looking around with a dim, unknowing kind of eagerness. What was happening on this fourth day? But nothing was happening. Things were the same as usual. Across five hundred yards of water the war junks were becoming visible, their gaudy colors muted in the silvery light. On *Volage* and *Hyacinth*, parties of sleepy seamen bugled while the Union Jack was run up the masts. From belowdecks on *Volage* rose the clatter of tin plates and mugs—the ratings were getting their breakfast. In the main cabin, breakfast would shortly be served the officers with more ceremony and less noise. It was all the same as usual.

But suddenly it was different. Around *Volage*'s bow a strange ship sailed out of the mist, making toward the line of war junks like a terrier busily intent on a trail. On *Volage*'s deck, all movement was arrested as heads turned to stare at the strange ship. There was a long, pulsing pause. Then, from *Volage*'s bridge, a bullhorn-magnified voice bellowed out an order to heave to. For a moment it seemed that the ship would ignore the order, but figures appeared to wrestle with her sails, and she slowed and stopped, wallowing, slewing to present her transom to the watchers. The name on it was *Royal Saxon*. The flag that flew from the stern mast was the Union Jack.

A short, fat bearded figure stamped to the stern rail, cupping its hands to trumpet a truculent shout across the water:

"Why for you stop me?"

"Where're you from and what's your business?" The disembodied voice from *Volage*'s bridge was that of Captain Smith himself.

"From Singapore, to load rice at Canton, if that be any of *your* business."

"Heave to and sail back to where you came from." Captain Smith's voice rolled across the water, calmly authoritative.

"Sod you!" *Royal Saxon*'s master shook his fist defiantly. His voice faded as he turned to shout orders at his crew, then grew audible again as he turned back. "I got nothing to do with opium. I be going aboard that Chinee flagship and sign what papers they ask me to sign, and be buggered to you. . . ."

His words were whisked away as the breeze caught *Royal Saxon*'s sails and rushed her forward, straight for the Chinese flagship, beckoned on by the red tassels that bobbed and shone in the newly rising light of the sun.

From *Volage*'s bridge came a bellow of a different nature, full of peremptory authority. From somewhere beneath Charlie's feet a loud rumble shivered the deck on which he stood, then came an ear-cracking roar. Something splashed heavily into the sea a few yards in front of *Royal Saxon*, gouging out a great gush of foamy water. An excited tumult of cheers rose all over *Volage*. Ellison's voice spoke sharply in Charlie's ear.

"Stand back, Charlie. Smith's giving that bantam cock of a captain a warning—"

His words were drowned in another roar that burst out of a flash of fire from the Chinese flagship. Something splashed into the sea so near *Volage* that a deluge of spray drenched the deck and everyone on it.

"By God!" Ellison's voice cracked like a whip. "The Chinese are replying!"

With a grip that threatened to crush the bones of Charlie's arm, Ellison rushed him down the ladder to the deck below, the gun deck, and pushed him back against the thickness of the mainmast. "Stay here—it's safer!" As Ellison rushed away, Charlie clutched at his sleeve, half gasping a question, but the words were torn from his mouth by the fury of *Volage* grinding up for action. It was a turmoil of ordered chaos. All over the ship, commands were bellowed in the echoing resonance of bullhorns, and all over men raced headlong to obey, avoiding collision by hairbreadths, yet never really getting in each other's way, in an economy of movement that bespoke the acme of training.

Great screeching creaks were the gun ports being opened. Great groaning rumbles were the cannon being rolled and levered into position. Great clanking thuds and clatters were the gun crews rushing to stack their armaments. In a sudden lurch and shudder, the wind caught *Volage*'s sails and sent her leaping forward. Through the narrow gun ports, Charlie saw a glimpse of *Royal Saxon* beating a retreat, then nothing but heaving, foam-tipped waves rushing past. It was quiet now on the gun deck, all in readiness, the broadsides squatting like giant black toads, the gun crews at their stations taut as wire. A signal came, glorious and terrifying—a roll of drums, caught up by drummer after drummer, and passed along the decks and down the ladders. From each end of the gun deck an officer raised his bullhorn and bawled *"Fire!"*

Afterward, Ellison said it took forty-five minutes by *Volage*'s chronometer for the two frigates to smash the Chinese fleet. Forty-five minutes to sail along that line of war junks at a range of fifty yards, once toward the Bogue, firing their starboard broadsides, and once back toward Lintin, firing the port guns, each shot hulling the junks with deadly accuracy, the junks' balls no more effective than if they were made of snow, flying high and wide, somewhat damaging the frigates' rigging and injuring one British seaman under a falling spar. That's all it took, Ellison said—forty-five minutes.

But to Charlie, crushed against the mast on the gun deck, all sense of time was lost in the pandemonium of the attack. A fighting machine, Ellison had called the navy, and Charlie found himself helplessly, monotonously, uselessly saying the words over and over in his aching throat—machine-machine-machine. The whole ship was a machine and the gun deck was the core of it, the gun crews the cogs that drove it, their bodies, arms, faces, blackly covered with thick, smoky grime, and through the grime their eyes glaring, their mouths snarling, red and ghastly, as they strained, arms flailing, tendons jutting, muscles rippling, to serve their deadly charges. Rolling, lifting, shoving home the cannonballs, ramrodding them tight, spilling gunpowder into the breeches, touching the bright little flares to the powder. Then the split second of high tension before the deafening boom of the explosion and the huge clatter of the recoil. Continuously, one after the other, again and again and again and again, the great guns roared and flashed while their demonic acolytes toiled to tend them. Unthinkable that the turmoil would ever stop—the head-splitting crashes, the nostril-searing smell of gunpowder, the roiling smoke and flame—it was timeless, it would go on forever, and Charlie floated about on it, stunned and mindless.

But suddenly, it stopped. The bawling of the bullhorns changed in tone and resonance, drums rattled, bugles blared, men shouted, and it all came to an end in quiet as stunning as the noise. The gun crews tottered, seemingly bewildered by the cessation of activity, then rushed to the gun ports, climbing over each other to peer through the slits. They began to cheer, their voices blowing back over their shoulders, and more cheering echoed down from the deck above, bouncing on the air, growing ever louder, wilder, more triumphant, more exciting. Charlie rushed up the ladder, pushed and shoved his way through the mob of yelling, jigging seamen, and stopped to stare, open-mouthed, tight-throated, at the bay.

The water was still bright blue, ruffled now by a strong breeze, and the sun still glinted off the waves, but otherwise the scene was spectacularly different. The long, gaudy line of war junks was gone. In its place was a strung-out mass of lumpy flotsam scattered on the water like a Sargasso Sea. Spars and masts and split timbers floated uneasily like the discarded matchsticks of a giant. The hulls of capsized junks reared bulkily, slowly sinking, sucked down by the waterlogged weight of their toppled superstructures. Waves nipped at them impatiently as though to urge them on their way to the bottom, and they shifted sluggishly, turning to reveal the jagged holes torn in their sides by the iron vomit of the British guns. One junk was going straight down, squatting on the water like a great, fat duck, its masts still erect, its yellow pennants still snapping in the breeze. As Charlie watched, the water reached for the lowest of the pennants, gobbled at it greedily, inexorably drew it under.

Only the Chinese flagship still floated, listing heavily, her crew working frantically to dislodge a cannon that was jammed against a bulkhead. *Hyacinth* made to tack toward the flagship, and voices on *Volage* began to shout, "Finish her off," but Captain Smith's bullhorn roared and *Hyacinth* stopped, poised on her keel, swinging slowly.

"Leave her be," Captain Smith bellowed. "She stood to fight us. She didn't run."

Silence fell on the two frigates as all eyes turned to watch the flagship's crew lunging and jerking at the cannon, slithering down the steep angle of her deck, getting tangled in the red-tasseled cords that dipped and swung toward the water, fantastically framing the straining men. Then suddenly the cannon came loose and plunged over the side with a great splash. The flagship righted herself, her masts swinging upright, the gay tassels bobbing back into position. She lay low in the water, for a great hole was torn in her side, but it was clear that she could limp to her harbor.

A cheer rose from the decks of *Volage* and *Hyacinth*. Turning, Charlie glimpsed Ellison's face, split in two by a fierce grin—but, by God, was he weeping? Everyone's face was fierce—grinning, glaring, dripping sweat—but, by God, Ellison's face was dripping tears!

Charlie turned away, his heart jerking, to stare over the litter of the murdered junks. Now he could see that many hands were hanging on grimly to the flotsam that heaved ponderously on the deep swell, and bodies bobbed about in the debris as though playing a game with the waves, a game that they had already lost. But Captain Smith was bellowing again, ordering a double tot of rum all round, his bullhorn voice barely audible above the jubilation on *Volage*. Turning abruptly, Charlie pushed his way through the crowd, clattered down to his cabin, flung himself on the tumbled bunk. Down here the noise sounded only faintly and he tried to ignore it, but once again the stink of his body and of the frowsty bedclothes began to invade him, a thick glue that assembled the sights and sounds of the day into a brilliant, brittle amalgam that covered his brain and barred the entry of a great and terrible thought clamoring for recognition.

All at once, the thought broke through. He must go at once to Ningpo! He couldn't afford to wait any longer! Months ago Yin-kwa had said that Wei was hiding the children because they showed their barbarian blood. Now, when news spread of this battle—this slaughter—the anti-foreign mood of the country would ignite, would burn white-hot. The danger to his children would increase a thousandfold—and even more, oh God, the danger to Ling-ling, for anyone who saw her children must know that she had lain with a barbarian. They would hate her for that, detest her, abhor her.

Hot fear bubbled in his blood. In his first anger at Wei, he'd sworn that once he had them back Wei would never see them again. Now, he'd give anything to know for sure that Wei still had them, that he'd be able to keep them safe, keep them breathing, keep them walking the earth! He'd let himself be persuaded to inaction by reason and logic, but there was no reason or logic to the flow of the events in which they all were now caught up. The flow was escalating of itself, catching fire from sparks struck out of the clash of iron wills—the will of the high commissioner to stop the traffic in opium, and of Carradine and his ilk to continue it. And in the middle stood Ellison, helpless to stop it. Ellison, who for all his fierce pride in the victory of his beloved navy could still shed tears. For what? For the defeat of justice?

A great yearning for Blogg swept Charlie—Blogg, to whom all things were simple and straightforward. He would go to Kolo-an as quickly as possible to beg Blogg's pardon for these cold months of silence, and to ask him to go with him to Ningpo. And Blogg would. Blogg would recognize that now, with the destruction of the war junks, the danger to Ling-ling and the children was too great for them to wait any longer. A prickling tide surged through Charlie as he thought of Blogg— a tide of love, gratitude, relief, humility. Had anyone ever had a friend like Blogg?

He felt the forward lunge as the wind caught *Volage's* sails. They were starting back for Hong Kong harbor, the victors sailing away, turning disdainful backs on their victims. Through his small, low porthole he saw the slap of waves, and then, very near, the sitting-duck junk, still upright but almost under the water now. As he watched, a whirlpool opened in the water and the junk's superstructure rushed down into it, swirling around and around, the last thing to disappear the topmost yellow pennant that, until the end, still snapped bravely in the breeze.

The frigates were spotted immediately as they sailed back into Hong Kong harbor. Swarms of small boats put out from the merchant ships, and soon a stream of men were hurrying up *Volage*'s ladder and the roar of voices grew louder and louder as a hundred accounts of the battle were shouted out. Excitement boiled so high it seemed to reach the peak of Hong Kong's mountain, and to echo in magnified waves as it bounced back on the water. When *Sylph*'s cutter came alongside loaded to the gunwales with bottles, the surge of cheering was deafening. The bottles came flowing up the ladder, passed from hand to hand like a river in reverse, and the sound of popping corks punctuated the babble like hail falling in a thunderstorm. A bawling voice made itself heard, calling for a toast to Her Majesty's Navy, and—"Navy! Navy! Navy!"—the toast was drunk and redrunk and drunk again, raised bottles splashing their contents into eyes and noses as much as into wide-open mouths. Jubilation spread like wildfire, snatches of words and sentences jetting up out of the storm of noise like gushes of spray from a heaving sea. The navy was great, the navy was wonderful! But soon—very soon—some trader shouted:

"By God, we can forget Lin's bond now!"

At once, the tide began to turn. The glory of the battle began to fade into the past, and men began to look into the future. There was no bloody need to sign Lin's bond now! Ellison had been right all along, after all! They didn't need to sign Lin's bond in order to get back to trading on Jackass Point. The *navy* would see them back there! The *navy* would put them all back on their feet again!

And then a new tide of whispers. . . . Ellison had said that if the Chinese didn't want to sell them tea, they couldn't buy tea. Who the devil cared about that? They'd be getting back to Lintin too! The clippers would start sailing again. The opium trade would flourish again. Under the guns of Her Majesty's

Navy, opium could be landed anywhere along the coast! What war junks, what admirals, what mandarins could stand up against the British navy?

"Hey, Ellison!" someone shouted. "What about that indemnity, eh? That six million dollars to be divided up among us for the chests we turned over to Lin? Now that opium'll be starting up again, I need my share *urgent!*"

Suddenly, everyone was looking at Ellison, breaking off whatever they were saying, falling silent to hear his reply. He stood in the middle of a circle of men, staring solemnly, blinking. He was very drunk, Charlie saw. But he spoke clearly, enunciating with care:

"You all know, I've had no answer from Palmerston. . . . Last I heard, he was waiting for Carradine to arrive in London to consult him before sending me new orders. . . ." He rubbed his hands over his face, shook his head sharply as though to try and clear it. "But . . . don't understand what you're talking about. What's the navy's victory over those war junks got to do with opium? Nothing! You'll be putting the navy to shame if you try to use it to start up your bloody, evil opium trade again. . . ."

"*Muck you!*" somebody shouted furiously, and the cry was immediately taken up.

"Muck you, Ellison!"

"You want to ruin us, that's what you want!"

"Won't be satisfied, you won't, till we're all penniless!"

It grew threatening. The wild, drunken gaiety was quickly turning into wild drunken fury.

But suddenly, Andrew's voice rang out. He was standing on a capstan, balancing himself with a hand on the shoulder of the nearest man, laughing, his teeth glinting whitely in the light of the flares.

"Makes no matter what the captain thinks, men! You heard what he said: Palmerston was waiting for my father to arrive in London in order to consult him. Well, you know what my father thinks!" A roar greeted the words, and Andrew, laughing harder, raised his voice to a bellow: "My father must've made London by September, and it's November now. We'll be hearing soon. The mail packets are coming through the Isthmus of Suez now, and that's much quicker. Tell you what, gentlemen! A toast to the Isthmus of Suez!"

It was drunken and feckless, but once again it turned the tide. The men swung full circle, from their growing anger to renewed joy in the new quick mail route through the Isthmus of Suez.

"Suez! Suez!"

The voices shouted, the faces relaxed, the bottles were raised again.

Charlie, standing quietly against a bulkhead, watched and listened. He had to find out whether *San Seb* was in the harbor, and if not he had to find some way of hiring a junk to sail him to Kolo-an. He had to do it soon. Later, when the news of the battle spread, the junk owners might not hire out to a Briton, or if they did, the Briton might find himself dumped into the middle of the bay.

But how the hell was he going to manage all that? The noise was growing louder every minute, the drunkenness more reckless. But then a man moved slowly to stand in front of him, his figure dark against the flares. He had a bottle in his hand, but he was standing quietly, not weaving. He wasn't drunk. In a moment, Charlie recognized him from the tangled outline of his hair—it was Robert Innes. It was like him not to be drunk! The violence of his nature had a shrewd kind of calculation to it. Charlie stretched a hand and touched Innes' shoulder. Innes swung round.

"Who's that? Tyson? What d'yer want?"

"Innes, is my ship in the harbor? *San Seb*?"

"The *lorcha*? Nay. Seen her a week ago, sailing out. Why d'yer ask?" He laughed slyly as Charlie hesitated. "If you got somewheres to go, seeing as how Cap'n Smith ain't likely to lend yer *Volage*'s cutter, yer might as well tell me. I might help, it be worth my while."

Charlie said bluntly, "All right. I want to hire a junk to sail

248

me to Kolo-an. I've not got much silver on me, just a few dollars, but you know my credit's good."

Innes snorted derisively.

"Yer thinks it's going to be easy to hire a junk? It'll be amazing, I reckon, after news of that battle come filterin' through, if any junk man be willing to hire out to a Britisher."

"That's why I'm so anxious to do it right away, tonight, before they hear about the battle."

"When d'yer expect to be back from Kolo-an?"

"I don't know—couple of months, I should think."

"Mmmmm."

Innes gave Charlie a long and speculative look, then suddenly made up his mind. He leaned forward and began to whisper in Charlie's ear, his breath spreading a sour little cloud around their heads.

"I'll tell yer. I can get you a boat tonight. Not a junk—a bumboat, one of them that's been bringing the vegetables from Kowloon. Not as fast as a junk, but it'll get you to Kolo-an in a couple of days, latest. I'll do it, but not for any note against yer credit. What I want is your promise to sell me *Merope* at a reasonable price."

"*Merope?*" The proposal was so unexpected that Charlie's voice rose in astonishment.

"Shhh!" Innes glanced around cautiously, but no one was paying them the least attention. He turned back to Charlie. "Aye. *Merope*. I'll tell yer true, Tyson. When the opium trade starts up again, I want to be ready. I'm not so young as I was, and I want to make it rich in the next two-three years. I cain't afford no clipper, but I already got a small ship, and I figure with *Merope* at Lintin, I'll be doing good. D'yer agree to sell her to me at, say, a thousand guineas? That's a bloody good price for that old tub!"

Charlie didn't hesitate. "All right."

"Good." Innes gave a brief nod of satisfaction. "Come on, then."

Innes turned and burrowed through the crowd, Charlie fol-

249

lowing. They clattered down *Volage*'s ladder, jumped from boat to boat in the mass of small craft tied up alongside, and finally got to Innes' dinghy. A silent row through night made darker by the flaring lights from *Volage*, and they were at the ladder of one of the merchant ships. Innes hitched up the dinghy.

"Wait here. Won't be long."

He scrambled away. Charlie waited, his head humming emptily, keeping time, it seemed, to the thin beat of the pulse in his throat. The rocking of the dinghy as Innes got back into it startled him. His heart leaped and, at the same moment, with the same little gasp of indrawn breath, he smelled the heavy sweetness of opium. He glanced sharply at Innes.

"What the devil . . ."

"Shhh!"

Innes' breath hissed unpleasantly in Charlie's face. He unhitched the dinghy, pushed off, rowed with swift, economical movements, sending the little boat neatly between the closely moored merchantmen. When they were in open water on the Kowloon side of the harbor, he seemed to relax a little.

"Yer knows danged well that water carries voices." His low mutter hardly reached Charlie's ears. "No bloody use letting everybody in on our business. . . . Aye, that be opium yer smelled. A whole ball of it." He chuckled softly, a chilling sound. "Supercargo on that ship I'm quartered on, he ain't got sense to keep the ship decent, but plenty sense to find out all sorts of things. He tried paying them bumboat owners in opium 'stead of silver. What that brought yer wouldn't believe! Spring water by the barrelful. Vegetables like you never seen, so big and new-plucked! Fresh-killed pork. Once even the carcass of a calf, though I reckon that danged animal died of something other than slaughtering! The supercargo was keeping it quiet, selling all that extra meat and vegs and water for a fat profit, but I found out. . . ."

He started again to row, glancing over his shoulder, altering course by some landmark on the dim shoreline of Kowloon.

"Them bumboat owners and farmers—they'll be mighty pious, swearing to revenge their war junks by starving us out, but by God they'll not resist payment in opium! There's a-many of us saved out a few balls when we gave up our chests to Ellison for Lin. Now I brung a whole ball. One of them bumboat owners be anchored somewheres 'round here—he'll take you to Kolo-an for a whole ball of opium. . . . Ah, there he be!"

Over Innes' shoulder Charlie saw a dark outline. A bumboat. He recognized the rounded shape of the roof—oiled paper stretched over half-hoops of split bamboo that could be slid over the well of the boat to shelter the crew or the cargo. Innes pulled strongly on his oars, then shipped them. The dinghy slid forward fast, the water whispering as her bow parted it, and a moment later the bulk of the bumboat loomed above them.

Charlie sensed a movement in the air—a rushing hiss. Instinctively, he dodged, his stomach tightening. Something hit his shoulder heavily. He sprawled backward, his head rapping against the thwart behind, and pain exploded dizzily.

"God rot it!" Quickly, Innes shoved his nearside oar against the bumboat, propelling the dinghy out of range. "You all right, Tyson?"

Lying half-stunned in the bottom of the dinghy, gazing up at the lightless sky, Charlie muttered vaguely. Innes took two or three strokes of the oars to widen the distance between them and the bumboat.

"It's the boatman's damned woman!" he growled angrily. "Supercargo told me she hates opium. She hit you with the bamboo they use to pole the boat in shallow water. Damn her! I s'pose her man's sleeping and she thought to get rid of us afore he woke. Must have rekkernized the dinghy—maybe even smelled the opium. . . ."

There was a scramble of movement on the bumboat, a curse, a yelp of pain, a heavy thud. Then a man's cautious voice called out. Innes brought the dinghy an oar's stroke nearer to the bumboat and replied, as cautiously:

"Brung yer *yar-pee*, yer bugger. Yer wantchee *yar-pee?*"

"*Yar-pee?*" Soft as it was, the whisper sounded eager.

"Aye." Innes brought the dinghy bumping gently against the bumboat. The boat's roof was slid aside a few inches. A hand reached out to clutch the dinghy's rope as Innes held it up. A low-voiced dialogue began.

Charlie struggled up from his prone position, propped his elbows on a thwart, laid his aching head in his hands.

Yar-pee. The Chinese word for opium. He'd heard it a million times spoken by Chinese to Chinese, but never before by a foreigner. Ellison would find significance in that! The English, getting closer to the scummy dregs of the opium trade, descending from the lordly sale of tidy wooden chests out of the holds of beautiful clippers, to the barter of stinking black balls out of dinghies!

"All right." Innes turned around. "He's agreed. Yer'll be safe with him, 'cause he knows if he don't carry out his part of the bargain, he'll be cutting hisself off from more supplies of *yar-pee*. We be the only suppliers now—we on the merchantmen in Hong Kong harbor. On land, all along the coast, that high commissioner's got every bit of it!" Innes laughed harshly. "Well . . . go ahead, Tyson. Get in the bumboat. He'll start off at once. And don't yer forget—*Merope*'s mine for a thousand guineas, come time the opium start up again."

"I won't forget."

Still giddy from the blow the woman had dealt him, Charlie clambered unsteadily onto the deck of the bumboat. A hand grasped his arm and propelled him toward the dark tunnel under the roof. He fell painfully a foot or so into the well of the boat, and landed on unexpected softness. A quilt was spread there, still warm from the bodies that had lain on it. With a groan, Charlie stretched out and was asleep in an instant.

When he woke, the boat was moving smartly. Bright sunshine shone out on the deck, though under the low, rounded roof over the well it was still dim. He was warm, sweating from some heavy weight that lay partially on top of him—the damned boatman's body! He pushed him off sharply, and the man rolled over and lay as he had rolled, inert, breath snorting in and out of his puffing mouth. He was drugged. He had already smoked opium! There was no smell, for the vapors must of course have been blown off by the wind, but on the quilt beside the man lay an opium pipe. Charlie stared, his skin crawling. He'd seen hundreds of opium pipes in shop windows in Macao—new ones of polished wood or bone or ivory, mouthpieces of silver or gold, even of jade. But this was a cheap used one—a two-foot length of ordinary bamboo, about an inch and a half in diameter, rubbed smooth and shiny from much handling, the bamboo mouthpiece dented as though from clenched teeth, the bowl black with dottle. No splendid ornament. A tool. An opium smoker's opium pipe.

Shivering, Charlie slid from under the roof out onto the deck. A sharp breeze was blowing and the boat's sails billowed full. An old man crouched in the waist of the boat, cooking on a round clay stove sheltered from the wind by a wooden board. In the bow, a girl of ten or twelve squatted on the deck, watching over the play of two toddlers. He turned toward the stern. On the gunwale a woman sat, balanced between her upstretched hands clutching guy ropes fastened to the rigging, and her strong bare feet on the shaft of the rudder, controlling its movement. She was sailing the boat alone, with expert competence! Charlie stared at her. She was young, round-faced and full-bodied, her thickly plaited hair bouncing in the wind. One of her eyes was swollen almost shut, the skin around it bruised a turgid black-green-yellow. As he stared, she turned from watching the sails, and glared at him with such ferocity that his breath caught in his throat. By God, if the shaft of her gaze could acquire the substance of hatred that she was willing into it, it would tear into his heart and kill him!

He turned away, swallowing, and sat with his back to the mast, out of the woman's sight. The old man and the children paid him no attention. The old man took bowls of food to the children, and then he took one to the woman, held the guy ropes for her as she quickly slurped its contents. He ate himself, washed his bowls and pots by dipping them over the side into the sea, put them tidily away into a box, and sat down, nodding into sleep. The girl wound the two toddlers into a long length of cloth and laid them down on the bow deck to sleep too. She stood squarely on the ends of the cloth so that they could not roll out, and turned to stare out at the sea ahead.

For a while, nothing happened. Then the girl gave a cry and bent forward, peering over the side at something she saw in the sea. The old man went to look too. He turned and signed to the woman, who rose, clinging to the guy ropes, one foot still clutching the rudder with prehensile toes, the other on the gunwale. Standing motionless, craning to one side to look into the sea, the wind flattening her thin garments against her strong body, she looked like some heroic statue, an Amazon, a Chinese Valkyrie. Charlie found himself unable to take his eyes from her. Then the child wailed again, and he too ran to look at what was in the sea.

Two almost naked bodies tumbled playfully together in the trough of the waves as though in some grotesque game of death. They were swollen to bursting, their flesh faded to a thick, whitish-blue color. The shreds of gaily colored clothing that still clung to their arms and legs marked them as sailors from one of the war junks now lying on the bottom of the bay.

Under some kind of spell, Charlie and the woman and the old man and the girl stood motionless, looking back until the bodies were far out of sight.

Then the woman moved. With a harsh rasp, she hawked up a clot of phlegm from deep within her throat and spat it over the side, jerking her head violently in a symbolic gesture as primitive, as savage, as the attack she had made with the bamboo pole. Her baleful eyes were once again fixed on Charlie.

He stepped quickly out of her sight and went to sit once again, his back to the mast, his blood prickling. With her man lying like a log under the roof, drugged into insensibility, the woman was in command. If he so much as closed his eyes, even involuntarily, she might attack him again, push him overboard, hit him over the head with a cleaver from the old man's box of cooking utensils, cleaving through his skull to the jawbone. He might attack her himself and subdue her, but then who would sail them to Kolo-an? He hadn't the vaguest idea of the direction. He needed the woman—her knowledge *and* her cooperation. There was only one way to get it. . . .

He set himself to watch. The woman had resumed her position on the gunwale and was sailing the boat, tireless and enduring. For an hour or more, nothing happened. Then, the sun on the horizon, the old man cooked again. He fed the children and the woman as before, and then he picked up the two toddlers and carried them toward the roofed well, passing behind Charlie. It was Charlie's chance: The girl was alone on the bow deck, with nothing between him and her. He sprang swiftly forward. The girl, seeing him come, cried out and tried to dodge, but he caught her around the waist and held her tight against him. He turned toward the woman, the length of the boat between them. For a long moment, they stared at each other. Then he said:

"Listen, woman. If I get safely to Kolo-an, your daughter'll be safe too, but if you try anything, she'll be drowning in the sea before you can reach me."

To make his meaning clear, he lifted the child and made as if to throw her overboard. The child whimpered. The old man, now standing again in the waist of the boat, cried out. But the woman made no sound. She was stretched toward Charlie to the limit of her grip on the rudder and the guy ropes, her fury and frustration, her hatred, vibrating in every fiber of her being. Then, abruptly, she gave in—nodded, drew back, forced her face to stony calm.

Sighing with relief, Charlie drew the girl down to the deck and tied her up with the cloth that she'd used on the toddlers. She was a sturdy little thing, face round as a moon, button nose, small black eyes staring fiercely in a mixture of terror and courage.

He smiled at her, trying to put reassurance and comfort into it. "Don't worry. It's a bluff. I would never throw you overboard!"

She went on staring without response or comprehension.

"I'm sorry," he said, touching her cheek with a finger. She flinched away. He sat back against the gunwale, hugging himself, for the sun was gone and it was getting cold, and willed himself to think of nothing.

In the silver light of dawn, Charlie woke from a light doze and jumped stiffly to his feet. The child rolled off his lap where in the night he had held her to keep her warm, and began to whimper. The woman still sat on the gunwale like a statue carved out of stone. As far as Charlie could tell, she hadn't moved all night. But now, as she saw his movement, she jerked her chin, pointing straight ahead.

He saw the island then, a dot rapidly growing bigger, and was convinced that it was Kolo-an, because he could see a bump on the beach above the waterline that looked like the roof of a house, and there was a ship in the little bay that, even in the dim light, he knew was *San Seb*.

In a short while, the bumboat served and stopped. With an expert twist of the rudder the woman had slewed it around, and it now hovered on the water, its sails sagging. With a jerk of her head she signaled to Charlie: She wasn't going to take him any nearer to the island; he'd have to jump out and swim. But it wasn't too far. He bent and unwound the strip of cloth from around the little girl. She was quiet now, still half asleep, no longer afraid. He drew from his inner pocket all the money he had left from his sojourn on *Volage*: six silver dollars. He lifted the girl's hands, cupped them together, and put the dollars into them. They were bright, new dollars, and at that moment the first rays of the sun shot over the horizon and glanced off them, making them sparkle. The girl laughed aloud. She wiggled her fingers, making the dollars jingle against each other, shooting more sparkles out of them. Then, still laughing, carefully holding the dollars, she began to scramble across the deck toward her mother on the gunwale.

Charlie let himself over the side into the water. It wasn't deep. A few strokes, and he was standing on the sandy bottom. He turned to look back at the bumboat. The woman had slewed it around again, ready to move off. The child had reached her and was putting the dollars into her lap, looking up into her eyes, laughing, delighted. She'd probably never in her life seen as many as six dollars all together, Charlie thought, smiling, nor had the woman, perhaps, for she had hitched the guy ropes over the gunwale and had taken the dollars into her hands. He felt his heart ease a little—at least she'd have some compensation for the roughness of the past two days!

She was on her feet now, balancing between the rudder and the gunwale, and she turned her head to look at Charlie. She was thanking him, he thought, and he smiled and waved. He heard her laugh, a light, contemptuous sound, and he knew that she hadn't looked at him to thank him, but only to be sure that she had his attention. As he watched, she threw the dollars into the sea, one by one, flinging them as far as she could. They spun in the air, flashing in the sunlight, and fell into the water with such tiny splashes that Charlie, bewildered, thought they surely couldn't be the cause of the ripples of grief that swept through him.

In the evening of that day, Charlie and Blogg lay sprawled on the beach after dinner, in a vast, quiet world lit by a gently setting sun, lapped by the merest whisper of surf. Charlie sighed and stretched. By God, it was good to be with Blogg again! When he had waded out of the sea, Blogg had simply picked him up and hugged him, dripping wet as he was, and then they'd walked up the beach to the little house, exchanging no words, silent and smiling. *San Seb*'s dinghy had come splashing through the surf with the mate and five crewmen to welcome Charlie, and there had been a great deal of laughter and chatter, although only the five old crewmen were left. The younger ones had gone off, tempted by the prospect of big-money jobs in the town of Fat-shan, where the high commissioner had had a metal foundry converted into a gun manufactory, turning out five-ton cannon that were being sent to the Bogue forts and coastal cities to strengthen their defenses. Right determined, that high commissioner was, Blogg said. And clever, attacking his job on all fronts.

While *San Seb* sailed off to Macao to tell Ah Sam of Charlie's return—no English were yet allowed in Macao—Charlie settled down to tell Blogg of the battle in the Bay of Canton. Blogg stared gravely.

"Trouble's growing like a typhoon! A small blow first, and then up and up to a great howling wind that sweeps everything away. Aye! What's the high commissioner going to do now? He cain't take that lying down, but what the devil can he do?"

"Nothing." Charlie shrugged. "At least, on the ships in Hong Kong harbor they don't expect any obstacle at all to opening up the opium trade again as soon as the clippers get opium to Lintin."

They had eaten a fine dinner of fresh fish cooked by Blogg, and now they lay quietly on the sand, Charlie preparing to say to Blogg: "We must go to Ningpo, Blogg. You realize that, don't you? They're in far greater danger than they were before. . . ."

Blogg sat with his arms propped on his drawn-up knees and gazed out toward the corals and greens and blues of the sunset sea. He said softly:

"Charlie, I know you want to go off to Ningpo right away. I know that battle will make the Chinee hate foreigners more than they ever done before, and that'll make it all the more dicey for your family in Ningpo. But still, Charlie, I think it can do more harm than good for us to go. Just think. Before, if any Chinee near Ningpo seen you or me, they'd just pass us by, even if in their heart they hated us. But what would they do now? Try to kill us! You know how Chinee mobs can grow right up out of the dust of the fields! It wouldn't be one to one, or even ten to one. Hundred to one, more like it. We wouldn't live, Charlie. And what good would you be to Lingling and your children, dead?"

Charlie sat bolt upright, shooting sand in all directions.

"And what the hell good am I to them sitting here on Kolo-an, Blogg?"

"No good, of course. But at least you'll be there, wherever it be, to take care of them once this is all over. . . .

"God!"

Charlie flung himself back on the sand and stared up at the stars gradually emerging from the dark blue sky. . . . Blogg was right.

But *San Seb* came sailing quietly back into the little harbor, and the mate came ashore alone, soft-spoken and subdued. He talked to Blogg a long time, and when Blogg turned to Charlie his own tone was somber.

"The news ain't good. The high commissioner's broke off trade with Britain 'forever,' but all the British ships are still in Hong Kong harbor living high on drink from *Sylph*'s stores, and food that the Kowloon farmers are bringing them for pay in opium. . . . And—you said Captain Harry Smith let the Chinee flagship sail back to her harbor? Well, she did. Got back to Chuenpi Fort all right, and as soon as she'd set her anchors the Chinee admiral ordered his crew on parade. Went up to his poop deck in his best uniform and stabbed his short sword into his heart, front of all his crew and all the men from the fort who'd come down to welcome him."

Charlie held himself very still and quiet, feeling that the fabric of life was stretching thinner. The boatwoman had flung away his gift of dollars, and the admiral had flung away the gift of life itself, refusing redemption to the conquerors. He let a handful of sand trickle through his fingers, and it seemed to him that grief trickled with it, sharp and prickly, hurtful.

Chapter IX

January-July

1840

I T WAS THE END of March. Charlie was sitting listlessly on the beach, when Blogg exclaimed and pointed. A junk was approaching. They got to their feet, shading their eyes. A figure standing in the bow was peering at them as they were peering at him. Even at a distance, Charlie could see the untidy rags of clothing swathing his body, and the maze of snarls that was his hair.

"It's Innes! By God, I forgot I promised to sell him *Merope!*" He cupped his hands and shouted: "Innes?"

"Tyson?" The hail echoed angrily over the water. "What the devil happened to you? You said two months you'd be back!"

"I'm sorry! I'll make good my promise!"

"You *better!*"

The junk was close now, and Innes jumped off, went completely under, surfaced again, blowing and puffing.

"Damn you, Tyson! You *said* two months!"

"I'm really sorry! I . . . I've had difficulties. Anyway, we can settle it immediately, now."

Innes stumbled up onto the beach. Blogg, trying not to laugh, handed him a square of cloth to dry his face with. The three of them trudged up the sand to Blogg's cottage, and Blogg poured grog for them.

"Well . . ." Innes settled himself on a stool, glowering. "You got papers for *Merope*, Tyson?"

"Of course not! She was an abandoned wreck when I took her over. But there's no need of papers. You can simply move aboard. Who'll ask questions?"

"She's in good condition?"

"She was last time I saw her."

"Is she—"

Wearily, Charlie broke in:

"D'you want her or not, Innes? If you don't, I'll be glad to keep her. If you do, you made a promise too, remember—to pay me a thousand guineas for her."

"You'll take my note on London?"

Charlie shrugged—what did it matter? "All right."

Innes scribbled swiftly on a piece of paper and handed it over. Charlie glanced at it: Bank of the Midlands. A thousand guineas. An illegible signature. He folded it and put it away in a pocket.

Innes relaxed a little, downed his grog, and held out his glass to Blogg for more.

"Well—that's all right, then. I'll move aboard in the next few days."

"You know the foreman already," Blogg said meaningfully.

"Aye . . ." Innes looked a little uncomfortable. "That's true—I did go aboard and give him some weapons to defend the opium case the viceroy tried to take it. After all, the opium was mine!"

"Except for what was Lee Kwok's," Charlie said sardonically.

"Wasn't nobody's after he died, was it?"

Innes began to sound belligerent, then thought better of it. He tried to alter his expression to one of mild interest.

"Well—wot yer two been doing? Thought yer'd have *San*

261

Sebastian in Hong Kong picking up some cargoes—plenty cargoes, there be! Should see that harbor now! Yer heared that Lin declared trade with Britain finished forever? Well!'' He chortled. "It's *bigger* nor ever! All that tea that was held up when he suspended the tea trade—twenty-four million pounds of it, credit it or not!—it all had to come out of Canton, and the Americans couldn't buy it all their selves, so they're buying it *for us!*" He cackled loudly. "Andrew's idea. Americans buying it and shipping it from Whampoa to Hong Kong harbor and we putting it on British ships in Hong Kong, for England. 'Course, those damned Americans ain't doing it for nothing! Charging us freightage for that hundred mile from Whampoa to Hong Kong same as they charge Whampoa to *Boston!* But all the same, we all be getting summat out of it—live and let live, that's wot I says!"

Charlie stared at him, fascinated. He was so incredibly dirty—there must be a million nit-nit in that tangled hair!—and so incredibly *smug*, sitting there, legs spread, broken teeth showing in a malicious grin.

" 'Course, Carradine and Dent and the likes of them're getting the lion's share of the tea, but we're all getting summat. Must say, Carradine's been generous 'bout advancing credit 'gainst that indemnity.''

Charlie sat up.

"You mean, Palmerston's paying the six million dollars Ellison promised when you gave your opium up to Lin?"

Innes' grin widened.

"Not Palmerston! The *Chinee*'re going to pay it."

"*What?*" Blogg and Charlie spoke together. Looking pleased with the impression he had created, Innes went on with a great play of nonchalance:

"Aye. That be one of the terms that Ellison's to demand from the Chinee after the navy's done its work."

"The *navy?*"

"Oh, aye! The two of yer don't know nothing of wot's happened, do yer? Well, I'll tell yer. . . .''

He leaned back, swelling with importance, sucking loudly at his grog.

"Ellison got dispatches from Palmerston. The Cabinet decided that the high commissioner's been treating Britons so disgraceful that they're going to send out an armada to teach him a lesson. Three ships of the line, sixteen or seventeen other ships, plus transports for three or four thousand fighting men, Scottish and Irish infantry and sepoys from the British India army. Can you credit it? A real *armada!*"

He looked around, as pleased and proud as though the ships belonged to him, and took a gulp from his glass.

"After the armada's done its work, Ellison's got from Palmerston a list of demands he's to screw out of the Chinee. First, that six million dollars. Then, four more ports to be opened up for foreign trade—Foochow, Amoy, Ningpo, and Shanghai. Then some stuff about diplomatic relations to be direct, no more going through the Co-hong. And Choushan Island to be taken for the British—the Portugees got Macao. And"—his smile became evil—"trade in opium to be made lawful."

There was complete silence. It seemed that even the sea stopped its murmur, the wind its lonely whistle.

Innes took a cheroot from an inside pocket, lit it with a sulfur match that he struck on the sole of his boot. The smoke puffed, thick and gray and swirling.

"When's the armada expected?" Charlie asked, his voice tight and thin.

"'Bout midyear . . . and the first clippers'll be along with the first warships. Andrew got a letter from his father in the same packet wot brung Ellison's dispatch from Palmerston. His father'll be right along with that armada in *Falcon,* and *Falcon*'ll be full of opium, I'll lay yer any wager yer likes. . . . Point of fact, seems old man Carradine had more to do with Palmerston's dispatch to Ellison than Ellison liked!"

"What d'you mean?" Blogg asked quietly.

"Well—yer remember Palmerston said he was going to wait

for Carradine to get to London to consult him? Seems it weren't no *consultation*. Seems it were more like *advice*—Palmerston took all the advice wot Carradine gave him, and that was plenty!"

He laughed again, and held out his glass.

"One for the sail, eh, Blogg? Long ways back to Hong Kong harbor—or maybe Lintin. Maybe I'll drop in on *Merope*, now she be mine. . . ."

Blogg poured him a full glass, and he downed it in a few swallows, his Adam's apple clicking. Then, with a jaunty wave of his cheroot, he was off, trudging back down the beach and wading into the water to jump onto his hired junk.

They watched him go. Charlie felt a balloon swelling in his throat, a balloon that would soon burst in a great explosion of triumph. Afraid to let it go, afraid that once again he was hoping too much, he restricted his breathing.

"Blogg . . ." His voice trembled. "Choushan Island's ten miles across the straits from Ningpo, isn't it?"

"Aye." Blogg's voice was quiet.

"And the first thing that armada'll do when it gets here will be to take Chousan Island? To use it as a base?"

"Reckon so."

"Blogg—if Choushan's occupied by the British, there'll be a lot of confusion, and our chances of getting into Ningpo will be much greater, won't they?"

"Reckon so."

"So, Blogg—we'll follow the armada to Choushan and take our chances of getting into Ningpo."

Blogg said, very low:

"By the Lord God, Charlie, you're bloody near as bad as Innes! For him the armada's to restore the opium trade and make him rich. For you, it's to get you back your wife and children. Nor you, nor he's thinking that that armada means *war*. Thousands of men killed, women widowed, kids orphaned, lives ruinated—and all of 'em *Chinee*. By God, Ellison spoke true when he said opium's evil! That's what this armada's about. No need for armadas to make the tea trade work!

Opium's the cause of it. I'm finished with it, Charlie. I'm finished with that black bloody trade!"

"Me too," Charlie said slowly. "You're right, Blogg. It's a black bloody trade."

Blogg poured rum, and they lifted their glasses and drank. On a common impulse, they walked down to the sea and flung their glasses into the water, watched them bob about, slowly filling, sinking lower, at last disappearing from sight. Charlie thought of How-kwa and of Wei, and wished that he could tell them. Could he shout it out on the wind? "I've no need of forgiveness anymore. I'm finished with opium!" But that wasn't true. He still had need of forgiveness for all the years, the long-gone years that he couldn't take back. But that wasn't true either. He had no more need to feel guilt toward Wei. It was Wei who had harmed him irrevocably, not the other way around. . . . Confusedly, he turned toward Blogg.

Blogg was rubbing his hands.

"Well, that's done! Now . . . we can't follow the armada to Choushan, Charlie. Warships'll outsail *San Seb* by days. We'll have to go before them—be at Choushan before they get there, to be sure of taking whatever chances might come of getting into Ningpo."

They made Choushan Island after a fine three-week sail in the refurbished *San Seb*. Careened, recaulked, reoiled, with new mast and sails, *San Seb* behaved like a jaunty youngster instead of the old lady she was.

Ah Sam was with them. Her help in getting into Ningpo might prove invaluable, and if Charlie himself could not get in, she surely could. She could look for Wei and Ling-ling and the children, bring news of them, or even bring them back to *San Seb*, hidden in any of the dozen little harbors in the string of small islands that dropped like a necklace from Choushan to the coast near Ningpo.

During the first part of the voyage Ah Sam had been so quiet, so remote, that Charlie, even while scoffing at himself, had felt some awe of her—the blankness of her eyes, the set of her lips, at once fierce and sad.

One day she had come to sit beside him where he sprawled on the deck, restlessly idle, watching a flock of screaming seabirds.

"Chahlee—why Inglis send many fire ship for kill Chinee?"

He hesitated, looking for words, and she turned to him, eyes wide with pain and puzzlement.

"Inglis people . . ." She paused, not finding the word she wanted, and finally acted out her meaning: Lifted her head imperiously, looked down her nose, flicked a contemptuous hand. "Inglis people think they more better than Chinee. But why they want *kill* Chinee?"

He could not bear the gaze of her eyes and turned away to stare again at the screeching, wheeling birds.

"Because opium," she answered herself. "Inglis want every man spoke opium. Chinee too. Chinee sell opium too. But Chinee not *kill* for sell opium."

Now, standing with Blogg and Charlie on the bridge, she watched as Blogg sailed *San Seb* around the point of a landlocked harbor and brought her sweetly to her mooring just inside the entrance. It was a sunny day toward the end of June and the harbor sparkled, big and deep, full of craft of all sizes, even great seagoing junks. Behind rose a hill on which the capital town, Tin-hai, was spread out, a biggish huddle of low, curly-roofed houses threaded through by a maze of steep lanes and surrounded by a tall, thick, five-sided wall. A prosperous, busy little town.

At the top of the hill was a pagoda—a joss house, Blogg's mate called it—and on a plain beside it the town's defense armaments were installed: six cannon in fixed emplacements, of the vintage from which balls were likely to trickle out and bounce down into the town. In addition to the cannon, Charlie had counted eleven small war junks anchored close to the beach.

"Pitiful, ain't it?" Blogg said quietly. "When you think of that armada!"

Ah Sam made a sharp sound in her throat and turned away abruptly.

"I go with mate for buy food. And wine. Tin-hai famous for *sam shui.*"

"Good," said Blogg. "And then we'll sail for a cove I know and lie there waiting. We'll see the armada from there, when it comes."

It was very quiet in the cove, and at night very dark. On the open sea there was always a shining off the water, a luminescence in the sky, even when moon and stars were hidden. In the cove it was so dark at night that even the nearby outline of the land did not show—nothing showed beyond the small radiance of the candle in the oiled paper lantern hung low on *San Seb*'s mast.

They spent the days quietly, resting or bathing in the warm water or fishing for fish that Ah Sam cooked up deliciously. In the evenings they sat around the lantern, dipping *sam shui* from the big red clay jar. Ah Sam had bought a long-handled ladle that exactly fitted the narrow neck of the jar. They dipped the liquor out with this and poured it into their own mugs, each time with a clink and a gurgle. These were the only sounds unless someone spoke. After a while, Ah Sam would go down to the cabin. The men slept in the open air, Blogg and Charlie in hammocks, the Chinese on the deck, on their sides or their backs, very neatly disposed and very still. A Chinese seaman could sleep soundly on a bamboo pole slung in midair, Blogg said, and never fall off.

On their eighth day in the cove—by Blogg's log book, the second day of July—the armada came.

Charlie woke very early that morning, while the dawn was still beyond the horizon. He lay quietly for a moment, then hitched up on an elbow to look toward the west, toward the town of Ningpo hidden in the distance and the darkness and the silence. He stared for long minutes while the darkness grew lighter, and suddenly was aware that the silence was no longer silent. There was a hissing murmur, the sound of the sound of movement, and still far away. He climbed out of his hammock and went up on the bridge, found the spyglass, peered through it toward the south. In the silvery grayness, so quiet and dim that they might have been only the ghosts of ships, he saw the ships coming.

By the time the first of the ships was in full sight, the sun was at nine o'clock and shone brightly on the ship's great white sails. Her name, seen through the spyglass, was *Alligator*. The watchers on *San Seb* were utterly silent as she sailed by. Charlie, glancing at Ah Sam, saw her face was expressionless—it might have been carved of stone.

Behind *Alligator* the other ships came, frigates, corvettes, brigs, sloops, transports, strung out in a line that stretched as far as the eye could see. Blogg named them as they sailed by. *Blonde*, first-class frigate, forty-six guns. *Conway*, frigate, twenty-eight guns. *Modeste*, corvette, eighteen guns. *Columbine*, a little ten-gun brig. *Calliope. Nemesis. Cruiser. Algerine. Pylades. Atlanta. Kite* . . .

It grew monotonous. Charlie stopped trying to count the number of guns, and counted only the ships instead. By the time three little brigs went by, fussily escorting a group of troop transports, he had counted forty-five. Forty-five beautiful, terrible ships, their combined firepower unimaginably awesome, going to pit themselves against eleven smallish war junks and six ancient cannon! Almighty God!

He shivered and rose, stretched himself, looked up at the sun. The ships had been sailing by for hours! The sun was going down to its setting. There was a pinkish tinge to the light, and the slow curling waves of the long swell were touched at their frothy tips with pink. He turned to Blogg, but Blogg, on the bridge, was still staring southward. "Look, Charlie!" he breathed, pointing.

Charlie turned back, and saw them—the three ships of the line. Involuntarily, he gasped, and he heard the hiss of indrawn breath from Ah Sam and the crewmen. They were magnificent! Huge. So tall that their masts seemed to pierce the pink clouds of the sky. They moved through the water at half-sail, leisurely, like greyhounds in restraint, untold speed and power held in control. God, they were beautiful!

Blogg, his eyes bright blue and shining, his voice tight with pride, handed Charlie the spyglass.

"Take a good look at three of the greatest ships of the world's greatest navy!"

The ships were sailing in a diagonal line: *Blenheim* ahead, farthest from the watchers; *Melville*, flying the admiral's flag, in the middle; *Wellesley* nearest. Under the glass, they lost none of the magnificence with which the vista of distance had endowed them. Their decks were huge, serried one above the other—more than enough space for the seventy-four guns each of the ships carried, and for all who served and tended and ministered to them. Charlie shifted the focus of the glass from one ship to another. Men moved about them smartly but un-hurriedly—no excitement, no great preparations. The taking of Choushan Island would be all in a day's work for these great ships.

The glass was trained on *Wellesley* when a face suddenly appeared, close up, seeming to stare straight into Charlie's eyes. A clean-shaven face, the skin pinkish in the light of the sun-set, a blue scarf wound around the head. Dark eyes, swivel-ing.

"By God," Charlie shouted to Blogg. "Gutzen's aboard *Wellesley!*"

Blogg took the glass and peered through it.

"You're right! The navy'll take the island by assault, but once it's taken, somebody's got to be in charge of civilian affairs, and who better than Gutzen?"

"Blogg . . ." Charlie shifted his gaze to the sun, resting now on the rim of the horizon in a brilliantly clear sunset. "It won't be dark for another hour. Let's sail to Tin-hai!" An intolerable excitement had seized him. There was the armada—that un-believable fleet of ships. They'd have Choushan anytime they bothered to take it. And then . . . "Blogg, we've got to be *where the action is happening.* We've got to be right there, so we can judge what to do next, and do it as quickly as possible. Blogg, let's go!"

Blogg stared.

"You're crazy-mad, Charlie! Take *San Seb* under those guns? We ain't going anywhere near those broadsides!"

They stared at each other for a moment, Blogg's eyes blue as fire, Charlie's black with urgency. Then Charlie turned away. Blogg was right, of course. But his heart pounded. He'd waited so long! A year since the day he'd heard the clack of Ah Sam's clogs in the empty house in Macao! A *year!*

In a fever of frustration, he tore off his clothes, plunged into the sea, swam the fifty yards to the mud flats, pushed his way through the tall marsh grasses, feeling them prick and cut till little spots of blood covered his limbs and he seemed clothed in the skin of some strange animal. He climbed the low palisade onto the uninhabited shore and strode naked over the coarse scrub. Somewhere he stepped into mud that squished between his toes—wet mud. Joyfully, he knelt and scraped with his hands until he had dug out a basin that slowly filled with fresh, clear water. He squatted beside it and washed himself, rubbing at his skin with the ball of a thumb, loosening scrolls of dirt that he carefully scraped off. When the water in his basin became too soiled, he scooped it out with his cupped hands and let the basin fill again with clean water that seeped up from some hidden spring. Again and again, he emptied it and let it fill, and washed himself, inch by inch, in a kind of orgy of cleansing, a ritualistic preparation. At last he laid himself down on the prickly grass, shivering, and fell asleep at once and slept dreamlessly until the morning.

The next day and half of the day after that passed quietly.

They waited.

Blogg busied himself with his log book. The crew fished and muttered to each other. Ah Sam sat under the stern awning making rice-flour cakes, frying them to a golden color in hot oil. Charlie lay on deck in the sun thinking of nothing, dozing, the sizzling sound of Ah Sam's frying cakes sliding weirdly through his dreams.

On the second day, when the sun was just past the zenith, they heard the broadsides—roaring echoes that sprang from the blue of heaven like the wrath of gods. They listened, all of them arrested in midmovement, staring into space, not breathing. For minutes it went on. Then, suddenly, it was over. Insects chirped and shrilled again. Small waves lapped *San Seb*'s sides. The mate reeled in his line with a flapping fish on the end of it. Ah Sam dropped another rice cake into the sizzling oil.

Charlie rose to his feet.

"Blogg, it's time to go."

"Aye," Blogg said. "It's time."

The sun was setting as they neared Tin-hai harbor.

"There'll be a moon soon," Blogg said.

But there was no need of a moon. As the last of the sun's light fell out of the sky, the light of the fires took over—the fires that merrily burned among the ruins of Tin-hai, rippling up and down the hillside, reflecting prettily in the water, pointing mischievous fingers at the craft that tried to hide, splashing fitful light on the stream of refugees who fled up the hill and around the joss house, abandoning the symbols of their lives to the flames and the barbarians.

Ah Sam took a single look and went below. Blogg ordered the crew, their faces chalky white under the reddish glow that the flames lent them, to the shadows of the stern deck, where they squatted on their haunches, silent with awe. Blogg sailed *San Seb* around the periphery of the harbor, keeping out of the hot dancing light, to the dark and deserted extremity of the seawall that bordered on the foot of the hill. There he and Charlie made the ship fast and then stood on the bridge, side by side, surveying the scene.

The central docks below the town, brilliantly lit in pulsing red light from the fires and from a row of flaming torches, were

271

alive with movement. Cutters were coming alongside in a constant stream, bringing men from the warships which were spread in the middle of the harbor. Like swarms of large black ants, the men could be seen climbing down from the ships and shuffling into the cutters. The water was pocked and pimpled with the endless beat of the cutters' oars. As soon as they touched the docks, the men leaped ashore, milled about, formed squads, marched off. The army of occupation, taking possession of its prize.

At *San Seb*'s distance from the scene, hardly any sound reached Charlie and Blogg, though the sorcerous light clearly revealed the ceaseless movement. It was mesmeric. They stared, fascinated, for a long time. At last Charlie shook himself:

"Let's go!"

They walked along the seawall, trying to keep out of sight as they neared the light. Sounds began to reach them—hoarsely shouted orders from the docks, the thump and shuffle of many feet, the loud hiss and crackle of the flames, and—faint under the babble—the voices of human plaint, the moans of the wounded, the lament of the bereft.

At last they reached the place where the lanes leading down from the town debouched onto the docks, and here, another kind of sound filtered out of the lanes—a loud, rough, brutal, mindless, rumbling kind of growl, a shocking sound.

"By God!" Blogg breathed. "The *sam shui!*"

Suddenly they were wading in it, their boots inch-deep in a mush of liquefied filth from which the fumes of the wine rose in choking waves as their feet sloshed it up. The jerky light revealed men in officers' uniforms wielding clubs, smashing red clay jars like the one Ah Sam had bought for *San Seb*, letting the wine gush out in streams that snaked their way down the lanes. But the officers were fighting a losing battle against their own troops. The rank and file of the conquering army were already out of control, roaring drunk.

Blogg and Charlie turned from the docks into a lane and entered a nightmare world. Clots of shouting, howling, shoving men fought each other to dip their hands, their cups, whatever they'd found that would hold liquid into the jars of *sam shui* that stood in shop after shop. Some snatched up smaller jars to drink direct from them, the liquid sputtering into their mouths and running over their chins, over their clothes, the smell of it almost tangible. It seemed that every other shop in Tin-hai had sold *sam shui,* and it seemed that, except for the fraction the officers had contrived to waste on the mud of the lanes, all of it would be drunk before morning by the men off the ships who this night would earn the epithet "barbarians."

Grimly, Blogg and Charlie shoved steadily forward and upward, out of the shopping lanes and into a district of small houses that seemed to crouch behind their tight-shut doors as though desperately hoping to go unnoticed. But the mob was close behind. It erupted, howling, into the district. Finding no red clay jars readily available, the men began to smash down doors and force their way into houses. Over the crash of rending wood and the drunken roars of the soldiers, there came now a high-pitched screaming that spread from house to house in a rising wave. There were people in the houses, hiding, and the soldiers were rooting them out, shaking them, hacking at them, throwing them out of doors and windows. Charlie was shoved off his feet by a surge of reeling men. Stunned for a moment, he lay where he had fallen, trying to avoid the feet that stumbled over him. Through the tangle of rushing, stamping legs he saw a great splurge of light—a new fire had flared ahead of them at the corner where the lane turned into another. The legs and feet came stumbling back toward him in wild confusion as the men retreated from the fire, the whole knot of them falling backward but somehow, for some reason, staying together, all clutching and pawing at something. For an instant, in the red glare, he saw what it was—the naked body of a girl twisting in frantic struggle, breasts small and tender, skin gleaming.

She might have been Ling-ling.

Anger such as he had never known surged through him in a tidal wave. He flung himself at the cluster of men, a tornado of fury, fists and feet flailing, head a battering ram. Pain zigzagged through his body as the men pounded back at him, but the fierce thrust of his attack was forcing them backward, back toward the fire, which in turn was jumping forward, jumping toward them, greedily gobbling at the masses of broken wood that lay in its path. Their resistance crumbled. Suddenly they were fighting each other to push back, to get away from the flames, to flee. In ten seconds Charlie was alone, the girl on the ground at his feet. He leaned into the fierce heat to pick her up, and at once she began again to fight, blindly, silently, wild as a terrified animal. He backed away from the fire, trying to get a grip on her, but it was like trying to hold a hurricane. The strength of her little body was incredible—the crazed strength of fear. He felt her teeth close on the side of his left hand and for an instant her body was still as she tore at his hand with her teeth. Pain flashing through his left arm, he took advantage of her momentary stillness to clutch her tightly in the crook of his right arm, and as he did so, words flashed into his mind—Chinese words from a jingle Ling-ling sang to the children about not being afraid of the great flying beetle, of the wild cat, of the tiger. "Don't be afraid." He remembered the Chinese words. "Don't be afraid," he said to the girl, over and over, over and over, closing his eyes in the intensity of his effort to imitate Ling-ling's intonation.

She understood. Somehow, through the frenzy of her fear, the words penetrated. He felt her quieten. Slowly her teeth separated and released his hand. For an instant longer she lay unmoving in his arms. Then she twisted to hide her breast against him and began to sob as though her mind had flown and her heart had broken.

Holding her close, he turned and fled the fire. Other shadows were running too, dodging out of the homes that could no longer keep them safe. They ran together, around corners, up and down other lanes, twisting back and forth. At last he found himself in a small square of houses, deserted because they had already been stripped—doors broken open, debris tumbling out of them and littering the lane knee-deep.

With an elbow, he pushed open a sagging door. Beyond was a small courtyard, and beyond that a ruined room. He entered, stumbling over something. A crumpled quilt. He laid the girl down on a corner of it, and folded the rest of it over her. Then, not knowing what more to do, he knelt beside her helplessly, watching the sobs convulse her slight body, hearing the sound of them rasp in his ears.

After a while, with a creaking and a rustling, an old woman crept out of somewhere. Watching him fearfully, she crawled on hands and knees, skirting him as far as possible, and sat on the floor and began to pat the girl, softly, gently. Tears rolled down her wrinkled cheeks and lost themselves in the girl's tousled hair. The girl turned and buried her head in the old woman's lap. One of her hands, fingers delicately curled, trailed from under the quilt and rested on the floor. Like a small white bird, Charlie thought.

He rose, then, and left them.

Outside, bedlam roared on in the flame-lit night, a tumult of terror and pain and loss and heartbreak and bestial glee. The conquerors were everywhere, the drunken conquerors, the triumphant despoilers and rapers, reeling up and down the lanes, breaking, entering, snatching what took their fancy, smashing what they didn't want or couldn't carry, roaring, shouting, stumbling, falling, retching, spewing, scrambling up again to reel on. Behind them, beyond and between them, fearfully dodging them, dim figures edged out of doorways, slid from shadow to shadow, made their way toward the tenuous safety of the darkness beyond the joss house. Some bore burdens, possessions so precious they endangered their lives to try to save them. Many carried children, hushing them frantically when they wailed. Other figures crouched in corners, cowering, whimpering, or staring dumbly, stunned by disaster. In a mesmeric sequence, an old man ran, despairingly calling, turning over bodies, staring at dead faces, never finding the one he sought so desperately. A boy, face contorted, tears pouring, leaped on the back of a conqueror and plunged a knife into his neck, again and again, as hard and quickly as he could, until other conquerors, screaming righteous fury, plucked him off and trampled him to death.

And over everything the fires raged, weirdly lighting the night.

At last Charlie, trudging uphill, came to a place only dimly lit by the fires, a place that seemed hardly touched—it was high up, and the despoilers had been diverted before they reached it.

Here the houses were well built, gracious. He passed a big white building with square windows whose embrasures revealed how thick were the walls. Beyond was a gate, the tall, blank kind that he knew must lead into a courtyard. He pushed it and it creaked open. He stepped into a courtyard that seemed to glow with pale light reflected from white flagstones, white walls, a tall white stele in the center—all marble, as in Howkwa's courtyards.

Drained to exhaustion, he flung himself down and leaned against the stele, closed his eyes, slipped into a state between sleep and waking in which his mind seesawed in a shifting black-and-red world.

After an unknown time he knew that he wasn't sleeping, and that he was sore and stiff. He opened his eyes. It was becoming morning. The color of the world had changed from black and red to gray—the gray of doves in his still-shadowed courtyard, and the gray of pearls in the luminescent mist glimpsed through the door that he had left open. He rose and stepped out into the lane.

He was high up on the hill. Below him the town was spread, so still and silent that it might have died of its wounds. The fires had burned themselves out; their black and sooty residue was broadcast over a vast waste of rubble. The walls that still stood seemed to lean toward each other, for comfort perhaps, or to shield from barbarian gaze the dead who lay between them.

Beyond, in the harbor, the water was still as a mirror, as a sheet of metal, and the color of metal. He could make out the dim shapes of the warships, masts spiky, hulls hunched mysteriously in the fog that swirled around them. In the midst of them, the bulkiest shape of all must be *Melville*, crouched like an ogre mother keeping watch over her deadly brood.

Heart thudding, Charlie reentered the courtyard, crossed it, pushed open a door on his right. It led into some kind of office—large, airy rooms opening into each other. Tall chests full of papers stood against the walls, and there were rows of desks also covered with papers whose readers might have laid them down a moment earlier, pushed their stools back, stepped out for a moment. But there was no one. The building was empty.

He crossed the courtyard to another building, smaller but more opulent. The first room in it was an anteroom, floor and walls of marble, chairs and tables of austere blackwood. A waiting room, in which no one waited. In the next room—large, square, deep-windowed—four old men sat around a marble-topped table.

Charlie dodged back out of sight, holding his breath. Had they seen him? Would voices now begin to shout? Would whistles be blown and guards come running?

But nothing happened, and after minutes of tense waiting, Charlie peeped back into the room. The old men had not moved. They sat erect in their blackwood armchairs, heads slightly bowed, open eyes staring at the teacups on the table before them. Slowly, slowly, Charlie tiptoed around the table, touching the hands of the old men, peering into their cups. The hands were cold as ice. The cups were empty.

He stood back, nerves quivering. The elders of the town. Even in death they were invested with sober authority. In life they must have been full of dignity and honor, wise, respected, trusted. The conquerors would have found them invaluable in restoring the town to order, would gladly have given them their lives. But they had disdained to ask. Like the admiral, they had flung their lives in the faces of the conquerors. The boatwoman had only had dollars to fling, but she had flung them too, flung them away and laughed as she did it.

Coldness pulsing in his body, he stepped back into the courtyard. It was full daylight now and the town was waking, recalled to life, not by the accustomed stirrings of the dawns of centuries, but by barbarian tokens—clump of leather boots, jangle of heavy weapons, loud voices barking orders in English. Listening, Charlie smiled grimly. The drunks of the night before who were still sleeping it off in the lanes below were being cursed awake by their officers.

But boots and English voices were very nearby too, approaching the courtyard in which he was standing. Suddenly, just outside the doorway, someone said loudly:

"This must be it! Very nice! This will do you very well, sir!"

The door of the courtyard was pushed open and Gutzen entered, followed by another. Charlie ducked behind the stele. They turned to enter the larger of the two buildings. Quietly, Charlie slipped out into the lane and began to walk quickly downhill.

The havoc began halfway down the hill, the incredible carnage that a few broadsides and a single night's pillage had wrought. Cascades of bricks and tiles streamed down from toppled walls and roofs. Smashed doors and windows gaped like blind eyes. Clutter lay everywhere, unrecognizable under the thick, oily residue of the fires. He picked his way, his boots squelching in the blood-soaked mud, trying not to step on the bodies.

So many bodies, some vague shapes under the debris, some sprawled on top of it, some alone, some gathered in heaps as though meekly trying to minimize the space they took up. His passing disturbed the hordes of flies that were already clustering, though it was not yet warm. They buzzed up, hovered a moment, settled greedily back to their monstrous feast. He had never before realized that the dead were so humble. None protested the flies. None bewailed the wounds, nor the blood, nor the dirt, nor the rending of their clothing, the exposure of their privacies. A woman lay on her back, arms upflung, her breasts pointing at the sky. He bent and tugged at her blouse to cover her, and dislodged the tiny infant she'd been clutching when death flung her down. The baby rolled down the slippery surface of the lane, gathering reddish-black stains on its brand-new skin. He scrambled after it, brought it back to its mother, covered her bosom, laid it in her arms.

Beyond lay an epicene heap of bodies—how many, how young, how old it was impossible to tell—and on top of them a small boy, one leg flung out, suspened in space: At any moment it would come thudding down to carry him on the desperate flight in which death had caught him. The boy was dressed as Jin-see was—as Wei wanted Jin-see always to be dressed—in a miniature long gown of satin.

So many. So many. He walked among them, panting, stumbling, trying not to look. At last he came to a clear place, a kind of park, a belvedere where citizens might take the air on summer evenings. It was untouched, unlittered. No one had died in it—no one had thought, in the terror of the night, to run to a place meant for pleasure.

Rough stone benches stood around the little park, and Charlie sat down on one of them. Below him, the harbor was spread out, the water blue now, reflecting the sky and the shimmering beams of sunlight. The warships were no longer dim shapes—they were real and solid. Five of them were anchored in a tight row across the middle of the harbor, their port broadsides presented to the shore. Charlie strained his eyes: *Wellesley*, *Conway*, *Alligator*, *Cruiser*, and *Algerine*. Behind them the main body of the British armada was clustered, *Melville* and *Blenheim* anchored on each side of the harbor's entrance.

In a little bay at the western end of the harbor a few Chinese craft were huddled, among them the eleven war junks, stripped of their flags and pennants. Across the mouth of the bay, a British brig tacked to and fro, on guard. In the harbor, as last night, a constant stream of British cutters ferried British men from the troop transports to complete the occupation of the Chinese city. And on the top of the hill a British-appointed civil magistrate had taken power from four dead Chinese sitting around a marble table.

Abruptly, Charlie jumped to his feet, marched out of the

park, continued downhill. No one stopped him. As he reached the docks, a cutter was unloading a new cargo of soldiers. With a little shock he saw that they weren't British—they were sepoys, Indian soldiers of the British army. Black Barbarians, for whom all Chinese had the same visceral dislike that Ah Sam had of the lascars, part of the army of occupation.

Charlie walked on toward the seawall, saw *San Seb*'s masts in the distance, and began to run, suddenly anxious: He'd taken it for granted that he'd find Blogg on *San Seb*—but, by God, would he? Had Blogg been hurt? *Killed?* Panting, he ran on.

In the periphery of his vision, on the seaside, a fast-moving object suddenly appeared: a cutter, rowed very speedily and precisely by a contingent of ten smartly uniformed British sailors. From the bowsprit it flew two flags—the Union Jack and below it another: a miniature of the flag that flew from *Melville*'s halyards, the admiral's flag!

Charlie stopped. The cutter was brought very smoothly and skilfully to the embankment. Two sailors sprang out with mooring ropes. And then another figure sprang out—a tall, thin man resplendent in naval officer's uniform, corn-colored hair clubbed in a short lock beneath his cocked hat.

"George!" Charlie shouted. At the same moment, he heard Blogg roar from *San Seb*, "Ellison, by God!"

When they had shaken hands and grinned at each other and slapped each other on the back and toasted each other in rum that Blogg poured, and when they had finally settled down on *San Seb*'s bridge, Ellison said gaily:

"And where the devil did you two come from? I just happened to catch a glimpse of *San Seb* as you came around the point last night. Wouldn't have recognized her, all dolled up as she is, except that you passed so close under *Melville*'s bows that I actually saw Blogg at the helm—and lucky for you that I did, or *Melville*'s watch officer might have called down fire on you!"

Charlie kept the smile on his face, but his heart sank as the realization hit him: In the purlieus of the British navy, he and Blogg were not free agents. A hint of their desire to get to Ningpo, and they could be ordered back to Hong Kong, or even interned here in Tin-hai harbor if it so pleased the navy. He glanced at Blogg and knew that Blogg was thinking the same thing, but Blogg said easily, smiling at Ellison:

"Well, as you saw, *San Seb*'s cleaned up from hull to masts, and we were anxious to see how she'd do at sea. Marvelous, she did, but we came farther than we meant to, and once we were in these waters I thought to take a look at the currents this time of year. Then we heard the broadsides, and of course we came to see."

Ellison said wryly, waving a hand at the ruined town: "Well—you saw."

"We talked to Innes," Blogg said. "He told us you'd had dispatches."

"Yes." Ellison's gay mood, his pleasure at seeing them, had fallen into eclipse. "The admiral on *Melville* is carrying a letter from Lord Palmerston to the Emperor of China complaining of the way the high commissioner has treated the British and demanding reparations. This expeditionary force is to convince the Emperor of the wisdom of granting them, and I'm in charge of exacting them. As soon as Tin-hai is secured, the main body of the fleet will be off to the Gulf of Pei-chi-li to present Lord Palmerston's letter. If it's received at once, and if the Emperor will appoint a negotiator without delay, I hope there'll be no further need of . . ." He gestured again toward the ruins of the town.

No one spoke, and after a moment Ellison went on painfully:

"It wasn't cut-and-dried, you know. I mean, whether or not an armada was to be sent out. There was a debate in Parliament. Sir Robert Peel proposed a motion of censure against Palmerston, and many spoke in favor. Sir James Graham pointed out that I had several times asked Palmerston for instructions about opium, and none had ever been sent me. Sir Sidney Herbert said that if we engaged in war over opium it would be without just cause and a disgrace to the flag. Gladstone called opium an infamous and atrocious traffic and said outright that in his opinion justice lay with the Chinese. But in the end the motion of censure lost by nine votes. Two hundred and seventy-one to two hundred and sixty-two. Just nine votes. And the armada came."

Charlie said: "Innes hinted that Carradine had a lot to do with it."

"A lot!" Ellison laughed bitterly. *"Everything.* Andrew had a letter from his father on the same mail packet that brought my instructions from Palmerston. He showed it to me. Carradine wrote that he'd given Palmerston a 'paper of hints' of which he sent Andrew a copy. Well, credit it or not, Palmerston's instructions to me exactly matched Carradine's 'paper of hints,' with a single exception: Carradine recommended that the armada should take Hong Kong, but Palmerston decided on Choushan Island instead."

Silently, Blogg poured more grog. Ellison sipped, then spoke again, his voice an even monotone.

"We got here day before yesterday. Anchored as you see now. With the admiral's permission, I asked Gutzen—we brought him along—to write a note inviting the Chinese commander to come aboard *Wellesley.* Wanted him to see for himself what he was up against—and hoped that he might decide to surrender the town. We let him take all the time he wanted inspecting *Wellesley*'s broadsides. Then Gutzen told him that unless he surrendered by morning, *Wellesley*'s broadsides, and those of the other four ships would be used against him. He said, 'It's terrifying. But I must fight.' Well, we gave him until noon yesterday. After that, it took nine minutes. Fifteen broadsides."

No one said anything. After a while, Ellison raised his glass to peer through the amber liquid at the spiky forest of the warships' masts.

"The purpose of this whole exercise," he said slowly, "goes much further, of course, than protection of the Jackass Point traders. Palmerston made that clear in his instructions to me. Our government's desire is to improve trade between Britain and China, which would benefit not only our two countries but the whole world, especially China herself, by bringing her into the comity of nations. It's essentially for that reason that we're trying once again to open up direct communication with the Emperor. The whole thing has advanced much further than the commission that was originally given to me as superintendent of trade. The British navy has no duty, or intent, to protect the Jackass Point traders—"

His voice stopped so abruptly that the air seemed to tinkle emptily. The hand holding his glass clenched so tightly that his knuckles whitened. He leaned forward, peering. Charlie and Blogg followed his gaze.

Clear in the sunlight, clear against the erect masts of the warships, the raked masts of a clipper could be seen moving into the harbor. She tacked to skirt the mass of battleships, veered to starboard, made for the open water where *San Seb* was moored, her half-furled sails flapping in the slight breeze. A seaman in her bow was swinging lead to take soundings, shouting back his findings to the bridge. His voice came to them faintly. It was all so slow and leisurely that it was dreamlike. They watched, hypnotized. At last the clipper released her anchor. It splashed down and she came to rest with a slight tug on the chain, began to swing in the current. The name on her transom came into view: *Sylph*.

Ellison jumped to his feet, turning his back on *Sylph*, draining his glass.

"Will you two dine with me tonight on *Melville*? Yes, do!"—as Charlie and Blogg looked down at their stained clothes. "I can lend you duds, Charlie, and there's a captain on *Melville* big enough so his clothes'd fit Blogg. You must come—it's important. The Admiralty has asked the admiral to chart the waters of the Yangtze estuary. When we sail north in *Melville*, the admiral intends to leave three or four of the brigs to take soundings between here and Ningpo. I've told him that you, Blogg, know more about the currents in the estuary than any foreigner in China, and he'd be most glad of your assistance."

"You mean . . . ?"

Blogg was looking sharply at Ellison. Charlie held his breath. By God, this might be the solution! What better excuse could they have for being in the vicinity of Ningpo?

"Well," Ellison answered, "he'll probably ask you to ship on one of the brigs and lead the exploration. Charlie could go along too, of course. You could leave *San Seb* here in this harbor."

"That'd be fine," Blogg said quietly.

"Good. I'll send a cutter for you about six, with the clean clothes."

Ellison waved and leaped off *San Seb* to stride back to his cutter, not turning his eyes toward *Sylph*. When he was out of earshot, Charlie turned anxiously to Blogg.

"But if we have to go on one of the brigs—"

"Hush!" Blogg broke in. "That'd be best, Charlie. Those brigs draw very little water; that's why they chose 'em. They can go very close inshore, closer nor what *San Seb* can go. We can leave *San Seb*, not here, but in a harbor I know on one of them tiny islands right near Ningpo. Ah Sam can get into Ningpo from there, easy, while we sail around on that brig. Give us reason to be right here in these waters. Then we can set a date with Ah Sam to meet back on *San Seb*. . . . Don't you see, Charlie, its the best damned chance we've had yet!"

Charlie's throat constricted so tightly that he could not answer.

When Ellison had gone, *San Seb*'s mate and the crewmen slipped out onto the deck. They had been with *San Seb* since that first trip to Namoa. None of them was young, and the mate was old—old and wrinkled, his eyes bright squinted slits from long years of staring at the sea. Now he stared up at the ruins and shook his head and licked his lips. Why had the English killed so many Chinese? Not the enemies of England. Not even soldiers. Merchants and shopkeepers. Housewives. Grandfathers and grandmothers. Children. All peacefully pursuing their lives amid the walls their ancestors had built and they had inherited, that were gone now, in an undreamed-of, inconceivable, unspeakable storm of destruction. It was foolish, the old eyes said, to rage at the gods who hurled the thunderbolts and blew the great winds of the typhoon. But this disaster had been wrought by men, not gods. It was incomprehensible. . . .

Watching him, his heart pinching, Charlie thought of the boy last night who had leaped on the back of the soldier and stabbed him in the neck. Was that the way it was? In the old ones, anger woke slowly, but the young did not wait to cry on heaven for vengeance.

Ah Sam came out on the deck and stood by Charlie and took his hand, held it in a convulsive grip, her stony eyes fixed on the ruins of Tin-hai.

The admiral's private dining room on *Melville* was all gleaming mahogany and brass, carpets, candles in sconces, gold-framed mirrors, shining china, silver and crystal on starched white damask. It was hard to envisage that just across the harbor a ruined town brooded, lightless, where, time out of mind, thousands and thousands of lights had sparkled every night to illuminate its bustling life.

The admiral, tall, fair-haired, looking a little like Ellison but older, sat at the head of the table. Opposite him, at the foot, sat *Melville*'s captain. Along the sides of the long board sat Ellison; the captains of *Wellesley* and *Blenheim* and the four brigs that were to take part in the survey of the estuary; Colonel Burrell, commander of the military force attached to the expedition; his aide-de-camp; and the four civilians, looking drab among the glittering array of military uniforms: Charlie, in a dark frock coat belonging to Ellison; Blogg, seeming afraid to move in case he should split the seams of an old greenish coat; Gutzen in his usual hybrid costume; and Andrew Carradine in sober black and white—the finest gabardine and cambric.

They had reached the end of dinner and the stewards in spotless white uniforms and white gloves were clearing the table. The dinner had been magnificent, including an enormous roast of fresh-killed beef. The admiral had graciously thanked Gutzen for that.

"Ingenious of you, Reverend, to produce such a treat so soon after taking over the administration of the town. There are shops open, then?"

"Er . . . no, sir." Gutzen's eye swiveled. "Some of my staff made a foray into the countryside to see the lay of the land and found a farmer who was—er—cooperative. He was paid, of course."

"Of course." The admiral inclined his head. "And how is the restoration of civil order proceeding?"

"It's early to say, sir. I have taken over the government office. As you know, I was able to persuade some of my good Chinese friends from Macao to accompany me here, so I already have the nucleus of a staff. In addition, we were fortunate enough to find four of the local clerks hiding near the government compound, and were able to persuade them back to work, which saved us a great deal of time and trouble discovering what we need to know about the records and so forth."

"You found none of the former administrators?"

"Er—no." Again Gutzen's eye swiveled.

"Cowards!" Colonel Burrell spluttered out the word in his loud, harsh voice. He was a red-faced, bull-necked man whose collar seemed to be half choking him. "Running away! Saving themselves, and the devil with the people they're responsible for!"

Gutzen's eye began to swivel wildly, but his tone remained quiet.

"I believe, Colonel, that running away in face of an attacking force fiercer than anything you've ever conceived in your wildest imagination is a normal, not a cowardly, reaction. In any case, the administrators did not run away."

286

"What happened to them?" Ellison's voice cut sharply from the other end of the table.

"They committed suicide," Gutzen said woodenly. "I found them sitting around a table in a private room of the government offices. They had drunk poisoned tea."

In profound silence, the stewards served port and brandy and placed cheroots on the table.

The admiral broke the silence, turning again to Gutzen.

"D'you think the people who fled the town will soon return? You understand that we must have the town back in working order as soon as possible. We may need to use it as a bargaining point, and a pillaged town, in ruins and empty of population, has little barter value."

Gutzen nodded. "From what my staff saw today, most of the people who fled are taking shelter in the countryside not far off. I believe they'll begin returning as soon as there is some semblance of normalcy—but that, of course, cannot be until the dead are buried." He leaned forward to glance down the table at Colonel Burrell. "May I take the liberty of asking the colonel when that will be?"

The colonel harrumphed and glared at Gutzen, his neck seeming to creak as he turned it against the tightness of his collar. "I ordered it done within two days. The sepoys are mutinous still—they didn't want to come to China, you know—but they'll buckle down. Damned fools think that in the *British army* they can pick and choose where they want to be sent!" He managed to sound sullen and threatening at the same time.

Gutzen said softly: "I believe the Chinese would also much prefer the Black Barbarians to remain in their own country. Anyway . . . I understand that your task is complicated by the very large number of bodies—larger than one would expect from the brief bombardment. My staff took a survey today. Many of the dead were killed, not by grape or balls or falling masonry, but by knife wounds."

"God blast it!" Burrell's face turned purple. "Am I to be blamed because the town was full of liquor?"

The admiral intervened.

"No one is to be blamed for that, Colonel. What we are all most sincerely hoping is that the town will be spared further *loot.*"

The color of the colonel's face grew frighteningly darker. He opened his mouth, but no sound issued. His aide-de-camp, beside Charlie, lowered his head and gazed into his brandy as though searching it for something.

"What's *loot?*" Charlie murmured.

"Hindi word," the aide-de-camp whispered back from the corner of his mouth, not raising his eyes. "Means 'pillage.' "

A uniformed officer entered the room, saluted stiffly, and, head in air, eyes staring at the ceiling, requested permission to speak to Captain Ellison. Ellison rose, excusing himself, and went across to him. After a moment of whispering, he came back to his seat. Charlie thought that he had paled.

"What is it, George?" the admiral asked.

"Sir." Ellison spoke evenly. "The Chinese commander. I learned that his legs were shot off during the bombardment. I suggested he be taken aboard *Blenheim* for our doctors to try to save his life. He died an hour ago."

"Well . . ." The admiral shrugged. "Fortune of war."

He rose, and everyone else instantly sprang to his feet.

"Good night, gentlemen. I hope you'll all retire soon. There's much to be done in the next few days. . . . Captain Blogg, I am grateful for your help in surveying the estuary. George, will you please complete the arrangements for Captain Blogg and Mr. Tyson to ship with Anstruther on *Kite.*"

As the admiral left the room, the men split into groups. Ellison came up to Charlie and Blogg with a tall, thin, pleasant-looking man whom he introduced as Captain Anstruther. Anstruther said, and sounded as though he meant it, that he was delighted to have Charlie and Blogg aboard *Kite.* He and Blogg and Ellison began a technical discussion. Charlie's mind turned to Ningpo. It would be soon! Anstruther and Blogg were talking about starting out tomorrow. *San Seb* could go across to that harbor Blogg knew of the same day. Ah Sam could be in Ningpo by the following day.

". . . a hundred dollars is a giveaway price, but that's just to encourage new customers, of course."

Andrew Carradine's voice carried clearly across the room. Ellison stopped speaking in midsentence and turned his head sharply toward the group among whom Andrew stood. Andrew was a little drunk, his words were slurred, but there was no mistaking the satisfied gaiety of his mood.

". . . *Falcon*, with my father and two thousand chests aboard, arrived at Lintin the day after the warships sailed into Hong Kong harbor. The day after that, *Jamesina* arrived with a thousand chests. Lintin's heavily stocked again, and my father thought we could well spare five hundred chests for the sake of being first in the market here."

Ellison strode across the room and confronted Andrew.

"What the devil d'you mean?"

"Why, George . . ." Andrew sounded amused. "What I say, of course. The house of Carradine and Son was first to restock the hulks at Lintin, and now we're first in the Choushan market. There're five hundred chests in *Sylph*, and as soon as Tin-hai's opened up again I'm going to offer them at a hundred dollars a chest—"

"Damn you!" Ellison's voice blistered with anger. "D'you think you can use the navy to protect your bloody filthy trade?"

"We're not *using* the navy, George. How could we?" Andrew's voice was blandly reproving. Pointedly, he turned to *Melville*'s captain, who, in the absence of the admiral, was both host and senior officer. "Isn't that so, sir? What did we have to do with the fact that *Druid* and *Larne* are now with *Volage* and *Hyacinth*, blockading the Bay of Canton?"

"Nothing whatever!" Melville's captain glared. "What could civilians have to say about the disposition of naval ships?"

Andrew shrugged. "There you are! So how can we be blamed if the mandarins are encouraged by the presence of those ships?

289

So encouraged, in fact, that they're defying their high commissioner and clamoring to get back on our rosters for bribes. Which, incidentally"—he turned to smile sweetly at stone-faced Ellison—"are back to thirty dollars a chest."

Melville's captain said impatiently: "What's all this got to do with the navy?"

"Exactly my point, sir!" Andrew bowed. "It's nothing whatever to do with the navy that trade's booming again along the southern coast. And that I'm here to start the boom up north. . . . Don't glare at me like that, George!" Andrew laughed teasingly. "It's not just the Carradines, you know. Its Dent and Innes and God knows how many others—even peddlers, like Tyson."

On the last words, Andrew raised his voice a little. Across the room, Charlie knew, without looking, that Andrew was smiling derisively. The beginning of anger stirred.

"Though I understand," Andrew went on, elaborately casual, "that Tyson's out of the market now. Sold that ancient hulk of his to Innes and went chasing after his doxy, who's left him. . . ."

For an instant, Charlie's ears rejected what they had heard: It was unbelievable! The next instant he was crossing the room, shoving through the group around Andrew and driving his fist into the handsome, smiling, mocking face. Andrew staggered back, and Charlie surged forward to stand over him, the jolt of the contact shooting joyfully up his arm, the explosion of anger buzzing around his head. In a smooth movement, Andrew recovered and leaped at Charlie, eyes blazing blue hatred, fists jabbing, knee seeking Charlie's groin. Charlie went down before the onslaught and they rolled together on the carpet in furious embrace.

Charlie felt a dozen hands laid on him, trying to pull him away, but he hung on to Andrew and knew that Andrew was clinging to him too. Once before they had confronted each other and been deterred. Now at last they were joined. Lust joined them, lust for each other's blood, and they would not be parted until it was spilled in orgasmic climax.

Panting, grunting, straining, gouging, jabbing, squeezing, they struggled in blind violence, their blood flowing and mingling indistinguishably. It might never have ended. They might have fought to the death, but inevitably, at last, they were dragged away from each other. Dazed and dizzy, Charlie found himself being hustled along passages and laid down upon a bunk. Someone was applying cold wet cloths to his face and head, and someone else was massaging his limbs. After a while the world stopped whirling, and the throbbing pain lessened. He opened his eyes. Ellison and Blogg were standing by the bunk, watching him worriedly.

"I'm sorry, Charlie!" Ellison leaned forward. "I should have warned you, but I never dreamed that Andrew would indulge in such damned bad taste! He knows, of course, that she's your wife! He was baiting you. Innes has been spreading some damned story that a boatman is supposed to have told him. Did he once get you a boatman to sail you to Kolo-an? His story is that on the sail across the bay you raped the boatman's daughter and then tried to pay the parents off with six silver dollars. Some rubbish like that. And the parents in revenge told Innes about your wife. . . ."

"Oh God!" Charlie tried to sit up but lay back again. "I did take the daughter hostage, sort of, to ensure that they took me to Kolo-an, and didn't dump me in the bay somewhere, but . . ."

The room began to whirl again, and he closed his eyes. Anger raced dizzily through his veins, but so did a wild and fierce satisfaction. He had spilled Andrew's blood!

"You all right, Charlie?" Blogg asked anxiously.

"All right," he muttered and sat up, wiping his hands over his face. "Come on, Blogg."

He staggered to his feet. There was no time to be lost. They'd be transferring to *Kite* tomorrow, and there were many plans and arrangements yet to be made on *San Seb.*

"Charlie . . ." Ellison's voice was determined. "I have to ask you. If I can, I want to help you. Where is your wife?"

Charlie tried to give him a straight look, but his eyes wouldn't focus. He mustn't tell him where Ling-ling was, for he would guess that they meant to get into Ningpo, and he would find a way to stop them. Blinking, he said as clearly as he could:

"My wife and I are temporarily separated."

Ellison paused a moment, then held out his hand.

"Very well. I hope the separation will soon be ended. . . . This is goodbye for now. You'll be going aboard *Kite* tomorrow, and a day or two later I'll be sailing north with the fleet. I suppose we'll meet again in Hong Kong harbor. . . ."

They formally shook hands. As Blogg helped Charlie from the cabin, Ellison said softly, "Good luck."

The cutter took them back to *San Seb*, the seamen dipping their oars with uncanny precision, sending the boat swiftly across the harbor. The water twinkled with the lights of the warships and bounced with the sounds of chat and laughter and singing. Above, the crippled town brooded darkly.

Chapter X
August-December
1840

I T WAS A STEAMING August day, the thirtieth day on *Kite*.
On leaving the harbor of Tin-hai, *Kite* had proceeded
south across the strait to the southeastern tip of the Bay
of Hangchow. They had worked their way slowly westward,
taking soundings in a range of about a mile from the shoreline
to as close inshore as they could get. They were now near the
coastal village of Chin-hai, behind which, twelve miles inland,
Ningpo stood on the bank of a river.

Charlie sat under an awning on *Kite*'s deck, surveying
the scene. Many fisher boats cruised the shallow gray-green
waters, and junks and ferries made their way east and west
along the coast, but there was little traffic through the archipelago of which Choushan was the main island—the occupation of Tin-hai had stopped traffic on that axis.

Charlie yawned as *Kite*, having reached the outer limit
of her survey range, turned once again inland. The sounding
of a body of water was one of the most boring businesses he
had ever known, involving the unending swinging of lead by

a succession of seamen, the monotonous calling out of their findings, constant readings of the sextant, and continual jottings on a hand-drawn map.

He turned to stare westward, where, somewhere behind the shimmering heat haze, Ningpo lay. Fifteen miles away? No more than that. He was that close to them. His body—the whole of his being—shifted in a surge of longing as strong and deep as the swell of the sea itself. Had Ah Sam found them? The day after Charlie and Blogg had transferred to *Kite,* the mate had sailed *San Seb* to Tao-hua-tao, one of the tiny islands that trailed southward from Choushan like a comet's tail. From there, Ah Sam was to have made her way into Ningpo. If she found Ling-ling and the children and could pry them away from Wei, they would all proceed at once to Tao-hua-tao and wait aboard *San Seb.* If she could not locate Ling-ling, or could not get her and the children away from Wei, she would return to *San Seb* after five weeks. In either case, after five weeks, the mate would sail *San Seb* back to Tin-hai harbor. By that time, *Kite*'s soundings should have been completed and Blogg and Charlie could reasonably ask Anstruther to sail them back to Tin-hai to their own vessel. . . . The plan was as full of holes as a sieve, but it had been the best they could come up with. At least it ensured thirty-five days for Ah Sam to try to locate Ling-ling and the children, and for Charlie and Blogg and *San Seb* to be close, very close, to Ningpo. Thirty days were gone already. Had Ah Sam found them?

A shadow fell across Charlie, and he looked up to see Captain Anstruther settling down on one of the stools under the awning, with his sketchbook.

"Blogg's taken over," he said, smiling. "By God, I thought to have been sailing north now in *Melville*'s wake, and I was glad enough to get detailed to this survey job—but to get Blogg on top of it!"

He laughed and opened his sketchbook. Charlie glanced over at a charcoal drawing of the head and shoulders of one of the seamen, a striking, full-bearded face, the eyes squinted intently, the arm raised in the typical gesture of swinging the lead. The drawing lived and breathed.

"By God, you're good!" Charlie exclaimed. "Don't know why you're in the navy!"

"Artists starve," Anstruther said, picking up a stick of charcoal. "At least, until they're dead and have no more use for food. Then maybe they begin to get known, in which case it's their descendants who get to eat." He began to sketch the head of one of the other seamen, throwing quick glances at him, his hand moving smoothly. Without lifting his eyes, he said obliquely:

"That to-do on *Melville* that night . . . I'm not prying into whatever may be between you and Carradine, but Carradine talked about 'chests.' Did he mean opium?"

For a moment Charlie was too astonished to answer. Was there anyone in these waters who could be in doubt that "chests" meant opium?

"Yes," he said at last.

"Mmmmm." Anstruther sketched in a line, rubbed it lightly with his finger to create a shadow. "There's more and more talk about it at home. Most people think, what the devil, it makes us a lot of money and whatever makes money must be good. But there's a lot now who're listening to Gladstone and the others who speak against it. They're saying not only that we shouldn't be selling it, but that we shouldn't even be *producing* it. . . ."

Kite lurched slightly. Anstruther looked up, not yet alarmed. Then there was a low, scraping sound, and Blogg went by them at a run, shouting to the helmsman. With an incoherent yell, Anstruther leaped up, sketchpad and charcoal flying, and rushed after him. *Kite* shuddered and seemed to struggle for a moment. Then, with a rending crash, she veered sharply and began listing heavily to starboard. As he fell from his stool and started slithering into the scuppers, Charlie saw Blogg and Anstruther and all the other men on deck stagger and flop to the boards, and start sliding helplessly.

*   *   *

At dusk, they determined that *Kite* would have to be abandoned. Crawling crabwise along the slope of the deck, clinging to projections, the crew had managed to launch the gig, and Anstruther and Blogg had gone to inspect the damage. *Kite* had speared herself on a jagged outcrop of rocks a few feet below the waterline. Even if she could be towed off, she was already filled with water up to her new waterline, and she would rapidly sink.

There was nothing for it but to wait for morning, hire a junk, or more than one if possible, and sail for Tin-hai harbor, where the troop transports were anchored. One of them would have to sail across and take off *Kite's* crew. It would take two or three days, during which the crew would have to get around by crawling on bulkheads that used to be vertical and were now almost horizontal. No cooking could be done. Rations would have to consist of dried beef and ship's tack.

Fortunately, the rum was intact. Anstruther ordered a double tot all around, and by the time it was fully dark, the men were squatting in a long row athwart the port gunwale, which was now pointed high in the air, cheerfully singing chanties.

Anstruther, his officers, Blogg, and Charlie sat on their haunches on the horizontal starboard bulkhead of the main cabin, chewing dried beef and sipping grog. Anstruther had recovered his sketchpad and now, by the light of a flaring oil lantern, was calmly sketching the head of his third mate.

Blogg said admiringly:

"By God, Anstruther, navy'd do well to have more like you! Some men'd be screaming for the helmsman to be keel-hauled!"

Anstruther, sketching busily, laughed. "Much good that would do!"

The first mate said conversationally—Anstruther seemed to inspire his officers to the same unworried calm that was at the core of his nature—"There's no more than seven feet at high tide inshore, near as we can get. No wonder there're so many fisher boats—must be marvelous easy fishing hereabouts."

The talk went on. Charlie sat silent, thinking that there were still five days left of the five-week time span of their plan. He and Blogg should be able, whatever happened, to keep the rendezvous with *San Seb.*

"Hoy!" One of the officers cocked his head, pointing upward. The singing out on deck, which had become one with the background sounds—the swish of water, the evening call of birds—was noticeably dying down. A moment later they heard feet scrambling to enter the narrow slit of the horizontal doorway.

"Cap'n, sir. Summat be 'appening. Best you come see, sir."

They all went on deck, scrambling for perches on the bridge ladders, which now lay on their sides. It was very dark. The heads and shoulders of the men astride the port gunwale made a jagged black line against the paler darkness of the sky. They were sitting strangely still, all staring in the same direction, out to sea.

"What's the matter?" Anstruther called.

No one answered—there was no need of answer, for all at once they all saw what was the matter. Surrounding *Kite* on the seaward side, a wide semicircle of lights was closing in. The lights were tiny yet, quite faint in the darkness, but there were a great many of them, and they were steadily nearing.

"I see," Anstruther said. "It's the fisher boats."

For a long time after that there was silence. The lights grew brighter. Then there was a burst of mutters.

"All our gunpowder sopping wet!"

"We bain't so far from shore, and it's right shallow. We could slide down and wade ashore."

"In a *'eathen land?'*"

"Wot then? Wait for they?"

"Wot else?"

"They be hundreds of 'em!"

"So we does for 'em with our cutlasses—ten or twenty head each."

There was no answer to that, and silence fell again. Charlie heard Anstruther say to Blogg, low-voiced:

"What are our chances?"

"For what?" Blogg answered softly. "For getting away by wading ashore? None—they'll be waiting for us there. For closing with them, killing a few of them afore they kill us? If you like. . . . But I reckon our best chance is wait till they come and let them take us. That way nobody gets killed, not them, but not us neither. If killing starts, I reckon it's us who'll be floating on our faces when it's over."

As though to agree with Blogg, *Kite* lurched, shifting on the ebb tide, and listed even more steeply. There was a thunderous rumble and a heavy splash as one of the cannon broke loose and tumbled into the water. Men fell off their perches like ninepins and went rolling after the cannon, their shouts cut off suddenly as they hit the water, then breaking out again as they rose in the shallows, gasping. Anstruther ordered a roll call, but the officer who went to fetch the roster returned to say that it was floating out of reach, so instead, Anstruther asked the men to call out if anyone missed a mate. After all the shouts and answers had died down, Anstruther raised his voice.

"We're all present and correct, then? Very well, listen. . . . There're thirty-one of us, and two or three hundred of them, more perhaps. The question is, what do we do? We can't fire our cannon at this angle, and not even our pistols, since the gunpowder's soaked. We could resist capture by using our cutlasses and other hand weapons, but it must be clear that although we'd kill a few fishermen, in the end we'd all undoubtedly be killed, since we're so heavily outnumbered. We could wade ashore, but we'd simply be walking into the arms of whoever's waiting for us—and you may be damned sure *somebody*'s waiting. . . . Well, men, what do we do? I for one am hoping to get home to my wife and children one day soon"—there were fervent mutters of "Hear, hear!"—"so I vote we do as Captain Blogg says—wait for them to come, and surrender as to a superior force."

" 'Ow do we know?" someone shouted. "Oo's to say they won't cut our throats once they's got a-holt of us?"

Blogg raised his voice:

"Men, I've been in these waters nigh on thirty years, and I'm certain-sure of one thing: Nearer our fleet gets to Peking, safer we are. They'll do nothing to risk bombardment by our warships so near to where their Emperor's at."

There was a moment of silence, then a rising murmur of agreement and approval interspersed with dissenting growls.

"Didn't you hear the cap'n?" someone yelled indignantly. *"Superior force.* 'Tain't no disgrace to surrender to superior force—'tis no but *common sense!"*

"We're all agreed then?" Anstruther called.

"We're agreed, Cap'n." The answers came from all over. "We're agreed!" "We'll wait for 'em!"

"Good!" Anstruther shouted. "Then let's try and keep as warm as we can while we wait. Everybody keep track of the man on the right of you—that way we'll know if somebody falls off. Cookie! Get your mates and go below. Get some nets and bring up rations. Share them out. Everybody's got to eat something now and keep some for later—put it safely in a pocket or stick it under your belt. And Cookie—bring the rum too."

There were cheers and laughter and chatter that lasted until the rations had been distributed and everyone had had a nip from a bottle. Then quiet fell. A wind rose and with it muttered curses as the men shivered and tried to find warmth in the clothing that had been more than adequate in the heat of the day. One by one, men lowered themselves carefully down the cliff of the deck, into the lee of the wind, clinging to the rigging, tying themselves to it if they could. There were murmurs and the scrabble of feet and now and then a cry as someone began to slip and scrambled to save himself.

Charlie bent cautiously until he was squatting uncomfortably on the rail of a ladder lying on its side. His heart was thudding dully, his mind blurring, flooded with inexpressible woe, loss, abandonment. More than a year of longing and dreaming and planning and striving to arrive on this cold, wet, painful perch on a wrecked ship, waiting to be picked off by Chinese fishermen!

"Charlie . . ." It was Blogg's voice whispering from a yard or so away in the darkness. "Charlie—you hear me? Wouldn't surprise me none were they to take us to Ningpo. . . . You hear me, Charlie?"

Through the hum of blood in his ears, through the tightness of his throat, Charlie managed to mutter, "Yes."

"Ain't nothing else they can do with us, far as I can see. Ningpo's no more than fifteen mile from here, and it's a big town. Must be a magistracy there, or something like that. Stands to reason that's where they'll take us."

Ningpo. *Inside* the city. Not hovering in the sea around. Not hanging about outside the walls. *Inside* the city itself!

"We won't be free, o' course," Blogg's murmur went on. "They won't let us wander about, that's certain-sure. But maybe . . . somehow . . ."

Maybe. Somehow.

Blood pounding, sweat suddenly pouring, Charlie rose to his feet, welcoming the rush of the breeze that cooled his body and swept his mind bright and clean. With new eyes he surveyed the scene. The lights were much brighter now, the circle much narrower. The fisher boats were closing in fast. Over the whisper of the wind, he could hear the swish of their oars. In these shallow waters, the fisher boats were small, flat-bottomed, with square decks fore and aft and a deep well in the waist in which the fish were deposited. They had stubby masts and small square sails, but their main means of propulsion was the single great stern oar that a rower standing on the aft deck rowed with a figure-eight motion to propel the boat forward as a fish is propelled by the motion of its tail. It was the swish of these heavy oars that came now to the listeners on *Kite*, as well as the low chatter of voices and the restless, shadowy to-and-fro movement of men passing before the lanterns that were suspended from the masts of the fisher boats, which were very close now, gunwale to gunwale, a solid phalanx encircling *Kite*.

There was a loud shout—a signal, for all at once a horde of men from the boats and from the shore hurled themselves into the thigh-deep water, churning it into a luminescent froth as they rushed toward the wrecked ship. Suddenly, hundreds of voices were shouting, turning the black night into a volcano of sound and fury. Fishermen trying to swarm up *Kite*'s cantilevered deck were being knocked back by sailors sliding uncontrollably down the deck, and all were plunging into the water, yelling, struggling, splashing, heaving like great stranded fish. Charlie dropped down and was immediately knocked over. He floundered, feeling the sting of salt water rush up his nose and spread behind his eyes. A dozen hands grasped him and pulled and pushed him along, he and his captors together in a tangled knot, stumbling, falling, gulping water, struggling up again to stagger on. At last he felt himself hauled up over the side of a boat and flung down into its well. Someone jumped down on top of him, crushing his face into the filthy bilge awash on the bottom, while someone else bound his wrists. He struggled to lift his nostrils out of the bilge, and another body came shuttling down on top of him, its owner kicking violently and cursing in English.

"Easy!" Charlie panted, and the man grunted loudly, then was still. Tensely, they lay together in the intimate contact of their tiny, pitch-dark prison while the noise of battle echoed hollowly around them and the overpowering stench of dead fish threatened to clog their lungs. Shoutings and splashings approached again, and Charlie braced himself for the descent of another body on top of them, but none came. Instead, the fishermen began to clamber back into their boat. The battle was over, but the shouting went on for a long time, the Chinese voices raging with excitement, blaring with triumph, apparently giving and seeking instructions. At last the boat began to move, in a line with other boats, it appeared, for the sound of oars squeaking in their rowlocks went before and behind them.

Lying on his stomach half over the legs of the other man, the right side of his face in the bilge water, Charlie squinted open his left eye and saw that light was approaching in swinging washes—someone had unhitched one of the lanterns from the mast and was carrying it forward. In a moment it was lowered into the well, brilliantly illuminating the black wash of the bilge water, the scummy boards covered with silvery flashes which were the scales of the long-dead fish whose lingering stink was almost tangible, and the man with whom Charlie lay entwined. It was the seaman whose head Anstruther had sketched. The beard was twisted under the chin, the eyes were closed, and there was a gash across the cheekbone that oozed drops, bright red in the light of the lantern, indistinguishably black as soon as they dripped into the bilge. The man was so pale that Charlie held his breath. Was he dead? But then he snorted and grimaced and muttered, "Gawd rot it!" and Charlie breathed again.

The lantern was raised, and the scope of Charlie's vision widened. He glimpsed five faces staring down at them, eyes darting about like the shining wings of moths when they caught the light: the fishermen examining their catch. They chattered excitedly to each other, pointing bony fingers at items of interest—the heavy beard of Charlie's companion, the shape of his nose. Then, suddenly, with a loud exclamation, one of them caught sight of something of tremendous interest, and fingers shot down at Charlie's head. Charlie squeezed his eyes shut and flinched away, but the fingers were aimed only at his hair. They clutched it painfully, as though they would detach it from his head, while their owners laughed and chattered and over and over again made the high-pitched, long-drawn-out expression of Chinese astonishment: *"Yeeeeeeeee!"*

"What be they doing?" Charlie's companion muttered, his eyes squeezed tightly shut.

"They're pulling my hair," Charlie whispered, not moving. "They like the color."

But suddenly the fishermen tired of their game. The lantern was withdrawn and placed on the deck. The angle of light altered into a cone that illumined a corner of their prison, leaving everything above and below in darkness. Through the cone of light, a bare, horny brown foot appeared, protruding from a faded blue cotton trouser leg. Charlie felt the foot place itself gently against the side of his face. Then, slowly, the foot increased its pressure, forcing his nose down under the water. He lay still until he felt his lungs were about to burst, then, with a sudden twist, he arched his neck to bring his lips above the water and gulp a great breath of the fishy air. He heard their laughter—childlike laughter, the laughter of children teasing a strange, captive animal. He felt the angle of the light change again, and flicked open an eye to see their laughing faces eerily lit by the lantern—red mouths, flicking tongues, broken brown teeth.

Then one of the faces changed. The laughter fled, the lips contorted, the eyes blazed with the black fire of hatred. The foot came down again, stamping this time, smashing the side of his head against the bottom of the hull. He heard the hollow sound and was astonished for an instant that he felt nothing. Then the pain exploded.

Later he was conscious that the man with whom he lay was nudging him and whispering: "Hoy, mate. You all right?"

"All ri—" he managed before darkness descended again. Still later, through the ear that lay pressed against the bottom of the hull, he heard the murmur of water, gentle and muted and somehow soothing, and he slept. Again later, hands hauled him up, scraping his back against the edge of the well, then against the boat's gunwale, and then against some kind of pier or jetty. Every nerve in his body and every sting and ache and pain screamed in protest. Then he was prostrate again, lying on someone's body, propped up on each side by other bodies, and all the bodies began jolting as whatever they lay on went bumping forward.

And at last, a long time later, someone beside him said clearly: "You all right, Charlie?" and he knew that it was Blogg.

"Are we in Ningpo, Blogg?" The words jumped from his mouth before he knew he was going to say them, before recollection had fully returned. He held his breath, waiting for Blogg's answer.

"Don't see where else we could be," Blogg said. "Reckon we're in the Ningpo magistracy or something like that. Take a look for yourself."

A giddy euphoria flooding him, Charlie opened his eyes. Daylight jangled his vision, but when it cleared he saw that he was sitting on the ground and that Blogg, beside him, his beard and hair streaked with sand and seaweed, was grinning at him.

Charlie grinned back. Immediately, pain sliced down through his cheekbone. He put up a hand to touch it gingerly, and blood oozed onto his fingers.

"Got quite a bump there," Blogg said, "but seems like nothing else wrong with you but for some scrapes along your back. We've had good joss. All present and accounted for, and not much damage done."

Charlie looked around. They sat in the middle of a huge courtyard paved with granite flagstones and surrounded by high walls. Blogg sat beside him, and on Blogg's other side was Anstruther. All around them, in a close-knit little group, were the officers and men of *Kite*, a filthy and bedraggled lot. Charlie looked down at himself and saw that he too was filthy, shirt and trousers torn and soiled, stained in great patches of gray and green and black and bloody red, speckled all over with silvery fish scales. And he stank!

They were all sitting so close together because they were tied to each other by the legs. Their hands were free—Charlie rubbed his wrists where the rope that had bound them had left a reddish burn—but their ankles were bound by long ropes wound loosely, in such a way that no man could move his legs without dragging on the legs of the men beside him.

On three sides of the court in which they sat were buildings three or four stories high with square deep-embrasured windows like those of the government offices that Gutzen had taken over in Tin-hai. On the fourth side was the entrance gate to the courtyard—a huge affair that now stood wide open, barred by trestles and guarded by soldiers with swords and blunderbusses. Behind the trestles the open gateway was stuffed solid, gatepost to gatepost and twenty feet deep behind, with a seething mass of people compressed so closely that they rippled and rolled like a single enormous body pimpled with multiple heads and legs and arms. And over the tops of the walls that surrounded the courtyard more faces loomed— row upon row upon row of faces, jerking into and out of sight as their owners shoved and pushed each other for a glimpse into the courtyard. And from all those thousands of faces came an enormous, buzzing, humming, rumbling, resonant roar.

"God Almighty!" Charlie muttered.

"Aye!" Blogg quirked his eyebrows. "We're a right curiosity!"

Anstruther leaned forward and smiled at Charlie. He had a cut over one eye to which blobs of dried blood clung, making him look raffish and piratical, but his smile was cheerful.

"Glad you're back with us!" He jerked his head toward the crowds of faces. "Wish there were some way of charging admission! We could get *Kite* repaired in no time. Extra charge for gaping at Blogg—took ten men to lift him out of the cart— and at you, Charlie. Seems you're the original Red Barbarian, so Blogg says. Did you see our own private personal guardians?"

He jerked his head again, and Charlie turned to see that a long row of soldiers was circulating slowly around their forlorn little group.

"They were just standing to begin with," Anstruther said. "But one of them came closer to take a look at your hair, and then they all did—ever since then, they've been walking around and around!"

He laughed cheerfully as nostalgia swept Charlie. It was Wei who had first fingered his hair and said, "Good-joss color!" Where had all the good joss gone?

The sun was climbing the sky. Where the group from *Kite* sat in the middle of the courtyard there was no protection from its merciless rays. They were going to be burned to a crisp. The soldiers were already beginning, by ones and twos, to back off into the shade of the buildings. Glancing enviously after them, Charlie saw for the first time that fifty or sixty other men were already sheltering against the thick walls. The drabness of their clothing against the gray-black shadows had made them hard to see. Blogg nodded toward them.

"Some of the fisher folk who brung us here." He smiled wryly. "They certain-sure don't like to give us up! Keeping their eye on us still! When we got here, everybody come running out to look—even the governor, or maybe the magistrate—anyway a big mandarin all dressed up in silk and satin and one of them peacock feathers in his hat. Never seen such excitement! Stood and chattered and stared at us a long time, then went back inside with some of the fisher folk. Reckon they're having a hard time deciding what to do with us. Now that they know what our warships can do, they certain-sure don't want to risk more ruination of their towns, and they know they'd call that down if they harm us. Anyway, we're better value to 'em alive than dead—they can use us for bargaining. But . . ." Blogg jerked his head toward the throngs at the gate and on the walls. "Listen to them. They want our blood and our guts. They want to cut our hearts out. And anybody who makes decisions is bound to take account of any crowd as big and noisy as they."

He shrugged and fell silent. Around them the men from *Kite* sat quietly. They had long since eaten the rations Anstruther had distributed last night. It was thirst that began to torment them now. Charlie's throat felt like sand—he could not even muster enough spittle to ease it by swallowing.

It was a long, long day. Nothing happened, except that the soldiers and the fishermen in the shade of the buildings took their ease, squatting down, lying back, falling asleep, although the throngs around the gate and the walls were relentless in their hating energy. The sun dragged through its orbit with infinite slowness. Sweat poured out of the men from *Kite*. Visibly, by the minute, their skins pinked and then reddened, became fiery-colored. The men drooped; some seemed to lose consciousness.

At last black shade from the building on the west began to

touch the group. They shuffled into it, shifting on their haunches, moving their bound legs in concert. The guardian soldiers woke up and came running, shouting harshly, raising their weapons, but they did nothing more than resume their patrol.

And at last, from the main building at the back of the courtyard, a small parade emerged. At its head was the mandarin in his robes and his hat adorned with peacock feathers, walking with measured stride. Behind him came other officials also grandly dressed and dignified, but none of them got the least attention from the members of *Kite*'s crew, for in their wake came two coolies bearing shoulder poles, from each end of which swung a heavy wooden bucket, glistening damply, oozing droplets. Water.

A deep groan rose from the group, a sound between torment and ecstasy. Every eye was fixed on the buckets, every head turned slowly to follow the progress of the coolies. As the dignitaries stopped in front of the group from *Kite*, the coolies plonked the buckets down on the flagstones. For an instant Charlie felt astonished that the buckets remained put— surely the concerted, the desperate desire of the men from *Kite* must lift them up into the air, carry them forward of their own volition! But the buckets remained, and the mandarin stepped forward. He held his head high. He was frowning. He extended his left arm in front of him and, with a slow and exaggerated gesture, passed his right hand over it, drawing up the sleeve to expose his wrist. He did the same thing with the right sleeve. He cleared his throat. Finally, he began to speak.

Even if they could have understood him, not a single Englishman would have listened. The buckets of water riveted their attention. The mandarin spoke at length, giving no sign that he knew that the people to whom he spoke couldn't understand him, but at last he stopped, stepped back, looking satisfied, and waved the waterbearers forward. As one, *Kite*'s crew strained toward them, eyes glazed, mouths open.

But it was not yet to be.

Anstruther rose to his feet. His face, his arms, the patches

of skin exposed by his torn clothing, were burned lobster scarlet. His bound ankles hampered him and his knees were shaky.
He had to clutch Blogg's arm to haul himself up. But he rose
to his feet, stood swaying for a moment, then gathered himself and bowed formally to the mandarin.

"Sir." His voice came out a croak. "I am Captain Anstruther of Her Majesty's ship *Kite*. You and I cannot understand each other, but it is my duty to point out that we are
here as your captives only because our ship had the misfor-
tune to run aground. To save the lives of my men, I ordered
our surrender to a superior force of fishermen who heavily
outnumbered us. Nevertheless, I must tell you, sir, that we
are loyal to Her Majesty Victoria, Queen and Empress, and
nothing you can say or do will undermine that."

He staggered, held to Blogg's shoulder with his left hand,
and turned toward his men waving his arm.

"Long live the Queen! Hip, hip . . ."

"HURRAH! HURRAH! HURRAH!"

The cheers echoed and reechoed, the men waving wildly,
staggering to their knees, their eyes shining through swollen
lids, their cracked lips grinning out of bright red faces already
beginning to blister.

The mandarin stared, drawing his head back and cocking it
like a great sparrow. Charlie saw his mouth form the inevita-
ble *"Yeeeee!"* The officials behind him stared too, shrugged,
waved their hands in astonishment, and so did the soldiers,
and the fishermen, and even—Charlie thought—the crowd
beyond the walls.

As the cheers died down, the mandarin turned to Anstruther. In a moment of dead silence, they bowed gravely to
each other. Then the mandarin turned and strode back to his
office at the head of his retinue. Anstruther collapsed, falling
half on top of Blogg, grimacing with the pain of his cramped
legs and his burned skin, but still grinning, weakly waving toward the waterbearers, gasping, "Bring it on! Bring it on!"

* * *

Used as bedding, the flagstones were rotten. Charlie slept restlessly, waking often, stiff with cold but at the same time feeling the painful warmth of his scorched skin. He heard the men from *Kite* muttering, groaning, snoring, snorting, and under their noises, listening carefully, he heard a kind of hum from around the walls of the courtyard. At nightfall the soldiers closed the main gate, forcibly pushing the spectators back, but it seemed that some were still there, crouching in the dark, keeping places for when dawn came and they could once more gape and stare and point at the hated barbarians.

At last, first light broke. With it came the same coolies who had distributed ladlefuls of water the night before; this time to distribute steaming hot soft-boiled rice, scooping it out of the buckets in bowls made out of dried gourds cut in half. There were no spoons, but the rice was soft enough to be slurped directly from the bowls, and *Kite*'s crew began busily slurping. Watching them, seeing the steam curl lazily out of the buckets, Charlie knew that he was ravenous. When his turn came, the gruel slipped down his throat like elixir. It wouldn't last long; boiled rice was a very insubstantial meal. But for the moment his stomach felt comforted and warm. The men were feeling as he did—they were cheerful again, grinning, gingerly touching filthy fingers to their lobster-red, cracking, blistering skin.

"By God," Anstruther whispered to Blogg. "One more day like yesterday and we'll be broiled raw!"

"Mmmmm," Blogg murmured, "but I reckon they'll be doing something to us today. The talk here is so different from the south! Yesterday I tried the lingo that my mate and me use on the fishermen, but they didn't understand a word. Anyway, I reckon that whatever it was that mandarin announced last night, that's what they'll be doing to us today."

"Reckon you're right," Anstruther said, pointing.

The patrol of soldiers was approaching—many more of them this morning, carrying ropes and cudgels. They dispersed, some standing guard, cudgels at the ready, while others began cautiously to remove the ropes from the prisoners' legs and tie them together arm to arm instead.

"Hoy! Going to move us!"

"Mucking time, by God! Out of that bloody *sun!*"

"Got corns on my backside!"

There was relief in the prisoners' voices, and the soldiers felt it. The cudgels were laid down, and all of them worked to retie the prisoners, in groups of six together. It was soon done, and the soldiers fell in around each squad of prisoners. They seemed anxious and hurried, the officer commanding them shouting orders with nervous harshness.

"Hoy!" someone behind Charlie said. "My name's Nick."

Charlie recognized the voice as the one that, on *Kite*, had said in a horrified tone, "In a *'eathen land?*" He grinned over his shoulder, and Nick said:

"Ain't so bad for 'eathens, they ain't! Give us water and that stuff to eat this morning. Ain't going to starve us, at least!"

He suddenly stopped speaking. The soldiers had led them from the courtyard in which they had sat the day before, around the main building, and into another courtyard at the back of it—an extension of the first, with the same walls surrounding it. The myriad voices of the mob, familiar now, had followed them around outside the walls, but as they entered the second court, the roar had taken on a new dimension. Another gateway stood at the end of the new courtyard, toward which the soldiers were leading the prisoners. When that gate opened, the prisoners would be within reach of the crowd, and they knew it. They were congregating there, waiting, the hum of their voices like that of a swarm of angry bees.

Nick said apprehensively:

"You think they aiming to take us out there? Where them 'eathen be waiting for us?"

Charlie said as reassuringly as he could:

"They won't let them at us! They want us live and healthy. If they'd wanted us dead, we'd all be dead before now."

"Aye . . . well, muck it." Charlie could feel from the tug on the rope that Nick was shrugging. "Reckon they's got a

right, arter wot we done to Tin-hai. Dunno wot it's all about—
sailing out to 'eathen lands, bringing ruination to their cities.
Some says it's account of that stuff, opium. Anyway, lads, far
as we's concerned, it's all for the Queen, ain't it?"

He was talking fast, trying to keep his courage up, and on
the last words he raised his voice, calling out to as many as
could hear him.

"Aye! Aye!" they answered. "The Queen! The Queen!"

The brave little cheer died away quickly, for they were at
the gate now, and the threatening roar of the crowd was louder
than ever. The soldiers halted nervously. Their commanding
officer came forward and began to give detailed orders. When
he had done, several soldiers moved up to the gate, lifted the
bar, and carefully allowed one of the leaves to swing open a
few inches. Immediately the crowd outside began pushing, but
the soldiers held the gate steady while a group of their comrades, carrying muskets, forced their way out, one by one. Then
the gate was pushed closed again, and those inside waited.
The noise from outside increased sharply and there was scuf-
fling, but at last a voice shouted louder than the others, and
the commander inside gave a sign that the gate was to be
opened.

Charlie, in the first group of prisoners, caught a confused
impression: a dusty yellow strip of roadway, on each side of
which soldiers with muskets at the ready held back the buzzing crowds. Beyond, a long, peaceful green field, and at the
end of that another gated wall. The soldiers immediately began to rush the prisoners through the pathway held open by
their comrades. Charlie caught no more than a glimpse of the
multifaced crowd boiling and bubbling behind the musketed
soldiers, but in the space of that instant the fear he held for
the safety of Ling-ling and his children doubled, tripled, bal-
looned a hundredfold. The hatred that spewed out of those
glaring eyes, those contorted faces!

"Mate?" Behind Charlie, Nick's voice sounded anxious. "You
all right, mate? You gone all pasty-like under your sunburn."

"I'm all right," Charlie muttered, feeling the blood flow

311

slowly back into his heart. Oh God, let Ah Sam have found them! Oh God, let them be safe on *San Seb!* Oh God . . . He stumbled along, Nick muttering worriedly behind him.

Then they were through the gate on the other side of the field—an old gate, splitting, canted on its hinges, set in an old, cracked, moss-grown wall—and in a small compound, sticks of dry weedy grass surrounding a bare, trampled area of stones and dust, in the middle of which was a round pool half full of brown lumpy sludge. A dirty, desolate place, but the soldiers were breathing sighs of relief—some were even smiling—as they got their charges out of sight of the mob. Everyone, guards and prisoners alike, seemed to relax, to take a little time for recovery. Then someone said loudly:

"Wot the 'ell's that smell?"

There was indeed a smell—a strong, heavy odor that seemed to rise from the sludgy pool. All the prisoners were staring at it, puzzlement, alarm, written on their faces. There was a small, tense silence. Then Blogg's voice was raised in a tone akin to awe.

"By God, I do reckon it's a cesspool! I heared about 'em, but I misbelieved it! Who'd believe such a thing? Someone told me they dig these big round pools for everybody in the village to use, and those who can't come to it, they empty their chamberpots into it. And they keep the cess to lay over the fields—makes the plants grow well, so they say!"

For a moment there was complete silence. Then, with concerted determination, the prisoners began to pull away from their guards, to back as far as possible from the pool. No one spoke but Nick. All he said, in a voice of wonder, was " 'Eathen!" but it was enough for the soldiers to pick him for their demonstration. Two of them cut the rope that tied him, took him by the arms, and urged him toward the pool, while a third made motions of taking down his trousers.

He broke into a wild struggle, shouting at the soldiers, close to hysteria: "I done it already! Wot d'you expect, keeping us a whole bloody day and night in that courtyard! We all done

312

it already right where we was sitting, you boobies! Leave me alone! Leave me alone!''

The violence of his struggle stopped the soldiers. They took a step back, panting, glaring at him as he was glaring at them.

A loud, long, heavy creaking sound broke the tension.

Instantly the soldiers dropped the confrontation with Nick, swung around with gestures of relief, began to push the prisoners toward the inner part of the compound.

There, a large door leading out from the building to which the compound was attached was creaking open. Out of it were coming a large number of guards dressed in uniforms different from those of the soldiers. They were coming forward slowly, eyeing the prisoners with caution and distaste. The soldiers lost no time in handing over the ropes that bound the prisoners and making their exit from the outer gate back into the field. Their duty was done. They had delivered the prisoners. Somebody else could take over now!

The new guards were nothing like the soldiers. They were untidy. They moved lethargically. Some carried short cudgels. Two or three had whips. With obvious reluctance, they picked up the ropes and began to lead the prisoners back into the building from which they had come. Nick, as though afraid of being left alone, picked up the rope where it had been cut from his arm and held it around him, sticking close to Charlie.

The room that they entered was very large and would have been quite dark, for there were no windows, except that great pieces of roof had fallen in, converting it from a closed room into a semi-open-air quadrangle. Rubble from the roof was strewn all over the paving, which was of worn old stones. Weeds grew from between the stones, and in cascades from the damp brick walls, encouraged by the light and the water that must come through whenever it rained.

It was a decrepit and desolate-looking place, but airy and cool. The new guards led the prisoners around the perimeter of the walls and gestured to them to sit. A universal groan arose as they sank down. It was exquisite relief to be off their feet, to be free of the pressure of the ropes and the unavoidable jostling of their neighbors, and to be in the shade! Even though the roof was broken, the tall walls kept out most of the sun.

Charlie leaned back against the cool, damp wall and closed his eyes, deliberately shutting out the images that immediately leaped up behind his lids of those screaming, hating mob faces. There was nothing he could do. Today was the thirty-second day of the thirty-five days they had allowed for Ah Sam to find Ling-ling and the children. Either she had or she hadn't. If she had, they'd be safe on *San Seb*. The mate would keep them safe. He knew all the ins and outs of the tiny little harbors in that comet's tail of tiny little islands. And if she hadn't . . .

"Mate . . ." Nick, beside him, was nudging him. "Wot be they doing?"

"Huh?" Charlie dragged his mind back from the hinterlands of his fear and leaned forward, peering. In the middle of the quadrangle a number of men were working with saplings or thin branches or short lengths of bamboo, tying them together in crisscross style with strips of split bamboo. Hundreds of times Charlie had seen Chinese use such fastenings—thin, pliable strips split from the outer bark of the bamboo. Wrapped around and across and across and across again, the ends tucked in, the strips were strong as the strongest rope. Whatever these men were taking must be for some rugged purpose. There were so many of the crisscross fastenings, like bars, formed into large squares like boxes, with plank bottoms . . .

Cages?

Cages?

"Blogg!" Trying to keep alarm out of his voice, Charlie craned his neck to see where Blogg was sitting.

"Aye!" Blogg called from farther down the row. He too bent forward and craned his neck. Their eyes met. There was a warning in Blogg's eyes, and he gave his head a faint shake. Charlie leaned back, breathing hard. Blogg knew too that the men were making cages, and Blogg had the same suspicion—that the cages were for them. . . .

About noon, coolies came through the inner door with water for the prisoners. Later, when the sun was low, they came again with another meal of soft-boiled rice, this time with bits of cabbage floating in it. By now the prisoners had discovered that the comfort brought to their stomachs by the waterlogged rice was illusory: It vanished very quickly and left hunger gnawing. They grumbled even while they were wolfing the rice.

When the coolies had gone away with their empty buckets, the inner door again creaked open and a slow procession began to come through, shuffling, limping, creeping toward the outer compound. In the growing darkness the procession seemed to be composed of dim gray wraiths barely able to drag themselves along. The prisoners stirred uneasily. There was something doomful and hopeless about the slow, sad movement.

"Oo's for the pisspot parade?" someone tittered nervously.

"Hoy, Nick!" someone else called. "Be they *'eathen* ghosts, you reckon?"

Beside Charlie, Nick sighed.

"Tain't no joking matter. We all be 'uman beings, but—"

He broke off, jerked back, drew a hissing breath. One of the ghosts had stopped and was shakily lowering itself to the ground before him and Charlie.

"Get away," Nick mumbled fearfully, squeezing closer to Charlie. "Get away from me, ghost . . ."

"It's a man, you fool!" Charlie spoke harshly to still the superstitious dread that stirred in his own breast. There was something weird about the dimly seen figure in front of him, about the way it grunted as its rag-covered limbs sank slowly to the ground. Reluctantly, he raised his eyes to look into the face that was thrusting toward him. A skeletal face. A death's head, but for the eyes. The eyes were living, burning.

The mouth quivered and words came.

"You . . . are . . . English?"

Nick gasped and Charlie stared, his own mouth gaping in amazement. Not only had the words been English, but the intonation had been very like Yin-kwa's! But for the rusty, faltering tone, it might have been Yin-kwa who spoke!

The burning eyes were fixed on Charlie's, insistent and anxious. Charlie found his voice, whispered "Yes" to the eyes.

"Ah . . ."

The eyes closed. The face twisted in a spasm of pain, and sweat popped out in great beads on the bony forehead. Involuntarily, Charlie touched the stick-thin arm.

"You're sick!"

A panting whisper: "I . . . am . . . better."

"Better?"

The tortured features began to relax, and after a moment the eyes opened again, looking straight into Charlie's.

"Yes . . . better. . . . Each day it gets better. . . . A month ago I thought I could not survive, yet here I am. I am an opium smoker who has been without opium for a month."

"What?"

The man nodded shakily, and his lips quivered in a ghastly smile.

"This is a prison for opium smokers. Those of us silly enough to be caught are thrown in here. Most die, but I am recovering. . . ."

The smile strengthened. He was proud of himself.

Two or three guards, standing nearby, had been listening, fascinated into immobility. Now one of the guards at the outer door shouted, and they hastily came to life, bent to haul the man up, push him toward the cesspool compound. At once the English prisoners began to shout excited queries at Charlie, but now the guards were alert, rushing about with their cudgels, yelling orders which clearly meant "Be quiet!" At the same time, men came from the inner building carrying torches and wooden stands in which to set them to illuminate the work of the men who were still making cages. And the first of the cesspool procession began to return from the outer compound.

When the confusion died down, Charlie saw that the man was approaching him again, this time led by a guard who wore red epaulettes—a chief guard? The man carried himself straighter, and his step was less faltering. It was remarkable how much the excitement—or whatever it was—had stimulated him. When he stopped before Charlie, his voice was strong enough to carry through the dead silence that had fallen among the listening prisoners.

"Sir . . . they have told me to give you a message. They want to make a . . . a *trade* with you. They—the guards—have been put in charge of keeping you alive, but the citizens of this town are trying their best to kill you. The guards will be in very much trouble if you are killed, so they are both angry and afraid. They have told me to propose to you that you help each other—they will help you by protecting you, feeding you, not beating or torturing you, if you will help them by promising to make no trouble, and not to run away."

From somewhere near Blogg, Anstruther's voice rang out.

"That makes good sense, Charlie. We want to stay alive as much as they want to keep us alive. Tell that man we'll cooperate. And thank him."

"You heard?" Charlie said to the man.

He nodded. His eyes gleamed.

"Yes. Good. I will tell the guards. It is a very wise decision. But there is one other thing. . . . After tomorrow, you will be taken inside the prison, where it is a little better than here. But tomorrow . . . tomorrow, you will be put into the cages that those men are making, and you will be carried around Ningpo to be shown to the people. . . ."

He had lowered his voice, but still some of the prisoners heard him. Gasps and cries of protest rose.

"Caged!"

"We bain't animals, to be put in cages!"

"They cain't do that!"

317

As the others heard, the tumult grew. The man put a filthy, bony hand on Charlie's arm, leaned forward to whisper, his foul breath creating a miasmic cloud:

"It's necessary to appease the crowd! Otherwise they may break in here to get at you!"

Anstruther's voice roared out:

"Quiet down, men! Quiet down! It's not much different from the pillory at home! Quiet down! *Listen!*"

The uproar died a little. Anstruther went on calmly:

"The guards are in a hard position. They're responsible to keep us alive, and they're afraid of what that mob out there might do. So they're trying to give the mob some kind of sop without putting us in danger. It'll just be for a day. A kind of *raree* show."

Blogg's great voice cut in:

"The cages'll *protect* us! Certain-sure I wouldn't like to be in a mob like them out there without a cage 'twixt me and them!"

There was a brief, heavy-breathing silence. Then someone said wholeheartedly, *"Right he be!"*

"Good!" Anstruther laughed easily.

"He's a good man," Nick murmured to Charlie. "Fears naught, and talk about carrying men with him!" His voice rose suddenly: "Hip, hip for our cap'n, men! Hip, hip . . ."

"Hurrah! Hurrah! Hurrah!"

The cheers resounded.

Under cover of the noise, Charlie said hastily to the man:

"Who are you? What's your name?"

"I'm called . . . Lee," he answered, hesitating over the name and ignoring the first question.

"Where did you learn English?"

"From Gutzen, the missionary."

No wonder he spoke like Yin-kwa!

"How did you—"

But the red-collared guard interrupted with a harsh question to the man. He answered, then turned back to Charlie.

"They are pleased that you've promised to cooperate, but

he says I'm talking to you too much. I will see you again after tomorrow, inside the prison. . . ."

The man's eyes still burned with fever or some fierce desire, but the burst of energy that had lent him life and color suddenly faded. He seemed moribund again, as the guard hauled him to his feet and dragged him off, tottering.

In the end, Blogg was spared the cages because the coolies couldn't fit him into one, or pretended they couldn't. After pushing and pulling assiduously for a minute or two, they stood back, panting heavily and shaking their heads, and the supervising guards reluctantly waved Blogg aside. He got to his feet, panting as heavily as the coolies, or pretending to, muttering: "They ain't stupid! They certain-sure don't want to carry *me* around all day!"

But all the other prisoners were fitted into cages by the small army of coolies who invaded the quadrangle as soon as the workmen had finished their task. The cages were made so that one side could be lifted open on rope hinges attached to the top bars. The prisoners were seated on the ground, back to the open side of the cage, and made to wriggle backward into it. Then the open side was fastened underneath the plank bottom of the cage, where the occupant could not reach the fastening. By the time the first streaks of dawn showed through the holes in the roof of the quadrangle, everyone but Blogg was sitting in a cage. Some, medium-sized like Charlie, could sit in relative comfort, cross-legged, backs straight, but Anstruther and the taller men had to sit crouched forward, the backs of their heads pressed against the top bars.

Lined up in single file, the thirty cages stretched across the quadrangle, into the compound, and around the cesspool. Charlie found himself in the middle of the line, Nick in front of him. Nick was philosophical.

" 'Oo can tell what 'eathen customs be! Though, mind you, when I signed on I never thort to sail to 'eathen lands! Well— it be all for the sake of the Queen, I s'pose. . . . Wot's keeping us? Quicker we start, quicker it'll be over!"

The coolies were waiting now, some squatting on their haunches, some milling about the line of cages inspecting the prisoners. The coolies were a motley lot, barefooted, queues wound around their heads, dressed in anything from faded rags to neat blue cotton. They seemed to like the job they had been given, for they talked and laughed cheerfully, peering at the prisoners, pointing, exclaiming. In the growing light, one noticed Charlie's hair. *"Yeeee!!!!"*—and in a moment a crowd had gathered around Charlie's cage and were sticking their fingers through the bars to prod at his head.

But a minute or two later a new group of men entered the quadrangle, dressed in shabby, gaudy uniforms, carrying gongs and cymbals. The band! Now the parade could start. The guards began shouting, the coolies hurried to their carrying poles, the outer doors were thrown open, and the procession started smartly out across the cabbage field toward the dusty road. In the lead, two men carried between them an enormous brass gong nearly five feet in diameter, slung from a carrying pole by red-tasseled cords. On each side of the gong a gong-beater walked, at every third or fourth step striking the gong with a flourish of huge padded gong sticks, drawing forth reverberations so deep that they seemed to stir up the guts more than the ears. Behind the great gong marched two cymbalists clashing their instruments, and behind them, like the tail of a dragon, four other gong-beaters, each carrying a small gong and smiting it with high-pitched tintinnabulations. Each man maintained his own rhythm, independent of the others. The resulting ear-blasting counterpoint rolled over the countryside in awesome dissonance. Charlie saw Nick turn to him, eyes wide, lips forming a word that Charlie knew was " 'Eathen!" although he couldn't hear it. He laughed aloud. There was something so crazy about being the subject of a *raree* show—like a performing monkey—that he felt fey.

His cage bobbed as the carriers stepped up from the field onto the dusty road, and he bounced and hit his head a glancing blow on the bamboos that barred the top of the cage. At the same moment, the sun broke through the dawn mist. It would be a fine day, the sky blue, the air clear. Here, where the procession turned right onto the dusty road, the new light showed both ends of it, the band in front vigorously beating the devil out of their instruments, then the long line of cages bobbing on their carrying poles, the coolies thud-thudding along, their bare feet stirring up clouds of dust, and behind a line of guards with whips and cudgels.

And beyond, approaching rapidly from both sides of the road, other and greater clouds of dust, and a sound that was not the beat of gongs or cymbals but the roar of voices. The roar of the mob.

Suddenly, as though by magic, the mob was there, milling around the cages, its roar a continuous, mindless turbulence like the pounding of storm-whipped surf. The guards hurried forward and closed in, waving their cudgels and whips to keep the crowd at a distance. For a while it worked. The procession moved forward unhampered, at a rapid pace, the guards marching close beside the cages, the people flowing by like a solid river a yard or two beyond them.

But suddenly they left the fields behind and were in a maze of streets as twisting as the lanes behind Jackass Point, as narrow as the Street of the Psychics. Here there was no room for the guards to swing their cudgels, and the crowd, growing ever bigger, closed in. Their noise became deafening, the thrust of their packed bodies suffocating. Charlie's head seemed to lose contact with his body, seemed to be tossing about on buffeting waves of sound. The air he breathed seemed to grow thicker as if compressed between the converging walls of people. He kept his head down, felt a stinging prick along one temple, squinted from under his lashes to see a slyly grinning face, a thrusting hand, the sharpened end of a bamboo stick jabbing at his eyes. In the nick of time he snapped his eyes shut and jerked his shoulder to deflect the stick. There was a shrill laugh and the stick poked into his ear. He threw his arms up, clasped them over his head, heard the laugh again, and felt the point of the stick jab along his wrist and forearm in a hundred little stinging cuts. Warm wetness dripped onto his face, and he smelled and tasted blood.

But the grinning stick-jabber could not keep his place beside the cage—there were too many fighting to get close. He was swept aside and his place taken by another and another and another—a thousand, ten thousand others, churning around the cages, screaming, staring, jibing, poking with fingers and sticks and fists, throwing stones and clumps of garbage, hawking up globs of phlegm and spitting them at the prisoners. It went on and on. It was endless. It would never end. They passed from narrow streets into wide ones, into and out of courtyards, into spacious places where the sun beat down without mercy, into lanes where the light was obscured by gimcrack gewgaws hanging overhead like the myriad sign-boards of the Street of Psychics. Charlie endured, eyes tight shut, face bowed, arms clasped over his head. At first he knew that Nick was still ahead of him, heard him calling out. Then he heard nothing but the mob, the screaming, hissing, hating voices, the words he could not understand but knew the meaning of. Felt nothing but the plop of spittle and excrement against his skin, the crunch of stones, the jab and poke of sticks.

And the touch of a hand.

He felt a hand brush his fingers, slip to his wrist, close on his wrist like a butterfly alighting.

He knew at once whose hand it was—knew by the clenching of his sphincters, by a bursting in his breast like the firing of cannon.

He lifted his head and opened his eyes and saw her, hurrying desperately beside the cage, one hand clinging to the bars, the other to his wrist, her eyes streaming tears.

He said: "Ling-ling. Darling," and turned his wrist to take her hand, but he could only touch the tips of her fingers, for, like the other thousands, she was swept away by those who pushed and shoved to take her place.

"*Stop!*" he yelled at the carriers, but they hurried on, unheeding. Frantically, he swiveled his body, craned his head against the bars to look for her, and got a lump of phlegm spat into his eyes. In despair, he pounded his fists on the plank floor of the cage and threw his body from side to side, screaming, "Stop! Stop! Stop! Stop!" The cage rocked as a dinghy is rocked on waves. He felt it lurch and slip from the shoulders of the bearers, felt it overturn as it tumbled, felt a crashing pain across the top of his head, then nothing more.

For a long time, it seemed, he was in a feverish, burning place where light and dark, noise and quiet, fear and a terrible anxiety came and pulsated and slipped away again, never near enough to grasp and drag forth into consciousness.

Sometimes he woke for a moment and knew he was lying on something rough and scratchy, knew that someone was beside him—Blogg?—but his eyelids were too heavy to raise and he slid into sleep again.

Sometimes he heard Blogg say, "He's still out," and he wanted to cry, "I'm not," but the movement of his facial muscles was excruciatingly painful and he lost himself in it.

One day, he woke and moved his shoulders, and Blogg said, "Charlie?" and he wanted to say, "Yes," but the word stuck in his throat and only a humming sound issued, but all the same Blogg said, "God be thanked!" with the same fervor as on that night when he'd returned to *San Seb* from How-kwa's deathbed. Water trickled into his mouth, and he swallowed, some of it spilling from the corner of his lips, down his cheek and around to the back of his neck. The water was cool and grateful, both inside his throat and outside on his skin, and he made a sound that meant "More" and more was given him. Then Blogg said, "I'll hold his head up, and you feed him," and his head was raised and food put into his mouth that slid down his throat and came to rest comfortingly in his stomach, and he slept again.

And then one day he woke and thoughts were stirring in his head. He opened his eyes and saw that dawn was showing through the roof, but the holes in the roof were only small, so it couldn't be the quadrangle. He turned his head and saw

323

that he was lying on a pallet of straw, on a broken stone-flagged floor, in a very large room—a hall. The silver light showed high walls, cracked and moss-grown, stained with damp. This must be the inner hall of the opium smokers' prison, beyond the quadrangle and the cesspool courtyard. He turned his head to the other side and saw that he lay by a wall, and that Blogg was sprawled against the wall, chin on chest, snoring lightly. Blogg looked very peaceful, and the great hall was quiet with only small murmurs and breathings and shiftings, so Charlie slept again.

When next he woke, nothing was peaceful. Harsh sunlight shone through the holes in the roof, beaming great bright spots on the broken floor that dazzled the eyes and made every-thing around them dark and grim. It was cracklingly hot. There were many sounds—voices and groanings and footsteps and a keen humming sound that he knew was made by flies. He saw them—swarms of them, darting and hovering, their iri-descent blue-green bodies catching the light. He flicked a hand at the flies around his head and struggled up on an elbow.

The hall was huge. It seemed to be divided more or less in half. On one side, the side away from him, there was move-ment, figures moving in and out of the spots of sunlight, one moment bright, one moment dark. He thought he saw Blogg and Anstruther standing together, talking, and around them some guards. But on the other side of the hall, the side on which he lay, there was no movement, though there were many lying down like himself, some on pallets, some on the ground with nothing between them and the broken flagstones. He fo-cused his eyes on the man nearest him and felt his heart give a great jump: The man was dead! The skin of his face was papery, his nose a bird's beak, his half-open eyes sunk so deep that they seemed to lie in the eye-holes of a skull. . . . God Almighty, was he lying in a place of the *dead?* He raised him-self higher to see beyond, and felt a hand on his arm, looked up into a face he slowly recognized—though it was different. It was still very thin, but there was color in it, and the eyes were bright, not burning.

"You're—Lee."

The face smiled. "That's right. I look better, don't I? I *am* better. Almost well. Not many opium smokers can say that!" His eyes gleamed. "Lie back, Charlie. Blogg asked me to look after you for a while. There's nothing to see, anyway. Just twenty-pipe men, dying."

Charlie lay back in a kind of terrible exhaustion. He longed to close his eyes, but they stayed open of their own accord, staring fascinatedly at Lee. What was he talking about? Not opium! Opium was *silver*, not the paper-skinned skulls of twenty-pipe men. . . .

Lee smiled again, unpleasantly.

"You've never before seen a twenty-pipe man? I'll make a guess. You've never before seen opium smokers at all, except perhaps in Macao—rich men entertaining their well-fed friends in those divans with brocade couches and pretty girls to prepare the pipes. And you thought that was opium smoking?" He laughed harshly. "Well, I can tell you that real smokers smoke *at home*. They can't afford divans because they need every copper to buy opium. Every copper, even the coppers that should be buying food for their wives and children. And when there's nothing left, why then they die—like that."

He pointed to the man beyond Charlie. Charlie turned. After all, the man was not yet dead. He was sweating—sweat was pouring down his face—and he was twitching, his limbs shaking so hard that it seemed the bones should be heard to rattle. Charlie's skin crawled. A dying twenty-pipe man. A dying, dancing twenty-pipe skeleton. Slowly, the shaking subsided and the man lay flaccid, a handful of loose bones held together for yet a while by his envelope of dry and flaky skin.

A small figure hurried up to the man. A boy? A *child*? Charlie looked around wonderingly. Children were everywhere, moving among the prostrate figures. . . .

Lee said, "The guards let the children in every day for a few hours. They do a lot for their fathers and grandfathers that the guards would otherwise have to do."

The child, waving a palm-leaf fan, had flicked off the flies that were luxuriating in the man's sweat and the gummy mucus that drooled from his lips. They rose and buzzed for a moment, then avidly swooped back. The boy transferred the fan to his left hand and waved it steadily, keeping the flies away. With his right hand he wiped the skeleton face, then began to pat the still-twitching back. His movements were quick and adept, his eyes gentle and calm. He settled back on his heels, one hand patting, one hand waving the fan, as though fly-specked agony and death were simple manifestations of everyday life.

Lee went away and Charlie closed his eyes, but sleep withheld itself and set him balancing on a razor's edge of nightmare. Children wandered through his dreams, waving palm-leaf fans, reproaching him with their gentle eyes. Why did they reproach him? Because there was something he had forgotten! He searched the corners of his mind, but memory eluded him, darting about like the flies, not settling anywhere, for the children's fans kept them on the move. If only the children would stop waving their fans he would remember!

"Charlie . . . "

Blogg was there again. The children were gone. The holes in the roof showed the pinkish orange light of sunset. Charlie blinked and saw that Anstruther and Nick were there too—thin and dirty and heavily bearded, but undoubtedly Anstruther and Nick.

"Well!" Anstruther grinned his cheerful grin. "You're looking better. Soon the guards will let you cross over to our side of the hall."

"It's better on our side!" Nick said, glancing over his shoulder and shuddering a little. Both he and Anstruther had their backs turned to the twenty-pipe men.

"You're right thin, Charlie!"

"We all are!" Anstruther laughed. "Even Blogg's less bulky. But we'll be eating better from now on. Charlie, when we left *Kite* I saved my sketchpad. Wrapped it in an oilskin with some charcoals and stowed it inside my shirt. Today I opened it up to sketch one of the guards, and what d'you think? A grandee came by who turned out to be the commander of this prison. He stopped to see what I was doing and instantly demanded that I draw his portrait. I'd have done it for nothing, but for Blogg. . . ."

Blogg was grinning. "Well, after all these years of sailing traders about the China seas, reckon I'd be stupid if I didn't pick up some notions of trading. I fetched Lee right quick, and we made a trade with the commander. Anstruther'll do his portrait, and any others that he orders, for thirty-one pork pies apiece. You know them pork pies, Charlie, like they sell on the streets in Macao? Right tasty! The commander's already ordered portraits of his whole family, and Lee reckons there'll be plenty others."

"And that's not all," Anstruther went on. "Lee was teaching English before the police caught him and stuck him in here. I don't know what his real business was, but he was teaching English to help out—suppose it takes a lot of money if you're buying opium. He says he's got a market for scripts—sentences written out in a good hand that students can use as models. The price for those is going to be ten pork pies per page, and Lee'll provide the paper. So get well quick, Charlie. We need you to write!"

They squatted there beside Charlie, filthy, tattered, haggard, laughing happily. Charlie tried to join in, but his throat was still too dry and his voice too croaky. Anstruther quickly put a hand on his shoulder.

"Keep quiet, Charlie. You were very sick. A bump as big as an apple on the top of your head that must have scrambled your brains good and proper, for when they brought you back here you were yelling and fighting so hard it took three or four of us to hold you. And then you went so deadly quiet you scared us all. You looked like a ghost, all black under the eyes. The guards thought you were dead, or near it, and insisted on putting you on this side of the hall with them. . . ." He jerked a thumb over his shoulder. For a moment he looked very sober, then his eyes twinkled. "By God, we're glad you proved them wrong! So all of us from *Kite* are alive and well enough, and we're starting a new life in terms of pork pies!"

"And not too bad neither!" Nick chimed in. "The 'eathen be better nor wot I thort—at least, *these* 'eathen. Lee says the guards in the prisons where be the bandits and murderers, they be cruel hard. But there be no need for hard men to deal with opium smokers." He half glanced over his shoulder and shuddered again. "Mind, the guards don't like us, but in a kind of way we be partners with they. We both—they and us—want us to *stay alive!*"

They talked awhile longer, Nick bubbling—pork pies were going to make all the difference in his life. Charlie listened, drifting, hearing and not hearing, and fell asleep before the talk was over.

In the morning when he woke, Blogg was beside him and sunlight was pouring through the roof, already hot and bright. He yawned and stretched, and suddenly, with a clanging like the beat of gongs and cymbals, the thing he had forgotten rushed into his mind, his heart, his blood, into the core of his being. Paralyzed, he stared unblinking into the sunlight.

Blogg said, "Charlie?" But he could not speak. It was not until Blogg sharply shook his shoulder that he could force words out of his constricted throat. The words came slow and harsh, as though someone else spoke them, some person in the depths of agony who was, after all, himself. . . .

"I saw her, Blogg. . . . She put her hand through the bars of my cage and held my wrist. She was weeping. Then the mob swept her away and I couldn't make those bloody cage-carriers stop."

Blogg said quietly, "Reckoned maybe you saw her. When they brought you back you were like crazy, yelling her name and fighting to get away. . . . Is that how the carriers came to drop you? You were fighting to get out of the cage?"

"Yes. You can't imagine what it was like to see her swept away and not be able to go after her. . . ."

"I can imagine," Blogg said.

They fell silent.

It was time for the children. They came fluttering into the prison hall, small and light and quick, like drab little moths in their faded, ragged clothes. They ran to the dying men and greeted them gently, though they got no answer. They wiped the sweat from their bodies, fetched gourds of soft-boiled rice and tried to make them eat, gave them water. They crouched and looked into the skeleton faces with soft, solemn eyes. They murmured and patted the limp shoulders, and waved their fans to keep the flies away, performing the little rituals that were still of use in this world—as, later, they would perform the rituals of the other world, the ancestral rituals.

The family is everybody, Ah Sam had said. The living, the dead, the not yet born. All one whole, one entirety. On that night, so long ago, when he had knelt before How-kwa's ancestral altar, he had felt solemn and mystical, and been surprised that no one else had. But the descendants knew their ancestors, lived with them in comfort, on familiar terms, doing for them what was necessary, as, in turn, their sons and the sons of their sons, would do for them.

Like a small, pure, white spot inside his head, budding out of anguish, Charlie saw a vision of how Wei must have felt when he learned that Jin-see was to be taken away to England. And who could guarantee that he would ever be brought back from that faraway place of arrogant, willful, headstrong people who cared so little for their sons that they sent them thousands of miles away at the age of thirteen to the mercies of strangers?

Charlie turned to Blogg, his eyes blank, his pain too great for emotion.

"If ever I get back my wife and children, it won't be to take them from Wei. It'll be to give them back to him. To put his family together again, so there'll always be honor for the ancestors and sons for the future."

Blogg sighed, a long sigh. After a time he said:

"Wish I could say better, Charlie, but we can't do more than our mucking best to get them back. It's war. And war's the

329

devil's chance to make a grand, god-awful mess. To break off bits and pieces—bits of families—and strew them all over, spin them off into the whirl of war, lost and gone."

On the hundredth day of their imprisonment, a day when rain dripped dismally through the holes in the roof and guards and prisoners alike crouched in whatever shelter they could find, and the dying twenty-pipe men lay oblivious in puddles, when the smell was worse than ever, and the misery more pervasive, the commander of the prison sent for Lee. He went apprehensively and came back smiling.

There was news from Peking.

The Emperor had appointed Chi Shan, viceroy of the Province of Chihli, to negotiate peace with the British. Chi Shan was on his way overland from Peking to Canton. The British fleet, which had been anchored all this time at the mouth of the Pei-ho River, was sailing back to Canton, where the British and Chinese negotiators would meet to hammer out a treaty. The British negotiator had already said, however, that he was prepared to return Choushan Island to the Chinese in exchange for the safe return of the *Kite* prisoners.

Kite prisoners cheered until their shouts bounced back from the moss-grown walls. The guards grinned. Nick yelled: "By Gawd, they be glad too! Wot they be saying, they be saying 'At last!' " Everybody laughed some more and yelled and shouted till Lee waved for quiet.

"It will be some time, of course, before you are released. They won't let you go until all the foreign soldiers are out of Tin-hai and all the British warships are out of the harbor. But in the meantime they will take you to a better place than this prison, and you will be given better food. And I am to go with you as a translator."

"Gawd!" Nick whispered to Charlie between cheers. "He'll wriggle himself out of all this yet and right straight into whatever 'tis he wants!"

330

Chapter XI

1841

I T's *Modeste!*" Anstruther cried.

The frigate lay neatly at anchor two hundred yards from the beach, waiting for *Kite* prisoners. The island of Chou-shan had been formally returned to the Chinese, and now the Chinese were formally returning *Kite* prisoners, and the British had sent *Modeste* to fetch them. Shouting, cheering, wild with joy, they tumbled over each other as they rushed down to the water's edge.

"Wait! Wait!" Lee shouted. "There's to be a proper exchange. The mandarin is coming and the captain from your ship is to come ashore to acknowledge that every single one of you is being returned alive!"

Modeste's cutter was already putting out, the Union Jack flapping briskly from her bowsprit. The mandarin's palanquin, carried by twenty bearers, was making its way ponderously down the beach. Anstruther shouted orders, and the men from *Kite* somehow restrained themselves enough to form a line. In their rags and tatters, gaunt, unkempt, burned brown by the sun, they looked like a company of tramps, but their faces beamed with the joy that had suffused them ever since it had been announced that a British frigate was on her way to fetch them.

Modeste's captain jumped ashore, and at the same moment the mandarin's bearers set down his palanquin. The mandarin stepped out, and he and the English captain bowed to each other. Lee stepped forward to translate their brief dialogue. Then the two of them, Lee following, walked solemnly down the line of men, counting. When they reached the end of the line, they faced each other again, and Lee asked *Modeste*'s captain:

"Do you agree that there are thirty-one?"

"I do."

"All who were captured?"

"Yes."

Lee spoke to the mandarin, and then turned back to the Englishman:

"They are hereby returned to you."

"I thank you."

Again, they bowed to each other, but it was too much for *Kite*'s men. They broke ranks, cheering and shouting, and rushed into the water. Quickly, in three trips of *Modeste*'s cutter, all thirty-one of them were embarked. As the last of them climbed up *Modeste*'s ladder, the mandarin stepped back into his palanquin.

Charlie, on *Modeste*'s deck, watched the mandarin and his entourage withdraw, Lee swaggering in their wake. Even at that distance, Charlie could see the little protuberance that Lee's stomach made under the black silk gown that he had somehow acquired. In the new prison to which they'd been transferred four months ago, Lee had grown sleek and fat. From the first day in the lightly guarded house of detention, he'd begun to organize a new life-style for himself. People had come at all hours to see him, to confer with him in whispers, to hand over mysterious little parcels, while the guards had willingly turned their backs, and started to grow a little sleek themselves with their share of whatever it was that Lee was harvesting.

On the day it was announced that a British ship was on its way to fetch *Kite* prisoners, Charlie had cornered Lee in the courtyard of the prison house while the other prisoners celebrated with wine that Lee had shown them how to make from fermented rice.

"Lee . . ." Charlie swallowed the balloon that had filled his throat. "When the others leave, I want to stay behind."

Lee stared. "You mean here, in Ningpo?"

"Yes."

"Impossible!"

"It's not impossible for you, Lee. You can arrange it. You can get someone to wear my clothes and take my place on the British ship. Blogg will cover for him until the ship leaves, and then will help him to get ashore. He won't come to any harm. I'll pay him well. And you too, of course."

"With what?"

"Silver! I have it! Plenty of it! Not here, of course, but Blogg will get it as soon as he gets back to Macao. How much d'you want? Ten thousand? Dollars or bullion, as you like!"

"Why do you want to stay in Ningpo?"

"To find some people. A woman and three children."

"*Find* them? There are two hundred thousand people in Ningpo! Do you know where they live?"

"In the house of a man called Wei."

"There must be fifty thousand Weis. What's the other name? Wei what?"

"I don't know!"

"Do you know the name of the street?"

"No."

Lee laughed.

"You must be mad! You offer me ten thousand in silver that I don't even know you have, to help you find some nameless people on an unknown street in a city as big as Ningpo. Do you know what you're asking me to risk? My head! The only reason the lot of you were kept alive was to barter you for the return of Choushan Island. They're certainly not going to risk spoiling that deal now! They're going to make very, very sure that every single one of you gets onto that British ship!"

Charlie grasped his arm as he turned on his heel.

"Lee, you've got to help me! I've got to find them! You can surely get somebody to take my place!"

Lee spoke over his shoulder.

"It's *impossible!* Apart from everything else, look at the color of your hair! What Chinese has red hair with a big white streak in it? I've no objection to earning ten thousand dollars—*if* you really have it—but it simply can't be done that way!"

Now, watching the swaggering black-clothed figure walk up the beach in the wake of the palanquin, Charlie felt agony sear his soul. He had *touched* her, brushed her fingers, felt her soft hand on his wrist. He had been that close to her. And now she was receding, farther and farther. Nothing, now, but the empty beach. . . .

On *Modeste*, festive meals had been laid in the crew's quarters and the officers' saloon, and wine and grog were flowing freely. Amid rejoicing, *Modeste* got smoothly under way. At his laden table, her captain urged Anstruther and his officers and Charlie and Blogg to eat hearty as he brought them up to date on what had happened during their imprisonment. When all their plates were full and their glasses overflowing, when they had settled down to eating and drinking as they had not eaten and drunk for seven long months, he leaned back and began to speak.

"First of all—those forts at the Bogue in the Bay of Canton have been destroyed."

Charlie's eyes jerked up to meet Blogg's startled gaze. Carradine's words come true after a quarter of a century—the Bogue forts destroyed by British warships. Charlie's heart seemed to double its beat as *Modeste's* captain went on:

"You all know, I suppose, that the Emperor appointed a peacemaker, Viceroy Chi Shan, to negotiate a treaty with Captain Ellison. The negotiations were to take place in Canton. The viceroy went to Canton overland, while our fleet sailed back.

Well, God rot it, that was all trickery! The Chinee were damned uncomfortable with our ships in the Gulf of Pei-chi-li, so near their Emperor, so they tempted us away by saying that the viceroy would negotiate with Ellison in Canton. When we got there, the damned man refused to negotiate! So, to force his hand, the admiral ordered the Bogue forts taken."

"How did it go?" Anstruther spoke with his mouth full, eyes shining.

Modeste's captain shrugged. "Took a couple of hours, that's all. *Modeste* had the honor of participating in the attack—the others were *Calliope*, *Larne*, and *Columbine*. It was on the seventh of January. The fort on the west shore—Tycocktow, it's called—went in less than an hour. *Modeste*'s broadsides claimed four direct hits. The other fort, on the east shore—Chuenpi— took a little longer. It was garrisoned by some kind of crack troops they call Tartars who refused to surrender even after their field batteries were completely done for by our broadsides and they had nothing left to fight with but swords and daggers—and some of them not even those, by God! When it came to burying them, we found some with nothing but brass gongs and cymbals that they'd been making the devil of a row with—to scare away the evil spirits, Carradine's translator told us. By God—crack troops, and brave ones too, refusing to surrender, and that's what they give them to make war with!"

He passed the port.

"Well, that brought the viceroy to the negotiating table pretty quick! In a week he and Captain Ellison had agreed to the first two terms—Choushan Island to be returned in exchange for you lot, and Hong Kong to be ceded to us instead."

"Hong Kong!" Charlie and Blogg exclaimed together.

"Aye. Ellison took it over on the twenty-sixth of January. When we sailed out of the harbor to come here and fetch you, the Union Jack was already planted on the bluff, and a lot of building had started. Carradine was building a great warehouse of stone, like a fortress, right there on the beach."

A commotion on deck brought them all to their feet and outside. *Modeste* was sailing past the wreck of *Kite*. *Kite* had

335

been stripped to her skeleton—everything was gone, from her cannon to the very timbers of her hull. While *Kite*'s men were exclaiming and bemoaning, Blogg drew Charlie aside.

"Look!"

At first Charlie saw nothing but the usual fishing boats and junks, and then the sails of one of the craft began to look familiar. . . .

"*San Seb!*"

"Aye!"

Blogg's eyes shone. He turned to *Modeste*'s captain, pointed out *San Seb*, and asked to be transferred to her. His voice through the bullhorn quickly brought *San Seb* close. *Modeste*'s gig was lowered. Everybody wrung hands. Nick had tears in his eyes.

"Take care, Charlie. Sometimes a bump on the 'ead like you got—why, everything seem fine for a while, and then suddenly you gets dinged out again. Take care, Charlie!"

On *San Seb*'s beloved old scrubbed-clean well-worn deck, the mate came running, tears streaming through the wrinkles of his face, to welcome them. It was an emotional time, Blogg and Charlie hugging the mate and the crewmen, who in turn bowed low, hands clasped, in deep kowtows of joy and welcome and thankfulness to the gods for their safe return.

But then the news had to be told: Ah Sam had not returned to *San Seb* on the thirty-fifth day, in accord with the plan. No one had come. The story of *Kite*'s capture had spread like wildfire, and on *San Seb* they had soon heard it. When Ah Sam did not come, the mate had gone into Ningpo to find out what he could. He had learned of the procession of cages and that the prisoners were housed in the prison for opium violators. He had heard the speculation that they would be kept alive and bartered for the return of Choushan Island. But he had found out absolutely nothing about Ah Sam or Ling-ling and the children. So he and the crew had decided to wait at Tao-hua-tao until something happened to indicate what they should do—and now, finally, after seven long months, Blogg and Charlie had been released!

While all the talk went on, they'd been sailing back to the little harbor on Tao-hua-tao. When they dropped anchor, evening had come. They gathered on the stern deck around a clay jar of *sam shui.*

Why had Ah Sam not come back to *San Seb?*

Because she had heard of the capture of *Kite?*

Because she had found Ling-ling and the children and was afraid to bring them to *San Seb* for fear that *Kite's* capture might lead to further retribution that might involve *San Seb?*

Because she hadn't found Ling-ling and the children?

And whether she'd found them or not, what had she been doing during the seven months of their internment? She hadn't even tried to get in touch with *San Seb!*

Was she alive?

Were they alive, Ling-ling and the children?

Had something completely unforeseen, unknown, undreamed-of, happened?

The questions churned around in their heads. They all knew them and they didn't bother to voice them aloud. They sat silently, gazing into their bowls of *sam shui,* or at the twinkling black water or the twinkling black sky.

There were no answers to the questions.

At last Blogg said: "Better sail back to Hong Kong, try to talk to Yin-kwa. Don't see there's nothing else to do than that."

Charlie didn't answer. There was nothing to say. Twenty months since he had lost Ling-ling, and they were back to the same old thing: talk to Yin-kwa. Ask Yin-kwa. . . .

"Eh?" said Blogg, but Charlie had no voice to answer. It seemed that the blood in his veins was hardly flowing, might stop soon, might curdle.

San Seb had lost the little burst of youth that her refurbishing had given her, and she sailed southward at a slow and dignified pace that neither Blogg nor his mate could peruade her to increase. It was not until the last week of May that they sailed into Hong Kong harbor.

337

As they entered Lyemoon Pass at the north end of the harbor, the mate, who was at the helm, suddenly let it go—if the sea had not been like glass, *San Seb* might have slewed dangerously. While Blogg ran to grab the helm, the mate jumped down from the bridge to join the crewmen, who, they too dropping whatever they were doing, were gathering on the foredeck, staring in utter silence.

Hong Kong was transformed. What had been a barren island was now a busy little town. What had been a great, empty spread of fine yellow-sand beach was now a kind of dirty forecourt for a long line of buildings stretching almost as far as the eye could see, dominated in the middle by a huge square stone warehouse that must be what *Modeste*'s captain had called Carradine's fortress. Behind this front row of buildings, and up on the bluff that stood at the foot of the island's mountain, more buildings were springing up, seeming literally to be springing from the hands of hordes of coolies who climbed like monkeys on bamboo scaffoldings. Streams of people, Chinese outnumbering foreigners a hundred to one, hurried up and down the beach and in and out of the buildings. Dozens of ships—warships, clippers, merchantmen of all varieties—sailed about the harbor or stood at anchor, almost motionless in the gentle water. Hordes of junks, sampans, barges, bumboats, cutters, gigs, dinghies moved from the mainland to the island and back, and to and fro between the anchored ships.

"It's like any port anywhere, except the harbor's more beautiful," Blogg muttered. "Who the devil would have believed it? By God, it's too much to believe!"

He and Charlie took *San Seb* to anchorage while the mate and crew, still standing on the foredeck, recovered enough from their astonishment to stare and point and nudge each other and utter *"Yeeeeee!"* over and over. When *San Seb* was made fast, they lowered the dinghy and rowed across to a wooden pier that protruded from the beach a hundred feet into the water. Where the pier joined the beach, a square stone building stood, a big sign marking it as the office of the harbor master.

A stiff, middle-aged man who, he said, had arrived from England two full months ago turned out to be the harbor master. He received them with cold courtesy.

Captain Ellison was not on Hong Kong—he had sailed for Canton a few days ago.

Yes, Canton was open—at least that part of it that, the harbor master understood, was called Jackass Point. Since the Treaty of Chuenpi had been signed between Captain Ellison and the viceroy, the tea trade had been resumed, and dozens of ships had been dashing up and down with tea from Canton. Very untidy, all these comings and goings in and out of the harbor without permission, without even proper notice. It was something that the harbor master was planning to deal with severely.

Now—who exactly were Captain Blogg and Mr. Tyson? What ship was it that they'd arrived in? Was the ship properly registered with the harbor master's office?

Cursing aloud, Blogg marched out of the office and back to *San Seb*'s dinghy. Charlie waited long enough to tell the angry harbor master that their ship was *San Sebastian* and that she'd been registered in Macao for twenty years.

Within the hour, they sailed for Jackass Point.

Ellison looked earnestly at them from across the scarred table in his old rooms in Carradine's factory. The factory was empty now—their footsteps on the wooden stairs had resounded eerily. The cobbles of Jackass Point itself had seemed to resound as they walked across it from *San Seb*, for all the factories were empty. The traders had moved en masse to Hong Kong.

Ellison was in his shirtsleeves. They had interrrupted him as he cleared out his desk and closets, piling clothes and files and papers into large open baskets, to be carried off to the frigate that had brought him here. Nevertheless, he had made them welcome and had poured brandy for them all. Now he sat, drumming his fingers on the tabletop. He was strung up taut as wire.

339

"Quite true!" he said. "The appointment of Viceroy Chi Shan to negotiate with me was just a ruse to get our fleet away from the Gulf of Pei-chi-li. The viceroy told us that he himself was now in charge of affairs with the British. High Commissioner Lin had been disgraced! For having been overzealous, thus causing the British to attack China!"

He gave a high-pitched laugh and shrugged helplessly.

"Can you credit it? Lin! Who damned nearly bested me, with his bond and his ultimatum! *He* was blamed by his Emperor for starting this war, and was arrested and bundled off in chains! *Incredible!*"

He sipped distractedly.

"Anyway—the viceroy then said he would meet me in Canton for negotiations to end the war, so we sailed away. My fault! I should have known better; I should have asked for guarantees. When we got here, the viceroy simply refused to negotiate—sat pat inside Canton for a whole month, and no number of 'petitions' budged him. So . . . " He shrugged and gulped brandy. "We took the Bogue forts."

He was silent for a moment. Then, broodingly:

"What the Emperor did to the high commissioner made it easier for me to swallow what we did to the Bogue forts. . . . You saw them on your way over."

They had. Blackened ruins that looked as though they were part of the bald hills themselves, as though they had been there forever, as though there'd never been walls and embrasures and cannon and Tartars. Ruins, lying sad and humble under the Union Jack.

"You realize," Ellison said, "that I had to do it, even though I knew that I was fulfilling Carradine's damned prophecy. By God!" He slammed a fist on the table. "There was no other way of bringing that damned viceroy to the negotiating table! But that brought him! Within a few days, we'd agreed on the return of Choushan in exchange for you all from *Kite,* and the ceding of Hong Kong to the British. I took Hong Kong over formally on the twenty-sixth of January. Then, in another month, the viceroy and I concluded the rest of the Treaty of Chuenpi and signed it. . . ."

He jumped up and began to pace the room.

"The treaty includes what I've told you—Choushan and Hong Kong—and two other items: payment of the six million dollars indemnity that I promised the traders; and direct negotiations to take place henceforth between British and Chinese diplomats—no more going through the Co-hong for anything except trade. *That's all.* There's nothing in the treaty about opening more ports for trade, and nothing about making opium legal!"

He stopped and faced them, his eyes gleaming in his long face, the corn-colored hair, dusty from the work he'd been doing, drooping in spikes on his forehead.

"I told you once, didn't I—*by no means* would I let Palmerston and Carradine make me their instrument for spreading opium. *By no means!*"

In an access of emotion, Charlie jumped up and flung an arm around Ellison's shoulders.

"By God, George, that was great!"

They stood, smiling at each other, Charlie a good deal shorter, his eyes black, his hair bright red with that strange white streak, Ellison taller, thinner, his hair pale, his eyes like the sky. Yet, for a moment, different as they were, they could have been brothers. Then Ellison laughed and broke away.

"Thanks, Charlie—but it's an empty victory. *I* can't stop Palmerston! What I won't do for him, he'll just get someone else to do. I've been dismissed. It hasn't been announced yet, but I got private information from London. I've been given the sack like an incompetent office boy. The government won't ratify my Treaty of Chuenpi. They don't consider the war to be over. They're sending out new commanders, new troops, and a new plenipotentiary to replace me as negotiator. The war will start all over again as soon as they arrive. . . ."

He sat down and leaned back.

"I tell myself it'll be a great relief to get out of this at last—

and it really would be if only Palmerston hadn't given a bad report of me to the Queen. I'm told Her Majesty wrote with her own hand agreeing to my dismissal for incompetence and disloyalty. She wrote I *tried* to let the Chinese off as easy as I could."

His lips took on a bitter little twist.

"Oh God!" Charlie mumbled.

They sat, not looking at each other. There seemed to be nothing to say. After a while, unable to sit still any longer, Charlie jumped up and went to stare from the window that looked out over the black roofs stretching all the way to the Petitions Gate. Was that the way life was? All mixed up between truth and falsehood and idiocy and wickedness, and no way to make things clear?

There was a commotion on the narrow stairs that led to Ellison's rooms: footfalls, voices, and—astonishingly—a child's happy laugh.

"What the devil?"

Ellison rose to fling open the door.

Yin-kwa walked into the room.

Charlie felt his knees grow soft. As soon as they had arrived at the splintering old wharf of Jackass Point, Blogg had sent his mate into Canton with a note for Yin-kwa, but Charlie hadn't expected to see him for days. How many long, long days had he spent on Jackass Point, waiting, watching, listening, longing for Yin-kwa! This time he'd expected no better—and here was Yin-kwa, within the hour! Yin-kwa, who might hold the key to the mysteries in Ningpo, Yin-kwa, who'd been hidden for so long behind the facade of war. He looked no different. He'd never look different, Charlie thought confusedly. He'd never be old or enfeebled—he'd only become more elegant, more exquisite.

Yin-kwa smiled at Charlie across the room, a warm and secret smile that in an instant took him back to the earliest days of *Merope*, of Ah Sam, of the days of golden youth when nothing had been impossible.

"I came as soon as I got your message, Charlie."

There was whispering outside the door, a shrill little laugh, a patter of feet, and a small girl ran into the room, flung herself on Yin-kwa, clutching him around the knees, while her amah, following, tried to disengage her. Yin-kwa picked her up, his face full of tenderest love.

"Captain Ellison, this is my youngest child, my only daughter, O-lan. I promised to spend the afternoon with her today, so, when I received Charlie's message, I had to bring her along. Now . . ."

He set her down and gave her a little pat on the bottom. She laughed again and took her amah's hand and went with her out of the room, turning to wiggle her fingers at the men.

Yin-kwa watched her go, the softness still in his eyes.

"Sons are a duty to one's ancestors. Daughters are for one's own delight. . . ."

He looked around, smiling, dominating them by his very presence.

"Blogg, it's good to see you. I thanked the gods when I heard you and Charlie had been freed from that Ningpo prison. Captain Ellison, I apologize for turning your rooms into a meeting place without your permission. When I got Charlie's message I thought I'd better come at once—the last two times Charlie came to Jackass Point, something happened to prevent me."

"What could happen this time?" Ellison was setting another chair at the table, pouring another glass of brandy.

Yin-kwa smiled at Ellison over the edge of his glass.

"It has already happened! Viceroy Chi Shan has been arrested."

"What?" The three Englishmen shouted in chorus. Yin-kwa nodded, surprised at their vehemence.

"Yes. Arrested and led off to exile in chains. The Emperor is furious with him for giving away Hong Kong. The Emperor will not ratify the Treaty of Chuenpi."

Ellison burst into helpless laughter, spluttering between whoops and gasps:

"The viceroy and I! Sitting together at the Lotus Wall, solemnly making treaties, solemnly signing them! Yin-kwa, if the Emperor's furious with the viceroy for giving away Hong Kong, Palmerston's furious with me for giving back Choushan! If the Emperor won't ratify the Treaty of Chuenpi, Palmerston won't ratify it either! I've been sacked too, like the viceroy. The only difference is that I'm luckier than he is—I won't be led off in chains. I'll be allowed to sail away quietly on one of our own ships, and I don't suppose I'll be exiled, I'll be allowed to live quietly in some village in England as long as I keep my head very low!"

Ellison was close to hysteria. With an enormous effort he controlled himself, folded his hands on the edge of the table, bowed his head. The others regarded him with somber compassion. At last Yin-kwa said quietly:

"The war is going to start again?"

"Yes." Ellison sighed and reached for his brandy. His face was pallid and sweaty, streaked with dust.

"When?" Yin-kwa prompted gently.

"They're sending out new commanders and a new negotiator to replace me. They should be here by the end of July, and they'll go north at once, I suppose, to start the war up again."

"What should we expect of them?"

Ellison hesitated, and Yin-kwa bent forward.

"Ellison, it must be clear to the whole world, if not to our Emperor and his advisers, that your forces can do anything they please in China and we can do nothing at all to retaliate—not even to defend ourselves! I am asking you to tell me what to expect, because it is not the Emperor nor his advisers nor the Chinese military who will rebuild China after the war is over. It's we—the merchants—who will have to do that. So I want to be prepared as much as possible. For example, I feel sure that Lord Palmerston's new negotiator is not going to be satisfied with the six million dollars indemnity that you got out of Viceroy Chi Shan!"

Ellison sighed.

"No. . . . Well, Yin-kwa, I can only tell you what I suppose

344

our commanders will do. I suppose they will go north from here, attacking the coastal towns en route—Amoy, Foochow, Ningpo. I suppose they will retake Choushan Island. It's Palmerston's contention that no matter how recalcitrant your Emperor might be, we can ultimately force our terms on him by commanding the entrance to the Grand Canal, thus menacing Peking itself by endangering the rice supplies. I suppose, therefore, that until your Emperor is prepared to come to terms, we'll go on attacking northward—Chapoo, Shanghai—if need be, up the Yangtze River—Chinkiang, Nanking, eventually the mouth of the Grand Canal itself. I suppose, when it's over, the new negotiator will demand a new indemnity. Apart from that, the main points not included in the Treaty of Chuenpi were the opening of four more ports to foreign trade—Amoy, Foochow, Ningpo, and Shanghai. And the admission of opium as an article of lawful commerce."

"Ah!" Yin-kwa looked very thoughtful. "That last item is foolish of your Lord Palmerston. Short-sighted. Once it becomes lawful to trade in opium, what's to stop Chinese farmers from growing it? They may not produce as good opium as Patna, but it will be very much cheaper."

"By God!" Ellison slammed a fist on the table. "You take it calmly! Opium is *evil!*"

"Of course it is." Yin-kwa raised a serene eyebrow. "If one of my sons were to touch it, I'd thrash him, and if he couldn't keep away from it, I'd kill him with my own hands. Better he be dead than a slave to opium."

They gaped at him. Calmly, he looked from one to the other. At last Charlie said:

"Then you'll agree with Blogg and me, Yin-kwa. We decided to quit opium."

Yin-kwa bowed.

"You and Blogg are free to do as you please, Charlie."

"You mean—you won't quit?"

"Of course not. The big O will be bigger than ever after this war."

No one spoke. Ellison sat, stone-faced. Charlie and Blogg

looked down at their hands. After a moment Yin-kwa went on, speaking gently to the empty air in front of him:

"Should the British be allowed to debauch our people, and should no Chinese even attempt to control them? My grandfather and Sir George Seaton were the first to regulate the smuggling of opium, long ago, before the turn of the century. Did they do it because they loved opium or wished to profit from it? Not at all! They did it in order to hold it under their own control, to ensure that the quantities for sale would always be small and the price always too high for ordinary people. For a long time they were successful. . . ."

He rose and began to pace the room with his usual dignity and grace, but there was a blandness in his manner that told Charlie how tightly wound up he was.

"Charlie and I," he said lightly, "thought for a while that we knew better than our elders, and we brought Blogg into it with us. Now, he and Charlie have decided to withdraw, and I have no objection—in fact, I am glad. But I . . ."

He turned to face them, the window behind him so that his face was shadowed, his expression hard to distinguish. But his words were clear.

"I will stay in the trade because, like my grandfather, I have a duty to my people, to bring to it what control I can. Not that I think I can do very much for the time being, perhaps not for a long time, but it is unimaginable that I leave the field clear to such as the Carradines."

Yin-kwa turned to look out of the window. His voice came back to them, soft but firm and calm.

"In the last two years, I've given a lot of energy and money to organizing hospitals for curing opium addicts. The high commissioner asked me to. I did it willingly, though even as I did it, he watched me like a hawk. He trusted nobody, but I trusted him. In a way I loved him, because he was the only man in China who might really have abolished opium. But he's been exiled to the frozen north by the very man he served so well. Now—who knows? The war is to start again."

He turned to Ellison, his lips lightly curled.

346

"As I said, if ever my country is to emerge from its fog of misdirection, it will be we, the merchants, who'll drag it out of the clouds in which our Emperor and his advisers have their feet so firmly planted. We stand in the real world. We know the nature of the barbarian. So there's no need to give me that granite look, Ellison. I'm no monster. I'm just a hardheaded realist, like your Palmerston."

In the silence that followed, Ellison nodded slowly and heavily.

Footsteps came clattering up the stairs. Ellison rose.

"There're the ratings from *Druid* to fetch my duffel. I'll start back to Hong Kong on *Druid* this evening, to wait until I get my sailing orders." He glanced at Blogg and Charlie. "I'll see you there before I leave?"

They nodded.

The sailors came into the room, and Ellison showed them what to carry away. Then he stood awkwardly for a moment, looking around the shabby, bare room. Blogg put a great arm around him.

"Come on, Ellison! You're certain-sure not *sorry* to leave here!"

They all laughed then and went down the stairs in single file. Outside, they picked their way across dirty old neglected Jackass Point, where loose cobbles set traps for unwary feet. *Druid*'s cutter was waiting, two seamen holding her steady to the pilings, the others at attention at their rowlocks, oars held straight up in the air. Yin-kwa bowed to Ellison, holding up his clasped fists in the ancient Chinese gesture of salutation.

"Goodbye, Captain Ellison. I wish you good joss, and I hope we will be as fortunate in your replacement as we have been in you—but that is unlikely, for men like you are hard to come by."

Ellison flushed with pleasure.

"I wish England looked on me as kindly as you say China does!" He turned and jumped into the cutter. "Goodbye! Good joss!"

The rowers dipped their oars. The boat shot off down the

river, debris that the wind had swept off crumbling Jackass Point tossing about in its bow wave. Ellison stood, his white shirt flapping, one hand raised in farewell. They watched until he was out of sight. Then they walked silently to *San Seb*.

The child, O-lan, was on deck with the mate and her amah. The mate's wrinkled old face was beaming as he showed her how to tie a knot in a thin piece of rope. With her little fingers she was solemnly trying, but when she saw her father she dropped the rope and went to him, held up her arms to be carried. Her eyes were dreamy. Yin-kwa lifted her in his arms like a baby. She seemed instantly to fall asleep. He held her, caressing her hair, his eyes soft as Charlie had rarely seen them.

"The fairies brought her to us," he said, not looking up, "and they still speak to her. Sometimes she's in the world with all of us, and sometimes she hears them call and goes off to stay with them for a while. The other children tease her because she's different. . . ." He looked up, smiling at Charlie. "But not Jin-see. When he came to spend his fifth birthday with us, from the first moment he became her protector. She adored him. . . ."

His voice died away. At the mention of Jin-see's name, the atmosphere had seemed to grow heavy. Now Yin-kwa handed the sleeping child to her amah, and he and Blogg and Charlie went below. Silently, Blogg poured *sam shui*.

Charlie said: "Yin-kwa, what do you know?"

Yin-kwa turned the glass around in his fingers, looking down into its contents.

"Very little, I'm afraid. My man has been to Ningpo three times since that first time when he found Wei at his brother's house. Wei was very careful—he kept moving and my man had a hard time tracing him. He managed to find him once more and spoke to him. He thought Wei might be softening, but he still refused to admit that he had Ling-ling and the children with him. The next day, when my man went back to try to talk to him again, he had moved. Since then, though I've

348

sent him back twice more, he hasn't been able to find him. Now tell me what you know."

Charlie told him. Yin-kwa listened silently, shutting his eyes when Charlie told of Ling-ling running beside his cage. After the telling, they were silent for a while, Charlie's heart beating heavily in a kind of fearful anticipation. Why did he always feel that Yin-kwa had the answers? Yin-kwa sighed and shrugged.

"A dozen different things might have happened. It's impossible to tell. As far as I can see, the best thing is for you to go back to that little harbor near Ningpo." He paused a moment, his face expressionless. "If Ningpo falls to British guns, you yourselves will have access to the city."

They talked some more, but nothing new was said—there was nothing new to be said. At last Yin-kwa rose.

"You'll sail tomorrow? I'll send a man with silver. You'll have need of silver in Ningpo."

They went on deck. It was growing dark. Jackass Point lay before them, its shabbiness hidden by the dusk. There were one or two lights in windows, and for a moment of time it seemed as it had always been, as they had always known it.

"But it's finished," Yin-kwa said. "Jackass Point is finished. The Eight Regulations are no more."

Their eyes soberly scanned it—the ghost of it, for it was finished, as Yin-kwa said, its vital energy, its hustle and bustle, the good and evil of it, the honesty and treachery and malice and drama, all gone. For a moment, in the shadows gathering on the old, broken cobbles, Charlie thought he saw the tiny, tottering, chain-draped image of old How-kwa. Yin-kwa seemed to guess what he was seeing, for he said softly:

"On the Day of the Dead when we honor our ancestors, I kowtow twice to my grandfather, Charlie, once for myself and once for you. . . . Charlie, you know that you and your children and your children's children may ask anything of me and my family. What you did for my grandfather will not be forgotten through the generations."

349

He left then, giving Charlie and Blogg the same formal bow and the formal raising of his clasped fists that he had given Ellison. With a lurch of his heart Charlie thought, When will I see him again? And he called out, "Yin-kwa . . ." But Yin-kwa only turned and smiled at Charlie and stepped into his sedan chair. The bearers lifted it and bore him quickly away, and behind another chair with the little girl O-lan, who adored Jin-see, asleep in her amah's lap.

From Canton they sailed to Macao, to have *San Seb* careened and to inspect the white house at the end of the Praya. After a week they sailed to Hong Kong, entering the harbor with renewed wonder. The town might have sprung full-grown out of the sea. There was nothing tentative about it. The people climbing the beach, striding in and out of buildings, clambering about the scaffoldings of new buildings, knew exactly where they were going and what they were doing.

"Incredible!" Blogg murmured.

A little gig bobbed up, rowed by a young Englishman whose face neither Charlie nor Blogg had seen before.

"Hong Kong's been discovered," Blogg said sarcastically. "Here's another new one thinks he owns the mucking place because he arrived all of two months ago!"

But the young man in the gig was nothing like the harbor master. He was friendly, with a big smile on a cheery, homely face.

"Newspaper, sirs? *Canton Register.* News from home no more than three months old, and local news only three *days* old! It's being printed in Macao until we get our printing press set up in Hong Kong, but it is the very first *Hong Kong* newspaper— although it's called the *Canton Register.*" He grinned cheerfully. "Sounds topsy-turvy, like many things over here—the way the Chinese write, for example. But Mr. Carradine's the owner—he's one of the oldest residents of that British colony outside Canton—and I expect he wants it called *Canton Register* for sentiment."

Blogg regarded the young man sardonically.

"I see you don't know Mr. Carradine."

"No, sir." The bright brown eyes flashed. "He's not senti-mental?"

"That he ain't!" said Blogg.

The young man grinned and offered his right hand to Blogg, clinging to *San Seb*'s scuppers with his left.

"Thank you! I'm learning something every day. My name's John Murray. My father's a publisher in London, and I'm out here to learn the business from the bottom up, and the out-side in, so to speak. I'm just the dogsbody now, but I'll be a full-fledged journalist before the year's out, d'you want to wager?"

"Nay!" Blogg laughed. "If you write as quick and as much as you talk, you'll be a journalist long before that! My name's Blogg, and he"—he pointed to Charlie—"is Charlie Tyson."

"Hoy!" John Murray beamed. "The original Red Barbarian! I'll wager the Chinese named the whole English nation after you, sir!"

Charlie forced his lips to a smile, although his heart skipped a beat.

"How long have you been here?"

"Two months, sir, and still amazed at how much there is to learn!"

Charlie passed over a coin and took the inky newspaper that John Murray handed him.

"How about tomorrow, sir? Shall I bring you out another?"

"Reckon not. We'll probably be sailing later this evening."

"Well, you'll be back! Hong Kong's the hub of China."

Expertly, John Murray wiggled his little gig around and pushed off, grinning and waving over his shoulder.

Charlie opened the newspaper, a single large sheet folded in the middle to make four pages. On the front page, under an elaborate Gothic-lettered title, were a number of announce-ments and advertisements, including, in a heavily outlined box, quotations of the day's prices for opium. Patna, as always, was most expensive. Malwa, from Rajputana, next.

With a grunt, Charlie turned to the middle pages. Here was

the news, both English and local. In another heavily outlined box was an editorial announcing the imminent departure of Captain George Ellison, whose services Lord Palmerston had decided to terminate. Hong Kong, the editor said, would be the loser. The well-known and popular Captain Ellison would be much missed. The article ran to several hundred words, all of them unexceptionable, many laudatory. But there was a certain lip-smacking quality about them that caused Charlie to throw the paper down. Blogg kicked it overboard.

"We'd best go today. See Ellison and say goodbye to him, then set sail tonight."

A message to the *Druid* brought Ellison at once. He was thinner than they had ever seen him, and tired-looking, but calm and, in a way, happy. He said nothing about his departure or the editorial in the *Canton Register*. He sipped a glass of grog with them and then asked them to go ashore with him. They landed from the *Druid*'s gig at the wooden pier and walked past the harbor master's office, that official saluting grudgingly. Ellison strode along, proud and smiling, pointing out the sights. If Palmerston had spurned the Treaty of Chuenpi, Victoria Regina et Imperatrix had not spurned the island that Ellison had added to her crown. It was to be called the Island of Victoria. Its mountain was Victoria Peak. Its first road, already being developed on the landward side of the row of buildings, was Queen's Road. A large flat piece of ground beyond the beach was to be the Parade Ground: Ellison thought a statue of the Queen might well be placed there. Beyond the Parade Ground was the bluff, a kind of foothill, where Ellison thought a house for the first governor should even now begin to be constructed.

They stumbled over rocky ground up to the bluff. The view was breathtaking.

"It's beautiful, isn't it?" Ellison looked wistfully around. "I hope one day Her Majesty herself will have the time and disposition to come and look at it. Of all the British possessions I have seen, Hong Kong is the most beautiful. . . . D'you know what the name 'Hong Kong' means? 'Fragrant Harbor.' Gutzen

told me. A name as beautiful as the place. . . . See over there?"
He pointed down toward a little bay where Chinese craft were
anchored. "It's a long way for the peasants from Kowloon to
row over and back every day—they provide all the labor for
construction, you know. So many of them are beginning to
settle here on the island—I've given permission. . . . D'you
know what the name 'Kowloon' means? 'Nine Dragons.' "

They walked with him and listened to him for a long time,
Blogg attentive, answering gently, laughing often, Charlie silent, feeling both sad and glad for Ellison. At last they started
back toward the beach. When they reached a narrow cleft between tall rocks where they had to walk in single file, Charlie
stepped in front, leading Blogg and Ellison. Turning a corner,
he almost bumped into Andrew Carradine.

They stood face to face, a foot apart, staring at each other,
both startled into immobility. Andrew was the first to recover.
His blazing eyes set alarm bells jangling in Charlie's brain, but
he was a second too late. Andrew's fist crashed into the pit of
his stomach. Pain and nausea flared. He gagged and fell forward, clutching at Andrew, ducking his head under Andrew's
chin, instinctively seeking time to recover. Andrew pushed violently, trying to shove him off, but he clung all the tighter.
For timeless moments they struggled, panting, grunting.

Then, in a flash, Charlie found himself clutching at thin air.
Andrew had disappeared! Charlie's momentum carried him
forward. He staggered and fell to his knees, his head sagging
as he gasped for breath. For an instant, the world was frozen.
He heard his own panting, the buzz of flies that his fall had
disturbed, the tiny chirp of scurrying insects in the coarse tus-
socks of grass below his face. Then he heard above his head a
whirling, hissing, clanking sound. His heart clenched with fear.
What the hell was it? He'd heard it before! Without thought,
by sheer instinct, he flung his arms up to protect his head, felt
fierce pain slash the length of his left arm, saw red blood splash
onto the ground below his eyes, knew it was his own blood—
and remembered, all in the same instant, what it was that made
that terrifying sound.

A fighting iron.

Behind him he heard Blogg roaring and felt Blogg's great arms lift him from the ground. Before him stood William Carradine, his eyes shiny as miniature green suns, his lips grinning evilly, the declivity between his eyes deep and dark. From his wrist dangled the fighting iron.

From where his father had dragged him backward and flung him aside, Andrew sprang to his feet, leaping to grab his father's arm, yelling, "By God, I told you not to bring that bloody thing along! I told you! I told you!" Tugging violently, Andrew drew him out of the defile. Carradine stepped slowly backward, foamy spittle drooling from the corners of his mouth, his shining eyes fixed on Charlie. As soon as they were out of the defile, Andrew swung him around and began walking him quickly away, keeping tight hold of the wrist to which the fighting iron was buckled.

Blogg, setting Charlie back on his feet, sighed deeply.

"God be thanked he missed your eyes! Let's see that arm. . . ."

The sleeve had been torn off and was dangling loosely. Almost from the shoulder to the wrist, two long cuts zigzagged down the arm, blood welling from deep within, spilling down in little rivulets, splashing to the ground.

Blogg tore off the dangling sleeve and wrapped it tightly around the arm above where the cuts began, found a twig to twist the wrapping tighter, like a tourniquet.

"Come on, we've got to hurry. That needs attention."

He pushed Charlie out of the defile, an arm tightly around him. Ellison followed quickly, eyes wide.

"He must be mad! Carradine must be mad!"

"He is," Blogg said tiredly. "He's coming to the end."

"The end of what?"

"Of his run. . . . He's got the pox, you know. Had it for many years. It must be in his brain by now."

"God Almighty!"

By some trick of the air around them, Ellison's awed gasp echoed, bouncing back from the rocks.

Charlie heard the tinkling "-ighty-ighty-ighty" and thought it sounded pretty. His head spun around and around with the sound. His arm felt dead, though at the same time it seemed to burn. He tried hard, but he couldn't keep pace with Blogg—his feet stumbled and his knees seemed unable to hold him up.

"Get hold of him on the other side," Blogg told Ellison.

They hurried on down to the pier, and after a while they were on *San Seb* and somebody—the mate? Yes, the nice, kind, worried-looking mate—brought a mattress up from the cabin and laid it on the deck, and at last Blogg and Ellison stopped hustling him along and let him lie quietly and softly, resting, and Blogg gave him a big swallow of rum and he felt calm and drowsy. But not for long. Ellison took hold of his left hand and stretched out the arm, which wasn't dead at all, because if pain could scream his arm began to scream loudly as the cuts opened up again and the dried blood fell off and new blood began to flow. And then Charlie himself screamed to heaven because Blogg slowly and carefully poured liquid up and down the arm, drenching it thoroughly—from the smell, the liquid was rum. Then the mate hurriedly began dabbing sweet-smelling ointment over the arm—herb medicine, he supposed drowsily—he was drowsy again, the pain was quickly disappearing—and then Blogg and Ellison between them were wrapping bandages around and around his arm, and at last, at last, they left him alone, with the mate sitting beside him waving a palm-leaf fan to keep the flies off, as in the prison in Ningpo, but those were opium smokers there, twenty-pipe men, and the fan wavers were children. . . . It was all confused and confusing, but all the same, the swish and coolness of the gently waved fan was wonderful because it kept away the flies and deadened the awful clanking hiss of the fighting iron and obscured the blazing eyes of Andrew, who for some reason had stopped blazing now—he was grinning and mouthing "Doxy!"

Ellison was speaking in a hushed whisper: "Why do they hate Charlie so much?" And Blogg said: "There're many reasons. . . ." They were glancing at him, Charlie knew, not wanting to disturb his sleep, and he wanted to say that he wasn't sleeping, but it was too difficult to speak.

Blogg said, "I came to know Charlie more than twenty years ago—1821, it was. Carradine had beached me for losing twenty chests of opium off his ship *Betsy* when he ordered me to transfer in high seas—in those days we delivered opium in Lark's Bay, transferring direct from the carrying ship to the junks. You can imagine how those hulks at Lintin were welcome when they came! Well, that was Charlie's idea—did you know that? It was Charlie's idea to anchor hulks at Lintin, and he no more than seventeen years old at the time. He asked Carradine for the money to buy *Merope*, and Carradine refused him, meaning to do it all himself, but Charlie managed to get the money elsewhere and beat Carradine to it anyway— the *Merope* was the very first hulk to be anchored at Lintin— and, you know it well, Ellison, Carradine don't like to be beat!"

There was the clink of glasses and the gurgle of liquor, and Blogg went on.

"Then Charlie picked me off the beach where Carradine stranded me, and gave me *San Seb* to captain, and made me partner. Carradine didn't think any too well of that neither. . . . And all the Chinee liking Charlie, just nat'rally taking to him, where they don't take to Carradine a-tall, nor to Andrew. They trade with him for the sake of the silver, and bow to him because he's so mucking rich, but he knows mucking well some Chinee would slit his throat the minute they'd have no more use for him. The Chinee arranged for him to get the pox, you know—arranged it *special*. . . .

"And that time Charlie went into Canton, pretending to be Carradine, not knowing a-tall whether the high commissioner would chop off his head. 'Twas for old How-kwa's sake, not Carradine's, but lots of the traders sniggered at Carradine for that, behind his back. He too afraid to face the high commissioner, and Charlie marching off in his place, careless-like, between four soldiers. . . .

"But mostly, I reckon, Carradines hate Charlie because of

his wife. You know for yourself, Ellison, how the British are: All hot to get a Chinese mistress, but *marry* one's another thing. Disgrace to the flag. Insult to English womanhood. All that horse muck. And Charlie ups and marries Ling-ling, caring damn-all what Jackass Point thought of it. Reckon it didn't even cross his mind he was going against Jackass Point and the Praya Grande too, something any other Englishman would think ten times afore doing. And acknowledging Ling-ling's children as his fathering, all legal, while the Carradines—God knows how many of their bastards've been dropped around the China seas. Look at 'em—Carradine pox-rotted, Andrew with that *hareem* on *Sylph,* and the lascars and the sepoys all snickering at him. . . . It's no wonder to me that the Carradines hate Charlie. They envy him with a black envy. He's got something they ain't got."

"I know," Ellison said. "That very first night, the night of the typhoon when you rescued us from *Lily,* and we had more to drink than I've ever drank before or since—that night I said to him something about his Chinese mistress, something that Carradine had told me, and he glared at me, ready to hit me, and said, 'She's my *wife!*' I hadn't been in China long then. I learned something that night. Charlie taught me something. . . ."

The voices stopped. Charlie, filled with a vague kind of wonderment, tried to remember what they had said, tried to bring it back and mull it over, but it slipped away. . . . Carradine frowned at him, froth at the corners of his lips, and growled: "Sucker!" And handsome Andrew grinned and whispered: "Doxy!"

Later, Ellison bent over him and said: "Charlie? Charlie? I have to leave now. Blogg says you're sailing tonight, so this is goodbye, Charlie."

Goodbye? Goodbye to tall, gaunt, corn-colored honorable Ellison, who had wept that day on the Bay of Canton to see the war junks sinking, who sounded now as though he might weep again. No, no, he mustn't weep!

Charlie tried to sit up, but Ellison held him back, his eyes shining with affection, and perhaps a little wet. Charlie said, the words coming out a mumble:

"We can't say goodbye, George! Not us. Not you and me and Blogg. We're going to Ningpo to fetch my wife, but we'll be back soon to your beautiful Hong Kong. . . ."

When Charlie opened his eyes again, Ellison was gone, and there was a lovely sliver of new moon in the purple sky. He heard *San Seb*'s timbers creak and moan as her sails pulled her out of the Fragrant Harbor, pulled her yet once again into the swells of the South China Sea. She lumbered and protested and at last settled down to her slow, comfortable wallow.

Blogg came and covered him with a quilt.

He murmured, falling back into sleep:

"Blogg, d'you think Ningpo will fall to British guns?"

And Blogg said, "Aye, that it will!"

But Ningpo did not fall to British guns: It was ransomed. When, in six violent hours, the British ships destroyed the castellated town of Chin-hai, twelve miles from Ningpo, the panicked city fathers pressed the British to accept ransom and spare their town. Three days later, with hardly a shot fired, the British took possession of it.

But that was on the thirteenth of October, nearly three months after the day Blogg and Charlie said goodbye to Ellison and sailed out of the Fragrant Harbor. Under contrary and fitful winds that sometimes disappeared altogether, it took them more than five weeks to reach the Choushan archipelago of islands, and by that time *San Seb* was in the vanguard of shoals of Chinese craft scurrying northward like small animals fleeing before a predator. The new British commanders had arrived, and the voracious British fleet was once again on its fiery way.

Anchored in the little bay of Tao-hua-tao island, the men of *San Seb* saw a thousand little Chinese craft flit in to rest awhile before fleeing onward. Heard a thousand tales, whispered in awe, shouted in fear, howled out in anger and despair. The fortress town of Amoy had fallen, in spite of the great granite barrier across the harbor that was armed by ninety-six embrasured cannon. So many British ships had come, there must have been *ten thousand,* some said. And at least a *hundred thousand* barbarian soldiers! The ships must have been devil ships, springing from the sea as tigers spring from the jungle, for what craft that depended on wind alone could have come so quickly from Hong Kong to Amoy? And when they arrived at Amoy, the sails of some of the ships must have turned into wings and they must have flown over the barrier, for the opening was small and well guarded by Tartars, so how else could they have got inside? The three great ships had stayed far out and had blown a red typhoon of fire against the town and the barrier. The barbarian soldiers had carried sticks that spat fire too—spat it out very quickly, much more quickly than any ordinary Chinese musket. And the barbarian fire sticks had had something else in them, something magical: snakes that, when they saw an enemy, writhed out and stung him to death. It must have been so, for how else could Tartars have been so quickly vanquished?

"Bayonets," Blogg said briefly.

And at the end, when he saw his men defeated, stung to death by the magical snakes, burned to death by the typhoon of fire, the Tartar commander had walked slowly down the bloody beach among the sprawled bodies, walked slowly along the granite path on top of the barrier, stopped once to look back at the burning town, at the leaping orange flames and the swirling black smoke, and then had climbed through one of his cannon embrasures and walked into the sea, walked toward the great fire-spitting ships, until the sea had closed over his head.

When the fleeing junks and fisher boats had gone on their way, the British ships came to the archipelago. Tin-hai was taken again, almost as quickly as the first time, although, as Charlie and Blogg had seen for themselves, the town's defenses had been strengthened by a battery of new cannon on the joss-house hill, manned by Tartars. The Tartar commander, unable to go to the harbor to drown himself in front

359

of the British ships, had cut his throat up there on the hill. And then the British had crossed the straits and flung their fire against Chin-hai's castle for six hours, and Chin-hai's commander had slit his throat, too.

It was becoming routine, Charlie thought. There was no longer horror in the telling and the hearing of the tales—only a kind of sad, heavy inevitability.

Lee came a short time after the cannons that destroyed Chin-hai fell silent. From the anchorage at Tao-hua-tao island, the broadsides had sounded like faraway thunder, except that thunder was never so regular and ordered. When at last they stopped, the small huddle of boats in Tao-hua-tao harbor seemed slowly to relax from a tense crouch, to lift their heads, sigh with relief, take respite. The wind blew again. The sun shone. The water sparkled merrily. On *San Seb*'s deck, Blogg stirred, and Charlie slowly rubbed the thick zigzag scars that Carradine's fighting iron had left on his arm.

Blogg said soberly, "That was Chin-hai. Ningpo's next."

Charlie, glancing at a sampan entering the bay, turned away and then swung back sharply, staring.

"Is that *Lee?*"

"Who?" said Blogg.

"Lee! From the opium smoker's prison!"

Blogg snatched up his spyglass and peered at the man standing in the sampan's bow.

"By God, it *is* Lee! He's fatter nor we ever saw him, but it's him all right!"

They stood, staring. The sampan had put out from a large junk that hovered outside the bay, its masts draped in white cloth, a large white flag flapping from its halyards. The sampan was coming straight for *San Seb*, approaching quickly with the curious wiggle that the single oar gave it. Lee was alone in it except for the oarsman. He was dressed all in white, the whiteness making his bulk seem larger as he neared. His face was round and smooth. His neatly plaited queue glistened. He looked prosperous, lubricious, polished, at the opposite end of the scale from the skeletal creature they had first seen by the cesspool in that Ningpo prison.

And he looked sly. He was smiling so slyly when he came aboard that instinctively Blogg and Charlie gave him no greeting but waited for him to speak first. He wasted no time:

"Just happened to catch sight of this ship. I saw you transfer to it that day from *Modeste*. Thought I'd come and see if it really was you."

He took a step toward Charlie, his eyes sharp and bright. "You offered me ten thousand dollars to arrange for you to stay in Ningpo when you were released from prison. Does that offer still hold?"

"What are *you* offering?" Charlie said. He felt cold and alert and sharp as a razor. Now the waiting was over. Now something was about to happen.

Lee said, "To get you into Ningpo within the next couple of weeks."

"Into prison again? Into cages?"

"No. Free, within reason, to search for the people you want to find."

"How can you do that?"

"Because Ningpo will be surrendered to the British. . . . " He flicked a quick glance at the dozing oarsman and at Blogg's mate, incuriously fishing over the stern. Though neither could be expected to know English, he lowered his voice when he spoke again.

"I'm on my way now to the British admiral. After they took Tin-hai again, the governor of Ningpo sent me to ask if they'd accept ransom for sparing Ningpo. The admiral agreed, but wanted ten percent of the value of all the properties in Ningpo and of all the cargoes moving to Ningpo on the river. When I told the governor, he and his people were shocked. They dithered, wanting to bargain for five percent. I told them they'd better make up their minds—the British have no trouble at all making up theirs! But they went on dilly-dallying until the attack on Chin-hai started this morning. Then they sent for me in a panic—wanted me to rush off and wave the white flag in the teeth of the broadsides. They'd have paid fifteen percent by then, the fools! Anyway, I'm on my way now. Ningpo is going to be ransomed, and I can get you in. Does your offer still hold?"

Something in the flicker of Lee's eyes set off a cautious tingle in Charlie.

"If Ningpo's going to be controlled by the British, what's to stop us from walking in without paying anybody?"

Lee's eyes flickered again. He was amused.

"Try it if you like. You might succeed, though I doubt it. You see, I'll be chief of police. That's part of the arrangement. The British stipulated that Gutzen's to be appointed civil magistrate, and *he* stipulated that I'm to be his chief of police." He couldn't resist a contemptuous little laugh. "So, you see—you might get through the gates without my knowing it, but you wouldn't be a day inside the city before somebody reported it to me, and then . . . " He shrugged and spread his palms.

Charlie glanced at Blogg, and Blogg quirked an eyebrow. There was nothing for it but to accept Lee's offer.

"All right. Ten thousand dollars."

Lee drew a small, satisfied breath. "You're smart. . . . How will you pay me?"

Thank God for Yin-kwa's foresight! His man had brought aboard *San Seb* a heavy chest of dollars.

"In dollars."

Lee's eyes glistened. "You've got them aboard? Good! Get them ready. When the time comes, I'll send somebody to fetch you—and the dollars."

They watched him climb back into the sampan. Charlie thought that his heart should be pounding, his blood sizzling. Two years of trying to gain access to Ningpo, and now it had happened, so easily and smoothly. But all he felt was a deep quietness.

It was three long weeks before Lee's messenger came, a tall, hatchet-faced, silent man, carrying an unsigned note:

362

"The bearer will lead you to a place where I will meet you. Bring what you owe me."

They went with the man. The mate anxiously watched them depart. He would wait in *San Seb* in Tao-hua-tao Bay until they returned, or sent him a message to do otherwise.

They went a long way with the man, first by junk past the black ruins of Chin-hai among which people scrabbled like a swarm of large ants, still searching for anything salvageable, then up the river to a place that they judged must be near Ningpo. The junk anchored inshore, and they had a meal of rice and cabbage and hot tea, and slept fitfully on the boards, shivering with cold. It was November. The clothes they wore had always been sufficient for the cold months in the south, but in these northern latitudes real winter was clamping down.

At evening on the second day they left the junk and walked, the man leading silently, through windy fields and small bleak villages, meeting almost nobody—the people must be sheltering indoors from the bitter dusk. By the time they reached city streets it was too dark to see or be seen by the bundled-up, hurrying passersby, and almost immediately they came to a little house, to which the man headed: a shopfront house with a stone step up from the muddy street and a high wooden doorsill, like the shops in the Street of the Psychics in Canton. There was no real door—just planks that could be slid into grooves along the doorsill to close the doorway. A narrow slit had been left open. Lee's man went through it, beckoning them to follow. They entered a dark room. The man slid the rest of the planks into the doorsill, closing them in, and lit a sputtering oil lamp. The room came dimly into sight: dirty walls, a scuffed floor, a couple of pallets, a few stools, a cupboard. In one corner, a staircase, steep and narrow as a ladder, leading up into blackness.

Blogg lowered himself gingerly onto one of the stools, which creaked loudly. He grimaced.

"By God, if it weren't for this bloody heavy silver weighing me down, I'd not believe Lee was coming, but I reckon he won't miss that!"

"You have the silver?"

Lee was descending the narrow staircase. In the sputtering light, his sly eyes glittered.

"We have it," Blogg mumbled. Silently, they unbuckled the money belts in which they had been carrying the dollars, and spilled them out onto the table. Lee counted, his fingers flicking like lightning, matching the dollars in stacks of ten, as Charlie had in those long-ago days on *Merope*.

"Good . . ."

He gestured to his man, who swept the dollars into a heavy canvas sack, which he dragged into a corner.

Lee adjusted the lamp. The light grew brighter, striking glimmers from the shiny skin of his face stretched smooth and unwrinkled over fat cheeks and jowls. He was magnificently dressed in a heavy black brocade long gown, and over it a short jacket lined with silver-gray fur and buttoned with round silver buttons.

He drew one of the stools forward and sat down.

"I'm sorry you had such a long way to come, but unfortunately, after all, I couldn't have you brought through one of the city gates, because a slight complication has arisen. The British insist on having British sentries at all the gates. Ningpo has been turned into a British military garrison for the duration of the winter. Gutzen, as civil magistrate, insists that he'll not have British civilians coming into the city. He doesn't want the opium peddlers from Hong Kong rushing to Ningpo with cheap opium, as they did in Tin-hai. So you're free to move around the city as much as you like—the Chinese expect to see foreigners around—as long as you're not seen by a Britisher, who would report you, not to me, but to Gutzen. Then I'm afraid you'd find yourselves thrown out." He laughed maliciously. "The situation's reversed, you see. You don't have to be afraid of the Chinese, but you do of the British!"

Charlie leaped to his feet. "By God, Lee, you took my silver! How the hell can I—"

"Wait!" Lee raised a commanding hand. "I'll make up for your lack of freedom. Perhaps you need not, after all, run around searching the city. I've not heard anything about the people you described to me, but I do have reports about a woman from Macao who was making inquiries about the same people: a man called Wei, a woman, and three children."

Ah Sam! By God, it must be Ah Sam! Charlie drew a long breath. Lee said:

"You know who I mean? I can have her brought here to this house. Will that help you?"

"*Yes!*" Charlie blurted.

"Good. Then I'll have earned your silver, and anything else between us will be *new*." He threw Charlie a taunting glance. "Next time, if you're unable to provide dollars, I'll be willing to take your note. . . ."

He rose, smiling, elegant, rich, powerful.

"This house is just outside the eastern gate of the city. . . . In that cupboard there's some rice and beans, a stove, charcoal. Water in that barrel. There's a room upstairs, but I'm afraid its not habitable. The rent of this house has been paid for six months, so no one will come bothering you. . . ."

He stepped to the doorway and waited while his man removed three of the planks—two planks would have left an opening too narrow for Lee to sweep through. Charlie thought with a flash of grim humor that he himself would not expect Lee to squeeze through a door. Lee should walk through grandly, be bowed through, be ushered.

Lee stopped in the doorway.

"By the way, it would be useless for you to try to get to Gutzen over my head. In the first place, he wouldn't believe anything unpleasant you might tell him about me. And in the second place, you wouldn't live long after you had told it." His eyes glittered. "Don't make the mistake of underestimating me. It's true that when you first saw me I was a miserable opium smoker, but I'm entirely free of that now. Not many people have the strength to free themselves from opium. . . ."

He smiled, a chilling lift of his upper lip, and was gone, his man dragging the heavy sack after him.

Chapter XII

1842

W AITING FOR AH SAM, they lost track of the days. It grew
colder. Snow fell. They woke in the mornings to a
beautiful white blanket that was soon churned up to
dirty slush. The bare little house was icy, wind whistling
through cracks in the wooden walls and floor. They lived entirely in the downstairs room. Upstairs was nothing but a low
attic well ventilated by cracks in the roof. The stove was one
of the small round clay cookstoves. They left charcoal smoldering in it all day and all night, and at least could warm their
hands over it. The supply of rice and beans was plentiful, but
they grew very tired of rice and beans.

At last they decided to take the risk of Charlie's going outdoors. Blogg was too big and noticeable, but Charlie, in a
Chinese long gown, his hair covered by one of the round
Chinese hats that Wei had used to disguise him, could pass
for Chinese in a casual glance by an Englishman. When Lee's
man came with a note from Lee saying that Ah Sam would
soon be coming, they gave him money and showed him by

signs what they wanted, and he brought the garments. Blogg shaved off Charlie's sprouting beard, and one evening, in the early dusk, Charlie slipped out of the house.

It was the first of many excursions. Charlie bought food and *sam shui*. He bought each of them a fur-lined jacket, second-hand, soiled, the fur badly cured and smelly, but *warm*. He explored the lanes and byways around their little house. The district they were in had spilled out of the city's eastern gate—a poor district, crowded with ragged, hungry-looking people, small shops, ill-stocked markets, yowling street vendors. The tall, bleak gate was closed and barred at nightfall; to see into the city, Charlie would have to venture out during daylight hours. He did so on a day when it was raining—a slow, steady drizzle that seeped through his clothes and even, it seemed, through his skin, for his very bones creaked as he moved slowly along the wall toward the gate.

Crowds of people were passing through it, in and out, under the inattentive gaze of two Chinese officials—Lee's policemen?—huddled under a single umbrella, and two musket-bearing British soldiers. On an impulse, Charlie joined four or five men who were hauling a heavily loaded cart and went boldly through the gate with them. No one challenged him. He walked along, keeping careful track of landmarks, so as to be sure of finding his way back. Few people were on the streets on this miserable day, and they brushed quickly by him, paying him no attention. He could saunter along and look about.

By God, whatever ransom had been paid to save Ningpo, it was worth it! The city was untouched. Its life was ticking along as though nothing were untoward. Shops and markets were open, housewives bustling in and out. Food would be cooked and placed on tables tonight, as usual. People would eat and drink and go to their rest, would fall asleep straightaway, or pause with their wives to make sons for the future, or lie awake dreaming of revenge on the British, maybe plotting it. But there were no terrible black ruins, no evidence of the panic that had infested Tin-hai, no pitiful scavenging as around the broken citadel of Chin-hai.

Charlie walked, seeing no Englishmen at all until he came suddenly into a spacious square surrounded by three- and four-story stone buildings with the thick walls and deep-embrasured windows that marked them as government offices. Here the British were ensconced. A huge British flag drooped soddenly from a flagpole in the center of the square, and smaller ones hung from short staffs clamped above every doorway. British cannon menaced the entrances to the square. British sentries paraded before the buildings. British soldiers marched about, crisscrossing the square, boots clumping on the flagstones, the swords of the red-coated officers clanking against their tight-trousered legs.

Charlie crouched down against a wall at the end of a line of Chinese waiting to enter one of the buildings. Every few minutes, the man at the head of the line was gestured into the building by a jerk of the sentry's thumb. When he came out again, the next one entered, perhaps seeking some kind of permit or license or favor from the British. The line shuffled along, and Charlie moved with it. It was stupid to risk discovery like this, but he was fascinated by the sight and sound of the British. Their confidence. Their arrogance. And, he suddenly realized, by the pleasure of understanding what was being said. Just snatches of conversation as men hurried by him, but every word intelligible.

They were bloody unlucky devils, these men stuck in a bleeding Chinee town for the winter while them high muck-a-muck officers lived off the fat in Hong Kong. They'd be here till March—spring—when the offensive would restart. . . . But it wasn't all that bad here, after all. The ice skating was fine—you ever bin skating on *ice* before, mate? Just think of doing it the first time in *China!* And the grub was better nor wot they got on them bleeding transports! Christmas party'd been a right good 'un too, though no dancing. Wot d'yer want, mate, a bleeding *ball?* 'Ow could it be, you jackanapes, there being no ladies about? Oh, 'course there's *ladies*—some mucking good 'uns too! Wot you say, Bill? Good mucking 'uns? Hoy, that be mucking good, Bill! (Laughter.)

Charlie listened until he was almost at the head of the line. Then he pushed himself off the wall, hitched the collar of the ratty fur jacket over his ears, shuffled off. He arrived at the gate as they were shutting it for the night, and was roughly pushed through by the British sentries, who then marched off, boots thumping in well-practiced unison. " 'Nother mucking day gone!"

Charlie double-rapped on the door planks of the little house. Blogg slid two of the planks out, and he squeezed into the room. Even its chilly atmosphere seemed warm and welcoming after the misery outdoors. The red glow of the smoldering charcoal in the little stove drew him like a magnet. He stretched his hands to it, but other hands were already there, held over the coals. Tiny hands . . .

Ah Sam's hands.

She was looking up at him, eyes wide. With a shock he saw that her eyes were old—filmy-rimmed, like Wei's—and her face, lit from below by the glowing coals, was heavily lined. Images of the young, the ageless Ah Sam, leaped through his mind, and his heart swelled with love and nostalgia. Gently, he took her face between his hands and kissed her. She touched his cheek with a finger. When she spoke, there was a kind of grim sadness in her voice.

"Chahlee, why you come back?"

"Ah Sam, how could I *not* come? Why didn't *you* come to *San Seb* when we got out of prison?"

She sighed deeply. Blogg passed them bowls of hot tea, and she cradled hers in both hands, bowed her head low to look into the amber liquid. She was gathering her resources. . . . Charlie ached, remembering her instant responses, the flash of her smile.

Still looking into her bowl, she said softly:

"I not come 'cause I think more better you go 'way, forget Ling-ling, forget chilluns, forget me."

"Ah Sam! *Forget?* How could I ever forget! Ah Sam, I think you'd better start from the beginning and tell me everything."

She drew a weary breath.

"Yes. Now I must tell. . . . I start from day you go to Inglis ship, and I come with *San Seb* to Tao-hua-tao, and then I come to Ningpo. I look for Wei everywhere, but I no can find. So after thirty day I think soon I must go back to *San Seb.* But then I hear everybody talking, so excited, saying fisher people catch all Inglis man from Inglis ship, take them to prison in Ningpo. So I not know what to do. I think more better I stay Ningpo, maybe I can find out about you *and* maybe I can still find Wei. So I stay. I go to see big parade with cages, but so many people I cannot see anything. I ask, I ask, and people tell me all Inglis man go to opium smoker prison, stay there till maybe Inglis give back Choushan Island."

She stopped and sipped the tea and sighed again and shook her head.

"Next day, I find Wei! Too late! He already fix up with Tartar general."

"*What?*" Charlie's voice exploded in the little room, and she covered her ears, wincing.

"Please, Chahlee! So hard to tell you this! Please, you only hear me, don't talk. . . . That day, when I find Wei, I see him walk in street, and I follow him to his house. When he open door, I quick go in, so he can't stop me. But no need, because he very happy see me. He cry! And Ling-ling too, and chilluns. All of us, we cry! And they tell me what happen. I cannot find them because they change house many time. Very much danger. Every Chinee hating Inglis, and chilluns look like Inglis. They try keep chilluns inside house. Little Sisters so small yet, they stay inside, but not Jin-see. Poor little Jin-see! He no like stay in house, hiding. He like go outside, he like *fight*. People see his Inglis face, shout to him 'Inglis devil chillun!' Shake his body. Smack his face. Throw stones to him. When Ling-ling run outside to save him, people shout to her, say they kill her because she have Inglis son, she make ping-ping with Inglis man. Oh Chahlee, *terrible!*"

She looked up at him, tears as red as blood in the red glow of the coals dripping onto her folded hands—dripping too onto his heart like searing splashes of fire.

"Ling-ling tell me she saw you when they show you in cage. She touch your hand. Then people push her away. She hear you shouting 'Stop, stop' but she cannot see you anymore. She cry so much. Many people follow her, ask why she cry for Inglis man, ask if she make ping-ping with Inglis man, say they kill her, they kill her. . . ."

Her voice choked on her tears, and she drew a long, sobbing breath.

"That night, we talk so much, we cry so much, Wei say he give us medicine for make us sleep. When I wake up, they gone. I never see Ling-ling and chilluns again. Wei come back, tell me he send them to Chapoo with Tartar general. Chahlee—shhh! shhh!"

She reached quickly as he started up and placed a hand on his mouth.

"Hear me first, Chahlee! This Tartar general no can make ping-ping. You unnerstan'? He *no can ping-ping*. He feel shame. He don't like anybody know. So he ask Wei, if Wei let Ling-ling and chilluns stay his house, everybody think, if he get so beautiful new wife, he must be still like young man, every night make ping-ping two-three time. And no more fear for Ling-ling and chilluns because he take care them very good. Nobody dare go near fambly of Tartar general! You unnerstan', Chahlee? Wei let Ling-ling and chilluns go with him for *save their life*."

He buried his face in his hands. His heart was ticking hard and fast: *not-true, not-true, not-true!* And his mind was bonging slow and solemn, like the cymbals that had heralded Howkwa's death: *true—true—true*—she's gone with a Tartar.

He sat unmoving, too stunned to move. The room seemed to thrum with quiet. The tiny sounds—hiss of rain, moan of wind, spit of coals in the stove—echoed loud as gongs and cymbals. Charlie's heart turned to ice. The blood moved sluggishly in his veins, like the melted slush out in the lanes. His entrails burned with cold. The air he breathed stung his lungs like the bitter north wind. Was death like this?

Her whisper came to him, light as a sparrow's chirrup.

371

"So Chahlee, now you know why I don't go to *San Seb* when you come out from prison. I want you go back Hong Kong. I want you forget Ling-ling and chilluns and me. Fambly finish. Everything finish."

"*No!*" he muttered violently from behind his hands.

She leaned forward and spoke as to a child.

"Chahlee, now is *war*. Everybody running everywhere. Everything upside down, broken, lost, like throwaway rubbish."

He wiped his hands over his face.

"No! Today I was in the town, in the British quarter, and I heard that they'll start their offensive again in the spring. Soon after that, the Emperor will make peace—he'll have to. There's nothing he can do to stop the British. Then I'll find Ling-ling and the children and bring them back. Wei will know where they are. Wei will surely keep in touch with the Tartar, and we'll keep in touch with Wei, and we'll get them back as soon as the war is over."

He was speaking very fast, eyes shining, optimism rising with every word.

"Ah Sam, I'm not angry with Wei anymore. In fact, I want to ask his pardon. In that prison, I came to understand who Jin-see is—*what* Jin-see is to the family. I want to give him back to Wei. I want us all to be together, because now I understand that the family is forever. . . . You see, Ah Sam? It'll be all right! But I must speak to Wei. Where is he?"

She shook her head slowly, pity in every line and shadow of her face.

"Chahlee, Wei not here. He in a town called Yu-yao, about twenty mile from here. When this chief police find me, tell me come here see you, I go first to see Wei. I tell him, 'Chahlee in Ningpo.' I tell him, 'Wei, please come talk to Chahlee.' First I think he will come, because his face happy, like sunny day. But then his face close up, and he say no, he don't want talk to you."

The light slowly died from his eyes, and her face curled in

distress. She put out a hand to clasp his arm and, suddenly, frowning, she drew back the sleeve, sucking in a hissing breath as she saw the livid, puckered scars.

"What this?"

"Carradine," he muttered.

"With fight-iron?"

"Yes."

She ran a finger slowly along the scars, then drew the sleeve down and buttoned it over his wrist.

"Take care, Chahlee. Carradine hate you."

"I don't care about Carradine," he said. "I care about Wei. I care that Wei still hates me."

"No!" she cried. "Wei never hate you. I *know* Wei love you. I don't know why he don't want talk to you. Maybe because— because . . ."

"Because what?" he said dully.

"Because something he is doing—and me too . . . I tell you what it is, Chahlee, but you must promise you never tell, and Blogg too."

She glanced at them each in turn, and they nodded. She drew her stool closer to the tiny, wavering warmth of the stove and leaned forward to whisper to them a story that unfolded like the wanderings of a disordered mind.

Yu-yao, where Wei was living, was the headquarters of General I-Ching, who had been commanded by the Emperor to recapture Ningpo. Wei was helping him, spying on the English and so was Ah Sam.

"What?" Charlie woke suddenly to anger. "Are you crazy, Ah Sam, getting mixed up in *war?"*

She shook her head, her eyes shining with the excitement of the secret she was telling them. She was running no risks. She had taken a job in the quarters of the British officers as wash amah, washing their clothes, cleaning their boots. None of them suspected she knew English. They didn't even notice her about. They talked freely in front of her. She listened carefully, and reported anything of significance to Wei. Two or three times a month he came to Ningpo, dressed as a beggar, and she went outdoors pretending to give him food or money, to make her report.

"God Almighty!" Consternation made Charlie shout. "You and Wei are both *mad!* The Chinese can't take Ningpo back from the British! They'll be annihilated if they try! Ah Sam, you're in terrible danger!"

She gave him a superior smile, and he felt his blood curdle. Had her mind come unhinged? But she went on speaking as calmly as if what she said made common sense. General I-Ching had gone to the Temple of the God of War to kowtow and pray for victory. An old and holy priest had taken omens for him, and had told him that he would be victorious if he had on his side humans with the heads of tigers. When he and his officers returned to Yu-yao, there they were! Humans with the heads of tigers! Warriors from the Golden River, come to offer their services in fighting the British. They wore uniforms of yellow with black stripes and on their heads caps of yellow with black spots. Caps like theirs had immediately caught on in Yu-yao: local sew-sew women were kept busy around the clock making them up. And the month of March, when the general planned his attack, was the month of the tiger. And four o'clock in the morning, when he planned to begin his assault, was the hour of the tiger. How could he lose?

Her head was cocked on one side, eyebrows raised, glistening eyes darting, like a bird's, from Charlie to Blogg and back again. Blogg bent his head in a gesture of sorrow. Charlie drew a long breath, forcing back the black cloud of dismay that was invading his mind. He put his hands on Ah Sam's shoulders, looked deep into her eyes, said quietly and emphatically:

"Ah Sam, you know better than to believe all that! You know it's nonsense, don't you? Omens and tiger-men and tiger-time. You don't believe all that, Ah Sam."

Her eyes flickered with sardonic amusement.

"Of course I don't believe! You think I crazy?"

Her eyes changed, became soft and luminous. Behind them he could see the memories fleeting. The long nights on *Mer-*

374

ope, the nights of love. And the long days in the white house in Macao, full too of love, a different kind of love. . . .

She smiled a little. "But I-Ching believe, and who can tell? Maybe he will win. . . . Chahlee, I am old now. I will die soon. When Chinee people die, ghost come—ghost with white dress and tall hat. He come to take dead people to King of Hell, and they must show King of Hell what they do with their life, good or bad. Some people go to priests to buy passport. But me . . . no, no. When I die, Chahlee, when white-dress ghost come to take me to King of Hell, I want show him one Inglis head. Inglis come with many fire ship and kill many thousand of Chinee. I want show King of Hell *one* Inglis that *I* kill."

She rose, and he rose too and put his arms around her lightly, hypnotized by her eyes, inscrutable now, showing nothing, not sorrow nor pity nor love nor remembrance. She stood in his embrace and looked up at him and said very softly:

"One Inglis head, for showing to King of Hell. . . . Chahlee, I go now. And you go home to Inglan'. Forget Chinee fambly. Make new Inglis fambly. . . . Goodbye."

She slipped from his embrace, flashed to the door, slid it open a tiny crack and slipped her tiny body through, vanished, all in a moment of time.

Charlie rushed to the door, but Blogg caught him.

"Let her go, Charlie. She wants it like that."

For long violent minutes, he fought Blogg's arms clamped firmly around him. In the end it wasn't Blogg, it was Ah Sam herself who stopped him: the memory of her "goodbye." Once before she'd left him, but never before had she said to him "goodbye."

He stopped struggling, and Blogg led him back to the stools beside the brazier. He sat down, staring, hardly breathing. The dim room, the glowing coals, the sounds of wind and rain, began to take on the quality of nightmare. . . . Wei hated him, Wei had refused to talk to him, Wei had sent Ling-ling and the children off with a Tartar. A Tartar who couldn't ping-ping? But clearly all Tartars, fantastical Tartars, Tartars who drowned themselves and slit their own throats and plunged short swords into their hearts rather than surrender—surely all such magnificent men must be able to ping-ping! But Ah Sam said this one couldn't. And surely Wei, even to save Ling-ling's life and those of the children, even though Wei hated him, surely he wouldn't force Ling-ling into concubinage. . . .

Blogg said, his voice matter-of-fact, "Drink this, Charlie."

It was a bowl of *sam shui* that Blogg must have held over the stove, because it was warm—warm and potent. Blogg held it to his lips and tilted it so that he had to swallow fast. While he was swallowing, Blogg said easily:

"Chapoo's no more than a couple of hundred miles across the Bay of Hangchow. *San Seb'll* make it easy. But I reckon we can't start out much before March. Winter winds and ice too dangerous."

Chapoo. Blogg was proposing to sail to Chapoo.

Was the nightmare true, then?

Were Ling-ling and the children in Chapoo with a Tartar?

Was this exquisitely painful night real?

"Drink up, Charlie."

Blogg tilted the last of the bowl of wine down his throat.

Later, he knew that Blogg was easing him down onto his pallet.

Later still he half woke, feeling the *sam shui* churning in his stomach, feeling under his cheek an icy little pool of wetness that he knew was made of his tears.

In early March, when Blogg judged that it was almost time for them to go, they went out early one morning to explore the route by which Lee's man had brought them in. Blogg reckoned to walk back the way they had come and, somewhere along the river, or at Chin-hai, hire a junk to take them back to *San Seb*.

They left the house together—now that they were about to leave Ningpo, it wouldn't matter if somebody reported to Gutzen.

The moment they were out in the lane, it was clear that

something had happened. Usually, the lane woke slowly. First, the vendor of the twists of fried dough that in this poor quarter constituted everyone's breakfast rolled out his iron-wheeled mobile kitchen, lit the firewood under his deep iron frying pan, poured oil into it, and, while it was heating, began to knead and shape his twists of dough, all the while crying out the three-syllable chant that advertised his presence. The early risers, coming out of their doorways, stopped to buy breakfast. Other vendors, each with his own distinctive chant, brought out their carts or their merchandise balanced on shoulder poles. More people left their homes . . . and the day began rolling.

But on this morning, so early that the breakfast vendor was still lighting his fire, people were already flocking out of their houses and down the narrow lane. The news that was drawing them was being passed from mouth to mouth, called out from those in front to those behind, shouted up at heads thrust out of windows. Whatever it was, the news was exciting, thrilling, frightening, enraging, embittering, pitiful, solemn— the faces of the people bore all kinds of expressions.

They were all hurrying in one direction—toward the eastern gate of the city. Charlie and Blogg went along with the crowd. Nearing the gate, they had to slow down. Everyone was slowing down, running into blockages created by the ever-growing mass of people who stood gaping toward the gate.

"Here," Charlie said to Blogg. "If we go through this side lane, I think we can get out of this jam of people."

"Wait a minute," Blogg said.

Something in his voice made Charlie stop short. Blogg was standing still, head and shoulders taller than the people, looking over their heads toward the gate. A moment later, he began to push his way forward. Charlie followed. People gave way, unable to resist Blogg's weight. As they approached the gate, the buzz of the crowd became a roar, and the mass of the people became so dense that there was no room to move, except for enormous Blogg, who made way for himself and Charlie by a series of convulsions. Then, suddenly, they were through the tumult and in a clear space at the foot of the gate, where, in hushed silence, some British soldiers and uniformed Chinese stood gazing upward.

Charlie shaded his eyes from the rising sun and looked upward too—looked directly at the severed head of a man impaled on a spear above one of the gateposts.

The head of Wei.

The eyes were slit open, their filmy-rimmed pupils just visible under the lids that drooped slyly, as though to hide a secret. The lips were clamped tightly shut, perhaps over the same secret. The wrinkles of the face were a maze of arcs and parabolas on skin like crumpled paper. The queue, disordered and ruffled, twitching a little in the rough morning breeze, was still attached to the back of the head. The executioners hadn't cut it off; they must have pulled it tautly forward to bare the back of the neck to the ax. A drop of dark blood oozed with infinite slowness from the ragged edge of the neck, dripped down onto a paper tied to the spear below the chin. Chinese characters covered most of the paper, but there were a few words of English scrawled at the bottom, as though in deference to the conquerors:

THIS MAN WAS A SPY

Charlie read the letters over and over. They were a message written specially for him, for Charlie Tyson: Your father-in-law is dead. His ghastly head hangs before you. He died hating you. It's too late now to ask his pardon. . . .

Grief swirled around Charlie like a dark enveloping cloud, blotting out the light.

Someone shoved him between the shoulder blades.

"What the muck're you doing 'ere? No English civvies 'llowed in this town! Get the muck off 'fore I marches you to that cockeyed magistrate!"

The soldier's hoarse shout died behind them as Blogg pulled Charlie back into the anonymity of the crowd.

* * *

Time was no longer a pattern of minutes and hours, of night and day, of patience or impatience. Time was a kind of time-lessness of endurance and waiting. Only Wei had known exactly who had Ling-ling and the children. While he was alive, even though he hated Charlie, there'd been a tenuous lifeline to them. Now there was only Charlie to find and save them . . . and only two clues: Tartar general, and Chapoo. He dreamed of Tartars—waking or sleeping dreams he did not know, but in his mind's eye he saw Tartars, the four fantastical men who had strode on Jackass Point on the day of Lee Kwok's death, tall and proud, muscles rippling beneath their gray satin garments, waists and ankles bound in brilliant scarlet, embroidered breastplates splashed vividly across their chests. Did he look like that, the Tartar who was protecting an Englishman's wife and children by the strength of his prestige alone, while he steadfastly pretended to virility, giving no hint of weakness? Was he like that? By what sign could he be found?

God in heaven, let me find him!

Lee swaggered into the room, followed by his servant. He sat down on one of the stools after the servant had dusted it off. The servant placed a low footstool that he had brought under Lee's satin boots and carefully lifted the hem of Lee's black brocade gown to clear the floor.

Lee tucked his hands into the fur-lined sleeves of his jacket and shivered.

"By God, it's cold in here! How do you stand it?" He grinned mockingly. "Well, it won't be for much longer. You've had your money's worth. I need this house back. You'll have to get out in the next few days."

"We're going," Blogg said.

"Good!"

Lee gestured toward the *sam shui,* and his servant hurried to pour him some. He sipped and grimaced and emptied the bowl onto the floor.

"How can you drink that rubbish? Well, I suppose Englishmen don't know better. . . . Did you hear all that noise yesterday?"

"We heard something," Blogg said.

"Something? All that musketry? All those cannon? All the crowds roiling about asking each other and the gods and spirits what was going on?" He gave a snorting laugh. "Some idiot called General I-Ching thought he could recover Ningpo for the Emperor by assault. Attacked at the south and west gates at four o'clock in the morning with some fantastic troops, no weapons beyond a few muskets and hand swords, but lots of fancy yellow-and-black uniforms. It was slaughter. More than five hundred Chinese killed, and not a single British devil even wounded!"

With a shock of sorrow, Charlie thought that Ah Sam had failed. She'd have to go empty-handed before the King of Hell!

Lee's suspicious eyes were probing his face.

"Are you sorry? You'd like to hear of British deaths? Well, I can't deny that I would too. But this time it was my duty to warn the British. I found out most of I-Ching's plans—as a matter of fact, I found out through you. . . ."

He grinned maliciously at Charlie, then at Blogg.

"That old Macao woman of yours. My men had a hard time finding her in the first place, and finally found her in the middle of the British enclave, washing British uniforms, shining British boots. Not one of the British suspected her—a tiny little old wash-and-clean amah! But *I* did, when I realized that if you wanted to see her she must be able to speak English. And if she could speak English, what was she doing in the British officers' quarters, pretending that she didn't understand a word? I had her watched and followed when she came back from her meeting with you. Found out that she was regularly meeting an old man who looked like a beggar—a running dog for I-Ching. Had him followed too. Then had them both arrested and questioned. Had the old man's head chopped off and stuck up on a pole as a warning to others with similar aspirations. But that little old woman was too quick for my men. Killed herself with a tiny dagger, and one of my men too, when he tried to stop her. Stabbed him in the eye, and then stabbed herself."

Charlie smiled at Lee—smiled widely out of the surge of satisfaction that welled up in his heart. She hadn't gone empty-handed after all! She'd taken a head with her—not an English head, but one just as good: the head of a Chinese traitor, a running dog for Lee!

Lee said angrily:

"What are you smiling about? What was your interest in the woman? I've got a damn good mind to have you questioned too!"

"Don't try it!" Blogg growled. "Gutzen wouldn't stand for having our heads chopped off."

Lee smiled evilly.

"He didn't want to stand for having that old man's head chopped off either. Recognized him, he did. Seems he belonged to a family who sent a son to Gutzen to learn English. But what could Gutzen do, when I insisted? A Chinese caught spying against the British!"

Blogg slowly poured a bowl of *sam shui,* drank it, slammed the bowl down.

"What the hell have you come for, Lee? To brag about your cleverness? Or be there something else?"

Lee flushed, then controlled himself with an effort, smiled coldly at Blogg.

"I came to tell you that you're to be out of this house within a week. . . . You'll have company sailing out of the bay. The British devils are going too—across to Chapoo. Another lot of fools there in Chapoo! The British gave them a choice—pay ransom, or have the city sacked, and they refused to pay! They still believe in the legend of the invincible Tartars! Tartar flesh can withstand British iron!"

"By God, Lee!" Blogg spoke with a tone of wonder. "Who the hell's side are you on?"

"My own," Lee said, with a flat smile. "Who else's? Nobody ever gave me a choice. I'm making my own choices now. . . . Gutzen got me when I was a baby, a few days old. Told me that my mother had given me to him, that she didn't know who my father was. A bloody, dirty lie. He knew bloody well that my father was Carradine."

They gaped at him, speechless. He laughed sarcastically.

"Surprised? I was too, I can tell you! The only sign of foreign blood is that my hair's not quite black, if you look carefully."

"How did you find out?" Blogg asked.

"Carradine himself told me, when Gutzen sent me on one of his clippers with a load of Bibles to be delivered up the coast. Told me I was Andrew's half brother, older than he by fifteen years. Laughed when he told me. Andrew with a suite on *Sylph* for his private tarts, and me a poor bloody catechist! Gutzen began to teach me religion almost before I could walk. Day in, day out. Chinese, English, and religion. I wasn't to have any fun in life . . . and I hadn't even missed the fun until then! Thought it was fine to be Gutzen's disciple! That's when I started smoking opium—that very same day when Carradine told me. . . ."

"But why did Carradine give you to Gutzen?"

"Sheer bloodiness, I think, although he said it was conscience. I am his oldest child. He claims he didn't know what to do with me, didn't want to leave me with my mother, have me become a Chinese coolie, maybe. So he took me from her and gave me to Gutzen. If that's true about his conscience, it's the last time it ever troubled him, damn him. I must have a dozen or more bastard half brothers and sisters around the southern seas, apart from legitimate Andrew!"

The servant, who had been standing by the door, made a sound. Lee swung round. They exchanged a few words. Then the servant began sliding out the door planks, all of them, leaving a wide opening. Lee gestured Charlie and Blogg toward a corner of the room, then lit a second taper from the oil lamp on the table and went upstairs with it. For one of his bulk, he moved very quickly and quietly.

Two men came in from the street. Roughly dressed, barefooted in spite of the weather, but not coolies—they had an air of authority. They conferred with Lee's servant in whispers, then went up the stairs.

Almost at once, other men came in from the street, discernible more by their movements than by their bodies or their faces. For a moment Charlie was puzzled, then light dawned. They were lascars, so dark-skinned that they were almost invisible in the darkness!

And the only place from which lascars could be coming, thus secretly, to the city of Ningpo was from one of the Carradine clippers. . . .

Opium. They were carrying in chests of opium, passing them from hand to hand up the narrow steps, to Lee's two Chinese (policemen in coolie disguise?), who received them at the top of the stairs and stacked them in the attic.

It took half an hour to move in about fifty chests. The small attic space must be crammed with them. Then the lascars disappeared back into the night, and Lee's servant closed the doorway. Lee came down with the two Chinese. He handed them the bottle of *sam shui,* which they emptied, drinking in turn. Then they too left.

Lee turned to Charlie and Blogg.

"You understand why it would be safer for you to go as soon as possible? It wouldn't be healthy if you were found here with those chests installed above your head."

"We understand," Blogg said easily. "Is that Patna up there?"

"Of course," Lee said and laughed. "A hundred dollars a chest, introductory price. I've already contracted to sell them at five hundred dollars. I'll have made a million out of the Carradines before they find out there's going to be no such thing as 'introductory' opium in Ningpo. They're clever-stupid. First on the market, first to organize supplies and shipments, and never for a moment doubting but that I'll be their good and obedient servant. I'm their son and half brother after all, bastard that I am!"

"You made your arrangements with Andrew?" Blogg asked mildly.

"Yes, but he's already left for Hong Kong. His father—my

father!—is in Tin-hai on their receiving ship. They've got one there that they'll keep supplied by clipper from Hong Kong."

The servant had picked up the footstool and was waiting by the door, but Lee lingered. It was giving him pleasure to answer Blogg's questions. There was no one else to whom he could pour out his bitterness and his pride in his own intelligence, Charlie thought.

"How's old Carradine?" Blogg asked conversationally.

"You know what's wrong with him, don't you?"

"Heard it's the pox. It's true, then?"

Lee made a sound between a sneer and a snort. "He's rotting, body and mind! Stinks to high heaven with pussing ulcers. Walks around talking to himself, with one of those old-fashioned fighting irons buckled to his wrist, swishing it about. I wonder Andrew dares to leave him, but I suppose he'd be too much of a scandal in Hong Kong. Andrew's got a big position to keep up now—head of the princely house of Carradine!"

Blogg clucked his tongue and moved casually forward, sat down on one of the stools at the table.

"Say, Lee . . ." He spoke as though he'd just thought of something. "D'you know Chapoo? Give us a bit of a description. What's the best sailing to get there?"

Lee answered without hesitation, giving bearings for going straight across the bay. Then:

"If the weather prevents you, you can continue westerly along the coast to Hangchow, and then come back easterly along the opposite coast to Chapoo. That would be much longer, of course, but safer for that old tub of yours."

"Thankee, that's very clear," Blogg said gratefully. "And the town? What's where in it, so to speak?"

"Why do you want to know?" Lee asked sharply. "You can't go into the town."

"Not now," Blogg agreed. "But after—if, as you said, the town's bombarded and falls to the British. Maybe we could get in then."

384

Lee's eyes sparkled slyly.

"You want to look for somebody in Chapoo, is that it? The same people you were looking for in Ningpo? Was that your interest in the old Macao woman? Well! Well!" He laughed, pleased that he had the answer to something that had puzzled him. "Well, that's nothing to me! You can risk your necks in Chapoo, for all I care. . . . The town's about half the size of Ningpo, not famous for anything but well placed for commerce, directly on the coast, midway along the bay. It's quite heavily garrisoned by Tartars. The town has the usual wall and gates all around it. The south gate, facing the beach, is the main one. It's guarded by a joss house, where the Tartars are positioned. Just inside the south gate, the Tartars have their own quarters where they live with their women and children. I can't tell you much about the rest of the town. . . ."

He had risen and was smoothing out his gown. His servant slid planks from the door. Outside, there was quick movement—Charlie glimpsed a sedan chair. Lee smiled quite pleasantly—things had gone to his satisfaction.

"Well, I hope this is the last I'll see of you."

The last they saw of him was the hem of his opulent gown flipping as he went through the door.

Blogg replaced the door planks.

"Well . . ." He grinned at Charlie. "Got more nor what I hoped for when I began to butter him up. We won't have to look far, once we get into that town. Special Tartar quarters, just inside the south gate."

Charlie stared at Blogg. Perhaps the red shine of his eyes was a reflection of the glowing charcoal. Perhaps the tightness of his smile was an illusion of the shifting shadows.

"Blogg, let's go tonight."

Blogg stared back at him. Their gaze mingled and combined. The shadows shifted and flickered, and from up the stairs the smell of opium came floating down softly, insidiously.

Blogg laughed.

"Aye! We'll go right now. If for no other reason, because we cain't trust that bastard Lee not to come back with some of his policemen, all horrified to find *opium* in our attic. . . ."

Chapoo looked like no other Chinese place that Charlie had seen. Canton had a kind of heavy, monumental symmetry. Lintin was elegant in its bare, austere way. Macao was lovely— the gracious old town, the flower-decked *praças,* the shady trees, the low-walled Praya above the fine, long beach. Namoa was comely, and so, in its way, had Tin-hai been before its ruin. Ningpo was dignified. Hong Kong, of course, was beautiful— the Fragrant Harbor.

But Chapoo was plain ugly. From *San Seb,* anchored half a mile at sea because of the shallowness of the muddy inshore waters, it looked like a large brownish toad squatting several hundred yards above a stony beach along a dun-colored coast-line. Its wall and the south gate, the only one that could be seen from the sea side, were utilitarian, the gate of heavy, weathered timbers, the wall, about twenty feet high, of thick granite blocks. The joss house was ungraceful, a hard thing for a joss house to be, for the intrinsic form of pagodas was fine. But this one was out of proportion, its roofs of dull yellow tile, the lowest perhaps thirty yards in diameter, the highest about half that size. Altogether, an ugly town.

But Charlie, staring at it, saw beauty. Blogg had said that British gunners who could so easily blast away big, solid targets like ships and towns would have a hard time scoring a direct hit on the slim joss house, and if they did not, if it still stood, any landing party storming the south gate would be highly vulnerable to bullets, arrows, spears, and boiling oil shot and tossed down from the five stories above them. And the gate was strong and solid, and the wall thick and tall. Blogg said that British broadsides could damage but could not penetrate such a thick, strong wall. Also, because of its height, the trajectory of cannonballs coming over it would carry them beyond the black tile roof that abutted the wall on the inside, which must be the roof of the Tartar quarters that Lee had said were just inside the south gate. People sheltering under that roof, in Blogg's opinion, were quite safe from bombardment from the sea.

Charlie lay on his stomach on *San Seb*'s deck, chin propped on his fists, and tried to imagine where, under that roof, Ling-ling and the children might be. The place must be bare and austere—it was, after all, a military barracks—but wherever Ling-ling was must become infused by the special loveliness of her, the quality, the essence that set her above all other women. Her physical beauty was matched by the beauty of her soul, of her spirit—her glowing innocence, the love she had for every one of God's creatures. By God, they were right, all those who had said that Charlie Tyson's joss was fabulously good! It was! It had been, and now it would be again, for he was soon, soon, going to get her back. It was pure good joss, for what had he ever done to *deserve* such a wife, such children—and, of course, Ah Sam? A wave of happiness and sorrow, inextricably mixed, lapped his spirit. Ah Sam was gone now, but she'd had the joy of the "fambly" she'd contrived for herself for a good many years, and she'd gone with her eyes wide open, knowing exactly where she was headed. He smiled gently, thinking of that sardonic "You think I crazy?"

Ling-ling would grieve at the loss of Ah Sam and of her father. But when they were safe again, back in Macao, he'd build an altar for Wei and have a soul tablet carved for him out of the finest marble.

"Look!" Blogg called.

Strange sails were rising over the horizon. Charlie jumped up to see better. Not the British armada. A single ship. By God, a clipper! The raked masts were unmistakable. But a small one. A new one.

"Never seen *her* before!" Blogg said.

The mate ran up to chatter with Blogg, and the crewmen followed him, to line the gunwale on the seaward side, staring at the strange ship.

Blogg spoke again.

"They say they've seen that ship before, when we was in Ningpo. Mate says 'twas sailing between Tin-hai and Chin-hai. Charlie, I reckon it's that receiving ship Lee said the Carradines have in Tin-hai harbor."

"You're right," Charlie said, staring. "It's coming here to wait like a bloody vulture till Chapoo's taken, and then it'll swoop down with cheap opium. First on the market, the Carradines. First to organize the distribution of supplies. . . ."

"D'you reckon old man Carradine's aboard?"

The question lay on the air between them, unanswered.

The ship, unhurried, graceful, made its way to an anchorage two miles east of *San Seb*, sank anchors aft and stern, and seemed to settle down to wait, like *San Seb*.

The armada came three days later. The day was fine, the sea calm, the wind steady. The ships came sweeping over the horizon, supremely confident. *Melville* and *Wellesley* and *Blenheim*, which had wintered in Hong Kong, were there again in the forefront of their squadrons, but they stopped at a distance from the shore, and only a few frigates and transports came on toward the town—the British high command did not expect to have to use much power to capture this little bump on the featureless coast, good only for servicing commercial shipping midway in their sailings. There were no Chinese vessels of any kind at the port now, nor had there been in the week since *San Seb* arrived.

"Why should the navy bother with Chapoo?" Charlie asked.

"To prevent its being used against 'em," Blogg said. "The British navy makes war *professional*, Charlie, by rule and regulation, not haphazard like Chinee war junks with fire rafts and gongs and shouting and grimaces. British seamen and marines and soldiers are *trained* for fighting. The commander's got a book that he goes by. Ain't his to choose to pass by Chapoo 'cause its a little old nothing town. His book tells him that he's got to take it, and that he'll do."

They fell silent, watching.

The navy was in no hurry. A mile from shore, sails were

furled and the ships slowed, rocking gently on the calm water. One of the smaller frigates, *Larne*, sails half rigged, inched slowly toward the shore, sailors in her bow swinging lead to discover how close the rest of the ships could come. The lead-swingers' monotonous calls were carried to *San Seb* across the water. At some point about parallel with *San Seb* but more than a mile eastward, *Larne's* sails dropped and she anchored. From her crow's nest, a flagman signaled to the other ships. Now five of them sailed forward slowly, maneuvering to anchor in a line with *Larne*, about four ship lengths apart, all with their port broadsides presented to the shore. The rest of the ships, ten of them, stood away, grouped around the transports.

By now it was dusk, and Blogg lowered his spyglass.

"Won't be nothing more doing till first light."

The ships seemed to shut down. Lights sprang up on mast-heads and began to wink across the quiet water like the lights that appeared in windows in the town. On *San Seb* no sounds were heard but the usual creaks and murmurs of a crowd of ships nearby. Blogg went below, and the crew slipped into the shadows of their quarters.

Charlie sat on deck all night, eyes fixed on the lights of the town, trying to guess which reflections came from the Tartar quarters. Tomorrow, death would rain down upon the town. To the town fathers who'd refused to pay ransom, that was still only a concept. They were far away from Tin-hai and Chin-hai, hundreds of miles from Amoy. They had heard the stories, but they hadn't seen for themselves. The violence of total war such as the British made was still unimaginable to them. And when they had seen and felt it, when they were able to imagine it, it would be too late. Their town would be debris, half their citizenry dead, the other half wailing their mourning to the skies. Their defenders would be dead, armless, legless, headless, bloodless, lifeless, and those Tartars who still had life enough in them to do so would slit their own throats or plunge their short swords into their hearts.

But, pray God in heaven, under that long roof that abutted

on the wall, the Tartar women and children would be safe, protected by the height and thickness of the wall. Terrified, perhaps. Clinging together, hushing crying babies, soothing children, their eyes wide, their hearts fluttering.

But, pray God in heaven, *safe*.

It seemed to Charlie that the day dawned very suddenly. One moment everything was shadowy, silver and dark blue, and the next moment, on the eastern horizon, absolutely clearly, he saw the top curve of the golden sun appear, and the world turned gold and red, the new colors rushing swiftly up into the sky. And the moment after that, the great gray burst of smoke from the first broadside put all the lovely colors to flight, and the roar of cannon came bouncing across the water.

The warships bucked and shivered with the firing of the broadsides, the cannon set off one after the other, in a sequence of seconds, so that their noise was not like thunderclaps but like rolling thunder. Each of the six frigates lined up in front of the beach fired six broadsides, and nobody, nothing, fired back. They had cannon, perhaps, in the town—cannon sitting in embrasures on top of the thick high wall, which they had thought, before they saw and heard a British broadside, could be fired effectively. But what Chinese cannon could think itself effective once it had witnessed a British broadside? Appalled, they remained silent.

Inside the walls, great puffs of black smoke burst forth, at the core of each a licking orange flame, and spurts and spoutings and gougings of debris leaped up into the air and fell again in a long, slow, silent, dreamlike sequence, like a juggling game of gods.

Behind the frigates, seen hazily in the blowing smoke, cutters were gathering around the transports and men were climbing down into them, in accord with regulations, ready to be rowed ashore for the assault on the city gate. As soon as the roar of the broadsides subsided, the cutters began to move forward, rowed swiftly and precisely, oars flailing, the soldiers standing packed together, muskets ready, bayonets fixed. As the little boats began to slow, their keels dragging against the shallow bottom, mud roiling, turning the water blackish brown, the soldiers leaped out and waded ashore, climbed partway up the beach, fell into formation behind their officers, everything proper, in accord with regulations.

And then something very irregular happened, not at all in accord with the British Book of War, something that raised roars of fury from British throats and howls of joy and exultation from the top of the joss house. The Tartars began firing from the joss house, muskets and crossbows, and British soldiers on the beach began falling to the sand. Thus far, in the six battles of the war, uncounted thousands of Chinese had died, but not a single Britisher. And now, here, on Chapoo's ugly, dun-colored beach, under the ugly, misproportioned joss house, British were falling dead at the hands of Tartars.

Officers began shouting orders, and the British retreated in a rush, back to their cutters. Bullets, spears, and arrows from the joss house hailed after them into the sea. The cutters withdrew quickly. Out of reach of the Tartars, they paused, and a fury of semaphoring began between the frigates, the transports, and *Melville*. In a few minutes, *Melville*'s broadsides opened up. Compared to the frigates', *Melville*'s cannon were like a lion's roar to the mew of kittens. The whistle of *Melville*'s cannonballs was audible overhead. They plunged viciously into the town, flinging debris about like pebbles tossed from the hand of an angry giant.

Under cover of *Melville*'s fire, more cutters put out from the transports, making in a wide V to land far down the beach on each side of the joss house, clearly to breach the town's walls in several places, or to try for other gates.

Now men could be seen slipping out of the joss house, slipping back into the town through the south gate: defenders going to oppose the new landing parties from within the walls.

At once, the frigates opened up again on the now depleted forces in the joss house, and the cutters went in again, directly to the beach in front of the south gate. But this time, the men did not wait to fall in on the beach behind their officers. As soon as they could, they leaped out of the cutters and rushed up the beach for the shelter of the lowest roof of the joss house itself. A wild fight developed, as the British strove to take the lowest story of the joss house. Bayonets, swords, spears, scimitars glinted and flashed in the sun. Blood flowed, jetted, spurted, soaked into the pebbly sand, staining great splotches of it while bodies fell and heaved and rolled and staggered up again or lay still. Slowly, the British gained. More cutters brought in more of them, solid phalanxes of them, charging, shoving, climbing over each other to get at the Tartars. Once, from above, a cascade of flame came shooting down, burning oil from a tip-tilted caldron, but it was badly aimed—by God, what genius could accurately aim a deluge of burning oil?— and most of it sizzled into the sand, and some of it fell on combustible material that burst into flame but did very little damage.

It was over when the south gate was flung open from inside and British soldiers erupted out of it, coming from inside the city to join their comrades at the foot of the joss house. The walls were breached. The town was taken. Piles of motionless bodies impeded those who still moved. Exhausted men staggered and stumbled and crawled. New troops arriving on the cutters found no fight to join, were yelled at by their officers, began to carry prone and prostrate men back to the cutters.

"Now," Blogg said. "We can go in now."

They got into the dinghy that the crew had already launched. Blogg rowed a cautious course, making away from the joss house before heading in toward the beach. Now the cutters pulling away from the frigates contained no ordinary soldiers but red-coated officers with epaulettes that glimmered in the sunlight, and cockaded hats like Ellison's.

"The high muck-a-mucks," Blogg muttered. "Going in to secure the town before *loot* starts. If they let it start, it'll spread like wildfire. . . ."

Loot. And rape.

But Charlie felt nothing. Nerves, muscles, sinews, veins, the cells of his brain, all the myriad parts that ticked and turned and meshed continuously to make up the life of his mind and body, were keyed to such a pitch of tension that they were incapable of humdrum sequences like feeling. He was an arrow poised taut in a bowstring.

The dinghy touched bottom, and they leaped out, dragged it up on the beach above the tide line. They were about a mile from the joss house, around a little arc of rocky beach. They went quickly toward the joss house, crossing the dry pebbles to walk along the hard-packed wet sand at the edge of the water. The sun was at about four o'clock, the rays striking their faces obliquely. They shaded their eyes. Blogg said suddenly, pointing:

"Look! That gig! That's *Carradine* in it!"

Charlie looked, and indeed it was Carradine. He must have come off that little rake-masted clipper, but it meant nothing, it was just a part of the high, keen thrum of dreaming that had replaced reality. Charlie walked on, not answering Blogg.

At the joss house, chaos had miraculously resolved itself into order. Men were falling into squads on the beach, being marched off by officers through the now wide-open south gate into the town. Other squads were clearing the beach, carrying fallen comrades to the cutters, collecting other fallen men into a pile under the roof of the joss house. Charlie saw strips and tatters of silvery cloth among the tangle of limbs and heads and torsos. Streaks of brilliant color, too—shreds of embroidered breastplates. Proud and fantastical Tartars being piled up like throwaway rubbish to await burial. Part of the dream.

The fires had burned themselves out. The town was flattened. The look of British-bombarded towns was familiar now: rubble and bodies and wisps of dust or smoke swirling gently. But the black tile roof of the Tartar quarters stood.

They walked through the south gate without challenge. Sentries were being posted down a broad main street leading away from the gate. A squad of British soldiers marched, headed by an officer who, every hundred yards or so, designated four men to fall out and stand as sentries. There was not a single Chinese in sight, and there was no sound but the thump of booted feet, the authoritative shouts of officers. A ghost town. A town in a dream.

Charlie darted down the left-hand side of the main street, along a thick, blank mud-brick wall that joined the black tile roof of the Tartar quarters.

About halfway down the length of the wall was a doorway marked by heavy timber doorposts and a broad high stone step leading up from the lane. A cluster of British soldiers blocked the doorway, their heads and shoulders thrust forward into it, gazing at what was inside. They stood strangely stiff and motionless—even the small ordinary motions, shuffle of foot, twitch of arm, were arrested.

Charlie tapped the shoulder of one of them.

"Let me pass, please."

No answer. No movement. The man had not heard him, wasn't aware of him—he was the dreamer, invisible.

"Let me pass!"

He shoved the soldier, but as in a dream the soldier did not give way. Instead, he stepped backward, stepped into Charlie, moving out of the way of three red-coated officers who were coming out of the doorway. Brought up short against Blogg's chest, Charlie, the dreamer, found himself paralyzed. The dream had reached a crisis. Something was about to happen, something terrible.

"Poison, don't you think?" one of the red-coated officers said calmly.

"I should think so." The second nodded gravely. "No blood. No wounding."

They turned to the third, who was younger, his face more human, more mobile. "By God, they must have only just done it! Perhaps when our flanking parties marched off around the beach. . . . By God, the ones I touched were still warm!"

One of the soldiers said hoarsely:

"Be they *all* dead, sir?"

"All," the young one said, and gagged, and hurried after the older ones.

"Gawd!" the soldier said, awed.

Now the dreamer found himself released from his paralysis. He could move again. He slipped behind the men and stepped over the high threshold into a very large room, a kind of common room, two rows of pillars upholding the roof. From outside, it had seemed quite dark in here, but inside it was only dim. It was possible to see quite well.

The women lay on the matting-covered floor in tidy rows, some on their backs, some curled on their sides, many holding children, some holding each other, some touching hands, some austerely alone. Their clothing fell about them naturally—the colorful skirts, the voluminous loose blouses. Their long, heavy locks of hair, shiny black, were not disordered. Fresh flowers pinned in them were still fresh.

The dreamer walked among them slowly, looking at their faces. He was looking for a beautiful young woman named Ling-ling and her children. He had waited a very long time and come a very long way to find them, and now he knew that he would find them, for they were here.

He found them at the end of one of the rows. She lay on her left side, her head turned upward so that the full beauty of her face was exposed. He knelt beside her and examined her beauty, remembered it, detail by detail—the skin like cream, the arched eyebrows, the eyes, closed now, that always seemed shadowed. The straight little nose. The lips that had promised heaven and had fulfilled their promise. He saw that she lay on two big white pillows, and he smiled: She had always slept in a nest of pillows. In her left arm, cuddled in the curve of her body, were the Little Sisters. Her right arm lay lightly over them, as though to keep them from harm. But no harm could come to them now, nor to her, for the ultimate harm had been done.

A hand fell on the dreamer's shoulder, and he looked up and saw Blogg.

"They're dead," he said, and Blogg nodded. As in a dream,

395

Blogg's face came and went and wavered and melted and became a face again, down which great tears were running.

"I don't see Jin-see," the dreamer said. "Did you see him?"

"No," Blogg said.

The dreamer rose from his knees, for he must find Jin-see and bring him here to this corner to lie with his mother and his sisters. Jin-see would be unhappy alone in the dimness.

The dreamer walked again among the tidy rows, looking at each face, but no face was Jin-see's. He turned toward the door. Blogg, behind him, held his arm and asked: "Where are you going?" But he didn't answer, for Blogg must know that he had to find Jin-see.

They left the hall. It was dark now, but torches flared from brackets stuck into the ground and they could see clearly. Looking carefully from side to side, they walked down the lane and then down the main road to the gate, but they didn't find Jin-see. Perhaps he was in the joss house. The dreamer, Blogg following, entered the joss house.

The lowest floor was a shambles of bodies and equipment tossed everywhere as though a volcano had erupted. Muskets, lances, spears, swords, knives, arrows, cymbals, gongs, a great crossbow, and in a corner, being piled one on top of another by two dark-bodied men, a lot of wooden cases. The dreamer knew that the cases contained opium and the men were lascars, but he didn't wonder how they came to be there, for in a dream anybody and anything can be anywhere. He walked among the bodies that lay about the floor and looked at their faces, but none of them was Jin-see. In the middle of the floor was a spiral staircase going up, up, through round holes in the five floors above, to the very top of the joss house. He craned his neck and looked straight up and saw between the wedge-shaped treads that someone was at the top of the spiral staircase, and he started up, for it might be Jin-see.

He climbed up and up, Blogg behind him, and when he was nearly at the top he heard a sound that he'd heard before, a loud, clanking, whistling hiss, and Blogg snatched at him and shouted in a voice of despair, "God have mercy!"

Startled out of his dream by the timbre of Blogg's voice and the words that he'd never heard Blogg use before, Charlie looked up and saw the vicious arc of the fighting iron descending.

Chapter XIII

October

1842

THE YOUNG MAN with the pleasant smile said:

"D'you remember me, Captain Blogg? My name's Murray. When I was dogsbody on the *Canton Register* I offered you a wager that I'd be a full-fledged journalist within a year. Lucky for you you refused, for that's what I am, come to interview you for the *Register*."

Blogg remembered him then, and shook the hand he extended. They fell into step along the wooden pier that led to the harbor master's office, which was now only one of four or five piers.

Murray looked back at *San Seb.* "Your ship, sir! If you keep her another few years you might sell her for a fortune to a museum that the Hong Kong government is thinking of establishing. Regular period piece, she is."

Blogg laughed. The old *San Seb!* Still sound in sail and hull, though wheezing louder and louder as time went on. *Lorchas* were almost nonexistent now. There were even a few steamships lying at anchor in Hong Kong harbor.

"May I ask, sir . . ." Murray said formally, but with an innocent look in his eye that implied that he was just pretending to be a journalist; at heart he was a nice, unimportant young dogsbody to whom anybody might safely tell anything. "May I ask, sir, what brings you to Hong Kong?"

"You don't know?" Blogg asked. "Then why are you here to interview me?"

John Murray laughed merrily.

"You have me, sir! I did hear a rumor that the Reverend Gutzen has returned from Ningpo, having given back civilian control of that city to the Chinese, and has asked for a meeting with the governor at which he wanted you to be present."

"You heard right."

"But the meeting's at one o'clock, and it's only nine now. Would you take kindly to a walk along toward Happy Valley? Lots of development that I think you haven't seen yet, sir, that you might find interesting."

They turned left off the harbor master's pier and walked along Queen's Road, a proper roadway now, cleared of weeds and stones and rubble, clean, smooth, sanded. On their left, the sea, only fifty yards away, was hidden from sight by a long row of new buildings.

"Never saw a place grow so fast!" Blogg marveled. "Last time I was here, about the time Captain Ellison left—a year ago?—there was just that line of buildings the other side of the harbor master's office, and Queen's Road was just a track."

"The number of buildings has more than tripled since then," Murray said, "and we've the governor's mansion that Sir Henry Pottinger moved into a month ago, and a race course being built in Happy Valley, and a cemetery too, there, and Statue Square, and a town hall—all kinds of things. You live on the island of Kolo-an, sir? Must be quiet there, compared to this!"

"Very! Just me and my mate and a couple of old crewmen, pottering around, bit of fishing, bit of freightage. In fact, it's so quiet that I don't even know exactly what's happened since the Battle of Chapoo. Just bits of news that fisher boats brought along to Kolo-an. Let me interview you. What's what?"

"Well, the Battle of Chapoo was the last big battle. When the fleet went north from there, Woosung and Shanghai were only too anxious to ransom themselves. There'd been no real pillage in Chapoo, nor in Amoy for that matter—Sir Hugh Gough, who took Colonel Burrell's place, was most anxious to avoid a repeat of what happened in Tin-hai. But there was quite a bit of free-lance looting—can't be avoided, I suppose, when an army's on the go. In Shanghai, which is a rich city, it was bad—not only our troops breaking into houses and threatening to cut their owners' throats if they didn't out with their valuables, but marauding Chinese gangs following our troops around to pick up what they left behind. By God, war's not nice, is it?"

"That it's not!"

"Anyway, our fleet stayed in Shanghai awhile trying to decide what to do. The Chinese had got all the rice up the Grand Canal before June, so we couldn't hope to paralyze Peking by holding up their rice. Admiral Parker finally decided to take *Cornwallis,* his biggest ship, up the Yangtze River with a small fleet of frigates and corvettes. There was a bit of a fight at Chinkiang, but by then we already knew that the Emperor was sending peace negotiators to Nanking. The Treaty of Nanking, Sir Henry Pottinger signing for our side, was concluded aboard *Cornwallis* on the twenty-ninth of August."

"And the terms?"

"Everything we wanted, except one. Twenty-one million dollars indemnity, in addition to the six million Ellison got. Nobody can say Palmerston's not greedy. Proper diplomatic relations to be established between Britain and China. Four more ports to be opened to foreign trade—Amoy, Foochow, Ningpo, and Shanghai. They're already being called the Treaty Ports. And some minor clauses. One of which"—he grinned—"is that the Chinese aren't allowed to call us Red Barbarians anymore."

"What was the thing we didn't get?"

"That?" Murray's voice changed subtly. "That was rather grand of the Chinese, I think. Their negotiators simply refused to discuss making opium an article of lawful commerce. Their chief negotiator told Sir Henry that the Emperor had said, 'Nothing will induce me to derive a revenue from the vice and misery of my people.' And nothing would induce the chief negotiator even to discuss the matter with Sir Henry. He had to swallow that. The Treaty of Nanking doesn't even mention opium, though that, of course, is what the war was all about."

They walked along in silence for a while. They could see the sea again, across a strip of lovely beach—the beaches of Hong Kong seemed all to be of the finest sand. The beach curved into a deep bay, in which many Chinese craft were anchored.

"That's what they're calling Typhoon Shelter," Murray said. "The safest place for small craft in all of this safe harbor when the typhoons blow. Half the population of Kowloon seems to have moved over to Hong Kong!"

They turned inland along a broad, sandy path.

"Happy Valley's up there," Murray said. "It's the only flat place big enough for a race course. The cemetery is just west of it—where Carradine is buried." He paused a moment. "Would you like to see his grave, sir?"

"Might as well, since we're here," Blogg growled.

It was elaborate—a great white marble monument, far too opulent in comparison to the few unostentatious granite stones that marked the place.

Murray said delicately, "He died at Chapoo, didn't he? Andrew has never said much about the circumstances of his death, but I understand that you were present, sir, and you saw what happened? This isn't for the *Register*. . . ."

Blogg was silent for a moment. Then: "Ain't no secret, far as I'm concerned, if it's not for print. He overbalanced and fell."

"Would I be correct in assuming that he overbalanced because he was leaning too far forward at the top of a high staircase, in order to strike at Charlie Tyson with that old-fashioned instrument of torture he liked to wear on his wrist—a fighting iron?"

"You could assume that."

After a while Murray murmured, "And where is Charlie Tyson buried?"

"At sea," Blogg said.

In the Bay of Hangchow, carefully wrapped in a piece of new canvas with Ling-ling and the Little Sisters. Blogg and his mate had placed Ling-ling on her left side, the two little girls in her arms, and Charlie on his right side, his arms around the three of them. Charlie looked hardly damaged. The fighting iron had not touched him. In his eagerness, Carradine had leaned so far forward that the momentum of the swinging iron had carried him over Charlie's shoulder, and straight down. His bloated body had cushioned Charlie at the end of Charlie's fall.

Blogg and his mate had folded them in the canvas, with a piece of heavy chain at their feet, and sewed up the canvas and balanced it on a board cantilevered over *San Seb*'s gunwale. Blogg had said some words: "I commit your spirits to God in heaven, as I commit your bodies to the deep." And the mate had said words that Blogg hadn't understood, and then he'd kneeled on the deck and made a deep kowtow. And then, each with one hand on the board, they'd tilted it toward the sea, and Charlie and Ling-ling and the Little Sisters had slipped with only the tiniest of splashes into the sweet, calm, blue water.

But not Jin-see. After they'd got Charlie and Ling-ling and the little girls aboard *San Seb*, Blogg had gone back again to search for Jin-see. He'd stood and watched as sepoys shoveled Tartar bodies into the great, deep grave they had dug. There'd been many small, boyish bodies, but as far as Blogg could tell, none of them had been Jin-see. And he'd walked the highways and byways of the small town and found some more Tartar bodies, some killed by musketry or bayonets, some by their own hand, and among them too there had been young ones, but none was Jin-see. . . .

John Murray rose from the stone on which they had been sitting in the cool of the graveyard (why were graveyards always cool?) and said respectfully:

"If you're rested, sir, we'd better start back."

The governor's mansion, white and gleaming, verandahed, porticoed, stood on a bluff.

"I've got permission to attend the meeting," Murray said. "And did you know that Mr. Yin-kwa has also been invited?"

Blogg's heart lurched. Although Yin-kwa undoubtedly already knew what had happened to Charlie—what escaped Yin-kwa?—the duty of sailing to Canton to tell Yin-kwa an eyewitness account had weighed heavily on Blogg's soul. He couldn't do it while the war was still on, but the peace had been signed weeks ago . . . yet Blogg shrank from seeing Yin-kwa without Charlie.

Murray held open the great door of the mansion. A secretary took their names, said, "Oh yes," in a superior way, and asked them to wait. Blogg sat down on a hard chair in the hall, but Murray waved him into a room overlooking the harbor, furnished with upholstered armchairs and little English-made tables.

"This is the waiting room. Don't let those pipsqueak bureaucrats bully you!"

Blogg grinned and arranged himself in an armchair overlooking the harbor. There were so many ships at anchor that he couldn't pick out *San Seb,* although he knew where she was moored.

Murray pointed to the biggest ship in the harbor.

"That's *Comanjee Hormunjee.* What a name, eh? Indian. Appropriate, because she's stuffed full of Patna opium. Carradine's. He's six receiving ships like her anchored along the coast from here all the way to Shanghai. He's eleven coastal runners delivering opium from the receiving ships to points ashore. And he's three crack clippers, in addition to *Sylph* and *Falcon,* bringing opium from India all year round."

The secretary came back, raised his eyebrows when he found them in the waiting room, but said only that his excellency the governor would see them now.

Sir Henry Pottinger was handsome in a heavy-faced way. Bristling eyebrows and a luxuriant waxed mustache compensated for his receding hairline. His eyes protruded a little. He wore a broad red ribbon across his white shirtfront, beneath a tight wing collar and a black bow tie. He rose courteously to shake Blogg's hand.

"Sorry that you've had the trouble of sailing over from your island home. Reverend Gutzen particularly asked that you be present at this meeting—though I don't even know what it's all about!"

The door opened again, and Yin-kwa was shown in. Blogg felt a heavy tug at his heart. Yin-kwa was bowing to Sir Henry, pretending not to see his outstretched hand, greeting him in the Chinese way by raising his own hands clasped together. He wore a gown more magnificent than any of the magnificent ones Blogg had seen him wear when he wasn't disguised as a coolie. His oiled queue slid thickly down his back. His face was growing more like his grandfather's, the ivory skin, very fine and unwrinkled, tightly stretched across the high cheekbones. The ultimate aristocrat, Charlie had called him. He was that!

Yin-kwa turned from Sir Henry to Blogg, the smile extending warmly from his lips to his eyes.

"Blogg . . . I know about Charlie."

The smile didn't alter, but a bland flicker of the eyes told Blogg, as it had always told Charlie, that Yin-kwa's heart was sore.

Yin-kwa went on politely:

"If I may be excused, Sir Henry—and Mr. Murray—I'd like to give Captain Blogg a piece of news that may be of interest."

Sir Henry nodded, and Murray said: "Anything you say, sir, is of interest. You're only the most important businessman in South China."

Unexpectedly, Blogg laughed.

"I can see why they promoted you so quickly!"

They all smiled, Sir Henry rather grudgingly—he didn't seem to be sure that Yin-kwa was what Murray had said. What about Carradine? Blogg imagined him thinking. But Yin-kwa had turned to him, his black eyes fixed and shining.

"Blogg, at Andrew Carradine's suggestion, I've decided to

become the Chinese partner of Carradine and Company—the *compradore,* as they say now."

Blogg met Yin-kwa's eyes and felt his own spark. He could hear in his mind's ear Yin-kwa's voice saying gently in Ellison's empty rooms at the top of Carradine's factory: "Should the British be allowed to debauch our people, and should no Chinese even attempt to control them?"

With a grim little smile, he said: "I'm glad. Charlie would be glad too."

Yin-kwa's lips flattened in satisfaction: They understood each other, Blogg and himself—and Charlie.

The door opened again and the secretary appeared, frowning. Before he could say a word, a little girl ran into the room, skirted him carefully, then rushed to Yin-kwa. Yin-kwa picked her up tenderly.

"My only daughter, Sir Henry. It's hard for me to leave the house without her, for she won't let me out of her sight. I'm sure you'll forgive me."

He set the child on his lap, and she seemed to fall asleep instantly, leaning her head against her father's chest. Sir Henry looked startled, Murray amused. Yin-kwa said to Blogg:

"You remember my daughter, O-lan? You and Charlie met her once before on Jackass Point."

Blogg nodded silently. The child whom the fairies had brought, who heard the fairies call sometimes and went away to stay with them awhile . . . the child who adored Jin-see . . .

The door opened yet again, and this time, at last, the secretary showed in Gutzen. He entered quickly, in his strange flamboyant garments, the blue scarf wound around his head, his eye, swiveling as he greeted Sir Henry.

Blogg heard Murray give a faint whistle and mutter under his breath, "Another one!"

Another what? Blogg glanced around.

Another child.

A boy of nine or ten, soberly dressed in a miniature long gown of dark cloth, black hair short-cropped. Nothing else could be seen of him, for his chin was sunk so low on his chest

405

that his features were completely hidden. But all the same, Blogg suddenly felt his heart drum against his rib cage. He knew—he *knew*—what Gutzen was going to say.

Gutzen said, turning to the boy, who was standing stiffly on the edge of the carpet:

"Sir Henry, I asked for this meeting in order to decide what's to be done about this child. He is Jin-see, the son of Charlie Tyson."

Blogg shut his eyes and felt the blood drain from his heart. Oh God! If Charlie hadn't gone up to the top of that joss house looking for Jin-see, who was nowhere near! Oh God! Oh God! Charlie, whom Blogg had loved more than any other except, perhaps, the right-gentle girl, the mother of his children . . .

". . . I recognized Wei at once," Gutzen was saying. "My chief of police brought him in, and I knew at once who he was—your grandfather's bond man, Yin-kwa. He used to bring you to and fro from Canton for your English lessons. But he *was* spying for General I-Ching, there could be no doubt about that, and when my police chief insisted that he be beheaded as a warning to others, I simply couldn't find an excuse to avoid it. But I did see him privately. I did talk to him. He accepted his death. In a way, I think, he even welcomed it. I had the impression that things had gone very wrong for him. . . ."

Gutzen paused, looking anxious and sad, as though he wished with all his heart that he could have helped. Then:

"He told me where to find Jin-see. He told me that he'd sent his daughter, Jin-see's mother, and her two other children, both girls, to Chapoo for safety. But at the last moment he couldn't bear to be parted from his grandson. He couldn't bear the thought that he might lose him in the debris of war. So he kept the child with him, secretly, in Yu-yao, where I-Ching had his headquarters. He told me that Charlie had been in Ningpo—I don't know how. Charlie had asked to see him, he said, and he'd longed to see Charlie. He'd done something that would seem very wrong to Charlie, and he wanted to ask his pardon. He loved Charlie. But he was afraid, having Jin-see hidden in Yu-yao, that Charlie might get the British after him in order to recover Jin-see, and I-Ching's plans would be discovered. They were discovered anyway, of course—it was slaughter!"

He sighed and gazed out of the window for a moment.

"Anyway, Wei asked me to promise, to swear by my God, that I would keep Jin-see safe until the end of the war, and then give him back to Charlie. I didn't know until I got back here three days ago that Charlie was dead."

As Gutzen's voice faded, Blogg rose to his feet.

"There's no problem. I'll take the boy."

"No." Yin-kwa spoke softly from his armchair. "My family is obliged to Charlie's family forever, for reasons that Blogg knows well. Charlie's son is my son. I will take Jin-see."

Jin-see still stood on the edge of the carpet, head bowed low, the tenseness in him jangling out loud, Blogg thought, if only one had ears to hear.

But Yin-kwa made no move to go to him or to call him. Instead, he bent over the little girl in his lap and woke her up, whispering in her ear. She rubbed her eyes sleepily and looked over at the boy. Then she gave a glad little cry, jumped off her father's lap, and ran to him. She was short enough so that by cocking her head to one side, she could look straight up into his face.

"Jin-see?"

She gave him a brilliant smile.

Jin-see lifted his head.